Granville County Library Sy
P.O. Box 339
Oxford, NC 27565

O9-BHK-365

THE
PROTOCOL

APRIL CHRISTOFFERSON

A TOM DOHERTY ASSOCIATES BOOK
NEW YORK

This is a work of fiction. All the characters and events portrayed in this novel are either fictitious or are used fictitiously.

THE PROTOCOL

Copyright © 1999 by April Christofferson

All rights reserved, including the right to reproduce this book, or portions thereof, in any form.

This book is printed on acid-free paper.

A Forge Book
Published by Tom Doherty Associates, LLC
175 Fifth Avenue
New York, NY 10010

Forge® is a registered trademark of Tom Doherty Associates, LLC.

Design by Lisa Pifher

Library of Congress Cataloging-in-Publication Data

Christofferson, April.
    The protocol / April Christofferson.—1st ed.
        p.   cm.
    "A Tom Doherty Associates book."
    ISBN 0-312-86638-0 (acid-free paper)
    I. Title.
PS3553.H749P76   1999
813'.54—dc21   99-33234
                                                                    CIP

First Edition: October 1999

Printed in the United States of America

0 9 8 7 6 5 4 3 2 1

ONE

JENNIFER ROCKHILL CRADLED the phone in the crook of her neck and took a deep, shaky breath before hanging it up. It was done. She'd actually talked to the bastard, had scheduled an interview for next week, on Wednesday.

She grabbed her briefcase, climbed into her car—a little green Volvo that Charlie had bought her just a few days before the accident—and headed for Fresno. She would spend the better part of the next few days at Fresno State University.

In preparation for the interview she'd just scheduled, she had become a self-taught expert on biotechnology. She devoured each issue of *Bioworld*—the industry newsletter, which was faxed to her daily—and used its articles to cue her on which topics she should master. She'd visited FSU so frequently that the librarian at the med school teased her about becoming a permanent fixture in the dank, clammy building that housed over two hundred thousand volumes of medical journals. It had occupied her time, dominated it, the past six months.

And next week it would all pay off.

She could hardly believe it when, after a half-hour telephone interview with the Director of Human Resources, she'd been put through to Sherwood Fielding.

His voice was exactly as she'd remembered. Cold, formal. Arrogant. Nothing in it hinted that he might have recognized *her* voice. Of course, they'd only spoken once before, years ago. And she'd been close to hysteria that time.

This time was different. This time she had been calm, rational. In complete control.

She had impressed him, of that she was certain.

Granville County
P.O. Box 339
Oxford, NC 27565

"Good biotech attorneys are hard to come by," he'd told her. "Where did you say you've been working?"

"In the technology transfer department at Fresno State," she'd answered. "I handle research and licensing contracts."

It was more a half-truth than an out-and-out lie, but aside from her concern that his uncovering the falsehood could thwart her plans, she had no problem whatsoever lying to this man.

"That's just what we're looking for," Fielding had said. "Someone with experience in the industry. We've had a couple of local employment agencies on this position, but they're totally incompetent. They've been sending us morons. Not one of them could pass the most basic biology exam. We'd just decided to list with a national headhunter. Maybe now, that won't be necessary."

"I'm confident you'll decide not," Jennifer had answered.

"It's a stroke of luck you contacted us," Sherwood Fielding had said to her before hanging up.

"For both of us."

A *stroke of luck*. As she negotiated the two-laner that connected her hometown of Visalia to Interstate 99, Jennifer had to smile. Luck had nothing to do with it. She'd been waiting, patiently waiting, for this day. It had taken her almost a year to locate him. But the moment she did, the moment she saw his name in an article in the *LA Times'* science and technology section, her plan had begun taking form. Once she learned where Sherwood Fielding was—in Seattle now, running a biotech company called BioGentech—she knew that with patience, she would find a way to get to him.

J. T. Ryberg had not only helped her find the way, but had paved it for her. An ad in *The Hacker Quarterly* promising "can penetrate anyone, anywhere" had led Jennifer to J. T.—a former Yahoo! employee who'd seen a brighter future working solo.

J. T. knew his stuff, and with his help, Jennifer was soon reading e-mail generated and received within the confines of the BioGentech building six hundred miles away, in Seattle.

An early memo from Fielding to his vice president of finance had given her the idea.

> Review of budget shows excessive outside counsel fees. In-house attorney may be warranted. Let's monitor and evaluate in six months.

Jennifer had put those six months to good use. Her forty-five-mile commutes to Fresno became part of her daily regimen. One day several months earlier, on her way off-campus from the library, she'd noticed the sign that read OFFICE OF TECHNOLOGY TRANSFER. Technology Transfer. She'd noticed that term time and again in *Bioworld*. She'd pulled into the parking lot and gone inside, where she'd introduced herself to one of two overworked staff attorneys.

"I'm a contract attorney interested in going into biotech law," she'd told Grace Bell. "I'll work for nothing. Literally. I just want to get some experience."

It hadn't been an official hire; but Grace knew a good thing when she saw it and soon Jennifer was drafting agreements—the same kind of agreements that a company like BioGentech needed.

Jennifer had continued monitoring BioGentech e-mails. Two weeks earlier she'd read one from Fielding to Carolyn Powell, the human resources person to whom she'd just spoken.

Have one of our local agencies start looking for an in-house contract attorney.

Jennifer was still vascillating about what step to take next when yesterday morning's e-mail from Carolyn to Fielding caused her to catch her breath:

Reminder: another candidate for contract attorney coming in this afternoon.

What if they hired this person? She'd have to start over, come up with another plan.

But Fielding's curt reply, written at the end of the day, placated her.

Don't waste my time with another worthless candidate.

It was time to make her move. Jennifer had picked up the phone, asked for Carolyn Powell, and explained that she was a California attorney about to move to Seattle. Since her background was in biotech, she was calling all the local firms to see if they might be hiring in the near future.

"This is amazing," Carolyn had responded, sounding almost giddy (most likely, thought Jennifer, at the prospect of redeeming herself with her boss). "We happen to be in the interview process at this very moment."

Forty-five minutes later, Jennifer had an appointment to meet with Sherwood Fielding. Next Wednesday, 9:00 A.M. In Seattle.

Now that the wheels had been put in motion, a sense of calm settled

over Jennifer. She had a lot to do in the next five days. An airline ticket
to buy. Loose ends to tie up for Grace, who—used now to Jennifer's
assistance—would undoubtedly fall apart at the prospect of her departure.
More studying to do.

Still, as she pulled off Highway 99 at the Fresno State exit, for the
first time in three years, Jennifer Rockhill actually felt the tide might be
changing; that things might finally be going her way.

HER FLIGHT ARRIVED at six-fifteen on Tuesday evening. Carolyn Powell
had arranged for her to stay at the Residence Inn directly across the street
from Lake Union. BioGentech's offices, Carolyn told her, were just two
blocks north of the hotel.

From her small balcony, Jennifer watched as the lights of the downtown district popped out, accentuating the city's futuristic skyline. She'd
heard Seattle was beautiful, but none of the pictures in articles she'd read
had succeeded in capturing *this*. To the south, skyscrapers piercing a vel-
vet sky. Beyond, mythical in proportion, the fading outline of Mount Rai-
nier. Due west, the sun dropping behind the jagged peaks of the Olympic
Mountains while in the foreground a lighted ferry streamed across Elliott
Bay's black expanse.

After a fitful night's sleep, she got up and showered. Usually she let
her thick, shoulder-length hair dry naturally, but on workdays she'd almost
always blown it dry to try to tame its mass of chestnut curls and present
a more professional image. She'd occasionally wondered if the exotic air
lent by her unruly tresses and a narrow, slightly arched nose, both of which
she'd inherited from a grandmother who was half Lakota, half Irish,
played against her in the whitebread legal world in which she'd worked.
Today she couldn't allow that possibility. Looking professional was essential, so she spent a little extra time on it, curling her hair under at its
ends with her brush. Long dark lashes eliminated the need for mascara,
but applying a touch of coverup to the circles underneath had become
part of her daily ritual these past couple years.

She chose a classic navy blue pantsuit for the interview. She still had
a closet full of similarly conservative suits from her years with Butera,
Jensen, Moe, and O'Connor, where she had worked for six years before
Charlie and Stacey's deaths. The size eight she'd worn then hung loose
on her frame now. The extra ten pounds that years of twice-weekly aer-
obics hadn't budged were, now that she no longer cared, long gone. She'd
sworn that she'd never put the suits on again. That her loss had robbed
her of the resiliency and simple faith in justice that she felt to be absolute

prerequisites to making a living in the spiritually draining legal world. When the insurance money ran out, she'd planned on doing something else, something entirely new. Maybe even going back to school to get a teaching certificate. But that was before she found out about Sherwood Fielding.

At precisely 8:45, she headed out the hotel's front door.

AS PROMISED BY CAROLYN Powell, the giant metal sculpture of a futuristic medical symbol rotating on a column in front of its entrance made BioGentech's offices hard to miss. After reading the directory in the lobby, Jennifer took the elevator up to the sixth floor, where it opened to a lavish reception area. The black marble surface of the counter encircling the desk behind which the receptionist sat matched the floor. On either side of the receptionist's area, long, wide corridors led to floor-to-ceiling windows showcasing the city skyline and the waters of Lake Union. Oversized artwork—an oil behind the desk, and an abstract of the symbol rotating outside—imparted a further sense of drama.

The receptionist, a vivacious brunette identified by a nameplate as Zelma Webster, chattered animatedly on the phone. She flashed Jennifer a smile and, pushing a clipboard across the counter to her, mouthed to her to sign in.

Jennifer wrote her name, the time, and left a blank under the column labeled "Company," then seated herself in one of three leather chairs.

When Zelma finished her phone call, she turned the clipboard her way.

"So you're Ms. Rockhill," she said cheerfully, "you're interviewing for the attorney position."

"That's right."

"I'll let Dr. Fielding know you're here."

After a brief, hushed phone conversation, Zelma came around from behind the desk.

"I'll show you the way."

Despite two-and-a-half-inch heels, the diminutive Zelma barely came up to Jennifer's chin. Jennifer followed her down the left hallway. At the end they made a turn, which took them past several offices exposed to the corridor by walls of glass, which enabled Jennifer to see not only the interior of each office, but all the way through to the outside windows— all of which provided the offices' occupants with incredible views. After working in the environment of a modestly successful law firm, she was struck by the opulence of the accommodations. Each office housed oversized cherry-wood desks and a separate sitting area, furnished with stylish chairs and settees.

At the end of the hall, Zelma stopped and rapped on a door that read SHERWOOD FIELDING, M.D., PRESIDENT AND CEO. Fielding's office, Jennifer immediately observed, lacked the glass walls that robbed the others of any sense of privacy.

Standing there, a sense of panic swept over Jennifer. Had she lost her mind? She had become so fixated on finding Sherwood Fielding that quite possibly she'd lost the ability to reason.

But then, as Zelma tentatively pushed the door open to announce their arrival, Jennifer heard the voice again—*his* voice, coming from inside the room—and the simple sound of it, the gut reaction it invoked in the core of her being, yanked her back on to steady ground.

Zelma pulled the door closed again.

"He's on the phone," she whispered apologetically. "I'm sure he'll be right with us."

They stood staring at the door until finally, it opened.

"Sorry to keep you waiting."

Sherwood Fielding stood before them, framed by the doorway.

He was nothing like Jennifer had imagined. As a child, she'd had a teacher—a slight, shrewish man named Mr. Mayhume—who had taken great pleasure in intimidating her and the other girls in her third-grade class. Without even realizing it she had, in her mind's eye, given Sherwood Fielding a face and body like that of Mayhume.

This man—tall, slick, obviously vain in his pricey Ralph Lauren pin-stripes—was actually attractive, and that very fact made him all the more odious to her. When Fielding stuck out his hand for her, Jennifer had to catch herself, stifle her natural reaction to draw back in repulsion.

"I'm Sherwood Fielding. It's a pleasure to meet you."

She grasped the proffered hand firmly.

"Jennifer Rockhill, and the pleasure is mine."

Fielding nodded at Zelma to dismiss her and waved Jennifer inside.

Fielding's domain made the other offices she'd just passed look paltry. At least three times the size of the others, it had a continuous wall of windows overlooking the water, and a large deck, furnished with a chaise lounge for sunning. At the far end sat a highly polished black mahogany desk and matching credenza. Bookshelves, featuring many of the same journals Jennifer had recently studied, lined the long wall opposite the windows. And at the end opposite Fielding's desk sat two overstuffed white leather chairs and a small sofa centered around a gas fireplace. The wall on either side of the fireplace displayed diplomas, certificates, and numerous photographs of Fielding. Though fifteen feet separated it from the doorway in which she stood, one photo immediately drew Jennifer's eyes. Fielding with another man, who, even at this distance, Jennifer thought she recognized. The urge to approach it was hard to resist; but Fielding had grabbed her by the elbow and now steered her to the other end of the room, where he motioned for Jennifer to take a seat and then proceeded to settle behind his desk.

"First time in Seattle?"

"Yes."

"What do you think?"

"I just got in last night, but from what I've seen so far, I like it very much."

Fielding pushed back in his oversized chair and studied her.

"Let me ask you something," he said. "Before we get into your background. Why is it you're interested in moving here—to a city you've never even visited before?"

Jennifer could feel the color creeping into her cheeks.

"I'm a widow," she said matter-of-factly. "My husband died of a heart attack a few years ago, at a very young age. I've had a hard time getting over it. I finally decided the best thing for me would be to move away. Start over fresh, where there aren't so many memories."

"Any children?"

"No."

"Family? It must be hard to leave them behind."

"I have no family. I was an only child and both my parents died years ago."

"I'm sorry," Fielding said without a hint of emotion. "Well, if you're looking for a great place to live, this is it. Seattle's not only one of the most beautiful cities you'll ever find, it also has a lot to offer in terms of culture, nature, sports. You name it."

"How about you?" Jennifer asked. "Have you lived here long?"

"Years," Fielding answered. "Practically forever."

He lied, Jennifer observed, with finesse.

"Now, let's get down to business. We need an in-house attorney to negotiate and draft all our agreements—everything from research and licensing agreements to the lease on this building. Sound interesting?"

Jennifer leaned forward. This was it. She had to sell this man on her.

"*Very* interesting. I've been a contract attorney for ten years, the last few in the biotech arena. It sounds to me like a perfect fit."

"Tell me what they had you doing at . . ." he pulled a piece of paper on his desk toward him and read it, "Fresno State? Office of Technology Transfer, right?"

Jennifer nodded.

"Fresno State has a strong research facility. Primarily genetic engineering, with a heavy emphasis on the treatment and prevention of cancer. Our scientists conduct their own studies, but also, as a means of providing funding for our programs, they do a significant number of collaborations with outside institutions. Smaller research centers, companies like yours. I handle the legal end of things, the collaborations, studies, whatever."

"Are you the only attorney on staff?"

"There are two." It was true; she just didn't happen to be one of them. "I listed Grace Bell as a reference on the application I faxed you after talking to you last week. We have a strong support staff, too. Several paralegals and an administrative assistant."

"Sounds like a busy place."

"It is. But I like it that way."

"This job would be a lot of pressure. We've been farming everything out, but if we hired you, you'd be expected to handle it all."

"That wouldn't be a problem. I'm a hard worker. I'm more than willing to put in extra hours, if necessary. Basically, my job is my life." She raised her eyes to his and with no small amount of effort, held them there. "You won't regret it if you hire me, Dr. Fielding. I'm good at what I do."

"I suspect you are," Sherwood Fielding said.

He was quiet for a long while, his eyes roaming from the resume and application in front of him to Jennifer, then back to the papers.

Jennifer shifted in her chair and pretended to be taking in the view outside the window as her eyes searched out the photo at the back of the room. There was no way she could get up to get a closer look—not unless he left her alone in the room, which was unlikely. But if she succeeded in today's mission, the opportunity would eventually present itself.

The sound of Fielding clearing his throat drew Jennifer's attention back to him.

"Well, Ms. Rockhill, it looks like you've just simplified life for us here at BioGentech. It won't be necessary for us to continue to search for someone to fill this position."

He still appeared to be studying her, but finally, Sherwood Fielding's expression warmed to a stiff half smile.

"I'd say you're just what we've been looking for."

CHAPTER

TWO

S WEAT BEADING ON HIS forehead, Dr. Geoffrey Spillman's molelike face broke into a grin. A Starbucks. Right here at LAX, just like Sea-Tac.

Why did that delight him so?

He wasn't even much of a coffee drinker.

Still, he detoured through the door and took his place at the end of the line, the reminder of home, Seattle, and his former cohorts at Bio-Gentech, for whom Starbucks was a daily ritual, making him downright giddy, causing a surge of raw power to course through his diminutive body. He shifted his brown leather attaché forward, a needless attempt to hide the near invisible hard-on that reflected his visceral reaction to this sense of . . . what? What was it he felt at that very moment? Omnipotence? Certainly the consequences of his actions in the next thirty minutes were in keeping with a feeling of tremendous power. Revenge? His smile widened. Yes, that would be an appropriate sentiment.

Fear?

That too. His brow and sweat-stained shirt provided ample evidence.

Still, when he placed his order—impulsively, a double shot sure to have him doubled over with cramps later—he could have sworn the nymph working the counter sensed he was someone important.

In response to her "Have a nice day," he dropped a dollar bill into the tip jar and gave her what he intended to be a meaningful look.

They'd agreed to meet at the seating area just beyond customs. Spillman checked his watch. The flight from Paris, due in at 2:52 P.M., would have landed by now. As he settled into one of the formed plastic chairs at the back of the waiting area, he kept his eyes glued to the hallway marked INTERNATIONAL FLIGHT ARRIVALS.

He had no idea who he was looking for. No name, no description. Nothing. The arriving passenger, he'd been told, would find *him*.

The one thing he did know—the only thing of importance, really, about the Frenchman for whom he waited—was *what* he was.

A spy.

Spillman's shoulders quivered with his stifled giggle. Dr. Geoffrey Spillman, renowned biomolecular scientist—whose previous excitement in life consisted of discoveries made in tissue cultures and test tubes— was waiting to meet a spy coming in from Paris.

It had taken days of gut-wrenching introspection to reach this point, to come to the decision to betray BioGentech; ever since he'd made it, Spillman had experienced an almost orgasmic state of mind. What better way to get back at him, at Sherwood Fielding? That Judas for whom he'd worked; to whom he'd dedicated his best, most brilliant research only to have his contributions go unacknowledged, unappreciated, and under-funded. Only to be left out of BioGentech's highest-priority research. Spillman, head of Medical Research, left out, cut out of the loop, on a project! And then, incredibly, fired. Literally locked out of his own laboratories.

He should have seen it coming. There'd been plenty of signs. The cuts in his budget. The failure to fund his last study. And, of course, his exclusion from Project X. Not just exclusion from the research team—his ego might have been able to handle that—but he'd not even known about the project itself until he'd found the memo to Sherwood.

It had really just been a fluke, one of those freak things that end up having consequences beyond anything one might have first imagined.

He'd dropped by the admin room to shred that day's paper waste, as he did at the end of each day. All discarded paperwork generated at BioGentech was routinely shredded. If someone had just a few pages, they would usually feed them into the shredder themselves. But time constraints dictated that the longer documents—research abstracts fre-quently ran twenty to thirty pages—be dropped into a tall metal bin marked SHREDDER that looked like a hooded garbage can. Once an item dropped inside, it took a key to retrieve it.

At the end of each workday, Jim Wilkes, head of security, fed the bin's contents to the shredder.

Two-and-a-half weeks earlier, Spillman had come upon Wilkes in the middle of the process.

"Working late tonight, huh?" Wilkes had observed.

"They're all twelve-hour days," Spillman had responded smugly. Everyone else had gone home, but as head of Medical Research, he prided himself in his long hours. "Want me to drop these in there?" He'd motioned toward the shredder bin, which stood next to the shredder, half full, its top removed.

"Nah, just hand them here," Wilkes said, reaching his free hand out to take the two inches of papers from Spillman. As he did so, the stack Spillman haphazardly gathered from the floor around his desk just minutes earlier literally fell apart, its pages scattering everywhere.

Wilkes, exasperated, turned the stack he'd been feeding to the machine over, facedown, and with a sigh and shake of his head, dropped to the floor to retrieve the loose papers.

The security chief's not-so-subtle attempt to hide information from him—didn't Wilkes know that, as a director of BioGentech, Spillman had access to all company data?—served to pique Spillman's interest immediately. While Wilkes was still on his hands and knees, Spillman reached out, and turned the top document over.

He'd expected to see a ledger page from accounting. Or a draft of some kind of agreement. Or perhaps a research protocol.

But this document was a memo. A memo from—and it was this that caused Spillman to surreptitiously slip the single sheet of paper into his briefcase before joining Wilkes on the floor—Ram Chandra.

Six months earlier, Ram Chandra had been fired from BioGentech. But here it was, a memo, on BioGentech stationery:

> To: Sherwood Fielding
> From: Ram Chandra
> Subject: Project X

After helping Wilkes gather up all the papers from the floor, Spillman had hurried home. It hadn't taken long to get there, for like many other BioGentech employees, Spillman had an apartment within walking distance of BioGentech's Lake Union location.

Once inside, document in hand, Spillman had dropped into his recliner. He pushed back and began to read, but after just one line, bolted forward, his eyes riveted to the words on the page.

> Surrogate #5: first adult donor (Donor B, female). Attempts at arresting cell cycle prior to nuclear transfusion not successful. Study director believes this to be the result of incorrect nutrient formula. Currently, four new formulas are in experimental stage with Donor B cells. Results to be available within the week.

The signature at the bottom of the page was all too familiar. Ram Chandra.

He and Chandra had once worked side by side, as part of Bio-Gentech's genetic engineering team. But Chandra had fallen into disfavor with Sherwood Fielding when his last mammal cloning experiment had come in over budget—350 percent over, to be precise. Things had come to a surprisingly volatile head in a weekly departmental meeting and Chandra had, supposedly, been fired.

Yet, in Spillman's very hands, rested a document indicating that Chandra's experiments—he'd helped pioneer the embryo twinning process now routinely used in the cattle industry—were not only continuing, but were still being reported to BioGentech CEO, Sherwood Fielding!

The next day Spillman had stormed into Fielding's office, demanding an explanation. Fielding, typically cool, had played it with a poker face, citing a provision in Chandra's severance agreement that obligated him to report periodically on his ongoing research results.

His explanation had infuriated Spillman. What kind of fool did Fielding take him for? As if any scientist, much less one of Chandra's stature, would agree to such a provision. A scientist's research was sacrosanct. It was, in a word, everything. Everything. He would no more share its results with a former employer than would a Microsoft executive discuss program glitches at the barbershop. And that's just what he'd said to Fielding that day. For the first time in his career, Spillman called bullshit on his boss.

"And why would the memo be written on BioGentech stationery?" he'd ranted. "Explain that one."

Fielding had simply stared at him. And remained silent.

And the next day, Spillman had arrived at work to find himself without a job, the lock to the laboratory door having been reconfigured overnight.

And so the decision to approach Bio La Rouche—to offer to sell the French biopharmaceutical giant BioGentech trade secrets—had, in the end, not really been that difficult after all. Especially once he'd seen the stingy severance BioGentech offered. The biggest problem had been deciding which European company to go to. English and German pharmaceutical companies conducted research in the same fields as BioGentech. However, the French's reputation for being especially aggressive—and especially willing to pay—in the area of biotech espionage had been the deciding factor.

It was, after all, just what Fielding deserved.

Passengers began to trickle out of the customs area. Spillman, as instructed, positioned his attaché on the seat next to him and kept his eye trained on the corridor's opening. The half-circles of perspiration under his arms had spread and now threatened to meet at his sternum. He sat forward on the chair to avoid another embarrassing wet blotch on the back of his shirt, for surely if he leaned against the seat's back, that's what he'd end up with. He should never have ordered that double.

The first wave of deplaning passengers consisted of older, affluent-looking types—several couples and a number of business executives in dark suits, one of whom immediately caught Spillman's eye. Middle aged, tall and dashing, obviously very fit, he walked briskly. There seemed to be a hint of danger about him. He paused at the seating area, looked around. Spillman's pulse raced. His eyes traveled to the man's briefcase. Awfully thin to be carrying so much money.

Certain this was his man, Spillman nodded, but his acknowledgement went unnoticed. Instead, the man surveyed the seating area one more time, then, obviously not finding whomever he expected to be there, joined the stream of people following the baggage claim signs.

Spillman's breath escaped in a sigh.

First class had cleared. The passengers now consisted mostly of young, college-student types, with their backpacks, sloppy clothing, and sleepy grins; parents with whiny young children; and the occasional lone adult.

The corridor had pretty much emptied when Spillman noticed a rather nondescript man, probably in his midforties, dressed in rolled-up shirtsleeves and khakis, seated a dozen chairs down from him reading the newspaper. He looked up at Spillman casually.

Had he been a deplaning passenger? Spillman could not remember seeing him come through the security gate.

As Spillman continued to wait, his anxiety suddenly shifted focus—from the specter of actually coming face-to-face with the French intelligence agent to that of the agent not showing at all. Had Bio La Rouche double-crossed him? He'd already given them some information over the phone. What if they'd decided it was enough to get them started, that with their agent—the French agents were rumored to be the best in the business—they could obtain the rest on their own? Without Spillman. Without having to pay him the small fortune they'd agreed upon.

He'd flown all the way down there, to L.A., because he hadn't wanted to risk being recognized at Sea-Tac. They'd warned him that he would have to leave Seattle, start over somewhere no one would ever find him—when the theft of trade secrets was discovered, the finger always pointed first to former employees, especially disgruntled former employees. If Bio La Rouche used the information he'd already given them to get their hands on BioGentech's top secret project, Project X, Fielding would surely blame him. He'd have to leave Seattle now, whether Bio La Rouche came through or not. But he'd already depleted his savings account. What the hell would he do if they didn't show up with the money?

He grabbed his attaché and began rummaging frantically through it, searching for the telephone number in France he'd used just three days ago. He would call and straighten this out right now.

Relieved at finding it, he began to rise, but a voice—a stern voice, with just the slightest trace of an accent—stopped him.

"Stay right there."

The khaki-clad stranger suddenly appeared in front of him, his hand on Spillman's shoulder, pushing him back into his seat.

Spillman collapsed backward.

The man sat down next to Spillman.

The terminal was quiet now, save for the occasional airline employee and, scattered here and there along the rows of chairs lining the area, a traveler passing time during an extended layover.

For appearance' sake, the man smiled pleasantly at Spillman, a familiar smile, but his voice, in stark contrast, brooked no nonsense.

"Geoffrey Spillman."

Spillman nodded nervously.

"Is the documentation all there?" He nodded toward the attaché on Spillman's lap.

Spillman cleared his throat. "Everything I have. As I told Mr. St. Antoine, I wasn't able to obtain much hard data on the current project, but I did put my thoughts, my er . . . suspicions down, based on what I read and what I know about Dr. Chandra's prior research. And I included data from several other highly confidential studies BioGentech's been conducting."

"And security information? A list of employees?"

"That's there, too. A list of personnel, computer manuals, passwords, even my passkey. Of course, a lot of it has probably already been changed, but Mr. St. Antoine thought it might have some value."

For the first time since the shock of this man's appearance, Spillman realized he carried no luggage. None whatsoever. Where was his money?

"Um . . ." he said, clearing his throat. "The money. Is it in an airport locker or something?"

The man snorted a half laugh.

"You get the money after I've gone through the information." The French accent was more apparent now. The lilt at the end of the sentence, the rhythm.

Spillman's grip on his attaché tightened.

The Frenchman simply stared at him, expectant, confident.

Finally, reluctantly, Spillman slid the leather pouch onto the other man's lap.

"When?" he said before letting go of it. "When do I get the money? And where?"

The Frenchman was already standing.

"Tomorrow morning. Nine-fifteen," he said quietly. "Just outside the Starbucks, the one where you were such a big tipper."

He snickered, then was gone.

Just then the double shot of caffeine hit Spillman. Really hit.

Or was it his nerves?

Pallid and soaked in a full body sweat, Spillman stood and raced to the nearest rest room. A red sign reading CLOSED FOR CLEANING blocked its entrance.

Shaken, he raced on in search of the next bathroom.

The Frenchman had been there all along! He hadn't even been on the two-fifty-two flight from Paris. Who knows how long he'd been watching Spillman, following him?

Who knows whether he'd even show up in the morning with the money?

Maybe, thought Geoffrey Spillman as he streaked into the next rest room, cutting ahead of several other passengers waiting for a stall to become available, this wasn't such a good idea.

No, he thought, slamming the stall door behind him without even taking the time to lock it, perhaps it hadn't been such a good idea at all.

CHAPTER

THREE

U NNOTICED, SHERWOOD FIELDING SLIPPED into the back of the cavernous conference room. The Symposium on Cloning had drawn a standing-room-only crowd. The whole world, it seemed, was in an uproar over recently proposed legislation that would permit the cloning of human body parts. Ever since the day the story broke about a Scottish biotech firm cloning a sheep, the anti-cloning crusade had been gathering momentum. It wasn't long after Dolly's arrival that the first cloned cow was announced. Just over a year later, Japanese scientists at the University of Hawaii succeeded in mass cloning three generations of mice from several different types of adult cells—clones of clones of clones. The refinement of the highly reproducible techniques used by the Japanese then led to the recent introduction of Immunocows—mass-produced cows immune to infectious disease.

All along, in keeping with long- and widely held scientific and ethical principles, a general prohibition against the cloning of human beings had been observed—on an honorary and voluntary basis—until recently when a Chicago physicist announced he'd moved to Mexico to set up a laboratory.

It's purpose: to clone a human being.

Who? Himself.

A huge public outcry, hysteria over the possibility that more human cloning would follow, had resulted in nationwide symposiums like this one: where legislators, scientists, and concerned citizens were taking the podium to demand a worldwide ban on all forms of human cloning experiments, including cloning for body parts.

"What's next?" a decidedly unattractive and fervent female speaker railed from the front of the room. "Mass production of blonde, blue-eyed children?"

Fielding rolled his eyes as dozens of spectators stood to applaud.

It was a fucking circus. Reporters everywhere, scribbling frantically; news crews scrambling for sound bites—"mass production of children," Fielding speculated, would undoubtedly make the cut—for the evening news. Religious types hoisting handmade signs, politicians manuevering to maximize their visibility.

And then the scientists.

Fielding's gaze scanned the room for his colleagues. Though they were vastly outnumbered, they were easy to pick out. Not just because he'd spent twenty-five years attending scientific seminars and symposiums with them, but because, no matter how hard they tried to avoid it, scientists wore their profession like a mantle. It wasn't just their clothing, though eight out of ten of those in attendance that day were dressed in near identical garb—dress pants that fell short of fashionable, short-sleeved work shirts (more practical than rolling up long sleeves), and your basic black or blue tie.

The few who broke the mold, as did Sherwood Fielding, who today was dressed in a navy blue Armani suit that accentuated his eyes, still managed to give themselves away with their comportment—a demeanor that inevitably combined equal parts no-nonsense sobriety, and superiority. Superiority that, they seemed to believe, flowed naturally from exceptional intelligence, and a lifetime of perceiving the world—*dissecting* the world—as though it were capable of reduction to a formula or theory. Fielding's first wife had once complained that making love with him was more an exercise in biological propagation than anything even remotely connected to passion. He'd never told her, but she was right.

After more dramatic speeches from an evangelist and a state representative, both of whom equated cloning with the devil himself, the room darkened dramatically.

The president of the United States' image appeared on an acre of screen above the podium.

"Science often moves faster than our ability to understand its implications," he said. "That is why we have a responsibility to move with caution and care. There is much about cloning we do not know. But this much we do know: Any discovery that touches upon human creation is not simply a matter of scientific inquiry, it is a matter of morality and spirituality as well."

"My own view," the president continued, "is that human cloning would raise deep concerns, given our most cherished concepts of faith and humanity. Each human life is unique, born of a miracle that reaches beyond laboratory science. We must respect this profound gift and resist the temptation to replicate ourselves.''

For the most part, lukewarm applause greeted these words, but one man seated in the middle of the audience stood and shouted, ''That's not enough. It's not enough to talk about *resisting the temptation*. We have to outlaw this abomination. Once and for all.''

The chant—which in Sherwood Fielding's opinion had obviously been orchestrated—began slowly, but as it spread throughout the auditorium, it grew, drowning out the rest of the President's words. The female who'd spoken earlier seemed to be leading it, cheerleading-like, from the front of the room.

''*Ban human cloning! Ban human cloning!*''

It was an awkward phrase, nothing like the *Down with America* chorus he'd heard fifty thousand Iraqis screaming on the morning's news, but when he thought about it, Fielding could come up with nothing more catchy. Perhaps cloning wasn't conducive to uprisings and mass demonstrations. He strode toward the door he'd entered just minutes earlier. He'd already seen enough. All these histrionics, talk of a worldwide ban on human cloning, did nothing but disgust and, to some extent, amuse him.

What did it matter?

Did anyone really think it would stop it from happening?

Did anyone really think it would stop him?

FOUR

A M I INTERRUPTING ANYTHING?"Jennifer Rockhill turned away from the window to face her unexpected visitor. How long had Angelique Mannington, one of BioGentech's top research scientists, been standing there? For some reason, Jennifer had the feeling it might have been a while.

"Of course not," Jennifer smiled. "I'm not being paid to enjoy the view."

"Hey," said Angelique, "you're only human. Right?"

"Oh so true," Jennifer chuckled. "Now, what can I do for you?"

Angelique slid a file on to Jennifer's desk. "Just wanted to drop this off. It's the protocol on that Lundgren study."

"You mean the retroviral vector research?" Jennifer asked.

Angelique raised her eyebrows.

"I'm impressed," she said. "You're catching on fast."

"I'm trying," Jennifer responded. "Of course, some things are done differently here than what I was used to at Fresno State, but overall, the transition hasn't been that difficult."

"How long has it been now? Seems like you've been here forever."

Jennifer didn't know how to take Angelique's comment, but her desire to get to know the scientist dictated a cordial response.

"Five weeks. And thanks, it's nice to know I fit in. This is a great place to work. How long have you been here?"

"Just over a year."

"Really? That's amazing. From what I hear, you're already in line to succeed the head of Medical Research. What was his name? I've seen it on several contracts but I can't seem to think of it now."

"Geoffrey Spillman. He left just before you were hired." Angelique paused, then went on, "So that's what you've been hearing? That I'll be the next head of Research?"

"That's the word. You've obviously impressed Dr. Fielding."

Jennifer didn't add that rumor also had it Angelique Mannington was having an affair with the married Sherwood Fielding—news which had prompted Jennifer to put befriending Angelique at the top of her agenda.

"Sherwood's shown a lot of interest in my research. He wants BioGentech to lead the way in using gene therapy to stimulate the immune system. It's one of our anti-cancer programs."

"And that's what your focus is? Using genes to soup up the immune system?"

"Exactly." Angelique sized Jennifer up for a moment, then, apparently caught up in Jennifer's interest and flattery, she said, "Listen, if you've got time, I could show you around the lab. Give you an idea of what we're up to. I need to get back there to check on a gel I'm running anyway. Want to join me?"

"I'd love to," Jennifer said.

WHILE MOST OF THE BioGentech offices, including Jennifer's, were located on the seventh floor, the labs were located on four and five. At the fourth floor, Jennifer followed Angelique off the elevator, and down a short corridor to a door marked RESTRICTED ACCESS, where the scientist used a passkey to gain entry.

Another short corridor greeted them on the other side. This one was flanked by doors, one of which displayed a sign bearing the warning CAUTION: RADIOACTIVE MATERIALS.

At its end, the corridor opened to one huge, well-lit room—almost warehouse-like in size. Partitions separating clusters of lab tables and desks created a maze-like effect. Scientists in spotless white coats stood or sat at lab benches and computers, making entries in large black three-ring binders, adding drops to test tubes, or peering into machines. There was an air of excitement in the room, a feeling that something important was taking place.

Angelique strode across the room's expanse confidently, her presence noticed by several of the scientists as she passed, though no one greeted her. She stopped at a counter upon which sat a row of four flat, square pieces of equipment that reminded Jennifer of a plastic leaf press she'd had as a kid.

"These are gels," Angelique announced. "Short for horizontal gel electrophoresis apparatus."

"Pretty impressive name for something that looks so simple." Each contraption appeared to consist of little more than two glass plates sandwiched together; however, a wire leading to each unit and the row of blue dots that appeared at a different place on each device hinted at more. "What are the blue dots?"

"Those are markers. That line just shows how far along the process is. The DNA is behind the line. What the gel does is separate it by the length of each fragment. Remember the OJ Simpson trial where they introduced the results of electrophoreses into evidence?"

Jennifer nodded.

"This enables forensic scientists to identify mystery DNA by comparing its migration across the plate to that of a known DNA sample. The gel is a material called agarose—it's like jello, only with starch instead of sugar. It sits in the upper tray. The lower tray, which is called the buffer chamber, is filled with a solution that conducts electricity. Because DNA has a negative charge, it migrates toward the positive charge at the other end of the plate. The gel acts kind of like a sieve. It's thick, and shorter pieces of DNA can get through it faster, so they reach the other end first."

"How do you get pieces of DNA in the first place?"

Angelique Mannington gave Jennifer an odd look.

"I'm surprised you don't already know," she said. "It's so basic. Enzymes. Particular enzymes recognize specific sites in a DNA sequence. They act like scissors, cut the DNA into fragments. Then you have to separate the fragments from each other. That's what this baby does. Didn't you get into the labs much at FSU?"

Angelique was right. Cutting DNA into pieces was basic. So basic that in all the research Jennifer had studied—research intended to be shared with other high-level medical professionals and scientists—no explanation had been necessary. She would have to watch herself more closely if she wanted to avoid exposing her fraudulent resume. A biotech attorney would be expected to know such things.

"We were in and out of the labs all the time. But I'm afraid our scientists weren't as generous with their time and knowledge. I didn't often get the chance to pick their brains. I still have a lot to learn. And this time I'll obviously be learning it from the best."

Jennifer breathed a sigh of relief when the scientist visibly brightened at this compliment and immediately resumed her lecture.

"Have you ever seen something like this?" She reached up to a shelf above the counter for what appeared to be a photograph. It was black-and-white, and printed on paper so thin it curled into a nicely rounded U, as if it were decades old. But there were no people or idyllic scenes in this photo. Only a sea of dull gray broken occasionally by short bright lines, maybe a dozen of them, scattered in what looked to Jennifer to be a haphazard pattern.

Jennifer bent to look closer. She wasn't sure how to respond now. Was Angelique testing her? If so, she was in trouble. Any guess she might make had the potential to reveal just how deficient her crash course in biotechnology had been.

"What is it?" she finally asked.

"A picture of DNA," Angelique answered. "After the gel's been run, you submerse it in a dye. There are several different dyes used; some of them are highly radioactive. The gel won't pick the dye up, but the DNA does. Certain dyes are specific to certain types of DNA. Then you take the stained gel in the UV room. The UV light is picked up by the dye. It's amazingly beautiful, really. The DNA glows, like psychedelic stars on a clear night. Maybe I'll show you how one of these days. You photograph it under the UV light. That's," she pointed at the photo, "what you end up with."

As she led Jennifer to her workspace—the biggest and brightest corner of the room—she pointed out other equipment used by the Bio-Gentech scientists.

"The gels are actually a pretty crude process. There are a lot more high-tech devices, like that magnetic resonance machine over there. It actually maps the protons in the DNA. But for ninety percent of the work done in this lab, the gel works just fine."

Somewhere in the lab, the shrill ring of a phone punctuated the hypnotic hum of all the combined lab equipment and machinery.

As they were settling onto lab stools for the continuation of Angelique's impromptu presentation, a short, balding scientist wearing jeans under his lab coat ran over to them.

"That was Sherwood," he said to Angelique. "He's waiting for you. In his car. Sounds a tad impatient."

The note of disdain was hard to miss, even for Jennifer, who had never before seen this man.

Angelique Mannington jumped up, looking at her watch.

"I lost track of time!"

She yanked open the cabinet below the lab counter and pulled out a purse. At the same time, she shed her lab coat, revealing a body-hugging white wrap-style blouse. Grabbing a pale blue blazer from the back of a nearby chair, Angelique all but ran out of the lab, calling back to Jennifer, "We'll have to continue this later."

Jennifer and the balding scientist exchanged an amused look.

"That'd be great," Jennifer called after her. "I've enjoyed it."

ON THE WAY BACK to her office, Jennifer noticed a woman's rest room in the hallway outside the lab. She detoured into it, but immediately after entering, she drew back.

There was a man standing at the sink. Their eyes made contact in the mirror, as Jennifer debated what to do. Turn around and leave? Demand that he leave?

Suddenly it occurred to her. She must have walked into the men's room by mistake. Embarrassed, she retreated. But when she'd reopened the door, still within sight of the rest room's other occupant, she saw immediately that the door said WOMEN.

"We both belong here," a voice—clearly that of a female—said from within the room.

If Jennifer hadn't known how to handle the situation before, she was at a total loss now. Her face flushed, she reentered the room and attempted a smile.

"I'm very sorry," she said. "I was just confused."

"About?"

About the fact that you're dressed like a man—down to the brown oxfords— and have a man's haircut.

"Nothing. Nothing at all."

Jennifer proceeded to one of the stalls.

Maybe, she hoped as she sat there waiting for footsteps to signal the other woman's exit, she's a visitor to the building and I'll never have to face her again. But the sinking feeling in the pit of her stomach told her she probably would not be that lucky.

CHAPTER

FIVE

GOOD MORNING, PHOENIX," the voice from the radio blared into the early morning stillness. "Ready for another scorcher?"

At least one of his listeners, Matthew Pace, was not.

"Record-breaking temperatures expected again today," the weather report continued. "Look for a high around a hundred and ten."

A hundred and ten. And it was only the first week of May. Matthew couldn't believe he'd committed to spending the upcoming summer in this blazing inferno. For heat, Matthew firmly believed, could make a man crazy. Put him over the edge.

He'd seen it firsthand. When he was still in the CIA, special operations training in the Mojave, 1982. Desert games, they called them.

His squadron had parachuted into the night. A moonless night, so black that, to the eye, earth was indistinguishable from sky. Gravity alone had given him some frame of reference from which to maneuver his free-falling body into position. He'd heard the terror in his comrades' voices. A jump that was supposed to be executed in absolute silence had been punctuated by several spontaneous, irrepressible *Holy Shits* that let Matthew Pace know he was not alone in finding this jump—the sensation of vaulting into nothingness—unique.

But there was one glaring difference between Matthew and the other free-falling soldiers that night.

Matthew Pace loved it. The absolute terror of having no idea, not a fucking clue, as to just how much distance separated his 185-pound frame from the night-cooled desert soil to which it hurtled at speeds over one hundred miles per hour.

Of course, in all fairness, he had to admit that it wasn't just the heat that had driven Edgar Banderas so crazy that he'd put a bullet through his head the second day into the mission. The ankle he'd broken in his jump was undoubtedly a contributing factor as well.

Still, none of the others had let the 125-degree sun get to them like Edgar had. Had allowed it to push them over the edge.

Yet, at this very moment, as he lay naked in his still-darkened room and listened to the KZZA weatherman announce the dawning of another record breaker, it occurred to Matthew Pace that if he had to spend the next two months here, in Phoenix, as he'd promised Nan he would, he might very well join the likes of Edgar Banderas.

Matthew rolled onto his back. His hand cupped his brow, as though shielding his eyes from glare; but, at 4:00 A.M., his room did not yet even hint at the approach of another day in the Valley of the Sun.

A sliver of moon shed just enough light to enable him to see the outline of Look Out Mountain. When he'd first moved into this fancy house, in the fancy resort community that fit the image World Therapeutics, Inc., wanted for him, he'd chosen the smaller of the two upstairs bedrooms to sleep in, just because of this view. He'd positioned his bed against the far wall so that Look Out was the last thing he saw at night. And the first thing in the morning.

It was the only thing he really liked about the house.

Matthew's hand moved across his chest, down his taut abdomen. And came to rest on his early morning erection. He stroked it, slowly. Methodically. Silently.

But soon he stopped. He wasn't really in the mood today. Maybe if the two idiots on the radio would shut up and put on some music. But no such luck. They kept up their moronic banter—was it his imagination or did every goddamn disc jockey these days think he was the next Jay Leno?—until his hand jerked from between his legs to the bedside table, where it smashed down on the snooze button of his clock radio, finally silencing the irritating banter.

It was just as well.

If he didn't get started on his morning run, it'd be into the nineties by the time he ended up on top of Look Out.

Swinging his long legs over the side of the bed, he sat, arms propped at his sides, allowing himself one more moment to fully awaken. Then he stood and walked to the sliding doors. Pushing aside the screen door, he stepped out onto a balcony that hovered twelve feet above his small, perfectly landscaped backyard. The motor to the self-cleaning pool—he'd insisted it be a lap pool, which ate up most the space in the postage-stamp-size yard—kicked in just then, its low hum the only sound in the predawn desert stillness. As was his ritual, he dropped down to the cement and pumped out a quick one hundred push-ups, his breathing on the last two or three just barely audible over the pump.

Matthew Pace's day had begun.

Like all others, it would start with his grueling workout regime. Matthew prided himself in being as fit at forty-one as he had been as a raw CIA recruit in the late seventies when he first entered a world in which physical fitness was a prerequisite, one that could literally make the difference between success or failure, life or death.

Of course, those days were gone. And while most people—if they were aware of what he did today, which they were not—would think the work he did now was still the stuff of James Bond movies, to a man who'd once survived a fiery plane crash while serving as a U.S. Far East spy, it was child's play.

Dressing quickly in gray cotton sweat shorts and white t-shirt, Matthew slipped out his front door and headed at a lope toward the golf course around which his community was built. A community Matthew chose because of his employer's dictum that he "blend in" with a certain kind of person. White, up-and-coming professionals. WTI wanted Matthew to look the role of a successful business executive. At the same time, it was essential that he maintain distance, a high degree of privacy. Mountain Estates fit both prerequisites. It was populated primarily by two-income yuppie families on the fast track, with just enough money and more than enough arrogance to ensure a community atmosphere of aloofness. When the realtor showed him around, Matthew knew immediately that so long as he drove the right car and adopted the right attitude, he wouldn't attract any undue attention. Two other factors solidified the deal: the fact that it was a gated community, and the location of the house. While virtually every other house in the development had sidewalks and drive-by traffic to contend with, Matthew's house, located at the end of a very private cul-de-sac, had neither. And it was one of only half a dozen homes with backyards that bordered the desert, at the base of the mountain. Of course, the price tag reflected the desirability of its location, but Matthew—single, childless, without any semblance of a social life—made good money and spent little. He could afford it. In short, though he could take or leave most everything else about it, Matthew ended up getting just what he most wanted in a house—one where there was no excuse for anyone to come within fifty feet without being invited.

He'd been there over a year now and no one, besides Nan and her kids, had been invited. Of course, he was gone a good deal of the time. Traveling on business. His last assignment, procuring a prototype of a blood sugar monitor from a Swedish pharmaceutical company, had him out of the country for three and a half months. It was his success at this assignment that had prompted WTI to "reward" him with two months off. A reward that felt more like punishment.

The last thing Matthew Pace wanted was time off.

No, that wasn't exactly true. The last thing Matthew Pace wanted was to spend a summer in Phoenix. And now, thanks to Nan, he had both—the next two months off and a summer in Phoenix to look forward to.

He'd only been off the job for two weeks and he was already ready to climb the wall. So antsy that, for the first time in his life, he thought he might just lose it. Go fucking crazy.

But Nan was dying of cancer, and when she heard he had time off, she'd asked him to stick around.

Nan was thirty-six. Matthew fully expected her to be dead before she reached thirty-seven, leaving behind two already fatherless children. She hadn't yet brought up the subject of the kids with him, but part of her agenda for asking him to stick around, Matthew suspected, was to encourage some bonding between them, in the hope that Matthew would step in when she died.

Matthew had no intention of becoming a surrogate father. He cared about Nan and her kids, but caring about them and changing his life for them were two different things. She should know that there was just so much she could ask of him, and right about now, it already felt like she had asked a little too much.

THE FIRST THING Jennifer did each morning, after logging on to the BioGentech network, was check her e-mail.

There were several messages this morning. One from Angelique Mannington, inquiring about Jennifer's progress on the Lundgren study, one from Jim Wilkes, informing all employees that the security system would soon be updated. And one from Dr. Fielding's secretary, Georgie Hill, asking Jennifer to drop by her office ASAP.

Jennifer wrote a brief reply to Angelique, informing her she'd have the first draft of the Lundgren study agreement done that afternoon, then she grabbed her empty coffee cup and headed toward the executive offices.

Passing the elevators, which she rarely used because they were ridiculously slow, Jennifer entered the stairwell. At the door marked "6," she used the security passkey that dangled from a chain around her neck to gain entry.

As she entered the reception area, she could see Zelma chatting with someone whose back was to her. Zelma noticed Jennifer right away.

"Hi, there," she said. "Have you two met?"

Jennifer's eyes traveled to the other person, who had turned her way. It was the woman from the rest room.

"Not *officially*," the other woman said with a tone so icy that it caused a look of startlement to cross Zelma's face.

Zelma graciously gestured from one woman to the other.

"Jennifer Rockhill, this is Patricia Lukins. Patricia, meet Jennifer. Jennifer," she told Patricia Lukins, "is the company attorney. Patricia," she told Jennifer, "is a research scientist."

Jennifer hoped her own expression didn't betray her horror at that bit of news.

Both women stepped forward, extending a hand, and muttered "Nice to meet you"s simultaneously. Then each stepped quickly back.

"I'm just on my way to see Georgie," Jennifer said, eager to move on.

She was almost out of sight when Patricia Lukins called after her. Jennifer stopped and spun around.

"I need to have a BMTA drafted. I hear you're in charge of that now. I guess that means we'll have to get together."

What was a BMTA?

"Of course," Jennifer said. "Would tomorrow be good for you?"

"How 'bout this afternoon? I'm kind of anxious to get to work on the study."

"I'm afraid the rest of my day's booked. But first thing tomorrow would work for me."

"What time do you get here?"

"By eight."

"Let's make it eight then," Patricia said. "In my lab, down on four."

Jennifer made a note of the meeting in her timekeeper, then continued down the hall.

Great. The woman she'd insulted in the rest room was not only a BioGentech employee, but a scientist—one with whom Jennifer would be forced to work. And it was pretty apparent from Patricia Lukins' behavior today that she had not forgotten, nor forgiven, Jennifer's blunder. What a way to start a working relationship. And just what was this "BMTA" she said she needed? Thank goodness she'd bought a little time to look into it. Something told her Patricia Lukins possessed a radar-like sixth sense. Jennifer had better come to the meeting prepared.

Jennifer stopped in the employee kitchen to fill her empty coffee cup on her way to Georgie Hill's office.

The BioGentech kitchen offered an assortment when it came to coffee: there were "Bed and Breakfast," "Raspberries and Cream," "Hazelnut," and plain old decaf. Bagels and fresh pastries sat on a tray. She reached for a banana nut muffin. A peace offering for Georgie Hill.

Georgie Hill was a sturdy, frequently sour woman, unmarried and in her midthirties. She made it a point to know everything about everyone at BioGentech and used her clout as Sherwood Fielding's secretary whenever, and as often as, possible. Like Angelique Mannington, Georgie's proximity to Fielding made her another person at the top of Jennifer's list. She'd heard Georgie could be very difficult, but so far Jennifer's and her relationship had gotten off to a good start.

Georgie was on the phone when Jennifer entered her office and did not look up, even though Jennifer was sure she'd caught her reflection on the computer screen.

Jennifer cleared her throat and placed the muffin on the desk, directly in front of Georgie, who glanced briefly her way, then returned to her conversation. Finally, after keeping Jennifer waiting several minutes, she ended the call and turned to her.

"Thanks for the muffin," she said. "I've had a taste for one all morning, but couldn't get away from that damn phone long enough to get one."

"Your job seems like a lot of pressure," Jennifer observed. "I can tell Dr. Fielding really relies on you." This technique had worked so well with Angelique Mannington that Jennifer couldn't resist giving it another try.

"Well, you know how these execs are. It's their secretaries who really do all the work." She giggled.

Jennifer laughed, too.

"I'm sure he'd be lost without you. Have you been here since he started the company?"

"Yep. From day one."

"How long ago was that?"

"Let's see. Just over two years. Two years and two months, to be exact."

So he hadn't wasted any time. He must have gone directly to Seattle after disappearing from Palm Springs. He'd undoubtedly felt that the distance, as well as a new city, offered some degree of protection. But Sherwood Fielding could have gone to China and she would have followed. It might have taken a bit longer, but eventually, Jennifer would have found him.

"That's hard to believe. Usually new companies struggle for years before they have this kind of feeling. You know, that aura of success. Where did BioGentech start out? I mean, before you moved into this incredible location and building."

"Actually, this is it," Georgie said. "This is what we started with. Two years ago, things looked pretty much like they do now. Of course, we have more employees now, like you, but somehow we managed to avoid that awful, struggling stage."

"Dr. Fielding must have lined up some impressive financing."

"Most of the money came from Sherwood himself. His medical practice before he came to Seattle was, apparently, extremely lucrative. And I've always had the feeling he has a couple of silent partners." She looked across the hall, in the direction of Sherwood Fielding's office, then lowered her voice. "I shouldn't be telling you this, but I think money's getting pretty tight now. That's why Sherwood's been trying to line up new investors. Of course, I'm not privy to company finances, but I think Sherwood wishes now that he hadn't been so extravagant to start with. He's been awfully uptight recently, and my guess is, it's got to do with money."

Jennifer lowered her voice, too.

"Gee, I hope my job's secure."

Georgie reached out and patted her hand.

"I shouldn't have said anything. You don't have a thing to worry about. You're actually saving us money. And I can tell Sherwood's very pleased with you. In fact, just this morning, he suggested that I take you out to dinner. He wants me to get to know you, to help you feel at home here, in Seattle."

"How thoughtful. I'd love to. Is that why you sent me that e-mail?"

"Partly. The other reason was to let you know Dr. Cannon called. He has the results of your physical."

Jennifer had been mildly surprised when, the first week on the job, Georgie had informed her that all new BioGentech employees were required to get physicals. When she'd acted surprised, even a bit resistant, Georgie had explained that their insurance carrier required it, due to the presence of hazardous materials on the premises. It helped keep premiums down.

"Well, did I pass?" she asked good-naturedly.

"I guess everything looked fine," Georgie answered. "Dr. Cannon said you can pick up the results at his office anytime after today."

"Well, that's good news," Jennifer responded. "Now how about that offer to go out to dinner? When would you like to do that?"

"Friday night might be kind of nice, don't you think?"

•   •   •

THE PHONE CALL had come in the middle of the night.

"Sorry to disturb you at this hour," the caller began, as he always did.

"No problem," Matthew had answered, sitting on the edge of his bed, his voice already surprisingly clear.

"I'm afraid we may have to interrupt the little vacation we promised you."

Wide-awake by then, Matthew had remained silent. Listening.

"Something's come up. Quite a fascinating matter. The company is actually quite interested." The voice, heavy with British accent, paused, letting the words settle in. "We need our best person on this one, Mr. Pace."

He'd worked for them five years now and was still addressed as "Mr. Pace."

Matthew could feel the rush that inevitably accompanied each such phone call.

"When," he said curtly. "And where?"

He knew better than to ask "what."

"Seattle," the caller answered. "You'll be receiving an over-night package in the morning. Usual procedure applies."

That meant a package containing all the details now known to WTI— details most likely concerning some new scientific discovery (perhaps in gene or drug therapy, for as a biotech firm, these were the areas in which WTI was most interested) that had apparently taken place in Seattle— would be arriving the next morning by 10:00 A.M. Also included, Matthew knew, would be a substantial amount of cash, enough to support him for several months, to enable him to acquire whatever equipment, services— whatever *identity*—he would need to fulfill his mission. A mission that would be spelled out with great precision in the package. The FedEx would also contain new telephone numbers and addresses that he was to use in communicating with WTI. As a matter of course, this always changed from assignment to assignment, to preclude the possibility that adversaries would stumble upon information being conveyed by Matthew to London. Adversaries who, like Matthew Pace, were most likely paid intelligence gatherers. Spies. Not your risk-your-life-and-limb-for-country kind of spies, as Matthew had once been. No, these were a different breed altogether. A new kind of spy, with a new mission.

Economic spies.

Some of them, like Matthew, had once been in the CIA. With the end of the Cold War, the agency's diminishing role had meant that hundreds of highly trained agents were let go. Perhaps that would eventually have been Matthew's fate as well, but Matthew had been the one to abruptly end his tenure with the agency.

For Matthew, a person on whom irony was never lost, the real irony of his new life was that along with other industrial spies, like himself but working for competitors, the CIA was now also his adversary. While critics of the beleaguered governmental agency were calling for deep budget cuts, even outright elimination of the agency, the President had come out strongly in support of it and advocated a new direction for the CIA, ordering the agency to make economic espionage of America's trade rivals a top priority. The agency had already reported success in uncovering bribes to foreign officials affecting over thirty billion dollars in foreign contracts. But while other nations, France and Japan in particular, were actively passing intelligence directly to corporations, the CIA, after vigorous internal debate, concluded that such a practice would be a perversion of the intelligence process. Besides, in the current era of multinational corporations, who would make the determination of which firms should be considered American and which should not? The CIA's role, it had been decided, would extend only to protecting American firms against penetration by foreign intelligence agents.

That meant today's CIA was out to get people like Matthew. People who were paid by foreign entities, even governments, to steal information from high-tech U.S. companies.

The knowledge that he was still competing with the "best and the brightest," as the agency liked to characterize its members, gave Matthew great pleasure.

Sleep had become out of the question. Matthew had gotten up and gone downstairs to the laundry room. He threw the wet clothes from the washer into the dryer and started a new load. Then he headed back upstairs to his bedroom, where he began to neatly fold shirts and slacks into his leather-trimmed canvas Pullman. When he'd finished packing, he reached under his bed and pulled out two very large, bright silver cases. They looked like that expensive, trendy luggage that went for over a thousand bucks in the Neiman Marcus catalog.

But the resemblance stopped there. These cases might look like something sported by the very wealthy, but it took more than money to buy them. It took the right job, with the right agency. Or, in Matthew's case, the right contacts.

One case contained a tactical audio recovery kit—two electret microphones and acoustic transducers, a scrambler, recorder, tube microphone, amplifier, and batteries. The other, an assortment of other highly specialized equipment. Equipment that Matthew knew well. So well that he had once trained other CIA agents in its use, at the "Farm," the secret CIA training center in rural Virginia. After leaving the agency, he'd had to establish new sources to keep up with the latest in surveillance technology. He'd entered a long-standing affair with an agent—carefully chosen for her position in the IEAD (Intelligence Equipment Acquisitions Department)—he'd trained years earlier. Students, he'd found, were always vulnerable and this one had fallen in love with him, making it that much easier to gain her cooperation. They'd only recently, when she became engaged, stopped seeing each other.

As he always did before setting out on a new assignment, the night before he'd come to Seattle, one by one, Matthew had carefully removed each piece of equipment from its case and inspected it. Maintenance of equipment, he'd always taught new recruits, was critical to success. It was an area frequently neglected, especially by older agents, because of its mundane nature. But one loose wire in a voice transmitter could sabotage an entire operation. It had never happened to Matthew. It never would.

By the time the sun had come up, he was packed and ready to go. He'd left for the airport as soon as the package arrived, after he'd called Nan. He had waited to the last minute to call her, knowing she would sleep in until her oldest son, Luke, woke her to say good-bye before leaving for school. Luke was a senior this year. His mother's pride and joy. Or at least, one of them.

Then Nan would get up and get breakfast for Tommy, a seventh-grader, and the other reason for her existence.

Matthew waited until Nan got both kids off to school, knowing as he did that she did not like to worry them any more than she already had. And then he made the call. Then he told her that work had, once again, beckoned and that he would not, after all, be able to spend the summer with her.

She had put up a brave front. Said she understood. That she would forgive him.

But what Matthew didn't know, even now, as he sat on a street in Seattle, observing the comings and goings at BioGentech's office building—as he had done for two days now—was whether he could forgive himself.

CHAPTER

SIX

BY THE NEXT MORNING, Jennifer knew that BMTA stood for "Biological Materials Transfer Agreement." She'd helped Grace with several material transfer agreements, so once she figured out the "B" stood for "Biological," she was able to relax somewhat about Patricia Lukins' request. And even though her first encounter with the scientist left her feeling apprehensive about having to work together, as she headed down to the labs, Jennifer had contemplated the possibility that Patricia Lukins could prove to be a good source of information.

She'd been pleased to find Patricia much friendlier today.

"The BMTA," Patricia Lukins—*Dr.* Lukins, Jennifer now knew to call her—explained, "is necessary for the next phase of my study."

They were standing at a lab table upon which sat a microscope, several small bottles of solution, an assortment of slides with specimens mounted, and a scattering of folders with a multitude of papers sticking out at odd angles.

"What biologicals are you working with?" Jennifer asked. The BMTA was a document used to cover the transfer of biological materials—which were then used by the BioGentech scientists in their preclinical and clinical studies—from one institution to another.

"It's a virus," Patricia Lukins answered. "A herpes virus that I need for my bystander effect studies. It's all here, in the file."

She slid a manila file across the tabletop to Jennifer, dismissing her.

Jennifer could have picked up the file and taken it back to her office to study, but she was intrigued. She found the work being conducted on the fourth and fifth floors of the BioGentech building fascinating. And if possible she wanted to undo the lousy start she and Patricia had gotten off to.

"Bystander effect?"

"Yes. It's a phenomenon I've been studying. Do you know anything about suicide genes?"

Maybe not leaving right away hadn't been such a good idea after all. Was Patricia Lukins testing her?

"Sure," Jennifer said, trying to project confidence. "That's when a gene is programmed to self-destruct."

Patricia Lukins gave Jennifer an odd look, but when she continued with her discourse, Jennifer assumed that if it had indeed been a test, she'd passed.

"Several years ago Dr. Culver—he's one of gene therapy's pioneers— came up with the idea of injecting an engineered herpes virus into brain tumors in rats. The virus contained what's called the HS-tk gene. HS-tk is only carried into a cell when it's dividing. In a mature brain, the cells have already stopped dividing, so in theory, the virus should only invade the dividing cells, which are the tumor cells we want to get at. Anyway, that's pretty much what happened. About sixty percent of the tumor cells incorporated the HS-tk gene. None of the normal cells did. Then Culver gave the rats ganciclovir—that's an antiherpes drug—and bang, it killed the tumor cells that had incorporated the virus."

"Sounds like a classic example of a suicide gene," Jennifer said, realizing now that her earlier definition had been off the mark.

"It was. But in this case the cells with the suicide gene weren't the only ones wiped out. Somehow a lot of tumor cells that hadn't even carried the HS-tk were also killed. One rat only had ten percent of its tumor cells take up the HS-tk, but the entire tumor disappeared. For some reason, the ganciclovir wiped out cells that hadn't even picked up the engineered virus. *That's* the bystander effect."

"Amazing," Jennifer said. "And that's what you're working on?"

"Yes. We're trying to understand the mechanism, why cells that don't even pick up the virus are wiped out, while healthy cells, cells side by side with those killed, are left alone."

"That must feel pretty good," Jennifer said softly, almost to herself. She had grown so jaded by the past couple years that she'd almost forgotten that people like Patricia Lukins devoted entire careers to trying to make a difference.

"Pardon me? *What* must feel good?"

"The knowledge that what you're doing could save lives. I mean, what I do—if it works—is keep people out of trouble. Out of court. What you do . . . well," she said, "that must feel pretty good."

For the first time, Patricia Lukins allowed her eyes to meet Jennifer's.

"My brother has inoperable brain cancer. He's enrolled in a University of Washington clinical study utilizing this same theory right now. So, yes, it does feel good to be doing something that could help. But the truth is, we couldn't do what we do without people like you supporting us. So don't give me too much credit."

Despite the awkward start they'd had, the two women seemed to sense in each other a common decency. Jennifer soon found herself seated at the table, listening in fascination to Patricia Lukins' history. Right out of her surgery residency she'd donated three years in the Dominican Republic as a medical missionary. Then, when her mother was dying of brain cancer, she returned to Seattle and changed career paths, dedicating herself to medical research. She made no mention of her personal life, but Jennifer assumed from Patricia's obvious dedication to her work that she was not involved in a serious relationship. Her brother's diagnosis one year earlier had clearly upped to a new level the scientist's determination to find answers.

"That's what drives me these days," she said. "And even if it's too late for David, there are plenty of others."

"I hadn't stopped to think how personal the work being done here is," Jennifer said. "It's easy to forget the human element of it. To think of it as mere science."

"Unfortunately, for some scientists, that's all it is. Science. Academia." Patricia let out a short, caustic laugh. "For some of the people who work here, the only human element involved in their work is ego. They're motivated more by the desire for recognition than by what this kind of work means to thousands of desperately ill people."

"That's a shame," Jennifer replied.

"You're telling me. But that shouldn't take away from their accomplishments. We've got some brilliant scientists here at BioGentech, people who stand to make a real difference."

"Sounds like I'm talking to one of them," Jennifer said.

"Let's hope so."

WHEN SHE'D FINISHED her meeting with Patricia, Jennifer headed over to Dr. Cannon's office to pick up the results of her physical. Dr. Cannon was nowhere in sight, but his receptionist cheerfully produced an envelope with her name on it. Emerging back outside, Jennifer decided not to go directly back to the office. It was another lovely day. Dr. Cannon's office was in the lower Queen Anne area, just half a mile from one of her favorite eateries, Larry's Market. Maybe she'd head over to Larry's for an early lunch. It felt good to be away from her desk and she was in the mood to play hookey a while longer.

In the month she'd been working at BioGentech she'd developed an appreciation for Queen Anne, the funky, off-beat district just north of downtown Seattle and west of Lake Union. It had so much more charm, she thought, than the polish and hustle bustle of downtown. Sidewalk cafes, pubs, antique furniture shops. Aside from the pricey condominium projects beginning to punctuate the skyline from the surrounding hills, no high-rises. And a blend of young (professionals who worked and lived in the area) and old (lifetime residents who'd lived in the area long before places like Larry's made it trendy) that made people-watching interesting.

Already thinking about Larry's clam chowder, she decided to leave her car at the Pay 'n Park next to the medical offices and started up the hill on foot toward the market.

She opened the envelope and read the lab results as she walked. Georgie was right, everything looked good—she was practically dead center in the "normal" range on every single test.

She found herself thoroughly enjoying the moment—the abundance of spring flowers mushrooming from planters along the sidewalk; the smell of freshly baked bread drifting her way as she passed the open door of a bakery; overhead, the call of seagulls as they rode the breeze coming off the waters of nearby Elliott Bay.

Larry's Market was fashioned after the European open-markets— stalls of exotic flowers at the store's entrance, food counters featuring multi-ethnic gourmet deli. Espresso and juice bar. An unsurpassed bakery. With its desirable location and all it had to offer, it was a happening place and came as close to providing Jennifer a social life as anything else these days.

She took her place in line at the lunch counter, then soon heard a voice raised in anger. Ahead of her, a well-dressed businessman was making life difficult for the woman taking sandwich orders by insisting that his turkey sandwich be on rye, which the cashier announced was not an option.

"Sourdough or wheat?" she repeated.

Pointing a manicured and suspiciously well-practiced finger in the direction of the bakery, the customer would not give up.

"You've got rye not ten yards from here. That's what I want. A turkey on rye."

His voice was loud, bullying, drawing the attention of several other shoppers, including an attractive man from the next line, who caught Jennifer off-guard by tossing her a smile and shaking his head in an "It takes all kinds" kind of gesture.

The cashier and irate customer had come to a standstill and now awaited the arrival of a store manager to settle the dispute. Meanwhile the man who'd smiled at her had moved to the front of the line at the juice counter. With his attention directed to the clerk taking his order, Jennifer took advantage of the chance to check him out. It was just curiosity, she told herself, a desire to see what kind of a guy he was.

She came to one conclusion very quickly. He was not hard to look at.

He was on the tall side, maybe six-one, with closely cropped sandy hair, a strong profile, and the tanned, well-lined face of an outdoorsman. He was dressed, however, in casual business attire—tan slacks and a blue denim shirt, sleeves rolled up, with a colorful floral silk tie. She was struck by his lean, taut physique and ramrod-straight posture, and would have guessed that he was an athlete of some sort if it weren't for his age, which she thought to be close to hers. She watched as he ordered a carrot and wheatgrass, but she was careful to turn away before he accepted change from the twenty he'd handed the girl in payment.

From the corner of her eye she saw that after leaving the juice counter he'd joined the line in which she stood. Still, she could have sworn there were several customers separating them. A few seconds later, when he spoke to her over her shoulder, it startled her.

"I hope you're not planning to order a sandwich on rye."

She turned. He was standing directly behind her.

"No," she said. "Just soup."

She had already turned her back to him again before she realized his comment had been an attempt at humor. She let out a short laugh and turned back.

"I just got it," she said, half-embarrassed. "Sorry."

He had piercing blue eyes that lacked much warmth, but they were offset by a nice smile.

"Wasn't really that funny," he answered, then added, "Seinfeld has nothing to fear."

"I'm not so sure about that."

They didn't talk more. While she stood waiting her turn to order, Jennifer found herself uncomfortable knowing he was behind her. Yes, he was attractive, but she wasn't interested. Period. That part of her life was over.

She finally made her way to the front of the line. Minutes later, soup packed to go, Jennifer turned away from the counter.

"Enjoy your lunch," the friendly stranger said to her.

She didn't even bother to smile.

"Thanks. You, too."

WHEN JENNIFER RETURNED to the office, she was surprised to find Angelique Mannington standing at her desk, leafing through an open file.

"Can I help you find something?"

Angelique turned, flashing her perfect teeth in a friendly smile.

"I was just leaving you a note." She hurriedly closed the file in front of her and reached for a memo on the desktop. "It's for the ADPRT study. The study director has been changed. Dr. Nguyen is replacing Dr. Gallagher."

She handed Jennifer the memo, which consisted of one line announcing the substitution.

"That was Dr. Gallagher's baby," Jennifer said. "I can't believe he'd give it up."

"Actually, he hasn't agreed to it. He had no choice. Dr. Gallagher's been let go," Angelique said matter-of-factly.

"Let go! But why? Dr. Gallagher was so enthusiastic about how the study's going. He said BioGentech has high hopes for the ADPRT drugs."

"That's right. So far we've seen that by inhibiting the ADPRT—that's a DNA repair enzyme—the study drugs seem to make tumor cells more sensitive to destruction by chemotherapy. BioGentech does have big plans for those drugs. No doubt about it. But Jeremy Nguyen can take over. He's worked under Gallagher for two years now and has almost as good a grasp on the ADPRT inhibitors as Gallagher did. And I'll be involved now, too"

"But that doesn't make sense. If Gallagher was the foremost expert on these drugs, why let him go?"

Angelique gave Jennifer a quick appraising glance.

"It all comes down to money. Gallagher's on a year-to-year contract. It was renewal time. He knew how valuable this study is to BioGentech and he tried to cash in on it. Sherwood didn't go for it. He never does."

Ever since last week when she'd rushed out to meet Sherwood Fielding in his car, Angelique had been more open in discussing BioGentech's CEO with Jennifer. It was clear that the scientist had access to privileged administrative information.

"Besides," Angelique continued, "if the joint venture with R&R doesn't go through, we'll be looking at layoffs pretty quick. Gallagher was already one of our highest-paid scientists. Getting him off the payroll is a big help."

"Layoffs? You mean BioGentech's in financial trouble?"

Jennifer feigned surprise. She'd given Georgie Hill her word that the information she'd shared would be kept in confidence. It looked like Angelique might be as loose lipped about the situation as Sherwood Fielding's secretary. But while Jennifer thought Georgie's disclosure had been made in an effort to bring the two women closer, she had the feeling Angelique's disclosures had more of a one-upmanship nature. Angelique wanted to make sure Jennifer knew she was in a position of power at BioGentech.

Angelique laughed. "Don't let looks fool you. This place is running on empty. We'd been thinking about going public, but with biotech stocks in a slump for months now, that's been postponed. Sherwood's been bringing investors in for the big sell for almost a year. Several have come close, but at the last minute backed out. R&R's one of our last hopes."

Jennifer knew that R&R was Roslyn and Roslyn, an American pharmaceutical giant that BioGentech had been talking to about a collaboration valued at more than $30 million, in which R&R would contribute development funding for BioGentech's anti-cancer therapies. At yesterday's company-wide meeting, all employees had been informed that dignitaries from R&R would be making a visit soon. The message had been loud and clear, everyone was to be on their best behavior. To Jennifer's amusement, the scientists had even been instructed to "spiff up" that day.

"But why cut back on our most valuable asset—people like Dr. Gallagher? The rent on this building must cost a small fortune, being on the water like this and right in the city. Why not move the offices? Cut back on administrative expenses? Or incidentals? Surely that's preferable to letting scientists go."

Angelique's condescending laughter was beginning to irritate her.

"You've got a lot to learn about this place. Ever work around a bunch of physicians before? There are two kinds of doctors working here at BioGentech. The research scientists, like me, and the guys—and they're all guys—running this place, most of whom were highly successful surgeons and medical practitioners. While we lowly and expendable scientists are used to working within tight budgets, these guys are used to nothing but first class—don't know anything else. Cutting corners is simply not a concept they can, or are willing to, grasp." Jennifer detected a bitterness in Angelique's voice that, in light of her rather privileged position within the company, surprised her. "But there's actually a practical side to how this place is run, too. In this business, image is everything. When you're trying to attract big-time investors, like R&R, or some of the Japanese groups we've had in, you've got to look successful. You've got to make them want to be part of what you're up to, make them believe you're a company going places."

"But they must do an audit."

"Of course. And that's when we usually lose them. But first impressions, an atmosphere of success and excitement, can blind them, maybe make them willing to take more risk than they initially thought existed."

Jennifer, still standing there with her to-go bag from Larry's, stared at Angelique in disbelief.

"Listen," the scientist said, "don't look so shocked. We're no different than any of the other biotech firms out there. It can cost over a hundred million dollars to take a single pharmaceutical from inception to the marketplace. Takes years. Biotechnology is in its infancy. Most companies are still in the research phase and will fold before they ever see one penny of income, much less profit. The name of the game is staying afloat until you get product to market. And if some expenses have to be cut until that happens, or until funding comes through, you can be sure there won't be any that directly affect Sherwood."

Angelique's next words echoed those spoken by Georgie just one day earlier.

"Hey, you don't have anything to worry about. Neither do I. Sherwood's not about to let either of us go. He thinks I'm indispensable. He's always saying he wishes he could clone me," she smiled coyly at that disclosure. "And before we hired you, we were spending three times your salary on outside counsel."

"Thanks for the reassurance," Jennifer said.

She put her lunch on her desk then stood there, waiting for Angelique to go so that she could eat it. But Angelique seemed in no hurry to leave. She stood for another moment, then reached casually for the file she'd been going through when Jennifer first returned to her office.

"You know," the scientist said, "on second thought, I should probably take this file with me. Dr. Nguyen may need to get up to speed on some of the data in it."

"I thought he'd already been involved with Dr. Gallagher's ADPRT work."

Angelique hesitated.

"He has. But now that he's in charge, he may feel a need to review its history. I'll just give him a chance to look at this, then get it back to you tomorrow. You don't mind, do you?"

"Actually," Jennifer said, "I was planning to work on it this afternoon."

Angelique, who by now had turned to leave—file already in hand—paused and threw just one quick glance back over her shoulder.

"Sorry about the inconvenience," she said. Then she disappeared out the door

TONIGHT'S DINNER WOULD BE the first time Jennifer had been out socially since before Charlie and Stacey died.

Georgie had come to her office earlier that day to make plans.

"Sherwood says the entire evening is on the company," she'd beamed. "That means the sky's the limit. Where would you like to go?"

"I'll let you choose. I'm easy to please. And I don't know any of the restaurants here yet."

"Well, how about starting at Cucina, Cucina. They have a great bar, and then we can either stay put for dinner, or, if something else sounds good, leave."

Jennifer did not usually drink. Her father had been a recovering alcoholic. She'd always figured that, coupled with her heritage, was reason enough to avoid alcohol. But tonight a few drinks might be a good idea.

"I'll meet you there at the bar. What time?"

"Seven okay?"

"See you at seven."

Now, as she sat waiting for Georgie on a padded bench inside the restaurant's entry, Jennifer felt like the proverbial fish out of water. She'd stuck her head in the bar, but immediately chose to wait outside instead. A steady stream of young, slinkily clad women, usually in groups of two and three, passed by her on their way inside, all of them hungrily checking out every male in sight. Equal numbers of males of every age—in contrast to the women, who seemed to be primarily in their twenties—joined the parade. Most looked to Jennifer like carbon copies of the others. White, clean cut, dressed in tailored slacks and crisp, long-sleeved shirts, most of which were worn rolled up. Ninety percent sported that half-wet, half-slick-backed hairstyle that was so big down in California. In the time she sat there, Jennifer saw only one or two couples. Cucina, Cucina was obviously a hot place for singles. Especially on a Friday night.

So this is what Georgie had in mind. Oh well, what difference did it make? The wilder and crazier the night, the looser Georgie's lips might turn out to be.

At 7:10, Georgie finally showed up. In the two hours since leaving the office, she'd managed to transform herself into someone Jennifer might not even have recognized had she not been watching specifically for her. Her usually mousey, shoulder-length brown hair was swept half up, with her bangs spiked to the side. Her lips and eyes were lined and heavily made up. Instead of the customary long skirt and flats Jennifer had grown used to seeing the secretary in, she had on a stylish pantsuit that, despite her ample figure, was quite flattering.

"Look at you," Jennifer proclaimed. "You're beautiful."

Georgie blushed.

"Sorry to keep you waiting. I got my hair done after work. And my makeup." She giggled then, and added, "As if you couldn't tell."

There were no empty tables, so the two of them made their way to the bar, where they were able to find adjoining stools. Georgie ordered a margarita. Jennifer chose wine.

The noise level was high, making it difficult to talk, but for two women just getting to know each other, it was awkward to remain silent for long, so they simply leaned into one another and raised their voices.

"So, are you happy with your job so far?" Georgie asked.

"Yes. I'm finding it really challenging."

"How about Seattle? I bet you're missing California. Where is it you came here from?"

"Visalia. It's a small town outside of Fresno, just south of the Bay Area."

"Lived there long?"

"I was born there," Jennifer said, which was true. What she didn't offer was that until she moved there after Charlie and Stacey's deaths, she hadn't been back in fifteen years.

"So you must have lots of family there."

"No, no family. None at all, not in Visalia, not anywhere."

Georgie seemed not to know how to respond to this answer.

"Oh," she finally said.

They sat, pretending to be interested in what was going on around them, for a while. The crowd was getting louder and more raucous. Jennifer found the whole scene extremely depressing. The noise made conversation difficult, so the one benefit she'd seen to starting out at a bar—a few drinks getting Georgie relaxed enough to talk freely about Sherwood Fielding—was looking less than promising. She hoped Georgie would want to leave Cucina, Cucina when it came time to eat. But from all outward appearances, Georgie seemed to be enjoying herself. When she ordered another drink, Jennifer declined. She still had half a glass of wine.

When the second margarita was delivered, Georgie opened her purse to pay for it.

"That gentleman over there picked up the tab," the barmaid said, pointing toward the middle of the room.

The room was packed tight with small tables, all of which were occupied, many of them with more than the designated four to a table. As Jennifer's eyes swept in the direction the waitress indicated, one table, one man, in particular, immediately caught her attention.

He was seated alone, about halfway between the bar and the window tables.

It was the good-looking man she'd seen earlier that week at Larry's. When their eyes met, he nodded.

"See, that's him," the waitress said. "Not bad looking either."

Georgie strained to get a look, her face flushed with excitement.

"Do you know him?" she asked, turning to Jennifer.

"Not really. But I recognize him. I ran into him at Larry's the other day."

"Well, we'd better go over and thank him."

"I don't think that's necessary. At least, not for me. After all, it's you he bought the drink for."

Georgie giggled.

"You're right. Guess I'd better go over there. Please, come with me."

Jennifer pushed Georgie jokingly.

"You don't need me. You're beautiful. Go get him."

Running her hand first over her hair, then reflexively down and across her midsection, Georgie rose from her stool.

"It would be rude of me not to thank him, wouldn't it?"

Jennifer nodded.

"I'll be right back."

Jennifer's curiosity made her want to watch what happened next, but she was annoyed at the man's actions and did not want to give him the satisfaction of her attention. She stared straight ahead, and realized that the wall behind the bar was mirrored. Over the reflections of a row of bottles, she watched as Georgie approached the table, then stood, gesturing nervously and smiling broadly. There were too many heads in the way for Jennifer to be able to see the man, who had remained seated. She saw Georgie turn and point her way, but then Georgie dropped into the sea of heads. She'd apparently joined the man at his table.

Shortly after that Jennifer became aware of the fact that someone had taken the stool vacated by Georgie. She looked to her left and came face-to-face with a red-faced, middle-aged man with a serious perspiration problem. Sweat rolled down his forehead in rivulets as he gave her a sloppy smile that made her think he was already half in the bag.

"Mind a little company?" he asked.

"Well, actually, my friend . . ." she started, but at that very moment, she felt a hand on her shoulder. She turned to see Georgie standing behind her. She looked absolutely radiant.

"Come on," she said. "He has an empty table and he's invited us to join him."

"But . . . but . . ." Jennifer stammered. "Maybe we should just go into the restaurant now and order dinner. Or try someplace else."

"He just ordered another round for us. We can't just leave now. It would be so rude. And he's really a great guy. I think you'll like him."

Jennifer tried to hide her anger. This certainly wasn't what she had in mind when she agreed to a dinner with Georgie. But it was clear that Georgie was having the time of her life and was not about to call it quits. And the prospect of sitting next to the slimeball that had just parked his rear end next to hers was decidedly less appealing than joining Georgie and the guy from Larry's.

"Okay," she finally said. "But just for one drink. I'm getting hungry."

Georgie couldn't get back to the table fast enough. When Jennifer arrived, she introduced her.

"Jennifer Rockhill, this is Matthew Pace. Matthew just moved here from Phoenix." Georgie had placed her hand on his arm, like they were old friends. "Jennifer is new to Seattle, too."

Matthew started to rise.

"No, please, sit down," Jennifer said. "It's nice to meet you."

"Same here," Matthew Pace said. He pushed the glass of wine he'd ordered for her in front of her. "So, where did you move here from?"

"California," Jennifer answered evasively.

"Big state," he replied.

"Yes, it is."

"Jennifer's our company attorney," Georgie chimed in.

"And what company is that?"

"BioGentech. It's a biopharmaceutical company here, in Seattle. I'm the executive assistant to its president."

Matthew raised his eyebrows.

"Biopharmaceutical? What the heck is that?"

Georgie giggled. She seemed pleased to have impressed him.

"It's like a regular pharmaceutical company, but instead of using chemicals our scientists use biologicals to come up with ways to treat diseases."

"I'm probably starting to sound pretty ignorant," Matthew Pace said, "but just what are biologicals?"

Georgie hesitated. "You know, genes and . . . and other living things. Jennifer, help me out here."

"Have you heard of genetic engineering?" Jennifer said, somewhat reluctantly, to Matthew.

Matthew nodded. "I've heard of it, but I'm not sure I know what it means."

"Genetic engineers," Jennifer explained, "like those at BioGentech, focus on the decoding of DNA. By studying the genes and manipulating them scientists try to block, or even reverse, the course of disease."

"Like cancer," Georgie added.

"So," said Matthew, his attention now focused solely upon Jennifer, "as the company attorney, do you get involved with all the scientific stuff?"

"I write the research agreements. BioGentech farms out a fair amount of research to various hospital and research facilities. I negotiate and write the terms and conditions of the arrangement between BioGentech and the institution that's actually conducting the experiments or clinical trials, or whatever. But before I do that, I have to get a pretty good understanding of what we're trying to accomplish, so I spend a lot of time studying the files."

"Fascinating," Matthew observed. Then, as if he sensed the expression of growing disappointment on Georgie's face, he turned back to her.

"Now, tell me more about what *you* do at BioGentech."

Georgie perked right up.

As Georgie launched into a glorification of her usually mundane tasks, Jennifer found herself studying this man, this Matthew Pace from Phoenix.

He was one smooth character. He had Georgie in the palm of his hand, and the truth was that at one time in her life, he might well have had the same effect on Jennifer. But right now, all that Jennifer felt toward him was resentment for interfering with her plans to pump Georgie for information about Sherwood Fielding.

Actually, the more she thought about it, the more she realized that her feelings extended beyond mere resentment. The room was full of attractive, obviously available women. Why had he chosen her and Georgie for the objects of his attention, when they were, after all, at least a dozen years older than most of the other women in the bar? Jennifer had once been considered something of a beauty, but since Charlie died, she had simply stopped caring about her looks and found it almost inconceivable that this Matthew Pace had chosen her out of the veritable banquet offered by the Cucina, Cucina singles scene. And despite her improved appearance this night, in light of the competition present—and it was a competition, of that Jennifer had no doubt—it was highly unlikely Georgie Hill had caught his eye.

So why had he picked them? Was he some kind of sicko, who considered the two oldest women in the room the most vulnerable?

"Jennifer?"

It was Georgie speaking.

"Matthew asked if we'd like to join him for dinner. We'd love to, wouldn't we?"

CHAPTER

SEVEN

EVER SINCE HE FOUNDED BioGentech, Sherwood Fielding had been holding the annual meeting of the management team in Las Vegas. Another junket financed by the company. This year he'd thought of telling the other four team members that the meeting would take place in Seattle; but he knew the conclusions everyone would jump to and he had too much pride to acknowledge just how much trouble the company was in. And so they'd all had two days of gambling, drinking, and lying next to the pool at BioGentech's expense. There was also, on the afternoon they departed, a brief meeting.

The current subject was whether to take BioGentech public.

"I know that biotech stocks as a whole shot up after the cloning news out of Scotland," Ralph Stockman, chief scientific officer, said.

"But don't forget Synertech." It was Marcus Fritz, chief operations officer, talking now. "Back in 1991, I bought at seventy-three dollars and sold at forty dollars. It could have been worse—it bottomed out at four dollars. I'm still staying away from them."

Sherwood Fielding cleared his throat. "But, Marcus, some biotech stocks doubled last year. What other industry is performing like that?"

Marcus took another sip of his afternoon martini before answering.

"Don't take offense, Sherwood. I'm conservative by nature. I just read that funds are so tight in the biotech industry, something like fifty-eight percent of all companies have less than a year of reserves left. All I'm saying is I don't want to be holding stock in any of those fifty-eight when the money dries up. And I don't think it's wise for BioGentech to go public in that climate."

"It's high-risk stock, no doubt about it," chimed in Craig Leff, newly appointed chief financial officer. Sherwood had recently hired Craig away from a competitor. Leff knew his stuff, and his opinion carried weight not just with Sherwood, but with the rest of the team as well. "Most biotech companies are one-drug research outfits. And we all know that only one in ten applications gets FDA approval. Plus there can be half a dozen companies working on the same basic treatment. It's just a matter of who wins the race. I read recently that only a dozen of the three hundred publicly traded firms showed a profit last year. Hell, the front page of today's issue of *BioWorld* tells the whole story. One headline was about Progenetics postponing its initial public offering because of the down market. The other was about Receptagen scaling back staff due to its cash crunch."

"There's no doubt that a lot of biotech firms will be out of business by the end of this decade," Fielding said. "But the ones that survive the shake-up are going to pay dividends that will make even Microsoft shareholders stand up and take notice."

"And BioGentech will undoubtedly be one of the survivors," Craig Leff said with diplomacy. "But a successful stock offering hinges on timing. And it would be premature to go public now, Sherwood. Especially in light of the Genome Tech news. Trust me. This just isn't the time— unless you've got another Dolly up your sleeve."

Sherwood's outward composure did not hint at his ire at the drift this conversation had taken. It was, for him, a touchy subject and, of course, hardly news. He didn't need to be reminded of the competitive nature of the business, not after the recent FDA approval of Genome Tech's late-stage prostate cancer treatment shot two years of BioGentech's research on a similar treatment out of the water. Odds of surviving in the biotech industry were abysmal. When he'd started out, he thought that the millions he'd personally invested, coupled with matching dollars from the Alpha Center, would be more than enough to see BioGentech's first drug to market. But at the rate they were going, BioGentech fell within the fifty-eight percent that would be out of funds within the year. And they were still at least two years away from product.

Venture capital might have been available in the past, but too many companies had been failing and that option for funding had grown tight. The discussion at hand was ample evidence of the fact that a public offering—another means of raising the millions needed to fund the ongoing research—was not, at this time, a practical solution for BioGentech either. That left contracting with partners like R&R for development, a project he'd been working on tirelessly for months now. But recently even that was looking shaky. He'd hired Craig Leff to polish up BioGentech's books for the R&R audit, but Leff had reported little success in being able to manipulate numbers to come up with a more attractive portfolio.

But Sherwood Fielding still had one ace in the hole. And he was counting on it to save BioGentech and guarantee the continuation of this lifestyle he'd built for himself.

After the meeting, everyone but Sherwood headed for the casino for one last shot at going home with a fat pocketbook. Sherwood, however, returned to his room, where he withdrew his laptop from its carrying case and set it up on the desk.

He could just as easily have picked up the telephone but he hadn't carried his address book with him, so he didn't have Tupeni Sanday's private number. He'd long ago, however, entered Tupeni's e-mail address in his laptop organizer.

An e-mail, he decided, was probably a better idea for now anyway, as he hadn't had a status meeting with Ram Chandra for a while. A telephone conversation could open him up to questions he wasn't prepared to answer. But after this afternoon's meeting he felt an acute need to be proactive. For that, e-mail would do nicely.

> Your Royal Highness, Tupeni Sanday:
> Just an update to report that we are progressing according to schedule and fully anticipate delivery by, or perhaps even prior to, the date previously agreed upon.
> As always, feel free to call me at any time.
> Yours sincerely,
> Sherwood Fielding, MD.

He read it twice. It was short and to the point, reaffirming their arrangement without saying anything that could prove to be of value to a hacker.

He clicked on the "send" icon and waited for confirmation, a sense of satisfaction at his business acumen settling over him. Sherwood had long ago learned that poor communication between parties to a business deal could spell its demise and with this one, he wasn't about to let that happen.

Next he picked up the phone and dialed the number of Ram Chandra, back in Washington State.

"Sherwood here," he said into the phone. "We need to meet. I want to go over everything you've got so far. The more promising results I can feed Tupeni Sanday, the hungrier he'll be to consummate this deal."

The voice on the other end, thick with Indian accent, did not sound pleased.

"Twice a week, I send you updated data. And I just met with Dr. Mannington yesterday and went over everything with her. Didn't she convey my message to you?"

So Angelique was poking her nose into things again. Maybe it had been a mistake to get her involved. But she was an ideal candidate, and Sherwood had known she'd be a more-than-willing participant. Especially when it gave her the leverage it did at BioGentech. She was one power-hungry lady. He'd recognized that in her from the start.

"I've been out of town. What message?"

"That I must have that solution. You get me the formula to that solution and I'll give you just what you ordered—what Tupeni Sanday ordered. Until then, there's not much point in a meeting. I'm already copying you on everything."

WHEN HE HUNG up the phone, Ram Chandra—stooped, his unruly black hair badly in need of a trim—let out a curse in his native tongue.

Yesterday's visit from Angelique Mannington had been bad enough. He didn't need Sherwood Fielding dogging him now, too. He was already frustrated. Frustrated and humiliated. To think that all his years of work, his brilliant research, now hinged on a formula devised by someone else—someone hardly worthy of holding his scientific jockstrap.

For days, Ram had devoured all the literature on Dolly the sheep, the world's first mammal cloned from adult cells. He had finally come to the realization that one missing link, a small but pivotal link, was the only thing standing in the way of his duplicating the work done by Ian Wilmut to create Dolly—only Ram's work involved an even more advanced species. And much to his chagrin, he now believed that that link could be provided by a rather mediocre scientist he'd been teamed up with earlier in his cloning work at BioGentech. Ram had spent years conducting embryo-twinning studies, work that had revolutionized the beef industry because of its ability to produce herds of genetically superior, identical cattle. Gregory Gallagher had been teamed with him on the cloning work for a while, but it had been Ram Chandra whom Fielding approached with a proposal. Fielding wanted him to produce the first-ever clone of a particular species. But what he *really* wanted was a clone from an adult. When Ram accepted, a public firing had been staged in order to enable Fielding to send Ram "underground" to work on this highly secret project. Gregory Gallagher had been left alone, floundering with his own ridiculous notions about cloning an adult cell. Never having achieved success, Gregory had finally redirected his attentions to the ADPRT studies.

The fact that Ram's work, his brilliant, groundbreaking work, could now depend upon another scientist—and a much inferior one at that—and something so utterly trivial as a solution was enough to drive him mad.

Angelique Mannington had picked up on it right away. He could see the pleasure it gave her. He'd never liked the wench, but the contempt he held her in now was going to make having to deal with her that much more distasteful.

She'd arrived at the lab yesterday unannounced, another unforgivable transgression. For Ram Chandra, the work he did in the lab was akin to that of the writer who requires solitude for his craft, or the painter who hikes miles to set up his easel in the middle of an idyllic mountain clearing. Interruptions, especially of the human kind, were not welcome.

These American scientists were a pathetic bunch. They had no true appreciation of the scientific process. They'd managed to corrupt it, commercialize it, use it for self-promotion and ego aggrandizement. For Ram Chandra, science, in its truest and most pure form, was an art.

But while there was no denying its position on the cutting edge, science in America had become an ugly political animal. And in the mind of Ram Chandra, no one individual personified this state of affairs more vividly than Angelique Mannington. Her visit yesterday was a case in point.

"I hear you're stymied," she'd started out as she reached for the sheet of paper on which Chandra had been making data entries.

"Sherwood told you that?"

She peered at him from over the glasses she'd slipped on soon after appearing in the doorway to his lab.

"Who else could have?"

Chandra didn't answer.

"So what's the problem?"

Chandra simply stared at her.

"Why are you here?" he asked.

Off came the glasses.

"You know damn well why I'm here," Angelique responded. "I have as much interest in this project as you." She chuckled then. "Maybe even more, considering what I've contributed to it."

When Chandra's eyes filled with fury, a fury he dared not unleash, she went on. "That drives you crazy, doesn't it? Well, don't let it. I'm not here to interfere. I want this to succeed every bit as much as you do. I have just as much riding on it. Now, tell me what's going on."

With a sigh, avoiding his fellow scientist's penetrating gaze, Chandra began.

"The embryo-twinning work is not, as you say, 'stymied' in the least. I've had considerable success in culture and even in early-stage implantation, which is quite remarkable, really, in light of the species. A pregnancy to term and successful delivery of a viable newborn would, as you well know, be a startling accomplishment, a scientific first. However, two of the three pregnant surrogates have begun showing signs of rejection and with the third, it's just too early to tell. I've been experimenting with anti-rejection programs and think I've come up with one that could solve the problem."

"Well," Angelique said dryly, "since the world will never be the wiser for it, and the chances of successful delivery seem remote right now at best, I wouldn't start writing that acceptance speech for the Nobel just yet. What about your most recent attempt? You know *that's* what really matters here."

Chandra decided to ignore the wisecrack about the Nobel—she was only telling the truth anyway, so how do you come back on that?—and continued.

"It's a mistake to assume the twinning work is not important. It's very valuable for the adult-cell work, too," he said. "By enabling me to work out a lot of the rejection problems I'm sure to experience using adult donor cells, it's laying the groundwork for success there as well."

"But according to Sherwood, you haven't had any success with nuclear transfusion. So it seems to me premature to worry about rejection."

"I'm literally one step away from success, of that I'm absolutely certain. I'd suspected as much for a while now, but the PPL work just confirmed it." PPL Therapeutics was the small Scottish biotech firm that had provided much of the funding for the work that led to Dolly's birth. "As cells mature and create specialized tissues, they gradually turn off thousands of genes that are no longer needed. It's always been believed that these shutdown genes were turned off permanently. But Dr. Wilmut and his team were able to induce a resting cycle in the adult donor cells. Then they fused the resting donor cell with an egg cell and somehow, the old genes from the adult were tricked into thinking they were young again." Excited about his subject now, Chandra was almost into one of his science-induced trances, any issues with Angelique Mannington temporarily forgotten. "The cloned cells began dividing and differentiating just as embryonic cells do. The only thing stopping me from having similar success, only on a grander scale, is finding the right solution to induce hibernation."

"You mean, Gregory Gallagher's solution."

"Yes, I believe Dr. Gallagher's solution would do it. It was based on the same theory apparently used by Wilmut—starving the cell, depriving it of nutrients. Not so drastically that its viability will be threatened, but somehow the low-nutrient solution induces a resting cycle. As I recall, that was Dr. Gallagher's finding as well. Only at the time, we didn't really appreciate what that meant. Of course, I know that with time I would be able to duplicate this solution, or come up with one that was even more effective."

"But time is something we can't afford to waste," Angelique said.

"So I'm told."

"Well, then, we'll just have to get you that formula," she'd said before departing.

Perhaps earlier in his career, Chandra might have probed a bit to see what Angelique Mannington meant by that comment. But now he had no real interest in how they got the formula. All he cared about was getting it, and succeeding at this quest.

In that respect, he realized he'd become a lot like his American colleagues. It was ego and money motivating him now. More money than he'd ever dreamed of.

But the difference between him and his American cohorts was what he would do with that money. He saw his share of the deal offered him by Sherwood Fielding as no less than a full-fledged, first-class ticket to scientific freedom. The ability to choose his work not by its likelihood of furthering an agenda set by someone other than himself, nor by the ever present pressure to publish and reap public acknowledgement for an ungrateful employer.

No, with financial freedom, he intended to focus on taking his work to an entirely new level. One where rules and restrictions had no place. Where the only obstacles to his success would be those imposed by his own limitations.

And since Ram Chandra firmly believed that no such limitations existed, who knew where that might lead?

EIGHT

THE FIRST MESSAGE on Jennifer's voice mail Monday morning had been left at 7:48 by Georgie Hill.

"Hope you're feeling better. Want to meet for coffee this morning? I've got lots to tell you. Give me a buzz."

Jennifer was relieved to hear Georgie sounding cheerful. She'd felt guilty all weekend and had even worried that something horrible might have happened when, on Friday night, Jennifer finally could take no more and, despite her silent vow to the contrary, she'd left a thoroughly inebriated Georgie on her own with Matthew Pace.

The three of them had spent more than two hours over dinner at Benjamin's, the restaurant next door to Cucina, Cucina—two hours in which Matthew Pace continued to order and pay for Georgie's drinks, while Jennifer made the switch from wine to coffee—and the evening had already begun to feel like it would never end when Georgie had suggested stopping by another bar, this one with a dance floor, before calling it a night.

"It almost feels like I'm coming down with something," Jennifer said in response. "Think I'd better get to bed."

This comment drew a suggestive look from Matthew Pace, which went unnoticed by Georgie.

"Come on, Jen," Georgie had slurred. Nobody had called her "Jen" in twenty years. "It's too early to go home. Just one more drink, and a dance or two."

Jennifer wondered whether her face revealed just how offensive she found the proposition. The more Georgie drank, the more turned off Jennifer became. And there was something about Matthew Pace that simply rubbed her the wrong way.

If her expression did, indeed, reveal all that, it was likely Matthew Pace had caught it, as all night he'd been studying her. She'd found it unnerving and rude.

"Really, I'm just beat," she'd reiterated. "I'm calling it quits."

After all, Georgie was a big girl. She could handle herself. She wasn't Jennifer's responsibility.

Yet when she'd finally climbed in her car and headed back to her apartment in Kirkland, Jennifer couldn't help but feel a little guilty. And worried.

After listening to two more messages, she dialed Georgie's extension.

"I'd love to meet for a break. Ten-thirty, lunchroom?"

"See you then."

Georgie was already in the lunchroom when Jennifer arrived. She looked like her old self again, the stylish hair and makeup gone, only there was something new about this Georgie. As Jennifer studied her, she realized what it was.

"I'm really sorry about Friday night," Fielding's secretary started.

"For what? There's nothing to apologize for," Jennifer said while actually thinking that an apology wasn't all that inappropriate.

"For abandoning you."

Now this was an interesting take on the evening.

"And," Georgie continued, "for making you feel like a third wheel. I was just having such a good time that I didn't stop to think how it must have made you feel."

"How *what* made me feel?"

"It wasn't until later, yesterday, that we realized you must have felt left out."

"*We?*"

"Yes, Matthew and I. We were talking about it. Yesterday. He was asking me about you, trying to understand you. You know, you were so quiet all night, and he just wondered if I thought there was something wrong or if that was just how you always are. We both realized that the two of us hitting it off so well Friday night had probably put you in an uncomfortable position. It's no wonder you wanted to go home so early."

So Georgie and Matthew had seen each other over the weekend. And they had been discussing her.

"It wasn't all that early," she said defensively. "It was after midnight."

Georgie smiled and touched Jennifer's arm.

"Well, I just hope you're not upset with me. I know we planned on it being a girls' night. I just hope you weren't disappointed."

"Not in the least. I had a good time."

"So did I," Georgie giggled. "He's really something, isn't he?"

"You mean Matthew?"

"Of course, I mean Matthew. Who else could I mean?"

When Jennifer was slow to answer, Georgie quickly turned combative. "What? What is it? You didn't like him?"

"No, it's not that I didn't like him. It's just that I like to take my time in getting to know someone. I've often found first impressions aren't to be trusted."

"What are you trying to say?"

"Just that in my experience, people don't always turn out to be what they at first seem. Especially when they start out seeming too good to be true."

Georgie bristled. She pushed back from her chair and abruptly stood. Several other BioGentech employees, also on break, looked their way as her voice rose in pitch.

"I suppose you think he's too good for me. That I was too easy for him."

"Georgie, that's not what I . . ."

"I suppose you think there was something wrong with bringing him back to my apartment that night."

So, that's what had happened.

"Well," Georgie huffed before Jennifer had a chance to recover, "maybe you're just jealous. That it was *me* he liked, and not you."

She'd turned heel, heading for the door.

"Georgie, please," Jennifer called after her. "You don't understand. I didn't mean . . ."

Georgie had already disappeared into the hallway when Jennifer realized that all eyes in the room were on her.

She could have run after her. But she'd already been embarrassed enough. And the truth was, she was angry. First, about Friday night. Now, about this.

Worst of all, it looked like her promising relationship with Georgie Hill had gone right down the tubes. And that *really* made Jennifer mad.

SOMETIMES HE ACTUALLY surprised himself by the depths to which he was willing to sink in order to succeed. It had been ingrained in him from the very start of his career. That kind of mentality toward his assignments. Only back then, such an attitude was easy to justify, for what was often at stake was no less than the security and well-being of an entire nation.

This, this was different. This he did strictly for money. No higher purpose. And, in reality, the money didn't even have much meaning to him. He had enough of it already. He was single, asocial, with no real use for material things. He could live on what he'd already put away for another fifty years, if he hung around that long.

So what it really boiled down to was that his job with WTI was just something to do. Something to give him purpose.

He had become a prostitute to a pharmaceutical company. A whore.

Matthew Pace smiled in amusement at the thought as he wiped away the coat of condensation on his bathroom mirror in preparation for his morning shave.

But in reality, he didn't find it very funny. In reality, he had been depressed ever since he'd departed the CIA. He'd always assumed he loved what he did because of the challenge of it. The element of danger. The high stakes. But to a large extent, he still had all of that in his current line of work. So that must not have been the real basis for his dedication. Maybe, he had, after all, been motivated by some sense of patriotism. Some belief he was making a difference.

Pretty noble notions. But it might just be possible.

Waking Saturday morning to the sight of a hungover Georgie Hill pretty much blasted any remnants of noble notions sky-high. He wasn't just a whore in the figurative sense. He had literally become one.

And the really frustrating thing was that he didn't think she was worth it. It wasn't that she wasn't willing to spill her guts to him, it was just that she didn't, as it turned out, have anything to spill. She was so fucking drunk by the time they got back to her apartment that had she worked at the White House, he could have gotten secrets of state out of her. Some of the information she'd given him on Sherwood Fielding—married, one child, having an affair with a BioGentech scientist, prone to masturbating in his office—might end up being helpful. But despite his obvious weaknesses, Sherwood apparently was smart enough to keep people like Georgie at arm's length from any of BioGentech's core technology. It quickly grew apparent to Matthew that Georgie Hill would have little to no access to information regarding any top secret, highly guarded work being done in the BioGentech labs. She might, however, prove useful at some point, probably as a ticket into the building, which is why he not only lingered after breakfast Saturday, but also returned to her apartment Sunday with a rented movie.

The one who had really piqued his interest, both professionally and personally, had been Jennifer Rockhill. She was not only stunning, but she had all but admitted that, as the company attorney, she was privy to high-level scientific information.

Oh to get inside the head—for starters—of that one.

But there was a significant problem with Jennifer Rockhill. She had a major chip on her shoulder. At least when it came to him. From what Georgie had told him about her, she didn't seem to have that attitude— an aloofness that Friday night bordered on downright hostility—at work.

But there was something else there. They'd barely been introduced when he picked up on it. It was more than a natural apprehension about strangers. She had an air of secrecy about her, the feeling of someone constantly looking over her shoulder. He'd seen it before, in his work with the agency. Jennifer Rockhill, he'd deduced by the end of the night, was not all she seemed. And that—the sense that she was hiding something—was what now dangled in front of him like a brass ring, waiting for him to grab it.

PATRICIA LUKINS DROPPED BY Jennifer's office later that afternoon.

Jennifer was sitting at her desk when she heard someone whistling a tune out in the hallway. Seconds later, Patricia's head popped through the partially opened door.

"Rolling Stones, right?" Jennifer guessed.

"Yep. *Vintage* Stones, if you need a clue." Patricia laughed, then challenged Jennifer, "Name that tune."

The scientist, dressed as always in a long-sleeved shirt and trousers, pursed her lips again and let loose with a couple more stanzas.

Jennifer's expression reflected deep concentration for a few seconds, then she broke into a smile.

"Can't Always Get What You Want!"

"I'm impressed," Patricia laughed.

"So how do I rate a visit today?" Jennifer's interest in Patricia had grown beyond merely seeing the scientist as someone who might prove helpful in her quest. She truly enjoyed Patricia Lukins' company. "Have a legal problem I can help you with?"

"Nope. I just wanted to share some good news with you. Remember I told you about my brother being in that clinical trial at the University of Washington?"

Jennifer nodded. "Of course I do. Have you heard anything?"

"Yes. He just called me. They told him there's been a measurable tumor response."

Jennifer jumped up and threw her arms around Patricia.

"That's wonderful. You must be thrilled."

"I am. I'm practically beside myself," Patricia said, beaming. "And it's not just David who's responding to the treatment. Five of the eight patients' tumors have shrunk. Only three of the trial's participants have been non-responsive. And it's still early. There's still hope they'll see a delayed reaction."

"Why don't we go have a beer to celebrate?"

"I've got too much work to do. Can I take a rain check?"

"Sure."

"Listen, I also wanted to let you know we're giving a lecture next week on the bystander effect. You seemed interested, so I thought you might want to attend."

"I'd love to," Jennifer said. "But who's *we?*"

For the first time since she'd arrived, Patricia's grin faded.

"Angelique Mannington and I," she said.

"Why Angelique? I didn't realize she was involved in your work."

"Involved?" Patricia snorted. "I'm not sure that's an appropriate description of her role. Let's just say she drops in from time to time to ask for updates. Apparently she and Fielding think that's good enough to get her name on the articles I've had published. And on the lecture credits."

Jennifer's jaw dropped.

"You've got to be kidding. And you put up with that?"

"I can't say I like it, but what difference does it really make? What matters is the work itself, not who gets credit for it. And my name's on there, too. What matters is the news I just got. Know what I mean?"

The outrage was spontaneous.

"But you can't let him get away with it. That son of a . . ."

Jennifer caught herself, but it was already too late. She didn't realize she'd balled both hands into tightly clenched fists until she saw Patricia's eyes drop to where they sat on her desktop.

"Listen to me!" Jennifer laughed uncomfortably. "Must be my PMS. Does it every time."

Patricia Lukins' eyes bore down upon her.

"Want to talk about it?"

"What? My PMS?"

"No." Patricia Lukins ran a hand through her closely cropped hair and with a sigh, dropped into the chair next to Jennifer's desk.

"Do you want to talk about what you're doing here?"

Jennifer's gasp was barely loud enough to be heard.

"What do you mean?"

Patricia's response came slowly, quietly.

"Look. You don't have to be afraid of me. If there's one thing I think I am, it's a good judge of people. And I know you're a good person. I can tell that. You must have your reasons for doing this, and I don't want to have to expose you."

"Expose me? I don't know what you're talking about."

"Let's not play games. Please. That day we were introduced, it was obvious you didn't know what a BMTA was. And for your information, a suicide gene isn't a gene that's programmed to self-destruct. It's a gene that's inserted into cancerous tissue—that, when treated with a killer drug, destroys the tumor."

Patricia's voice was patient, even kind.

"A biotech attorney should know that. My suspicions were aroused from the start, but I liked you, so I just wrote them off, decided you'd just fudged a little on your resume and there was no harm done. But your reaction just now . . . well, you'll have to admit it was a little extreme for someone who's only worked here a few weeks."

Jennifer had diverted her eyes to her hands, but she knew Patricia's gaze remained fixed to her.

"You're obviously a lawyer, and probably a damn good one. I'd wager you could get yourself a good job at any number of law firms, but for some reason you wanted to work here. My guess, from your reaction, is that it has to do with Sherwood Fielding."

When Jennifer did not respond, Patricia went on.

"Listen," she said, reaching halfway across the desk. "I don't want to have to go to Sherwood and tell him what I suspect. The truth is I have my own issues with Fielding. But I also have a professional responsibility. Tell me what's going on. Don't put me in this position. *Please.*"

Jennifer stood and walked to the door.

As she saw it, she had no choice. It was either trust Patricia Lukins with the truth, or be found out. Luckily, if anyone she'd met so far at BioGentech seemed capable of understanding, it was Patricia Lukins. In confessing, Jennifer would be playing Russian roulette, but she really had no choice.

She stuck her head out the door and glanced down the hallway in both directions.

Then she shut the door and turned to tell Patricia Lukins her story.

DRIVING BACK TO KIRKLAND that night, Jennifer debated whether to fix dinner at home or eat out.

Home. To call the one-bedroom unit in a complex of dozens of others identical to it "home" was pushing it. The only thing home-like about her choice of apartments was its location on the east side of Lake Washington. Kirkland's strips of beaches and upscale shops and eateries had reminded Jennifer of La Jolla. The generic apartment several blocks from the water had been all she could afford. Of course, she could have made some effort to personalize it, but she wasn't exactly feeling like Martha Stewart these days, when it came to decorating *or* cooking.

An empty space at a meter in front of her favorite restaurant, a place called Wraps, decided the matter. She pulled in and minutes later, was ordering a vegetarian wrap and fruit smoothie.

"To go, or will you be eating here?" the boy behind the counter asked.

She glanced at the window counter. It was empty. Why hurry home to a deafeningly silent apartment?

"I'll eat here," Jennifer answered.

She went back outside, dropped fifty cents into a slot, and returned to the counter with a *USA Today*.

This is actually kind of pleasant. It beats sitting alone in front of a TV.

She was lost in an article about a class-action suit against the tobacco companies when a voice roused her.

"Hello there."

She looked up, expecting to see the kid from behind the counter with her meal. But instead she found herself looking directly into the blue eyes of Matthew Pace.

"What are you doing here?"

Matthew grinned.

"Now that's the kind of greeting a man likes to hear."

At that instant, the boy who had taken Jennifer's order appeared, tray in hand.

"Here you go," he said to Jennifer. Then to Matthew, "Yours is next."

"Thanks," Matthew said, settling onto the chair next to Jennifer's.

Jennifer simply stared at him.

"*What?*" Matthew said. "I take it you're not exactly pleased to see me."

"Are you following me?"

His reaction, the fact that there was not a hint of defensiveness to it, threw Jennifer off.

"Now why would you think that? Are you used to being followed?"

When she didn't answer, he continued.

"Okay, I'll come clean. I was across the street, at that bar"—Jennifer's eyes followed the direction of his finger to a place called Laguna's— "when I saw you walk outside and buy a newspaper. So, yes, I guess you could say I followed you. But it wasn't just your exceptional looks that drew me in here. I was hungry, too. Now, when my food is delivered, if you'd like me to take it elsewhere, I will certainly do so. But I'd hoped that maybe if I got another shot at it, I could change your mind about me."

"Change my mind?"

"It was obvious the other night that you didn't like me. Call me an egotist, but that bothered me. When I saw you tonight, I saw it as a chance to start fresh."

Jennifer didn't know what to think. She'd had a draining day. A confrontation first with Georgie, then one with Patricia. Thank God Patricia had agreed not to expose her. But even so, she simply didn't have it in her to square off with Matthew now. Besides, just what was she afraid of? Worse-case scenario, he was attracted to her and had followed her, though if that were true, why would he have gone home with Georgie? None of it made sense, and she was simply too tired to try to sort it out.

As the boy placed his tray on the counter in front of him, Matthew looked at her questioningly.

"Well?"

"Feel free to stay," she said.

"Thank you."

They ate pretty much in silence. She had no desire to work at conversation, and it appeared Matthew knew better than to push her limited tolerance for his company.

"Care for some coffee?" he asked as they were both finishing up their wraps. "I think I'll go order a cup."

"Decaf would be nice," Jennifer answered. "Thanks."

He was just returning with two styrofoam cups in hand when he caught the toe of his boot on a chair and stumbled, sending a spray of steaming coffee Jennifer's way. The shoulder and back of her blazer took the biggest hit.

Matthew hurriedly placed the two cups on the counter and reached for napkins.

"I'm so sorry," he said, mopping at her shoulder. "I'll pay the cleaning bill."

Jennifer pushed his hands away.

"It's okay," she said. "Really."

She looked down. The shoulder and arm of her wheat-colored jacket now sported zebra-like stripes.

Matthew had borrowed a dishcloth from the kitchen. He was dipping it in his glass of water, then determinedly dabbing at her.

"Coffee will stain," he said. "Maybe if we get it right away . . ."

Jennifer pushed back from her chair.

"I'll run it under the faucet for a minute." Desperate to escape his touch, she made a beeline for the rest room.

When she got back, the counter had been wiped dry and Matthew was working on the streaks his mishap had left on her briefcase—which had been sitting on the counter next to her. She grabbed it from him.

"I'd better get home and soak my jacket," she said, holding it up for emphasis.

Matthew looked so embarrassed at what had happened that she almost found herself feeling sorry for him.

"Promise you'll let me take care of the cleaning bill," he persisted.

Why bother arguing? After all, she had absolutely no intention of ever seeing him again.

"Yes," Jennifer finally said. "I promise."

CHAPTER

NINE

MATTHEW WAS GROWING IMPATIENT. He'd been sitting in the rented car, a Ford Taurus wagon, for three hours now and—though the transmission from the frequency-synthesized receiver sitting in the attaché case on the seat beside him was remarkably clear—he hadn't heard a damn thing worth his while. Stakeouts, he'd once taught CIA recruits, were the bane of an agent's existence. More often than not they were so tedious that even the best agents risked losing focus. And as soon as that happened, a life could well be put in danger.

Relax not, die not, was the expression he'd drummed into their impressionable heads, knowing that six months from then, his words would most likely have faded into oblivion.

Of course, today's situation presented little danger, but still, Matthew would not allow that to affect his vigilance.

He'd been pleased at the ease with which he'd been able to get the pen—in which was hidden a state-of-the-art internal electret microphone that could be activated remotely—into Jennifer's briefcase. His only fear had been that when he doused her with coffee, she would either up and leave that minute or take the briefcase into the bathroom with her. But as he'd hoped, she was too rattled by the prospect of him pawing at her to think about the briefcase.

The line that had formed at the counter ensured that the employees were too busy to pay attention to what he was up to. He had just enough time to rifle through the briefcase's contents and plant the bug.

The first thing he perused was her wallet. There was a photograph of Jennifer with a good-looking man who had one arm around her and the other draped over the shoulder of a teenaged beauty who had Jennifer's eyes and lush mouth. Matthew was struck by how happy and at ease they all looked.

A social security card also caught his eye. He'd removed it from its plastic window and slid it into his back pocket.

When he unzipped a side compartment inside the bag, he really hit pay dirt. A security passkey. It had no identifying marks on it, but chances were it was from BioGentech.

Everything else was just what he would expect to find. A pen, lipstick, an address book, a small brush. A pad of tiny yellow Post-it notes. Ibuprofin. He substituted a generic-looking ballpoint pen for the one already in the briefcase and by the time she returned from the bathroom, he was making a show of wiping the coffee stains from its surface.

Well before 8 A.M. today, he'd positioned himself in the Taurus just across the street from BioGentech's offices, waiting for Jennifer to start her day. He'd decided off-street parking would be preferable to the parking lot adjacent to the building, though he was concerned that street traffic could present a problem with noise—"static" as he'd called it all those years of teaching surveillance technique.

So far the only problem, however, was that in over three hours, Jennifer had uttered less than a dozen words. She apparently worked solo in her office. He could hear her moving around. The click, click of her fingers, lightning quick as they struck the keyboard, was crisp and clear, indicating to him that she'd withdrawn the pen from her briefcase and placed it on her desk, just as he'd hoped she would. The microphone was actually sensitive enough to pick up sound from inside the case in the event she'd not taken it out, but the transmission from its current placement was near perfect.

Good girl, he thought.

Before that lucky day he'd been sitting outside BioGentech, when Jennifer's Volvo had emerged from the employee underground parking lot and he'd followed, first to some medical complex in Lower Queen Anne, then, on foot to Larry's, he'd had no success in penetrating the company's unusually restrictive barriers—barriers that indicated to him that something, indeed, was taking place there, just as WTI had suspected.

The "something" that was taking place was thought by WTI to be advanced cloning experiments. Cloning had been around for a long time now, but with the announcement of Dr. Ian Wilmut's success with Dolly, the first adult mammal to be cloned, it had become the hottest new field in the highly competitive world of biotechnology. Wilmut's work had established the unthinkable, that an adult cell was capable of reverting to embryonic stage and producing an entirely new, but genetically identical, creature. Biotech firms were in a frenzy, scrambling to get a piece of the lucrative pie that cloning represented. Cloned cows could produce more and richer milk—even, through genetic engineering, milk containing drugs for treatment of human disease. Cloning could produce organs used for human transplantation. By eliminating genetic differences that might impact test results and reliability, cloned monkeys could provide increased accuracy in drug studies. The potential was mind-boggling and, as Dolly had demonstrated, progress was being made at breakneck speed. And with so much at stake, economic espionage—the theft of trade secrets—was rampant.

The incentives WTI offered Matthew for finding out what Bio-Gentech was up to were extraordinary. In addition to his six-figure salary, a performance bonus stood to make him a wealthy man. If WTI actually used the information he acquired from BioGentech in WTI's own technology, he would be awarded an additional $200,000. And if WTI were successful in obtaining patent protection for the technology, that figure jumped to 1 million. Which is why the day he'd met Jennifer, Matthew had celebrated by pulling out one of his prize cigars—a Sancho Panza he'd bought in London. He'd savored its sweet, roasted nut flavor from his balcony.

The sound of Jennifer's phone ringing drew Matthew's attention back to the present.

"This is Jennifer," Jennifer's voice announced from the receiver sitting on the seat next to him. Then, after a pause, "Today? At noon? Yes, that's no problem. Tell Dr. Fielding I'll be there. Do you have any idea what this is about, so I can come prepared?"

The caller's response was very brief.

"Another thing, Georgie, if my passkey doesn't turn up today, how long will it take to get a new one?"

This time the response went on for a while.

"I've done that. I've retraced my steps from yesterday. As far as I can remember, I only used it once, and that was when I met you for coffee. Maybe I left it in the lunchroom. I used it to get down there but I didn't use it to get back up to the seventh floor—Mario was just heading downstairs and I remember he held the door open for me. The rest of the day I had so much to do that I stayed put." More from Georgie, then, with a hint of irritation, "Yes, I know that I'll have to pay twenty-five dollars for a replacement key. That the purpose of the fee is to serve as a deterrent to employees' losing them. That's not a problem."

It was clear from Jennifer's end of the conversation that something, perhaps Matthew, had cooled the friendship between her and Georgie.

After she'd hung up, Matthew heard Jennifer pick up the phone again and punch in four digits.

"Patricia, this is Jennifer. I just got a call from Georgie telling me Dr. Fielding wants to meet with me at noon. Guess that means I won't be able to make lunch after all. Sorry about that. Maybe tomorrow? Please call me to confirm that you got this message."

Matthew looked at his watch. Eleven-fifteen.

Maybe, just maybe, Jennifer would take the pen with her to Dr. Fielding's office. Wouldn't that be a coup?

With the exception of a call back from this Patricia person, nothing transpired in the next forty-five minutes. Matthew was disappointed to hear Jennifer's high-heeled footsteps, followed by the sound of her office door being closed, then locked from the other side, at just before twelve. She'd left the pen behind.

Matthew decided to grab a quick lunch while Jennifer was away from her office. He debated briefly whether to drive to a decent restaurant or just walk the two blocks to a 7-Eleven and pick up a sandwich. The audio transmission from where he now sat was so good that he hated to risk losing his parking spot. And with Jennifer tied up with Fielding, he needn't be concerned about her seeing him. The only other person who could recognize him, were she to see him on his way to the 7-Eleven, would be Georgie, and if that happened, he'd tell her he'd come down to Lake Union specifically looking for her. She'd eat that up.

Just before slipping out of the Taurus, he reached into the open attaché next to him, which housed his intelligence system, and, with the flip of a switch, activated the cassette recorder.

Even though the attaché left behind in the car also had a phone inside, when Matthew reached the 7-Eleven, he stopped outside to use the pay phone. Cellular calls were easily intercepted. He never used them for business, especially when calling Jack Eberhardt.

"Come up with anything yet?" he asked Eberhardt.

"Don't I always? Your lady friend was born Jennifer Alice Rockhill. She applied to the Social Security Administration for a new card with the name Jennifer A. Banks in 1977. The application cites her then-recent marriage as a basis for the change. Interestingly enough, records show she requested to have it changed back to Rockhill just two months ago."

"Divorce?"

"Sounds like it, doesn't it? And a less-than-amicable one. But I'm still checking. So far my gal in California hasn't found any record of proceedings in either of her names, so we might be barking up the wrong tree. I also ran a check with the California DMV. A year and a half ago she moved, from La Jolla to Visalia. Then, just a little over six weeks ago, she applied for another name change: from Banks back to Rockhill."

"Wonder why she'd bother changing in California when she was just about to move up here?" Matthew mused. "You'd think she'd do it all at once, when she went in to get her new Washington license."

"Maybe she needed to move up there as Jennifer Rockhill, not Jennifer Banks."

"Could be. Think you could get me some information on her husband? Or ex-husband. Chances are they got married in California."

"I'll try, but I've got other things on my plate. All hell's about to break loose because of these biological weapons rumors out in your neck of the woods. And every time I run one of your little data checks, I'm putting myself at risk. You know that, don't you?"

"Yeh, I know it," Matthew said tersely. "And you know I wouldn't ask if it weren't important. My offer still stands. Take me up on it anytime."

There was a pause before Jack Eberhardt responded.

"You know this isn't about money. I didn't mean to be an asshole. This place just gets to me sometimes. Sometimes I think you're the lucky one to be out of here."

"That's one way I don't think of myself."

"What?"

"As lucky."

They arranged to talk again the next day.

It was twelve-fifteen when Matthew arrived back at the Taurus. At first as he climbed into the car, the sound blended in with that of traffic, but once he closed the door, he realized the receiver was transmitting.

After checking to be sure the car windows were tightly closed, he reached into the attaché and turned the volume up. It took a few moments to recognize it, but finally, it came to him. It was the sound of pages being turned, shuffled through. What was odd was how long it went on. And why was Jennifer in her office, when she'd told him she had a meeting? Surely it wasn't already over. Had it been cancelled at the last minute?

The next second, Matthew got his answer. He heard the phone being picked up, numbers dialed (four again), then a voice, one which clearly did not belong to Jennifer.

"I can't find any trace of it," a female said, in hushed tones. "Are you still in a meeting with her?"

A pause, then, "I'm almost done. I've gone through all but one file. Be sure to warn me if she leaves and might be heading up this way."

More rifling through paper followed, then, finally, Matthew heard the scraping sound of a chair being pushed into its place under the desk, footsteps—high heels like Jennifer's. The click of a door. Then silence.

What the hell was that about?

He stopped the recorder and pressed the rewind button. He wanted to hear everything that had transpired in Jennifer's office since he left for lunch. Keeping one ear tuned for any further live transmissions—but the office seemed to be empty now—he waited for the tape to rewind, then pressed the play button and listened to everything that had taken place while he was gone.

There was silence for the first several minutes, then the jiggle of a doorknob—someone checking to see if the door was locked? The fact that it was apparently presented little in the way of deterrence, as the next sound was that of a key being used to open the door.

Then began the search through the files, which is where he'd first come in.

Who would be going through files on Jennifer's desk? Whoever it was, this person had a key to her office. The call she'd made had obviously been to Sherwood Fielding, which indicated his involvement, too. Was the meeting Fielding set up with Jennifer a sham, meant to keep her away while the search through her files took place?

And if so, just what was it they were after?

WHEN ANGELIQUE MANNINGTON entered his office, Sherwood Fielding's back was to her. He sat hunched over the powerful telescope that had been positioned on the credenza behind his desk, purportedly to indulge his interest in astronomy. But the instrument was rarely pointed skyward. Directly across Lake Union, on the western shore, the dock to one of several condominium projects showed signs of life. It was the start of a hot summer's day. Though Angelique couldn't make out the figures lying prone there, she had no doubt they were female, and clad in bikinis.

"What's wrong, wifey didn't put out this morning?"

Sherwood lingered at the telescope another moment, just to irritate her, then swiveled in his chair to face her.

"Very funny." He settled back in his chair, the picture of pomp and GQ high fashion, even at this early hour. "I don't know why I let you get away with talking to me like that. No one else dares to."

Angelique, her short skirt sliding up as she lowered herself into the chair opposite him, smirked.

"Just one of the perks, I guess."

They stared at each other a moment, a test of wills, then Sherwood spoke again.

"Did you find it?"

She shook her head.

"No trace of it. I went through every file on her desk. Gallagher has to be lying."

"I suspect you're right. Still, he swears he didn't take it with him when he left, that it's in his lab somewhere. Or that one of the assistants must have accidentally placed it in another file."

"Well, it's not in any of the files Jennifer has. I'm certain of that."

Fielding grew silent.

"Maybe Jeremy Nguyen can help," Angelique said.

"He was never involved. The only ones who worked on that cloning project were Gallagher and Chandra."

"I can't believe Ram doesn't have it then."

"Arresting the cell cycle to induce hibernation was Gallagher's concept. Chandra never bought into it. He and Gallagher practically came to blows over it. That's when Chandra came to me, threatening to quit. He refused to work with Gallagher anymore. Thought he was wasting their time and my money on this hibernation theory. In fact, he pretty much convinced me he was right. In light of how Ram felt about it, I'm not surprised he didn't keep any of the documentation, which is a damn shame since now he's convinced it's the key."

Fielding paused to pick at a strand of blond hair on the arm of his navy blazer. It could have belonged to either his wife or Angelique, but since his suits were dry-cleaned after each use and this was the first time he'd seen Angelique today, most likely this one came from his wife's thick head of hair.

"Looking back," he continued, "I think the real explanation for Chandra's skepticism may have been that he was threatened by it. He knew how big it would be, the acclaim Gallagher would have gotten had the theory worked. Hell, if it had worked, it would have been Gallagher announcing the first cloning of an adult mammal, not that Scottish yokel. I think that was why Chandra was so eager to break off from Gallagher, why he accepted my offer to continue the cloning work alone and in secret, and why he worked so hard at convincing me Gallagher's research was a waste of my money.

"That's why I stopped Gallagher, shut that research down," he continued. "Because of Chandra. He wanted to be the one that perfected the cloning technique. He didn't want to believe Gallagher's theory could work."

"But apparently now he does believe it," Angelique said. "He told me it's the one thing standing between him and success on this project. The one missing link. Sounds like you went with the wrong man from the start. Maybe it should be Gallagher out there, not Chandra."

"No amount of money would have bought Gallagher's cooperation on something like this. He's too straight an arrow. And at that time, I was inclined to agree with Chandra. Arresting the cycle seemed nonsense back then to me, too. But that's apparently what worked with Dolly. Gallagher knew it. Knew how valuable that formula became the moment the news broke about Dolly. Between that and the ADPRT study, he thought he had me over a barrel. Thought he could get just about anything he wanted from me. If there's one thing I'm absolutely certain of it's that there's no way he would have left BioGentech without that formula. And, apparently, he also decided there was no way he was going to leave it here for us to use. No, despite his insistence that it's still here, somewhere in one of his files, I'm convinced he has it."

"What are you going to do about it?"

Sherwood smiled then. He was a person who should never smile. Somber, he looked imposing, sophisticated. Powerful. A smile made him look almost stupid.

"Don't worry your pretty little head about that." His eyes strayed to her legs. "How about lunch today? I missed you yesterday."

"You could have fooled me. That meeting between you and Jennifer lasted almost an hour. I told you I only needed you to keep her out of her office for fifteen minutes."

"Jealous?"

Angelique snickered. "Hardly. She's not your type."

Fielding leveled his steely gaze at her.

"That's true. I like my women a little on the wild side. You know I can't get enough of you, don't you?"

"We might just have that problem solved, haven't we?"

"I'd like to think so."

TWO DAYS LATER, Matthew was again stationed outside the BioGentech building and listening in on Jennifer when someone dropped by her office.

"Have you heard about Dr. Gallagher?"

It was a woman's voice, throaty and deep, but not in a sexy way. Not the same one he'd heard in Jennifer's office the other day.

"You mean that he'd been let go?" This voice he knew. It belonged to Jennifer.

"No. Read this."

There was a sound of a newspaper being opened, then folded.

"There," the voice said, "that's the article."

There was silence for a moment, then a cry from Jennifer.

"Is that our Dr. Gallagher? Are you sure?"

"Yes. Zelma called the police department and they confirmed it. It's tragic, isn't it? . . . Hey, are you okay?"

"Yes, of course." Jennifer didn't sound quite right. "He seemed like a nice man. I felt badly when I heard he'd just been fired. But really, I hardly knew him."

"Listen, I'm sorry," Jennifer's visitor said. "I didn't mean to upset you. I just thought you'd want to know."

"Patricia, it's okay. I appreciate your telling me. It's just that . . ."

"Jesus, Jennifer," the other voice—apparently belonging to someone named Patricia—said suddenly. "I'm so sorry! What was I thinking? Your husband and daughter. They were in an automobile accident, too. Why didn't I think of that?"

"Their car went off a cliff just like Dr. Gallagher's." Jennifer's voice had grown so small that Matthew had to strain to hear. "It killed Stacey instantly. And I told you what happened to Charlie. A week later, he was dead, too."

The transmitter fell silent before Jennifer spoke again.

"Please, Patricia, don't feel bad. I had to learn about Dr. Gallagher somehow. And I'd rather hear it from you than someone else."

"I feel like a real jerk," Patricia said. "I hadn't thought about how this could affect you."

"Listen, you've been incredible. I'm the one who should feel bad. Laying what I did on you the other day. I want you to know, I have no intention of dragging you into this. Just knowing you're willing to keep my secret, well, I've probably asked too much of you already. But there's no other way."

"I've been giving it a lot of thought. Maybe I can help. At least be another pair of eyes and ears."

There was a long silence. Long enough for Matthew to reach for his transmitter and turn the volume knob. He didn't want to miss a word. Then Jennifer spoke again.

"I can't ask that of you," she said. "You have too much at stake here."

"Hey, I'm not saying I'll break into Fielding's office and start rifling through his files or anything like that. Hell, with that new security system they're putting in, none of us will be getting away with anything. But maybe I can help in some way."

"That means more to me than you could know."

"This place is starting to give me the creeps. We probably shouldn't even be talking here. Who knows what else is involved in this new security system they're putting in. If they can scan your irises, they can sure as hell bug our offices."

Just then Jennifer's phone rang. Before she picked it up, she hurriedly asked her visitor, "Want to get together after work? Go somewhere and talk?"

"I have to visit David at the hospital tonight," Patricia answered. "But maybe tomorrow."

When Jennifer answered the phone and began discussing an agreement she was drafting with her caller, Matthew reached to turn off the transmitter and started the car.

So Jennifer wasn't a divorcee, she was a widow. Why would a widow, one who was apparently still grieving, change back to her maiden name? And what secret had she confessed to her visitor? From the other woman's comment, it apparently had to do with Sherwood Fielding.

Finally, what was the deal with this Dr. Gallagher?

At the same 7-Eleven he'd made the phone call about Jennifer from two days earlier, he bought a *Seattle Times*. He found the story immediately, on the second page.

> Preston. A Seattle man was killed last night when his car, traveling at high speeds, failed to negotiate a curve on Highway 203 and plummeted 75 feet into the Snoqualmie River. Thirty-five-year-old Gregory Gallagher was alone in the vehicle at the time. He was pronounced dead at the scene by emergency personnel.

The first question that came to Matthew's mind had nothing to do with the accident. Why had Gregory Gallagher been fired? And what, if anything, did it have to do with this "accident"? It was highly unlikely the two were unrelated. Matthew had long ago learned to approach what others might consider "coincidence" as anything but. Taking everything else he knew into consideration, it was easier for him to believe some connection between the two events existed than it was to believe Gregory Gallagher's luck was so piss-poor that he could be fired, then killed in a car crash all within—what was it? a week? Maybe even days.

From the parking lot of the 7-Eleven, Matthew drove straight back to the apartment he'd rented on upper Queen Anne.

It was a penthouse unit, already furnished, of a six-story complex. Modern, good security. Pricey. The view of Elliott Bay was breathtaking, though Matthew rarely noticed it.

He went directly to a small back bedroom where he kept his equipment and set up his laptop. He dialed an 888 number to get on-line, then punched in his code word. Once connected, he went to the Internet equivalent of a phone book, "SearchEZ," and entered the name "Gregory Gallagher," and the city "Seattle." Seven listings popped onto his screen. Next, choosing the age-range button, he selected "30–40" and clicked. All but two of the names disappeared. He jotted down the address for both listings, exited the program, changed clothes, and was back in his car within five minutes.

The first address ended up taking him north to the Green Lake area. The path along the popular, mile-long lake was already buzzing with runners and skateboarders. He turned off the lake road, went one block west, made another turn, and found the address. It was an old two-story, colorfully painted frame house, typical, it appeared, of the neighborhood. On the porch sat a young woman wearing a tank top and oversized cutoffs, a fat orange tabby cat in her lap.

He parked the Taurus and approached, a friendly smile on his face.

"Hi there," he said, bending to pet the cat, who had jumped from her lap and was now winding himself around his legs.

"That's Toby," she said. "Hope you don't mind."

"Not at all," Matthew answered. "I'm looking for a Gregory Gallagher. Is this the right place?"

"Greg? Yeh. He's in the upstairs apartment. He's probably sleeping. He plays in a band. Didn't get in til three this morning. Want me to see if he's up yet?"

Not his man. His Gregory Gallagher was resting comfortably, but not in bed. Mumbling something about coming by again later, Matthew departed without delay.

The other address was in West Seattle: 1432 West Forty-third, 3C. It turned out to be a gated condominium complex on a hillside that overlooked the bay and undoubtedly charged a pretty penny for the views of the Seattle skyline.

He got out of his car and walked along the sidewalk to where the white cinder-block fence surrounding the condominium property ended. Glancing around quickly, he followed it when it turned and climbed up the hillside, and once out of sight of street traffic and neighboring houses, he hoisted himself easily up and over at a spot hidden by an overgrown spruce. It occurred to Matthew that he probably could make a good living as a security consultant, he was so used to searching out and finding the flaws in security systems. This complex went in for showy screening devices at the gate, then blew any chance at effectiveness by relying on a five-and-a-half-foot perimeter wall—one that was obscured by overgrown shubbery no less—to protect the rest of the premises. It was an expensive joke.

There were five separate three-story buildings, all that bleached white stucco, deserty look that he was used to seeing in Phoenix. He looked for one marked "C," then, finding it, entered its small vestibule, where he found six mailboxes and, next to each, a doorbell. He pressed the button labeled "Gallagher," but there was no response.

As he walked around the south side of the building, he nodded at a young woman whose dress and demeanor indicated she was on her way to work, and probably late.

Matthew had learned long ago that the best means of avoiding suspicion was to look people straight in the eye. Be forthright.

"Can you tell me where Unit 3 is?" he asked the woman apologetically.

"Dr. Gallagher's?" she responded, stopping. Her features immediately transformed to a look intended to convey sympathy or sadness, but which he read, unmistakably, to be more curiosity than anything else. This was one of those people, he suspected, who slowed traffic by gawking at serious freeway accidents.

"Yes," he answered. He was glad he'd changed into a suit when he stopped by his apartment earlier. She would likely think him there on official business.

"It's so sad," she said.

"Yes, it is. Are you a neighbor?"

"Actually, I'm housesitting for his neighbor. I only knew him from seeing him come and go. Did you guys find his next of kin yet?" she asked then.

So, she thought he was with the police. They must have been there earlier, asking around.

"No. We're still working on it. That's why I'm here."

"The accident sounded just horrible. He went off a cliff, didn't he?"

"Yes, he did. His car went up in flames upon impact. Pretty much an inferno," Matthew said, feeding her morbid curiosity with his lies. "Guess he was pretty hard to identify."

There, that seemed to be a little more than she wanted to hear.

"Well . . ." she paused, momentarily lost for words, "his unit is just around the corner. Up the stairs." Then, recovering quickly, she added, "Good luck."

Matthew climbed the stairs. At the top there was a landing with several potted geraniums. He swiveled 360 degrees and determined that he was totally hidden from the view of any other unit. An oversized paned window dominated the top half of the door to Gallagher's condo. He peered through it. To his right, a dining room opened to a living room. Off that, there was a deck. Just to the left, a large island with a wet bar and several stools surrounding it separated the dining room from the kitchen. He stood quietly, watching, until he was certain the apartment was unoccupied.

He moved left, to the window above the kitchen sink and examined it. He was pleased to see it was a jalousie, which meant it would be easy to slip out of its metal frame. He went to work and in less than a minute had gained entry to the apartment.

The kitchen, dining room, and living room indicated Gregory Gallagher was fastidious to the point of being anal. Matthew walked down a short hallway to the bedroom, pushed the door gently open. What he saw there was another thing entirely. Drawers stood open, clothes hanging out. Books were strewn haphazardly across the floor. Either Dr. Gallagher was a schizophrenic (neatnik by day, slob by night) or someone had turned this room upside down looking for something—something that they must have found, Matthew reasoned, or else the rest of the place would look just as bad as the bedroom.

Was what they were looking for—what they had apparently found—the same thing that had been the subject of the search through Jennifer's files the other day? It had to be. It all had to be connected in some way—his assignment to find out what was happening at BioGentech, the search through Jennifer's files during her meeting with Sherwood Fielding, Dr. Gallagher's firing, his apartment being ransacked, and then, last night, his death. Poor sucker obviously refused to cooperate with someone at BioGentech, probably Fielding, got fired, thought he could hide whatever it is they wanted in his apartment. Had he come home to discover the information missing, and then been killed when he'd gone after whomever took it? Or had he been killed to get him out of the way, then his apartment ransacked? Either way, the poor sucker obviously didn't have a clue as to what he was up against.

Matthew had seen it before. A disgruntled employee becomes bent on getting even, taking matters into his own hands. It was nothing new.

But what was new, what most of the people like Dr. Gallagher failed to take into account, was that in this day and age, and especially this industry, the stakes were so great—a trade secret might be worth millions of dollars—that a new mentality, a new breed of player was being drawn to the game. One that could make losing a very dangerous—in Gregory Gallagher's case, even deadly—proposition.

MATTHEW KNEW THE new security system being installed at BioGentech well. All it took was the mention of a system that scanned irises for him to be able to identify the technology. It had been developed by the military. He knew it meant monitors would be set up at all the key points of entry in the building—lobby, executive offices, lab entries. A picture would be taken of each BioGentech employee's eyes. Each monitor would have its own database of those authorized to enter that particular area. The digitized image òf the iris of any person attempting entry would be compared to the pictures in the database before a release on the locked door was triggered.

With this in mind, Matthew knew another thing. That once this system was in place, the chances of his gaining access to BioGentech's labs were drastically diminished. He'd been planning to wait and gather as much information as he could from the audio surveillance he'd set up of Jennifer's office before attempting entry onto the premises. But news that a sophisticated security system was being installed changed all that.

Between this thing with Gregory Gallagher and the new security system, things were definitely heating up. Matthew Pace felt the old adrenaline rush that came with being back in action.

It was just past midnight. He cruised slowly by BioGentech's office building twice, then parked two blocks away at a busy restaurant. The parking lot was still three-fourths full, most of its patrons having come late from a Mariners' game that had gone into extra innings.

There were several pedestrians, mostly couples, coming and going from the restaurant, but once he'd gone a few hundred yards, Matthew found himself alone on the waterfront path.

He continued on the path til he'd passed BioGentech, keeping his head directed forward but his eyes focused sideways, on the building. Most of the windows on the fourth through seventh floors were darkened, but on six, there was one room that was well lit. That, he concluded, must be the lounge. He knew from Georgie that BioGentech had a security guard during the day. Most likely, the night guard was sitting up there drinking coffee and smoking a cigarette at that very moment.

He'd decided to attempt accessing the building through the garage. After passing once then doubling back, just before the BioGentech building he cut across a patch of grass and continued along, hugging the blackness of the buildings, which were packed tightly along Lake Union's shores.

He approached the garage. A large metal door covered its entrance. He looked for signs of security cameras but saw none. As he approached, he saw a pedestrian ramp leading to another, smaller door. His hand fumbled in his pocket for Jennifer's security passkey.

Pressing the two-by-three-inch plastic card to the monitor, Matthew watched as the red light turned green. He reached for the doorknob and opened it, pausing briefly before entering, to listen for an alarm. Nothing.

He slid silently inside and found himself at the top of a ramp.

Flattening himself against the cement wall, Matthew crept downward. At the bottom, the ramp opened to a mammoth, subterranean garage. It was perfect. Loud—the noise decibel indicating the mechanical room containing the building's heating and air-conditioning systems had to either be adjoining the garage or directly above it—and providing plenty of shadow to allow him to move about. He established a plan. The best way to pinpoint the security guard's location was to stay in the basement—check it out and ascertain the best means of accessing the rest of the building from there—until he showed up on his rounds.

After a quick survey of the layout, Matthew concealed himself behind a two-foot concrete support pillar and waited for the guard. It was almost an hour before he heard the door marked "Stairwell" open. He waited, not moving, until the footsteps headed off, in the direction of the garage door through which Matthew had entered. Then Matthew peered out, saw the guard's back disappearing around the corner of the L-shaped garage, and made for the stairwell.

Assuming the guard would work his way back up the building floor by floor, Matthew decided to head for the seventh floor. In her drunken stupor, Georgie had told him Jennifer's office was located there.

On seven, he extracted a pen-sized flashlight and, walking briskly down the corridor, flashed it at each nameplate next to the row of locked doors. Jennifer's name was the fourth door.

He picked the lock in less than fifteen seconds. Inside, he removed his jacket, shoved it up, tight, along the seam between door and floor, and went directly to Jennifer's computer. Flipping it on, he was welcomed by a BioGentech logo that said, "Greetings Jennifer Rockhill. Please enter password."

He paused, trying to remember the conversation he'd overheard earlier that day.

He typed CHARLIE.

Network does not recognize password flashed before him on the screen.

He tried CHARLES, knowing that if BioGentech's fire wall—the system put in place to prevent computer break-ins—was even halfway sophisticated, his failed attempts to log in would show up sometime in the near future on a security report. A good system alerted security after a designated number, usually four or more, of consecutive failed log-ins.

Just what was Jennifer's daughter's name? He'd heard it earlier today, when Jennifer was telling Patricia about the accident that took the lives of both her husband and daughter. Was it Amy? Or Tracey?

Suddenly it came to him.

He typed STACEY.

Immediately the system kicked into gear.

Once inside Program Manager, he clicked on "File Manager" and scrolled down the screen, passing "admin," "acctg," "exec," "legal," "ops." At "scntst" he stopped and pressed the enter key.

ACCESS DENIED.

Damn. It didn't make sense. Jennifer had told him she had access to lab files in order to prepare agreements. Assuming the search he'd overheard on his audiosurveillance equipment was for a scientific document—not a difficult assumption to make considering it had to belong to Gallagher—also confirmed that fact. So why deny her on-line access to the scientist directory? It could only mean that there were certain scientific files kept highly confidential—so confidential as to be off-limits to the company attorney.

Scrolling back up, he clicked on "exec." Within the directory, he scrolled down to "Fielding," and clicked on the first file in that listing.

ACCESS DENIED.

Frustrated, he went next to "legal," and scrolled down, hoping something in a file name would catch his attention since he didn't have time to peruse all the files in the system. Most of the files appeared to be named for the scientist conducting the study, but there was one that caught his eye. It was named "BMTA/Cln."

Matthew clicked on it.

BIOLOGICAL MATERIALS TRANSFER AGREEMENT

This Agreement is by and between BioGentech and Dr. Ivan Natarajam of the Agnes Waterford Research Center.

*Whereas, BioGentech research scientists **Dr. Gregory Gallagher** and **Dr. Ram Chandra** are conducting mammal-cloning* *experiments for which they require genetically engineered bovine mammary cells; and*

Whereas, Dr. Natarajam of the Agnes Waterford Research Center has developed a line of bovine mammary cells genetically engineered to produce human proteins for use in medicines and is willing to transfer said cells to BioGentech for said research . . .

The agreement went on to detail the logistics of the transfer of cells between the Waterford Center and BioGentech. According to the agreement, the purpose of the studies being conducted by Chandra and Gallagher was to "develop novel gene therapy for human disease." It included detailed legalese regarding confidentiality and intellectual property rights.

Matthew knew instantly that the document had significance. Dr. Gallagher had been involved in cloning research before his death. Matthew's instincts told him the connection between the two—the scientists' work and his untimely death—could not have been a coincidence. And who was this Ram Chandra? His eyes scanned the room for the printer. When he saw it, on a side table, he flipped the switch, turning it on. But immediately, he decided he risked its motor being heard from the hallway and flipped it back off.

Before exiting the program, he clicked on the e-mail icon, then went to the electronic address book, where he perused the employee directory. He wanted to find out where the labs were located. Gregory Gallagher's name had not yet been deleted from the list of employees. He saw that his office and lab were on the fourth floor. He scrolled up again, searching for Dr. Ram Chandra, but the other scientist's name could not be found. Noting that Dr. Fielding's office was on six, Matthew finally logged off.

Matthew checked his watch. He'd been in Jennifer's office a total of fourteen minutes. He stood with his ear pressed to the door before opening it, then eased his way out into the hall and, using a different stairwell than the one he'd already used—the one the guard had also used to enter the underground garage—he descended directly to the fourth floor.

He was relieved to find that Jennifer's passkey gave him access at the entrance to the lab. He'd expected a higher level of security at the labs.

As the signal on the monitor turned from red to green, he slid quickly through the door. He was inside a corridor, with doors opening on either side. He could see that at its end the short hallway opened into one large room, which must be the lab. Matthew moved forward.

Inside the lab, the darkness was broken only by an occasional pea-sized light indicating that a piece of equipment was in operation, and digital clocks in cubicles housing the lab workers' desks, which lined the perimeter of the vast room—just enough light to maximize the effectiveness of his night vision goggles. He unzipped his cloth backpack and withdrew the headgear. Once on, the room transformed, enabling him to read envelopes and memos sitting on desks, labels on equipment. He scanned the room for the filing cabinets and located them along the far wall. Based on the Biological Materials Transfer Agreement he'd just seen, he moved directly to the "C" and "G" files—Chandra and Gallagher. For, of all the files he'd quickly perused and all the information he'd been able to glean from Jennifer thus far, that agreement—the BMTA—was the first to mention the subject that had brought him to Seattle in the first place, the subject that was the focus of WTI's interest in BioGentech: cloning.

Taking half a dozen files with him, Matthew crawled under a desk and, for the next hour, using a microcamera the size of a cigarette package, photographed their contents. He had no idea what he was photographing, or whether it would be of interest to WTI. Time did not permit him to be discriminating. The task of determining its value would fall to his cohorts in London. Matthew's job was to get information, hopefully relevant information, and pass it along. He was pleased to have had a modicum of success already tonight, but deep within him, there lay a certainty that the information for which he'd been sent would not show up on the photos he snapped. After all, it was obvious that Dr. Gallagher had removed some very valuable documents. What was left was probably pretty generic stuff that WTI would already have access to.

Still, maybe there was something there. Something that would help put the pieces together.

The files under Dr. Chandra's name—there were only four—were older than Gallagher's. Had Dr. Chandra gone the way of Gallagher? Somehow, he would have to find out, perhaps from Georgie, if this Chandra chap was still at BioGentech.

From what he could see in his hurried viewing, nowhere in either scientist's files was there anything on the cloning work that was referenced in the BMTA agreement to obtain bovine cells from the Waterford scientist. That file, the one detailing the actual cloning research, must have been removed from the cabinet.

Matthew had just stood to return to the filing cabinet and look further for the cloning file when he heard the lab door open. He quickly dropped back under the desk. Light suddenly flooded the lab, before he could rip the night vision goggles off, almost blinding him with the goggles' amplification. Since any movement might lead to his detection, he was forced to close his eyes and rely upon his ears to tell him if he were in danger of being discovered. The guard's footsteps, however, never came closer than several yards from where he sat huddled on the ground, and soon the blinding light—even with his eyes closed he was aware of it—was gone.

He waited several minutes, then rose and stole once more to the filing cabinets. He returned all the files he'd withdrawn, then systematically ran his thumb along the file tabs of the files in each of six drawers, looking for a name or subject that might mean something to him. He came up with nothing, and the process was beginning to consume too much time, so finally, he exited the lab and reentered the stairwell, headed now to the fifth floor.

On the fifth floor a large metal door opened to darkness. He slid the headgear back in place, stepped inside, and was immediately bombarded with an odor, then the sight of cages, endless cages, stacked three and four high, covering every square inch of the floors and tables. Inside were mostly mice, sometimes as many as a dozen of them to a cage. Huddled together, immediately aware of him. Probably, he thought, waiting for him to reach in and inject them with some deadly disease, or slice them open to determine just how long it would take for the toxin they'd been ingesting to eat away their guts.

He passed a cage of guinea pigs and stared, with equal parts disgust and fascination, at stomachs that had been surgically removed from the abdominal cavity, dragging along the floor of the cage beside them.

"Poor little fuckers," he murmured under his breath.

The sixth floor proved to be too well lit for him to risk an attempt at breaking into Sherwood Fielding's office. One of the things that had contributed to Matthew's success as an agent had been his sixth sense about when it was time to call it quits. Satisfied that he'd accomplished as much as he could safely accomplish that night, he was back outside just minutes later slinking through the dark shadows between buildings.

But now that same sixth sense alerted him that he was not alone.

He'd entered an alleyway that separated the BioGentech building from what appeared to be a warehouse for a shipyard. An untrained ear would not have picked up the solitary footstep that echoed after his. But he'd heard it, clearly. Someone else was in the alleyway, lagging behind him, frozen now, as was he, like a cat midway through its nocturnal hunt.

He assessed his options quickly.

If his pursuer were a guard, the best thing to do would be to lose him. ASAP.

But his instincts told him that this was no run-of-the-mill security guard lurking behind him.

No, his pursuer was a professional of another sort, of that—the longer he remained still, waiting for the other to move—he grew more certain.

CIA?

If it were, it might be kind of fun running some of his old cronies around a bit. Reminding them of the real meaning of the "best and brightest."

Matthew eased along the wall, pausing with each step to listen. When he reached the building's end, he tightened the straps on his backpack, then broke into a run, heading the opposite direction of his car. Crossing the strip of grass that separated the buildings from the asphalt path that ran along the water with a single stride, he hit the path at a full-out run. It was just seconds until he could hear a second set of footsteps on its surface.

Not bad, thought Matthew, upon hearing his pursuer's pace.

He turned it up a notch then, and soon he could hear the difference in their rhythms, his being quicker by a heartbeat. He felt safe in staying on the path, knowing he was losing him, for a hundred yards or so, then, once the path took a turn around the lake's shoreline, taking Matthew out of sight, he veered off. The street, residential now, was lined with cars. He shimmied on his belly under a dairy truck and watched as his pursuer, a capped figure of medium height and build, faltered on the path, turning this way and that—trying to determine where Matthew had gone—before continuing along the lake's shore.

CHAPTER

TEN

THE DISPOSAL OF toxic and biological wastes is tightly regulated by the DEA, FDA, EPA, and other state and federal agencies," Dave Maynard said.

The husky scientist, who looked more like an ex-football star than a highly trained scientist, half-stood, half-sat on the edge of Jennifer's desk. Dave, Jennifer had observed, was more comfortable in motion. But for half an hour he had been patiently explaining the subject of biomedical and radioactive waste disposal to her.

"Reading this thing," Jennifer said, raising the lengthy agreement Dave had asked her to review, "I can see why. It's amazing what companies like BioGentech dispose of: syringes, toxins, biological materials, chemicals. Pretty dangerous stuff."

Dave smiled broadly.

"Now you know why I don't sleep at night. I'm the one responsible for seeing that nothing goes wrong with any of it. That's why we contract with companies like Safety Disposal, to make sure we stay in compliance."

"Have you worked with them before?"

"No, but I checked them out. Always do. Their record is spotless. They know their stuff and they take it seriously."

"It's good to know that no one will end up exposed to some ungodly disease as a result of a study we're conducting here."

"Not only that," Dave said, "there's another reason for using companies like this. You'd be amazed by how much information can be derived from examining the waste that comes out of a lab."

"Really?"

"Seriously," Dave went on, "a skilled analysis of BioGentech's waste could give away some of this company's most-guarded trade secrets."

"Does that actually happen?" Jennifer asked, incredulous.

"Within the pharmaceutical industry?" Dave asked. "Absolutely. There are people who make their living stealing trade secrets from companies like ours. And they'll do it by whatever means they can, including going through the garbage. But it's never happened here, not at Bio-Gentech. At least not since I've been in charge of disposal. And it never will. That's the other reason you do due diligence before contracting with a disposal company. To ensure that waste products don't fall into the wrong hands."

Jennifer shook her head in amazement. When she first conceived of her plan and even later, after interviewing for the job, she knew that in Sherwood Fielding she would be dealing with a figure from the dark side. But she had no idea that the pharmaceutical industry in general had this cloak-and-dagger aspect to it. Sometimes she felt as though she'd entered a strange new world, whose reality bore no resemblance whatsoever to the world she'd always lived in and traveled in before.

The call that interrupted their session the next minute confirmed it.

"Dr. Fielding wants you to report to his office immediately," Georgie announced. Georgie was always brisk with her recently but something about her tone today gave Jennifer a serious sense of foreboding.

Jennifer apologized to Dave for cutting short their meeting and headed for the sixth floor. She glanced its way as she passed Georgie's office, but found it empty. When the door to Fielding's office opened in response to her knock, it was Jim Wilkes with whom she came face-to-face, not Sherwood. She noticed that Jim, who was usually very friendly, did not make eye contact. She also noticed that he was not wearing his trademark navy blue sports coat—which is probably why she'd never before realized that he sported a small pistol in a shoulder holster.

He stepped back to usher her in. Sherwood Fielding, seated behind his desk, wore an expression that was anything but welcoming.

"Please, sit down," Fielding said.

Jennifer seated herself opposite him. Wilkes stood, arms folded, alongside the massive desk, his back to the wall.

"What is it?" Jennifer asked.

She leveled her gaze first at Sherwood, who remained stone faced, then at Jim Wilkes, then watched as Sherwood gave Wilkes the go-ahead nod.

"We'd like to ask you a few questions," Wilkes said.

"Such as?"

"Such as where were you this morning at one-fifteen?"

Jennifer drew back in her chair.

"Pardon me?" she asked, her voice rising. "Where was I at one in the morning?"

"One-fifteen," Wilkes corrected.

She looked at him, incredulous, then at Fielding.

"In bed. Where I always am at one-fifteen in the morning. Why would you ask such a peculiar question?"

"Because our records from last night indicate that you logged on to your computer at one-fifteen. Can you explain how that's possible?" Fielding asked.

"*What?*"

Fielding reached for a printout on his desk.

"One-fifteen A.M.," he read. "Jennifer Rockhill. You logged off thirteen minutes later."

He extended the hand holding the printout.

"That's ridiculous," she said, taking it from him.

"The printout is clear," Jim Wilkes said. "It shows you logged in at one-fifteen and logged off at one-twenty-eight."

"This can't be," Jennifer protested, staring at the sheet of paper. "I was home in bed. How could I have logged on to my computer? And why, why would I?"

"Have you given your password to anyone?" asked Wilkes.

"Of course not," Jennifer snapped.

"Do you mind telling us what it is?"

Jennifer took a deep breath. It seemed unlikely that he knew Charlie's daughter's name had been Stacey, and even if he did, it had been Stacey Banks, not Rockhill. Still, she did not want to risk it.

And there was another consideration. She had told Fielding she had no children. She could try to explain that she'd meant no children who were still alive. But just the fact of offering an explanation bore the imprint of deception.

Still, what choice did she have? Surely they had the means to find out what her password was without her cooperation.

"My password," she said hesitantly, "is Stacey."

"Stacey?" Fielding asked. "Is that a relative?"

Seeing the expression on both men's faces, she realized that her hesitation had served to fuel their suspicions.

"Just an old friend," she said.

It was time to go on the offensive.

"Look, this is ridiculous. You obviously have a problem on your hands, but you're wasting valuable time here with me. I'm an attorney. That stands for something. At least it does to me. I don't appreciate having my integrity questioned like this. I don't know how to explain this," she gave the paper in her hands a decisive shake, "but I can tell you right now. I did not log on to my computer last night. Nor have I ever given my password to anyone."

She could not read either Fielding or Wilkes' reaction.

"If there's anything I can do to help you figure this out, how this could have happened, I'd be happy to. But if my word is not good enough for you, now or anytime in the future, then I'll have no choice. I will not stay, will not work for someone who doesn't trust me. It's as simple as that."

She'd shifted her weight forward, as if ready to rise from the chair and walk out of Fielding's office.

Fielding's eyes widened at her response, and he cleared his throat.

"Now, wait a minute," he said. "You can see for yourself what that printout says. Surely you understand the need for us to investigate a report like this."

Jennifer did not respond.

Fielding turned to Jim Wilkes.

"Jim, I want a full investigation. Find out how this could have happened. It looks like we owe Jennifer an apology."

Jennifer flushed.

"Thank you," she said. She suddenly felt as though she were about to be sick. Wanting out of there as quickly as possible, she rose and, sliding the printout back on to Sherwood Fielding's desk, nodded at both men curtly.

She hurried down the hall to the ladies' room, hoping it would be empty. But inside she saw high-heeled feet beneath the door of both stalls. Having no choice in the matter, she rushed to one of two sinks, where she leaned over and, quite unceremoniously, retched—losing, in the process, what few shards of dignity remained from her meeting in Sherwood Fielding's office.

ONCE JENNIFER WAS GONE, Fielding motioned for Wilkes to close the door behind her.

After doing so, Wilkes returned and lowered himself into the chair Jennifer had just vacated.

"You went awfully easy on her," Wilkes said.

Fielding shot him a scornful look.

"What choice did I have?" he said. "She looked like she might quit."

Both men grew silent, then Fielding spoke again.

"What did you think?"

Wilkes shook his head.

"I don't know. She'd seemed pretty sincere. I mean, she's either a helluvan actress or she was genuinely surprised. *And* upset at having her integrity questioned like that."

"But why would she hesitate to give us her password? Did you notice that?" Fielding said.

"It would have been hard to miss. I don't have an answer for that one. Maybe she's got something on there, on her computer, that she doesn't want us digging into."

"Good point. Check into it. If she goes back to her office now and deletes a bunch of files, you'd be able to pick up on that, wouldn't you?"

"You bet. I could restore them and take a look. But, you know, I just thought of another thing that fits with her claim that she didn't know anything about what happened last night," Wilkes said, reaching for the printout. "See here. It shows three attempts to log in. If it was Jennifer here last night, why would it take three tries? Two attempts show up all the time on this report. Typos. But three? For a six-letter password, that's a lot of typos. And the first two tries were seven letters."

"Good point," said Fielding. "So where does that leave us? Who logged in to her computer last night?"

Wilkes shook his head slowly.

"She's not close enough to anyone here at BioGentech to give them her password, I'm pretty sure of that. And my impression has been that she's just as much a loner away from the office."

"I know. I encouraged Georgie to buddy up with her, but she apparently did something to piss her off, cause Georgie doesn't want to talk about her right now. She's downright touchy about the subject."

Fielding grew silent, absorbed in his own thoughts, for a moment.

"I want you to keep an eye on her," he said finally to Wilkes. "See what she has in her computer files, or what she deletes in the next couple days." He paused. "Maybe the person who logged on really didn't have anything to do with her. Maybe her office, her computer was just picked at random."

"Could be," Wilkes replied. Then an unlikely laugh percolated to the surface.

Fielding looked at him, startled and contemptuous.

"What's so goddamn funny?"

"We know it wasn't Gallagher."

•   •   •

IT TURNED OUT to be fortunate that the parking spot he'd grown used to using hadn't been available this morning. He had, of course, been a little later getting there than usual. Last night's adventure had kept him up until after 3:00 A.M. and then, for the first time he could remember, he'd overslept.

By the time Matthew got himself settled outside the BioGentech building, it was after ten o'clock. Jennifer was already in the middle of a meeting about a toxic waste agreement with someone named Dave. The meeting had been interrupted by a phone call, which prompted Jennifer to call it short, and for the past twenty minutes, her office had been empty. Had he not been forced to park a few spots north of his usual spot, Matthew might not have seen her use BioGentech's side exit.

She was on foot, and appeared to be headed toward the path he'd run down last night. Matthew turned the recorder on and climbed out of the Taurus. He lost sight of her briefly, but when he reached the asphalt path, he could see her up ahead, walking briskly in the misty rain. It was an unusual day, and time, for a walk. Especially in those high heels. He allowed himself the pleasure of watching her for a while, until they were well out of sight of the BioGentech building, then he caught up to her.

"Hello, Jennifer," he said from behind.

Her entire body seemed to go rigid. She stopped and turned.

"You!" She glared at him. "I've had about enough of this. There are stalking laws to deal with creeps like you."

Matthew couldn't help but smile.

"Stalking?" he answered. "I hadn't thought about it, but I guess technically speaking—legally speaking—you might have something there."

The rain had picked up, and was beginning to turn her brown waves into a tangle of corkscrews. Jennifer simply stood there staring at him. A new expression suddenly took hold of her features.

"It was *you*, wasn't it?" she said.

"Pardon me?"

"Last night. In my office. That was you, wasn't it?"

"Well," he said, "now that you mention it . . ."

Without warning, her hand shot out and slapped him hard on his left cheek.

"You *bastard*."

She didn't seem the least bit concerned for her safety. After all, they were alone out there. She was being either incredibly brave or incredibly careless. Or, if what Matthew had suspected for days now was true, incredibly desperate.

"I'll turn you in. Breaking and entry *and* stalking. I'll have you put
away."

"I don't think you want to do that," Matthew said.

"Why wouldn't I? You think I'm going to play the role of the helpless
victim? You picked the wrong lady."

"No. I hardly think that," Matthew said. "I'd say you're anything but
helpless. I'd say you were a lady with a plan. A mission. Is that how you
see yourself?"

She stared at him.

"What are you saying? What do you mean?"

He reached for her elbow. "Shall we keep walking?"

She jerked out from under his touch.

"Are you crazy? I'm not going anywhere with you. I want an explanation. Right here. *Now*. Why are you following me? And why did you
break into my office last night?"

Matthew leveled his gaze with hers.

"We can help each other," he said. "I know you're not all you seem.
I know you're hiding something. If you tell me what it is, I'll help. And
you're in a position to help me. We can team up, work to . . ."

"Are you out of your mind?" Jennifer said, practically screaming.
"Who are you? What are you talking about? You don't know anything
about me."

"That's not true. I know that your married name was Jennifer Banks.
That you changed it back to Rockhill, your maiden name, just before
moving up here. I know that your husband and daughter were killed in
an automobile accident."

Jennifer was backing away now, her hand held over her mouth.

"Who are you?"

This time when Matthew grabbed her by both arms, she did not resist.

"I'm a businessman. I am not going to harm you. You have no reason
to fear me. In fact, I can help you. I'm not sure why you're here, what
your agenda is, but believe me, I'm someone who can help you achieve
it. No questions asked, no judgment passed. And I'm willing to do that.
In exchange for your cooperation."

"Cooperation with what?"

"Cooperation in helping me obtain information. That's all."

"Go away. Leave me alone," she said, but her voice had lost much
of its fire.

Matthew still had a hold on her arms.

"Think about it."

He reached into his pocket and withdrew a piece of paper with a number on it.

"This is my pager number. Call me anytime." He slipped it into the pocket of her blue blazer.

Then he turned and left her standing alone in the rain.

ELEVEN

RAM CHANDRA WAS a bundle of nervous energy. His tan suede Hush-puppies tapped perpetually as he sat on a lab stool, answering questions. He did not like to be still. Meetings had always been hellish for him. His long fingers fumbled purposelessly with a pen in the pocket of his white lab coat as Sherwood Fielding reviewed the file that lay open on the lab table.

"The solution seems to have made a big difference," Fielding observed as he pored over the data before him.

There it was again. Gregory Gallagher's solution. All the other work that had gone into this experiment—two decades of research that built up to it—had been brilliant, and entirely his own. Still, without the solution, he had been able to go just so far. Gallagher's formula had upped the odds of success considerably. The past two weeks had proven that.

The irritating drum of his shoe against the stool's metal leg ceased.

"I believe the difference in results has to do with the fact that this clone was derived from an adult cell. To the extent the solution facilitated the nuclear transfusion, yes, it was helpful. Clearly Angel's response to this embryo is dramatically different, dramatically more positive, than any other response we've had to date.

"While the embryo twinning looked good in culture—I achieved an eighty percent success rate—once they've been implanted, hyperacute rejection has been the rule rather than the exception. The problem with the twinned clones appears to lie in rejection by the surrogate; while the problem with the adult cell donor was at the other end of the process—nuclear transfusion. With natural fertilization, the sperm and egg are naturally in synchronization. But I was unable to achieve synchronization of the adult nucleus donor and the egg cell until I obtained the proper formula. In *that* respect, the solution has made a difference. But the most promising, and surprising, finding with the adult-donor work is that the surrogate, Angel—that's her file, there," he pointed at the file Sherwood Fielding was reading, "seems to be tolerating the foreign fetus remarkably better than any of the other surrogates tolerated the fetuses that were cloned by the embryo-twinning process."

Chandra strained his gooselike neck to read along as Fielding turned in the file to several charts, all of which were labeled "Angel."

Angel was Chandra's pride and joy.

She was also a baboon—as were all the surrogates housed in the cathedral-sized vivarium adjoining the lab in which Fielding and Chandra now sat.

"All the others have aborted?" Fielding asked after several minutes studying the data about Angel.

Chandra nodded.

"All but three. Pamela just started her second trimester, but yesterday's ultrasound showed the fetus to be grossly deformed. She's likely to abort. Then there's Tea." Chandra had a habit of naming his baboons after TV stars on whom he'd developed a crush, in this case Pamela Anderson and Tea Leoni. His beloved Angel had been named after his all-time favorite trio of beauties, Charlie's Angels. "Until recently I'd been encouraged about her chances. Early on, she showed minor signs of rejection but I was able to counter it quite effectively with anti-rejection drugs. Ursula's pregnancy still shows promise. She's in day forty-four. Of course, the fetus she's carrying is a result of the twinning process, but still, I'm optimistic that it will survive."

His gaze traveled to a dirty chalkboard next to the lab's main entry. A line was drawn down the center of the board. On its left side, under the heading TEA, the number 107 was circled. On the right, under ANGEL, the circled number was 32. But Chandra could have recited these numbers, and a whole host of others, without reference to the board.

"Today is day number 107 for Tea. But for the past two days, Tea's been showing preliminary signs of rejection. The anti-rejection drugs may have been ineffective. I'm afraid she's about to abort."

Fielding removed his glasses and turned piercing eyes on Chandra.

"What matters is Angel. What makes you think you'll have more luck with her? We need a full-term fetus from an adult cell. Everything—enough money to make us rich men, to keep BioGentech in business for years—is riding on that."

This was the part Chandra hated the most. Having to justify his work, defend it from constant attacks that—though in the game of scientific one-upmanship, his work was head and heels over all the rest and Sherwood Fielding knew it—it still wasn't good enough, wasn't happening fast enough. He sucked in a deep breath, calling upon the patience his Indian upbringing had instilled in him.

"There are several factors that contribute to my optimism," he said. "First of all, we know what we're getting with this clone. We've got a healthy adult donor, a proven entity. As you well know, since you were integral in producing them, the other donor cells, including Tea's, were all taken from embryos. It's possible that the abortions we've seen so far were the result of defective fetuses. Fetuses that would not even have survived in the natural mother. After all, they all came from the same embryo.

"And we not only have a clone taken from an adult cell, one that did very well in culture and appears to be thriving *in utero*, but we're also using our best primate, in terms of her immune system, as the surrogate. Historically, Angel's immune system has shown itself to be more accepting of foreign cells than any of the others, which, of course, is not a desirable characteristic in any other setting. Plus, there's also one more contributing factor," Chandra added, "particular to this subject only. This is the first time I've utilized my tolerance-building theory."

"To avoid rejection?"

Chandra nodded.

"It's a system I've been working on for the past three years, to increase a recipient's tolerance to transplant or, in this case, embryo implantation. Ideally, bone-marrow-stem cells from the donor are injected into the recipient. Then, when they mature in the recipient's body, it's hoped that they will suppress the recipient's immune reaction to the transplant or implanted embryo. They're basically teaching the body to tolerate the foreign tissue. Of course, we had no means of obtaining bone marrow directly from the donor, but I was able to use the blood samples we did have. For a month prior to implantation, I injected small quantities of refined serum, some of which consisted of stem cells, into Angel, in the hope that her immune system would develop a tolerance to the foreign cells. That may have contributed to the success we've had so far. There have been absolutely no signs of hypercute rejection. I know it's still early, but by this point in every other implantation, we'd seen preliminary signs of rejection. Based on the results to date with the other implanted clones, I have good reason to think that Angel will carry this embryo a full six months, and then some. Long enough for the fetus, with some assistance, to survive."

Fielding pushed back from the lab table.

"Well, let's just hope you're right," he said.

"Would you like to take a look at her?" Chandra asked, standing. "At Angel?"

Fielding glanced at his watch.

"Don't have the time right now, I'm afraid. But I'll be back soon. I plan to monitor your work closely the next few weeks."

CHANDRA CLOSED THE FILES and tucked them under his arm. His boss disgusted him. He doubted that Fielding had anything pressing to do. No, he was probably rushing off to screw his latest slut. Angelique Mannington. He'd known Angelique Mannington's predecessor. He had, in fact, had a bit of a crush on her. She was much classier than Angelique. Too classy to be taken in by Fielding's act for long. Though Chandra knew he would miss her, he had been happy for her when she announced to him that she was leaving, going east, to a Boston research center.

But her absence hadn't seemed to faze Fielding. Within weeks, Fielding had hired Angelique Mannington and begun a lurid affair with her. Worse yet, he'd disclosed their project to her. Chandra had been furious, but Fielding had pointed out the advantages of Angelique's involvement, advantages that Chandra could hardly dispute now.

His spirits picked up as he strode down a long hallway, stopping midway at a closet to extract a mask and sterile gloves. Just outside a door marked STERILE—KEEP OUT he donned them.

Fielding hadn't even wanted to see any of them, Chandra reflected bitterly. Not Tea, Pamela, or Ursula. Not even Angel. All he'd wanted was to review the charts and data. What kind of a scientist—what kind of a person—was he?

As he opened the door to the vacuous, septic-smelling vivarium, seven bright pink faces turned Ram Chandra's way.

"Hello my sweets," Chandra beamed.

Several long hairy arms extended through the vertical bars of the row of cages that flanked an entire wall. Chandra walked along, stopping at each cage, withdrawing a Tootsie Roll from his coat pocket and offering it, along with lavish words of affection and praise, to each occupant. Often, he would reach in and pat a head.

They were his girls. His *papio hamadryas*—Chandra's favorite subspecies of the baboon family. Chandra was not alone in his enchantment with this animal. Ancient Egyptians held the "sacred baboons" in high esteem, keeping them as pets and glorifying them in monuments. They believed the hamadryas to be incarnations of Thoth, god of scribes and scholars.

Chandra had always had a love for primates. As a child in India, his parents had chastised him when he tried to befriend the bandar—wild monkeys—by offering them fruit and nuts. One of his friends had undergone a painful series of rabies shots after being bitten by a monkey that jumped down from a tree as the boys walked to school. But that hadn't deterred Chandra.

Baboons, the largest and most intelligent of the Old World monkeys, simply fascinated him. He felt blessed to have found an area of research where he was not working with the traditional fare in scientific subjects—rats or mice, or even worse, the dreaded fruitfly. These odd-looking creatures, mastiff sized, their shoulders and backs covered with long grizzled hair, their faces pink and doglike, were like family to him. The males, of course, were known to be savage. But a tamed, young female, as were all his charges, could be affectionate, even trustworthy.

And of all the *papio* subspecies—including also the chacma, the yellow baboon, the anubis, the guinea, the rhodesia—he'd chosen the hamadryas to work with. Oddly enough, for Chandra was the ultimate loner, the attraction was in large part based on their social structure, which differs markedly from that of other baboons and is remarkably similar to that of humans. The hamadryas were the only primates that had integrated permanent marriage, loving and protective behaviors into their society. But there was one significant difference between their society and that of humans, and it was perhaps this that especially appealed to Chandra. Within a family of hamadryas, which includes a dominant male, his harem, children, and follower males (all of whom are celibate), the leading male rules by fear and abuse. His sudden rage is so terrifying to other hamadryas that it allows him to bring a family member into line with no more than a glance. Intimidated females don't flee—instead they rush toward the male, their pasha, flinging themselves into his arms.

Chandra had studied these behaviors for years and always they had stirred conflicting emotions in him. Sympathy for the females, whom he'd developed a protective attitude toward. And a perverse envy of the pasha. For a man who could not bring himself to even approach a woman for casual conversation, what erotic fantasies were evoked by the sight of the females, in attempts to placate the pasha, presenting their brilliant red behinds for mounting?

What a stroke of good luck it had been when Sherwood Fielding approached him with his proposal. How many in this world are so fortunate as to be able to combine a lifelong passion with challenging professional work? As Chandra's own affection for these creatures grew, he even deluded himself into thinking his work—in giving the hamadryas this vital role in a process that Chandra believed would one day be commonplace—could help save their dwindling numbers, provide a financial motive for saving the species, replenishing its populations.

If only he could successfully combat the potential for rejection.

But Angel had now given him reason for hope on that front.

His approach was on the outer edge of this new frontier, using his tolerance-building injections and powerful anti-rejection drugs. Great strides had been made with anti-rejection drugs, extending the tolerance period many times over. The beauty of this work was that it involved implantation, rather than transplantation. Transplants were meant to last years, the remainder of the recipient's life. But with this work, the attempt to produce a viable clone, all that was necessary was to get these baboons to tolerate the implanted fetuses long enough for the fetus to survive.

The downside to the anti-rejection drugs was that they tended to disarm the animals' immune systems, making a sterile environment—gloves, masks, and filtered air system—critical.

At the last cage, Chandra unlatched the door and offered not one, but two, pieces of candy.

"How is my Angel today?" he asked, as the closely set eyes of the animal in the cage honed in on his offering.

Angel turned her hand over, revealing a calloused palm.

When Chandra hesitated, she looked up at him, raising her heavy, overhanging eyebrows to afford her a clear view of him.

Chandra laughed.

"Okay, here it is," he said, placing both candies in her hand.

He watched as she adeptly, with great precision, removed one wrapper, then the other, before placing both pieces in her mouth at once.

He gave her a couple minutes to finish, then reached inside and lifted her in his arms, like an oversized toddler. Docile and cooperative, she grasped onto him, ringing his neck with her long fingers.

"Time for work, young lady," Ram Chandra said as he gently carried Angel over to a sterile examination table. He handed Angel a Mattel's *See 'n Say*. The hollow sound of a horse's whinny filled the room, turning the heads of Angel's sisters, as Angel pulled on its string.

A security camera in one corner of the ceiling monitored Chandra's movements as he withdrew several instruments from a silver cabinet, placed them on a tray next to the exam table, then flipped on the screen attached to the ultrasound machine. A guard, one of whose duties it was to respond if Angel were to become especially uncooperative—an event that had yet to occur—watched from another room. Chandra had long since grown oblivious to the camera's presence, so focused was he at times like this, when he was working with one of his subjects.

At times like this, there was only one thing on Ram Chandra's brilliant mind. And that was the tiny life taking form within the womb of its surrogate mother.

He tickled Angel, then rolled her onto her back, as she licked the yellow plastic toy.

Rubbing the cold face of his stethoscope briskly between his palms to warm it before pressing it to Angel's chest, he smiled down at her.

"Now," he said eagerly, "let's see how mama's doing today."

TWELVE

ACCESS DENIED

Jennifer stared at the two words, which flashed in red on a deck-of-cards-sized black screen mounted just above the door handle to the lab.

"That can't be right," she muttered to herself. "Damn this new system."

She removed the eyeglasses she wore for reading, then stepped to the right, positioning herself once again in front of the two cameras that were mounted on the wall next to the door. She checked to be certain she stood within the one-to-three-foot range from the metal box holding the cameras, as she and all the other BioGentech employees had been instructed to do when the new system first went in, then waited for it to identify her and grant her passage through to the labs.

The security system representative who had conducted the training sessions told them this new system could make identification through eyeglasses and contact lenses, but apparently he was wrong.

ACCESS DENIED the screen flashed again.

Exasperated, she rapped on the door.

It was opened by a pleasant-faced young man whom she'd seen many times and assumed, from his lab coat, to be a scientist. But she had never actually met him.

She smiled and said, "Thanks. For some reason it wouldn't clear me."

She stepped forward, but the young man stood his ground in the middle of the doorway.

"Uh . . ." he stammered, clearly embarrassed. "I'm, uh, really sorry but . . . but we've been told we can't allow access to anyone not authorized by the system."

Jennifer laughed.

"But I *am* authorized by the system," she said. "How do you think I got into work today? And yesterday, and the day before that?"

He hesitated.

"Well, actually, each monitor has its own base of authorized personnel," he said. "There are quite a few employees who don't have access to the labs."

"But I'm not one of them. I'm down here a lot," Jennifer said, her voice rising. "You know, working on research agreements. You've seen me here before, haven't you?"

He nodded. "Yes, I have. But I'm afraid our instructions were very specific. Maybe I can get you what you need, if you just wait here?" He made it sound like a question, but there was no doubt in Jennifer's mind. This was not negotiable.

Jennifer released a deep breath.

"Not *what*," she said. "*Who*. I came to talk to Angelique Mannington. Do you know if she's in her lab?"

"She is," he said eagerly. "In fact, I just saw her. Let me go get her for you."

"Thank you."

The door closed, leaving Jennifer standing in the hallway. She moved out of the way and tried to make herself inconspicuous when a lab assistant, carrying a shipping box with a large red label proclaiming CAUTION, TOXIC MATERIALS ENCLOSED, approached hurriedly, stood momentarily in front of the cameras, then, casting an eye in her direction as if to make sure she weren't following, turned the knob and disappeared into the lab.

As she stood in the chilly corridor, she became aware of her knees shaking.

She was angry.

She knew her emotions were easily ignited these days. She hadn't had a decent night's sleep ever since that day she'd been called in to Sherwood Fielding's office and confronted with a list of computer log-ins. Ever since Matthew Pace had followed her on the running path, and suggested they work together. She hadn't seen him since, but somehow she never escaped the feeling he was nearby.

Who was this man? He'd all but admitted he'd been the one to break in to her office, but had offered no explanations. He'd obviously been snooping, quite successfully, into her past. How much more did he know? What did he want with her? Tormented by such questions, she'd even picked up the phone one night and dialed the number on the paper he'd given her. She would confront him, demand answers. But her innate fear of him had caused her to hang up before the call went through.

Nothing would have given her more pleasure than to have turned him in to Fielding and Wilkes for breaking into her office, but his threat to reveal what he knew about her, though veiled, came through loud and clear. She dared not. If she had, *this*—her being denied access to the labs—would never have happened. She was sure of it. Fielding was watching her now, no longer trusted her. All because of Matthew Pace.

Angelique Mannington finally showed up and stepped into the hallway.

"Jennifer," Angelique said flatly. "What can I do for you?"

Jennifer studied Angelique closely to see how she would handle the situation.

"I needed to talk to you about one of the research agreements," Jennifer said.

"Why don't I come up to your office," the scientist said. "Would this afternoon be okay? After lunch?"

"Wait a minute," Jennifer said. "Why can't we just use your office? Why is it I'm suddenly denied access to the labs?"

Angelique stared at her before answering.

"You of all people know how sensitive the information in the labs is," she said. "We've just instituted a new policy, that's all. I hope you're not taking it personally."

"Does this have anything to do with . . ."

"With *what?*"

"Nothing," Jennifer answered. "Nothing at all. Listen, I'll be in my office all afternoon. See you then."

She turned and walked stiffly away, leaving Angelique standing alone. She could feel the other woman's eyes upon her until she turned the corner.

BACK AT HER OFFICE, Jennifer was so angry she found it hard to concentrate on her work. All her patience and hard work had paid off when Fielding hired her. Finally, after months of preparation, she'd maneuvered herself into a position where she stood to find the answers she needed to bring Fielding to justice. But now this Matthew Pace had threatened it all. She had to stop him. She couldn't allow him to interfere with her plans. She had to find out who he really was.

Her thoughts were cut short by a soft rap on her half-closed door. Patricia Lukins' head popped through the opening.

"Hey there."

"Come on in," Jennifer said, forcing a smile.

"Actually, I wondered if you had time to take a quick break."

Jennifer looked at the stack of files on her desk.

"To hell with it," she said, standing. "Let's go."

As she stepped into the hallway, Jennifer automatically turned left, the route she would take to the lunchroom on six. Patricia grabbed her by the arm of her jacket.

"This way."

Jennifer followed Patricia to the south stairwell. They descended one flight, then reentered the corridor. A short distance down the next hallway Patricia opened an unmarked door. They passed through a small, crowded storage room. The door at its opposite end opened to brilliant daylight. They found themselves on a tiny balcony, six floors above the waters of Lake Union.

"What's this?" Jennifer asked.

"My little secret. I have no idea why this is here, but no one else seems to know about it or use it. Except Tom, the maintenance man. He's the one who showed me. He and I are buddies. This is where I go to get away from everyone. Maybe I'm getting paranoid, but I just don't feel safe discussing anything in the offices anymore." She hesitated. "Especially after what just happened."

"*What?* What just happened?"

Patricia stood quietly for a minute or two, leaning over the railing. The beauty and serenity of the midday sun on the still lake stood in stark contrast to her visible turmoil. A baby blue sky, cloudless except for a few cotton balls that billowed above the Seattle skyline, when reflected in the water below turned indigo. A lone kayaker passed behind the rainbow-colored sails of a catamaran slowed by a lack of wind, then reappeared on the other side. The Space Needle looked like a toddler's playtoy just out of reach.

"I shouldn't be doing this, telling you this, but I'm going to. My instincts have never led me astray before and I'm going to trust them now." Patricia took in a deep breath. "I was down in Sherwood Fielding's office just now. Apparently Georgie's sick today. We were in the middle of this rather unpleasant discussion when someone knocks on the door. It was this skinny kid from the courier service. You know, the one with the bad complexion?"

Jennifer nodded. She couriered documents over to the patent attorney's office from time to time and had had the same kid pick them up on occasion.

"Well, he has this package that he wants Sherwood to sign for. Sherwood gets this look on his face, like he's about to lose control of his bowels or something, and snatches the board from the kid to sign it. The kid says something like, 'It's from your lab in Preston.' That's just what he said. 'It's from your lab in Preston.' Sherwood shoves the kid into the hallway and shuts the door so I won't hear, but there's no way I could miss it. 'I didn't ask you where the fuck it came from, did I?' he yelled at him. I sit there for a minute or two, then Sherwood comes back in, without the package, and he's put this poker face on. You know, like none of it ever happened."

"I didn't know we had a lab in Preston," Jennifer said.

"We don't."

"Did you ask him about it?"

"You bet I did. He insisted the kid was confused. That the package had come from our supplier, BioSystems, in Bothell. He made it clear he wasn't going to discuss it any further. And I'd already pissed him off, so I wasn't going to push it."

"Pissed him off about what?"

"Oh, that's a long story. I just told him I'm sick and tired of providing blood for his validation studies. Told him to get another guinea pig. This one's all dried up."

"You give blood?"

"I have. Three times now. For some top secret genetic work Sherwood himself has been conducting. He expects me to donate blood, but when I demand information about the study, he gives me some bullshit answers. But that's another issue entirely. The point is, there's no way that kid confused Bothell with Preston. And he's not going to refer to BioSystems as 'your lab.'

"After I left Sherwood, I stopped at Zelma's desk to ask her why she hadn't signed for the package. After all, she signs for everything. She told me the kid's been given explicit instructions that only Georgie and Sherwood can sign for certain deliveries. This was one of them."

Jennifer fell silent as she tried to make sense of what Patricia had learned. Why would Sherwood Fielding have a secret lab in Preston? *Preston.*

"Oh my god," she said, raising a hand involuntarily to her mouth. "Preston! That's where Gregory Gallagher had his accident."

"Holy shit. You're right."

"Could there be a connection? Between the lab and Dr. Gallagher's death?"

Patricia Lukins closed her eyes and ran her hand through her hair.

"I don't have a good feeling about this."

"I have to go out there," Jennifer said. "I have to find it."

"You're not going out there alone. It could be dangerous." Patricia Lukins hesitated. When she spoke again, her tone made it clear that she'd made an important decision. "We'll go together. Tomorrow night. I have to be with David tonight. He's been having a reaction to the treatment. On the days he has his injections, I spend the night there. He's having a treatment this afternoon. But if he's doing okay, I can go with you tomorrow night."

"I can't let you do that," Jennifer said.

"Just try and stop me."

ON THE RIDE DOWN to the underground parking garage as Jennifer was leaving work that afternoon, the elevator stopped on six. To Jennifer's horror, when the doors opened, on stepped Sherwood Fielding.

He gave Jennifer one of his tight-lipped smiles.

"Haven't seen you for a while," he said.

Jennifer gave him her own stingy smile and said, "Awfully busy these days."

She was relieved when the elevator stopped again immediately, on the fifth floor, where it picked up several other employees.

She did not direct her gaze at Fielding the rest of the ride, but had the distinct feeling he was watching her.

Since they were at the back of the elevator, they were the last to get off. Fielding waited for her, then held his hand in front of the elevator door to keep it from closing before she exited.

"Have a nice evening," he said as she stepped off.

"Thanks," Jennifer answered. "I plan to."

MATTHEW WAITED UNTIL after six to head out to the Eastside. Traffic was a pain in the ass until then.

Time to check out where Jennifer Rockhill lived. He'd gotten her address off her driver's license the night he'd tailed her to the Eastside and spilled coffee on her.

The address led him to an apartment complex. He could see her Volvo from the road, but continued past. He would return in a few minutes and cruise through the parking lot to check things out. Then tomorrow while she was at work, he'd break into her apartment and plant a couple bugs. One in the phone and one in the bedroom. Maybe she had a boyfriend she confided in.

An Italian restaurant in the strip mall just down from Jennifer's complex caught his eye. He hadn't eaten since lunch. He went in and indulged in the first good meal he'd had since coming to Seattle. Homemade spaghetti and meatballs, like Nan cooked.

An hour later he emerged.

He had just pulled into the apartment's parking lot when he saw her. The hatchback of her car was raised and she was bent over, apparently looking for something in the back of her station wagon. She had changed into jeans and t-shirt, both black, and she now wore sneakers.

Odd attire to change into at the end of a long day. Was she going somewhere?

She never looked up as Matthew cruised slowly by. As he passed, he could see she was busy rummaging through a toolbox. A flashlight lay next to her other hand, the one bracing her weight.

Matthew circled back around, reentered the parking lot, and pulled into a spot at the far end, near the second apartment building. After a few minutes, he saw Jennifer straighten, shut the hatchback, walk around the passenger side with the flashlight in hand. She opened the car door and dropped the flashlight on to the seat. Then, using her keyless remote, she locked the car again and went inside a door marked "I-D."

Matthew turned off the car, then settled back to see what would happen next.

THIRTEEN

BEFORE PULLING HIS ball cap down over his eyes for a quick catnap, Ken Hammer took one more glance at the three TV monitors mounted above his desk. He'd worked night shifts before and always had trouble adjusting to the way they turned his sleep cycles topsy-turvy, but this one was the worst. At the wood-processing plant—a big twenty-four-hour operation—there had been plenty to keep him busy on the graveyard shift. This place was just the opposite, so damn quiet that it was all but impossible to stay awake. Sometimes he regretted going into this business. When all the police departments turned him down for work because of his background check, he figured being a security guard was the closest he'd ever get to putting all that covert military training he'd gotten over there in North Idaho to work. Maybe he'd just have to find himself another militia group in these parts. He sure as hell hadn't seen any action around here.

His eyes moved from screen to screen. The first monitored the gated entrance to the property. The second, the building's main corridor. It was the third—a camera mounted in the lab—that he paid the most attention to. Those baboons were the damnedest creatures. He got a kick out of them. After his nap he might go in there and see them, give them some of the candy that Dr. Chandra kept in a glass bowl on the counter. But he would stop short of opening their cages. When he'd first been hired, Chandra had given explicit instructions for working with these animals.

"Don't let their size fool you," Chandra had told him. "These little ladies are powerful. And their incisors could rip you apart." Ken could feel him watching him for signs of fear. "And don't make eye contact. You have the advantage, because you're bigger—and they associate bulk with strength. But if you challenge them by making eye contact, you could get yourself in big trouble."

Ken had taken to visiting the baboons nightly, tossing the treats into their cages from a distance of two or three feet. He never bothered with the gloves and mask that goofy scientist told him to wear. He'd been conducting an experiment of his own lately. Been making eye contact with the ape he'd determined to be the most timid—Tea. He could hardly believe it one recent night when, in response, she'd turned her red bottom toward him.

Leaning back in his deluxe, spring-mounted chair, Ken lifted his boot-clad feet up on to the desktop. What he wouldn't give for a little excitement. Maybe tonight he'd try it again and see if Tea was still in the playful mood. If that theory about man being related to the apes was true, it's too bad *that* behavior hadn't been passed on down to human females. Yes, later he'd go see Tea. But for now, he was simply too damn tired to move an inch.

The last thing the night guard at the Preston lab did before nodding off was turn down the sound of the monitor so the noisy apes—who had a tendency to smack their lips playfully and call to one another during the night—would not disturb him.

JENNIFER WAITED UNTIL after dark, then she headed out the door. She had already put the flashlight in the car, when she went out there earlier to see whether there was anything in the toolbox that looked like it could help her pick a locked door. A screwdriver was the closest she could come, but as she stood there analyzing its potential, a sense of surrealism came over her. Could she actually pull this off? Maybe. But the Phillips-head she'd grasped onto wasn't going to get her inside anything. Not unless she used it to remove a door's hinges.

As she walked to the car, she tucked her hair inside a navy blue ball cap.

The last time she'd been in Preston it had been a day she'd explored the Snoqualmie region east of Seattle, in the foothills of the Cascade Mountains. When she first moved to Seattle, someone had told her the TV show "Northern Exposure" was filmed out near North Bend. She'd been a big fan of the show, so one day she'd taken off to see if she could find any of its settings. She'd meandered around the country roads and had, at one point, ended up driving through the little town of Preston, which was only identifiable as a town because a sign labeled it one.

She couldn't repeat the circuitous route she'd taken that day if she tried, and she didn't like the idea of driving those isolated, winding country roads alone at night, so this time, she headed instead for the interstate, which she knew had an exit for Preston. She had been relieved when Patricia Lukins told her she had to be at her brother's bedside tonight. As much as she would have liked company and support, she did not want to drag Patricia into it. This was something she had to do alone.

The night was clear, but brisk. Just a sliver of a moon hung in the sky, but the farther out of the city she drove, the more stars seemed to pop out. Also, the further east she drove on I-90, the higher and more rugged the outline of the surrounding hills became. Traffic was light. She noticed that the cars that passed her seemed to contain more couples and families than those she was used to seeing in the city. It must be nice, she thought, to live out here. If Charlie and Stacey were still alive and we lived in the Seattle area, this is probably where I would want to be.

Charlie and Stacey.

Were they watching her now? Did they think their mother and wife had gone crazy?

She slowed at the sign for Preston, then followed the arrows that took her back over the freeway and into the surrounding blackness. The two-lane road paralleled the interstate for half a mile before swinging north. She followed its curve, eyed the sign declaring PRESTON, POPULATION 953, then passed quickly by an antique shop, a little market, and a row of old frame houses, some well maintained, others that appeared long deserted. She'd passed through the town itself in less than thirty seconds.

Jennifer continued along the main road. It was dark, the thick branches of the forest on either side of the road hanging over the roadway, blocking out what little light the stars and moon might have provided, with just an occasional car passing in the other direction.

Nowhere was there any sign of any commercial facility like a lab. About ten minutes out of Preston she saw a sign announcing she'd entered the town of FALL CITY. She pulled into a Texaco at the edge of town and turned around, then headed back down Highway 203 again—back toward Preston.

This time as she traveled the distance between the two towns she slowed at side streets, looking for signs of . . . what? She did not know. She turned onto several narrow roads, even drove two or three miles down one, but was getting increasingly nervous about being in such remote surroundings alone, so she eventually turned around. She passed back through the town of Preston, then headed toward I-90, resigned—and, if the truth be known, somewhat relieved—at having failed in her mission.

Driving back along the portion of the road that hugged the freeway, she suddenly noticed a real estate sign. "Zoned Commercial," it said at the bottom. An arrow indicated the property, 5.2 acres, was located up a gravel road that angled off the route she was driving. Impulsively, she veered onto it. A facility like a laboratory would have to have commercial zoning, too.

The road took her past a little enclave of newer, upscale homes—country versions of those oversized brick Tudors in which Seattle's baby boomers liked to live—then began to climb. There were a few side streets, narrow gravel or dirt roads leading into a black void, but Jennifer did not have the heart to explore them. She was driving very slowly now, her car kicking up stones as she went.

A glint of light in her rearview mirror caught her eye, but when she looked closely she saw nothing. She shuddered when the road leveled out and an opening in the woods to her right revealed a small, unfenced cemetery—very Ichabod Cranish. But still, she continued, determined to at least make it to the property that was posted for sale.

Finally, up ahead, she saw another real estate sign. As she neared she saw that it matched the one she'd read at the bottom of the hill—same company, same ZONED COMMERCIAL message. At the far edge of the property for sale—a heavily wooded parcel—her headlights picked up a chain-link fence. Jennifer creeped forward.

The fence looked new. It was tall, much higher than the standard chain-link fence.

Jennifer followed it as it paralleled the road. It went on for two hundred yards, then was interrupted by a paved drive. She paused opposite a heavy-duty galvanized steel gate that bore a sign warning PRIVATE PROPERTY, KEEP OUT. In front of the gate was a post upon which she could see what looked like a security monitor, bearing a speaker and a number keypad. A camera was mounted at the juncture of the gate and the fence.

This had to be it.

Other than a nondescript, three-foot-high pole bearing the numbers 21932 at the mouth of the drive, there were no markings whatsoever to identify the property or its owners. It was *that*, more than anything else, which convinced Jennifer she had the right place. If Sherwood Fielding had a lab out in Preston, a lab no one at BioGentech seemed to know about, he would hardly post a sign advertising its existence. And what other business would not post its name?

The idea that this might be a residence popped briefly into Jennifer's mind, but she quickly dismissed it. Anyone that wealthy would put up an attractive wall, or at the very least, a wrought-iron gate.

This was it. She was certain.

But now, *what should she do about it?*

She had come to Seattle to uncover Sherwood Fielding's secrets. This was one of them.

She eased her car forward. Seeing a narrow opening in the forested parcel of land adjacent to the fence, Jennifer turned her headlights off and eased her car into it. She found herself on what appeared to be an old logging or utility road, basically just two parallel ruts, almost overgrown now with scrub grass and weeds. She didn't dare go far, just deep enough into the woods to be hidden from the road.

Before getting out of her car she'd withdrawn her old BioGentech security passkey from her wallet—the one that had been made outdated by the new system—and slipped it into her pocket. It just might come in handy. She climbed silently out of the car, leaving the door slightly ajar, and worked her way through the woods, cutting directly toward the fence line. Once her eyes adjusted to the dark, she could see well. She came upon the fence within minutes, then hung back to survey the situation.

As frightened and incredulous—at her own actions—as she was, as she stood there in the night forest, a sense of empowerment washed slowly over Jennifer. For the past two years, she had borne the frustration of planning, waiting. But tonight was different. Tonight, she just knew, held great promise.

She couldn't remember ever experiencing such silence. The only thing punctuating it was the drumming of blood coursing through her temples.

The fence was eight feet tall. Just a plain old chain-link fence—the kind she'd scaled as a kid—nothing more. No sign of barbed wire or of electric currents. If she could do it back then, as the klutzy kid she'd been, why not now?

With that thought in mind, and the help of an overload of adrenaline, she was up and over in a time and form that would have made Stacey proud.

The grounds were wooded, dark, and silent. However, it wasn't long before she picked up a glimmer of light through the trees. She honed in on it and soon found herself less than ten yards away from a sprawling white cement block structure. It appeared to be entirely windowless. The sole light came from a pole between the building's entrance and the parking lot. Jennifer couldn't tell if the building was occupied, though a lone car sat in the small parking lot in front of the building.

Staying under cover of the trees, Jennifer eased her way to the back of the building, which turned out to be considerably larger than she'd first thought. There were two separate entries on the back wall of the building. One was a steel double door that must have been used for deliveries. A short distance away, in an open clearing separating the building and the wooded areas, stood two large green garbage dumpsters. Another door was smaller. A sidewalk led from it to the far corner of the building then disappeared around it, paralleling the paved drive that led to the double doors.

Within a ring of twenty to thirty feet, everything, all trees and growth of any kind, had been cleared from around the building. Jennifer darted from the shelter of the trees to the dumpsters. She was hit immediately by a stench but as she huddled down behind the gigantic containers of waste, she realized the ripe odor did not originate in the dumpsters. She looked around and saw, behind her, several more yards out, a large pile that looked almost like the compost pile she'd spent years cultivating in her own garden, though this one was easily six or eight times as large. It seemed to consist primarily of straw but the odor reminded her of the barn where Stacey had taken riding lessons—the manure, which, to Charlie's horror, she'd actually hauled to their home by the wheelbarrowful each fall and spring. And urine. It was oddly out of place here, next to this building, with no barn or animals in sight. Jennifer wondered if she were mistaken, but since the pile lay in relatively open sight, she did not want to venture closer to examine it. Trying to ignore its stench, she focused instead on the building.

Again, there were no windows on this side, although on the top of the building she could see several domes. The light emanating from them indicated they were skylights. Jennifer reasoned that since she'd been able to scale the chain-link fence and cross the perimeter of the property and come this close to the building itself without detection, security precautions were minimal. Maybe, she thought, that's because no one even knows this place exists.

After enough time to establish the fact that no one was around, she crept forward, approaching the smaller of the two back doors. There was a six-inch metal box mounted on the door's frame, level with the handle. She switched her flashlight on and trained it on the box. It looked identical to the security stations she'd used for months at BioGentech, with the exception that it did not have a signal light on it. Preparing herself for failure and readying to flee if she set off an alarm, she withdrew her passkey from her pocket, then, pausing just briefly to take a deep breath, swiped it through the thin channel on the box's surface. Without a light, there was nothing to signal her success or failure, but she heard a distinct click immediately following the scanning of her passkey. She reached tentatively for the doorknob and turned slowly.

The door, miraculously, opened. Bright light instantaneously blinded Jennifer, causing her to fall back. Squinting, she stepped forward, through the door and into a corridor. It was long, bright, and empty, and made her feel enormously exposed. When the door closed behind her, she felt a momentary panic, as though she were trapped now inside the building. She reopened the door, then gently eased it back to where it stopped just short of engaging. For some reason the knowledge that it was still open—giving her quick access back outside—lessened the sense of entrapment and gave her a sense of security.

Stay calm, she coached herself. *Keep your head.*

Jennifer picked her way silently down the corridor to where another, shorter and less brightly lit, corridor intersected it. She took the turn. On her right was a door. Through its uncovered window, she could see a single lamp burning on a counter that looked much like those in the labs at BioGentech. Jennifer could make out a sink and, above the counter, shelves of what appeared to be periodicals and textbooks. There was a computer at the end of the long counter and several stools along it. A telephone sat next to the lamp.

Jennifer tried the doorknob but found it locked.

She moved on down the hall, passing an open closet that contained boxes of rubber gloves, surgical masks, and folded lab coats.

At the end of the hall was a door marked "Caution: Sterile Environment." There was another security panel mounted next to the door. Jennifer pressed her ear to the door, then, hearing nothing, again used her passkey. She listened for the telltale click. There it was.

She turned the knob.

The smell of disinfectant was the first thing to hit her. The next was the sense that she was not alone.

As she stepped inside, seven pair of closely set eyes were centered squarely on Jennifer.

She gasped.

The sight of the row of female baboons staring out at her from their cages horrified her at first, but that reaction quickly turned to repulsion at the recognition of the poor animals' fate, and compassion. It was their eyes that got to her. They were so incredibly human, so sad. She wanted to set them free.

She walked along the row of cages, mesmerized, drawn somehow to them. Above each door there was a nameplate.

At the last cage she paused a bit longer than she had at the others.

"Angel," she whispered. The cage's occupant cocked her head in response, in a gesture that struck Jennifer as being ridiculously human. She seemed to be measuring Jennifer with her liquid brown eyes.

"I'll come back for you," Jennifer found herself promising.

She turned to the rest of the vast room. In its center was a large stainless-steel table like that used as an examination table by her vet back in San Diego. Medical instruments were strewn about. She could have sworn one of the larger pieces of equipment was an ultrasound, though it had been so many years since she'd seen one.

Along one wall was a long counter; above that, metal cupboards with makeshift labels, crude penmanship scrawled on masking tape, denoting their contents.

She opened one marked *histological samples*. Inside, one shelf was labeled—again crudely, with masking tape—*brain*; another, *spinal cord*. From the size of the samples, Jennifer knew the subjects had been small rodents, most likely mice. She turned and looked back at the apes again.

What are they doing to you?

As she was turning back, once more, to the cupboards, a large barrel in the corner of the room caught her eye. It was stamped "Lab Waste."

Instantly, Dave Maynard's words came back to her:

You'd be amazed by how much information can be derived from examining the waste that comes out of a lab.

She started toward the barrel, a fifty-five-gallon metal industrial drum with a flat metal lid secured by a ring and clamp, then pivoted abruptly and returned to the cabinets. She opened the rest of the doors, looking for a container of sorts—she would need something to carry a waste sample back with her. A plan had now formulated in her mind. She would take a waste sample to an independent lab for an analysis that might very well give her the information she was after.

When her search of the cupboard turned up nothing but test tubes, culture plates, solutions, and samples, she began opening the drawers located in a row just under the countertop.

"Perfect," she mouthed when the second one revealed several boxes of plastic storage bags, in a number of different sizes.

She extracted a one-gallon zipper-locking bag from its box and headed purposefully back to the barrel.

There was a door on one wall that connected the lab to the room she'd just peered in through its window. She was so absorbed now in her task—so excited about her plan and how smoothly things were going— that she failed to hear its knob turn slowly. She could not have seen it, as her back was turned to that wall.

She struggled with the lid on the barrel for a few moments, trying to figure out how to remove it. There was a clasping mechanism, attached to a metal strip that circled the top of the barrel, fixing the lid in place. It required considerable strength to disengage and as Jennifer strained to force it open, she inadvertently leaned into the barrel. Suddenly the catch gave way and the lid, free now, clamored to the ground. As she shifted her weight away, a liquid sloshed out of the wobbling barrel.

The solution splashed over her hands. Several drops even reached her face.

Horrified that it might be some kind of acid, Jennifer mopped at it frantically with the sleeves of her sweatshirt. She'd pulled them long, to cover her hands, and was wiping her face with them when something floating on the barrel's surface drew her attention.

She stopped, sweatshirt-covered hands still pressed to either side of her face, and leaned closer.

"Oh my god," she cried out.

THE SCREAM—JENNIFER'S anguished, terrified "Oh my god"—jolted him from his task. He'd just finished installing two transmitters—a telephone transmitter and an internal electret microphone built into a surge protector power strip for the computer—in Chandra's office. These days the latest developments made it possible to plant bugs in a matter of minutes. All he had to do with the surge protector was plug it into the wall. The AC outlet provided an indefinite power source, eliminating the need for batteries and replacements. And the fact that there was a computer on the counter already using the same kind of strip meant the chance for detection of the replacement was almost non-existent.

He had carried both transmitters along for planting in Jennifer's apartment. He hadn't planned to use them until tomorrow; but when Jennifer's car had pulled out of the apartment complex, he'd fallen in behind and tailed her, hanging back several cars, as she headed east on Interstate 90. Where was she going at this hour of the night?

When she pulled off at the Preston exit, he immediately made the connection. Dr. Gallagher had driven his car off the road, falling to his death over a steep ravine, in this general area. Was this related to Jennifer's excursion tonight? Had the same thing that had drawn Dr. Gallagher out to the area late at night now drawn Jennifer?

Tailing conditions were not good on the sparsely traveled country roads Jennifer had taken. He would never have gotten away with it had he been following an experienced criminal—or, for that matter, an experienced agent. But he knew that turning his headlights off and hanging back a bit would most likely work with Jennifer. And, on desolate roads like the ones they'd driven, he was not likely to encounter a police car.

After following her to Fall City and back, Matthew had watched from an eighth of a mile behind her as Jennifer's car crept past the unmarked fenced compound. Watched as she paused opposite its entry, then continued on. When he saw where she pulled her car off the gravel road, into the cover of the woods, he turned around and expeditiously ditched his car on the other side of the property, the side from which they had both approached.

When he found himself in situations like this, Matthew automatically turned into the closest thing possible to a living, walking intelligence manual—his mind always two steps ahead, planning for every possible contingency. Policy often dictated that agents working in pairs split up. That way, if they were being pursued and were cut off in one direction, they'd still have transportation waiting in the other. In this situation, if their presence were detected, Matthew could distract pursuers away from Jennifer's parked car.

Even though Jennifer had parked first Matthew had beaten her to the building. Hidden in their shadows himself, he'd seen her weaving her way amongst the trees, watched as she made her dash to the dumpsters.

When she'd used her passkey to gain entry to the building's back door and the door had closed behind her, Matthew's heart had sunk. He wasn't surprised that her card had worked. This facility was apparently connected in some way to BioGentech. It was not surprising to discover that they had shared a security system—before, that is, BioGentech's installation of the newest technology. But Jennifer's good fortune, if he could call it that, at having access was apparently not to be his.

He was surveying the situation, eyeing the roof, where he could see domed skylights, when suddenly the door reopened, just a fraction of an inch, and remained propped slightly ajar. He waited thirty seconds, then followed Jennifer inside.

The door to the lab at the end of the first corridor to the left had just closed when Matthew made the turn. He hurried after her. But the lab door was locked and required a passkey. He retraced his footsteps to the lab/office he'd already passed. This door did not require a passkey; however, it, too, was locked. Matthew withdrew a sharp instrument—the proverbial "pick" used for covert entry—from his pocket and was inside within thirty seconds. He pulled the shade down over the window, the same window Jennifer had peeked through just minutes earlier.

He scanned the room and quickly saw that it was connected to another—most likely the lab into which Jennifer had just disappeared. He
tried the knob, but found it locked. He debated about picking it, too, but
feared that the commotion that would ensue when Jennifer saw him there
would bring a guard running.

There was a guard on duty, of that he was certain. The car out front
and security camera mounted in the hall meant that somewhere there was
a room where a guard monitored the premises. He was not surprised,
however, that his and Jennifer's presence hadn't yet been detected because he knew the habits of these low-paid, commercial guards all too
well—knew with jobs like this one, jobs where night after night passed
without incident, how complacent, sloppy they could become. This guy,
thought Matthew, must either be passed out somewhere or making it with
a female visitor on some lab floor. Still, you could only push your luck so
far. Deciding for the moment against forcing entry to the lab, Matthew
used the opportunity to plant the transmitters. He'd just switched the
wired surge protector for the one already there when he heard it. Jennifer's scream.

SHE WAS OFF, running at top speed, flying first through the door she'd entered to the lab, down the short corridor, then, turning, back down the long
one. The door she'd left propped open was closed now and as she ran toward it she thought her heart would give out on her if she were to find it
locked. But it opened readily and in the next second, she was back out in
the night, gulping fresh air as though she'd been underwater too long.

She ran through the night, toward her car, branches whipping at her
body and face, but oblivious to anything but her terror. *The terror of what
she'd seen.*

Her lungs felt on fire and her legs were already shaky, both from
physical strain and shock, when she reached the fence. Still, she cleared
it even faster than she had the first time.

Once in her car, she punched her foot down on the accelerator, shoot-
ing wildly backwards, almost getting herself stuck in soft ground, but
frantically rocking the car back and forth between reverse and first until
it once again rocketed backwards. Once on the gravel roadway, she drove
like a demon, reaching speeds of seventy miles per hour on the dangerous
little road—but still, it wasn't fast enough, couldn't take her far enough
away from what she'd seen.

When she finally reached the on-ramp to the interstate, she dared a
look in the rearview mirror. Nothing. No one had followed her.

She'd escaped. She was safe.

But safety, she knew intuitively, was strictly a physical concept.

For nothing could actually provide her with the kind of safety she really needed right now. A mental safety. Protection from what she'd just seen—what she knew she would continue to see, not just that night and in the days to come, but for the rest of her life.

THE SCREAM CAME from the adjoining room.

Matthew bolted for the door separating the two rooms, tried to force it open. When it failed to give way, he jerked the pick out of his pocket and inserted it into the keyhole. By the time he succeeded in opening the door, the lab was empty—well, not exactly empty, as he found himself surrounded by apes—but Jennifer was no longer in it. In one corner stood a barrel labeled "Lab Waste." Its lid lay nearby, on the floor, a puddle of brownish liquid surrounding it. He raced for the only other door—the one that Jennifer had just exited. As he opened it, he could hear the approach of running footsteps.

He shut the door and turned the flimsy lock on the handle, then pulled the heavy examination table over in front of the door. It would not stop the guard altogether, but it might buy Matthew a little time.

A quick assessment told him he could try to flee through the adjoining room, but its only exit opened to the hallway in which the guard now was located—a fact confirmed when the guard's initial attempt to open the door was quickly followed by the loud thud of his entire weight hurtling against it.

Matthew's eye swept to the ceiling.

The skylights. One happened to be directly above the row of cages lining the wall. Eyeing a microscope on the countertop, Matthew lunged for it, then, using the agility he'd honed on his frequent ascents of Look Out Mountain, he quickly scaled the eight-foot-high barred door of one of the baboon's cages. Once on top he could just reach the ceiling.

As the examination table tottered under the force of the guard's repeated assaults, Matthew tightened his grasp on the microscope, then bringing to bear all of his strength, he smashed it through the skylight. He repeatedly struck at the glass around the perimeter of the frame, each time closing his eyes as a torrent of razor-sharp shards rained down upon him.

The guard's progress at the door meant time was running out. Despite the needles of glass that still remained around the dome's frame, Matthew reached up, grasped firmly onto it, and hoisted himself through the hole.

He had just cleared the opening when a bullet sang through after him.

Matthew vaulted to the edge of the roof and jumped, falling sixteen feet to the ground, but managing to land on his feet. Assuming there was only one guard, he would have an edge on him. His pursuer would either have to climb on top of the cages and hoist himself through the skylight or run down at least two corridors before exiting the building, at which time he would have to decide which direction his subject had fled.

With any luck, Matthew would be deep into the woods by then.

But would Jennifer have been so lucky?

JENNIFER CLOSED HER EYES as she waited for the last traffic light before she reached her apartment complex to turn green. But it did not help. Nothing could ever erase the sight, the horror of those tiny figures. Floating on the surface of the barrel labeled "Lab Waste."

She'd recognized them immediately. She had, after all, when she was expecting Stacey, been one of those women who devoured books on pregnancy.

At any point during the nine months she could, and did—mainly with Charlie, she tried not to be boorish about it with her friends, but with Charlie she indulged herself, her absolute joy at the miraculous process—describe with amazing accuracy the stage of Stacey's fetal development.

At three weeks, rudiments of eyes and ears, as well as a pulsating heart. At eight weeks, all internal organs already formed. Also by the eighth week, the formation of twenty digits, ten perfect fingers and toes.

Yes, she'd taken such delight in educating herself about it, all of it, that Charlie had begun to jokingly refer to her as Dr. Rockhill.

And that explained why—despite the pandemonium prevailing due to the circumstances, despite the fact that the little lifeless forms were grossly discolored, almost black in hue—there was no mistaking precisely what they were. And Jennifer knew it.

Human fetuses.

Two of them. Floating, like bars of soap, on the surface of the formaldehyde heavy solution with which the drum was filled.

And with that discovery, Jennifer Rockhill knew that the suspicions she'd been harboring—the fears she'd lived with for several weeks now—were absolute child's play compared to the reality of the nightmare she'd actually, somehow, stepped into.

FOURTEEN

BACK AT HER APARTMENT by 2:00 A.M., Jennifer did not even attempt to climb in bed and get some sleep. What was the point? Right now she doubted she'd ever be able to sleep again.

She had this burning urge to pick up the phone and call someone. Call for help. She could not bother Patricia at the hospital. Her brother needed her. And despite Patricia's having been the one to tell Jennifer about the existence of a secret lab, Jennifer was reluctant to drag the scientist into this. Patricia had her career to think of. And her brother's situation, which obviously weighed heavily upon her.

But who then could she turn to? She had no one. Just the friends she'd distanced herself from after Charlie's and Stacey's deaths. She hadn't even bothered to bid them farewell when she left La Jolla for Visalia. In fact, one of her motivations for going to Visalia, for returning to the hometown of her childhood, was to get away from them, from the pity she saw in their eyes each time she happened to run into one of them. She could just imagine ringing them now, in the middle of the night, to tell them she was in a bit of trouble. She'd just broken into a secret lab in the boondocks outside Seattle and had found human fetuses discarded in the waste. They'd think she'd finally gone over the edge.

That left two possibilities.

One was the police. Would they even believe her? What did she have to offer as proof? Surely after what just happened whoever ran the diabolic lab out in Preston would dispose of the fetuses. After all, she'd left the lid of the waste drum lying on the floor, leaving no doubt as to just what she'd seen. The only other evidence she could offer the police to substantiate her claim that something hideously evil was going on was having been called in to Sherwood Fielding's office to explain the late-night log-in at her computer. Pretty flimsy stuff. And, perhaps more importantly, what explanation could she offer for her own trespass, breaking, and entry? With her luck, a call to the police would result in her being arrested, not Sherwood Fielding.

If she couldn't turn to the police, that left just one more option. Matthew Pace. From the day they'd met, every fiber in her being told her to stay away from him, but maybe Matthew Pace was just what she needed. After all, she'd turned to the good guys in the past, and what had they done for her?

For the first time it occurred to her that she was no match for the evil game she'd stumbled upon. And how many shots would she have at Sherwood Fielding before he figured out who she really was? Once that happened, she'd be lucky to get out alive.

She went to her briefcase and found the paper Matthew Pace had given her that day he'd followed her in the rain. Then, without wasting more time second-guessing, Jennifer picked up the phone and dialed. After a generic recorded message, she punched in her telephone number and hung up.

Next she went to the stove and turned the front burner, upon which sat a stainless steel kettle, on high. Maybe herbal tea would calm her. As she waited for Matthew Pace's return call, she sat staring at a column of steam that had begun snaking its way toward the ceiling from the kettle's spout.

Suddenly the middle-of-the-night quiet was shattered by a knock at her front door.

Jennifer jumped up and stood, silent, waiting to see what happened next.

Another knock, this time louder, more demanding.

She walked over to the wooden block that housed her cutlery and grabbed the largest white ceramic handle protruding from it. Butcher's knife in hand, she crept down the hallway to the front door.

Just as she got there, there was another insistent rap.

She raised herself up to see through the peephole.

It was *Matthew Pace!*

"How did you know where I live?" she demanded to know through the door.

"Let me in."

Jennifer did not respond.

"Listen, we need to talk. You could be in danger. Maybe serious danger. Let me help you."

"Yeh," she said, "like you helped by breaking into my office that night?"

There was silence, then Matthew answered.

"I admit it. I'll explain. I'll explain everything. Just open the door."

If she had any other options, any place or anyone else to turn to, she would not have done it. But the truth was, there *was* no one else.

Jennifer slowly undid the chain lock, flipped the dead bolt, and opened the door.

There stood Matthew. When he stepped through the door, Jennifer reflexively stepped back.

"You're bleeding."

His hands, which he held palms up, were slashed everywhere. Blood seeped from the deeper cuts, dripping on to the welcome mat covering the worn beige carpet.

"Sorry about that," Matthew said.

Jennifer locked the door behind him.

"Follow me," she said, leading him down the hall to the bathroom.

Inside, she placed the knife on the counter and turned on the faucet.

"Stick your hands under there," she ordered. As Matthew complied, she opened the medicine cabinet and withdrew iodine and sterile gauze. She lowered the toilet lid and made him sit down while she wrapped both palms.

"Do I dare ask how this happened?"

He looked at her, watched as she wound the white material around each hand, then secured it with tape.

"Thank you," he said.

Her only response was to stare at him, waiting for an answer to her question.

"I followed you tonight," he finally said.

Suddenly she remembered the glint in her rearview mirror on the way out to Preston.

"Just who the hell are you?"

Matthew studied her.

"I'm the guy you paged a little while ago. Remember? I presumed that meant you finally saw the wisdom of the two of us working together."

"How can I make that decision before I know who you are and what you're after?"

"Good point. However, if I answer your questions, I have to get some answers in return. Deal?"

She studied him before answering.

"Deal."

Still seated on the toilet seat, Matthew Pace made no attempt to dodge Jennifer's scrutiny.

"I work for a British pharmaceutical company," he said. "That's why I'm in Seattle. I was sent me here to investigate rumors that something big was happening at BioGentech."

"You mean you're a professional thief?" Dave Maynard had told her about people like this. "They sent you here to steal trade secrets? Intellectual Property?"

"That's about it."

"And that's why you were following me? You thought I knew what's going on?"

"Either that or that you could lead me to it. Which, I believe, is just what you did. Tonight."

Jennifer could not contain her loathing for this man. Aligning herself with him was out of the question.

"Get out of here."

Jennifer turned for the door.

Matthew jumped up and, in spite of the bandages on both hands, grabbed her by the shoulders.

"What did you see tonight?" he asked.

She twisted out from under him and stood, glaring at him.

"You have to tell me," he said.

"Why? Why would I help you?"

"Why? Because you're in danger. The same danger Gregory Gallagher was in the night he died. On the same road you drove not more than an hour ago. And because if you help me, I'll help you. I know that you came to Seattle for a reason. That it has something to do with your husband and daughter. What is it? This is what I do for a living. Don't you see that together we can accomplish a hell of a lot more than either of us could separately?"

This time, when Jennifer did not respond, it was Matthew who started to leave.

"You have my number," he said from the hallway.

"Wait!"

He swung back around and measured her with those cold blue eyes.

"We made a deal. That if I came clean, you would, too. I've kept my end of it. Now it's your turn."

Jennifer stared blankly at him while she tried to process all that had happened this night. Any way she looked at it, she came to the same conclusion. He was right. There was no escaping it. The possibility that Fielding was still involved in his heinous schemes hadn't really occurred to her until now. She'd assumed her accusations two years ago would have scared him straight, that he'd run to Seattle to make a fresh start. As hardened as she felt she'd become these past three years, she suddenly realized that she had still retained enough naivete to believe that she could follow him to Seattle and bring him to justice. It had never occurred to her that she might stumble into yet another of his twisted schemes. One apparently so dangerous (if, indeed, Dr. Gallagher's death were not accidental) that the possibility existed, she, too, could lose her life before she'd been able to put the pieces of the puzzle together she'd collected here in Seattle. *Before accomplishing what she set out to do.* She would do anything to avoid that happening and to prevent Fielding from getting away with what he had done to Charlie. If that meant working with Matthew Pace, so be it.

Heavy with the sense of resignation that had just settled over her, Jennifer lowered herself to the edge of the bathtub. Then she began.

"Three years ago . . ." she said.

IT WAS THE first time she'd had a day to herself in ages and, the truth was, she enjoyed it—which, after the fact, contributed to the unreasonable, almost unbearable guilt she'd carried around ever since. Actually, she'd even begun the day feeling a little guilty about not being there for Stacey's big tournament, but she'd quickly been able to reason that she'd made the right decision. After all, she had to work the next morning, and the way soccer tournaments went, the championship game might not even get started until seven or eight o'clock. By the time they made the drive back from Palm Springs, it could be midnight. And Jennifer had an important deposition in the morning, one she dared not go into tired.

Stacey had understood.

"Mom, you never miss my games. And you'll feel crummy all day tomorrow at work if we end up playing for the championship, which, of course, we will." Jennifer had always loved her daughter's confidence. "Besides, Dad cheers loud enough for both of you."

"You sure you don't mind?" Jennifer had asked one last time as she walked Charlie and Stacey to the car.

"Of course not," Stacey had told her, giving her a big hug. She was tall now, even taller than Jennifer's five foot seven.

"Be careful," Jennifer had told Charlie as he reached for her.

"We will," he'd assured her. "Don't wait up."

Once they'd pulled out of the driveway, Jennifer had puttered in the garden for a while. A month earlier, she'd turned over a section of grass and sprinkled one of those ready-made cans of wildflower seeds over the fresh soil. She wanted to recreate a mountain meadow they'd seen the summer before on a trip to Jackson Hole. She'd first seen signs of sprouts a week ago and now she delighted in checking their progress each day. Down on her hands and knees, she pulled out the weeds that had already begun to take hold and felt almost jubilant at the prospect of the relaxing day ahead.

The clouds had rolled in while she was weeding. She'd looked up and been startled to see the sky to the west filled with a roiling, ominous wall of black. Her first thought was that Stacey's game might be rained out, but then she dismissed that possibility. They were playing a hundred miles north and east, in Palm Springs. San Diego's storms never moved that far inland. And who was she kidding? Soccer games weren't called for rain. How many downpours had she stood in over the past ten years, watching as Stacey, knees and elbows caked with mud, defended the goal from the other team's assaults? Too many to count. Just once in all those years could Jennifer remember a game actually being cut short, and that was only after lightning had struck a nearby tree.

When the rain began in earnest, Jennifer had gone inside and turned her attention to the laundry that piled up during every work week. Later that afternoon, after the storm had passed, she went to the market, then stopped to browse the downtown La Jolla shops, where she was pleased to find a white sweater—one of those shorter, cropped cardigans that were just coming in style—that would be perfect for the sailing outing next weekend that she and Charlie had been invited on.

To this day, she'd never removed the sweater from the bag in which she brought it home.

Dinner was pleasurably simple. A small green salad topped with strips of the chicken breasts they'd had the night before. She ate it in front of the TV, watching "Sixty Minutes," then the last half of *Casablanca*, as she sipped wine and indulged in chocolate chip cookies she'd bought that afternoon. By the time the movie ended it was almost ten. Despite Charlie's admonition not to wait up, she decided to read in bed until they returned home. But the serenity of the day and the wine soon combined to make her so heavy lidded that, after the first chapter, she put her book down. Maybe she would just close her eyes for a little while.

Later, she decided that it was the silence that woke her.

At first, she assumed she'd dozed no more than a few minutes. The book lay, still open, on her chest. The bedside lamp was still on. But the moment she gave in to her still sleepy state and closed her eyes again, she knew. Something was wrong. The quiet—a middle-of-the-night kind of quiet, not the early-evening stillness she'd last known—told her she had slept hours, not minutes, and a frantic glance at the clock confirmed it. Three-fifteen.

They hadn't called. Charlie always called from his cell phone if he was running late.

It was the longest two hours of her life, pure hell. But later she realized that at least then there had still been just the tiniest glimmer of hope—maybe they'd pulled over on the side of the road to take a nap and hadn't wanted to call and disturb her—which was forever shattered by a knock at her door. It was just after 5:00 A.M.

She'd always felt sorry for the young police officer who brought her the news.

It was a passerby on Highway 74 who first noticed the car's headlights, just outside the town of Chihuilla. Charlie's Jeep had gone off the winding mountain road, made slick by its first rain in over a month. Later, when they reconstructed what happened, they realized that Charlie and Stacey had been there at least three hours before anyone noticed. The tournament had ended at 9:00 P.M. According to teammates, Charlie and Stacey had joined the rest of the team at McDonald's for a victory dinner—true to her prediction, Stacey's team had won the championship game. The rest of the team planned to take Interstate 10 west to I-15, but Charlie knew a shortcut that would take them directly southwest and cut half an hour off the trip. He was anxious, he said, to get home to his wife.

By the time ambulances and state troopers arrived, Stacey was already gone. Charlie was unconscious, with dangerously weak vital signs, but he survived the difficult, cliffside evacuation and trip to Chihuilla General, which is where the officer at her door offered to drive her.

At Chihuilla General, Charlie hovered near death for five days. He never regained consciousness, though the morning he died, Jennifer swore he'd squeezed her hand when she whispered to him, "I love you, Charlie Banks." She would not leave his side that day, so certain was she that he would come back to her, would help her bear the unbearable loss of their daughter.

"Have you found Dr. Treecedale yet?" she'd asked one ICU nurse after another that morning. Finally, just after noon, he showed up.

Two days earlier, he'd begun allowing Jennifer to stay in the room during his daily examinations of Charlie. Today, after hearing her story, Treecedale's exam seemed to Jennifer interminable.

Sitting on the opposite side of Charlie's still form, her eyes never left the internist's lined, kindly face.

Finally, he raised it to meet her gaze.

"*What?*" she said. "What do you think?"

"I don't want to give you false hope," he began. "But he does seem stronger today. And his pupils are more reactive to light."

When he saw the tears spring to Jennifer's eyes, he was quick to add, "But I've seen this happen before. It can mean nothing, absolutely nothing. It's premature to celebrate, please bear that in mind. But I'll have to say, I'm encouraged."

"Thank you," Jennifer mouthed.

"I have to drive up to Santa Barbara this evening," Dr. Treecedale told her then. "My granddaughter is graduating from UCSB tomorrow. But I'll be accessible at all times. The staff knows how to contact me."

"Who will take care of Charlie?"

Jennifer felt sheer panic at the prospect of Dr. Treecedale leaving.

"The nurses, of course, and another ICU doctor—Dr. Fielding, who covers for me from Palm Springs—will handle anything that comes up in my absence," he'd answered. "I'll be back the day after tomorrow."

For the first time since being given the option, Jennifer regretted her decision not to have Charlie flown via Medivac helicopter to San Diego General. The decision had only been made after consultation with Dr. Treecedale and a long telephone conversation with their family physician at home, Dr. Sriram. Both had told her that in his current state, the only thing medical personnel could do was sustain Charlie, keep him alive, a task for which Chihuilla General was more than qualified. If he came out of his coma, it would be imperative to move him to a more sophisticated facility, like San Diego General.

"Dr. Treecedale is a first-rate internist," Dr. Sriram had assured her. "He's well known and respected in the San Diego medical community. Spent two decades as an ICU doctor here, before deciding that he was ready for something slower. I'm confident Charlie is in good hands."

And so she'd rented a room at the Chihuilla Inn and spent all her waking hours at Charlie's side. Now she wondered if that had been the right decision. Still, she knew it would be unreasonable to expect Dr. Treecedale to miss his granddaughter's graduation.

"Have a safe trip," she'd told him as he squeezed her shoulder before parting.

Visiting hours ended at eight o'clock. That was when Jennifer usually walked from the hospital to Bud and Shirley's Cafe for dinner. But tonight she stayed longer, hoping to meet Dr. Fielding and be able to go to bed that night with a sense of peace from knowing that Charlie was still in good hands.

About eight-thirty, a nurse, one Jennifer had never before seen, came into Charlie's room. When she pulled back the curtain that surrounded Charlie's bed, she looked startled to see Jennifer.

"Visiting hours are over," she said.

"I know," Jennifer answered, "I usually leave at eight, but I was hoping I'd get a chance to meet the doctor who's filling in for Dr. Treecedale."

"Dr. Fielding's busy right now," the nurse answered curtly. "I'm afraid you'll have to leave. Hospital rules."

It was then that Jennifer noticed the syringe in her hand.

"What's that for?"

Clearly annoyed now, the nurse replied, "It's a routine antibiotic."

"I've never seen him get a shot that looked like that before. Especially at this hour."

"You just said you're usually not here this late. Maybe that's why."

She was right. How would Jennifer know what medications Charlie received each night after she'd left?

With the woman watching impatiently, Jennifer bent over Charlie and kissed him on the forehead.

"Good night, my love," she whispered to him.

It was the last time she would ever see him.

They told her they'd tried to call her. But there had been a mix-up. They'd tried the Desert Inn, not the Chihuilla Inn. Jennifer could never understand how such a mistake could be made. The first night she left Charlie's bedside, she'd written the Inn's phone number and her room number on a slip of paper and hand delivered it to the nurses' station. There were only two motels in town. When the Desert Inn reported they had no one registered in the name of Jennifer Banks, why hadn't they tried the other?

"We had a medical emergency on our hands," the same nurse had told her the next morning. "What do you think was more important? Finding you, or trying to save your husband's life?"

Charlie, it seemed, had begun hemorrhaging internally during the night. In an attempt to stem the bleeding and save Charlie, Dr. Fielding had operated. The form Jennifer had signed when she'd made the decision to keep Charlie in Chihuilla had given them the right "to perform emergency, life-saving procedures" without any further consent from Jennifer. When they were unable to locate Jennifer, they'd proceeded with the surgery. Charlie had not made it through the operation.

•   •   •

"I WANT TO SEE him," Jennifer said in her state of shock.

For the first time, the nurse—the same one who'd run her off the night before—seemed to soften.

"Please, dear," she said, placing her arm around Jennifer's waist. "Don't do that to yourself. Remember him the way he was. He's not there anymore. It's not something you'd be doing for your husband. It's something you think *you* need. But I've been in this business a long time. And it won't help. In fact, it can be devastating. Just devastating."

Later, Jennifer would discover that by the time they were having this conversation, Charlie's body had already been picked up by the local mortician.

MATTHEW HAD MAINTAINED an almost robotic quiet and stillness the entire time Jennifer was speaking. Once she'd started telling her story, Jennifer Rockhill's entire persona had visibly transformed from the aloof, self-contained woman he'd been relentlessly pursuing for weeks now to someone quite different. Someone vulnerable and in pain.

It only served to heighten her already considerable appeal to him.

"So you blame Fielding for not being able to save your husband," he finally said, when she'd fallen silent.

"No. I blame him for killing him."

"Killing him? Surely it was possible that no one—not even Dr. Treecedale, not even the best surgeons in San Diego—could save him after he'd begun hemorrhaging."

"I don't believe he was bleeding."

With any other woman grieving the loss of her husband and daughter, Matthew might attribute such a response to hysteria. But Jennifer Rockhill was not the hysterical type.

"If he wasn't bleeding internally, why would Fielding operate on him?"

"To remove his kidney. Or perhaps even both kidneys. I've never learned which."

"Just why would Fielding do that?"

"You're the last person I'd expect that kind of naivete from. Just why do you think he'd do it?"

"To sell it on the black market."

"Exactly."

"What evidence do you have to back it up?"

"A letter. One letter that failed to convince anyone but me. If I had evidence," she said bitterly, "the kind you're referring to, I wouldn't be here now. Neither would you. Or Sherwood Fielding. If I had the evidence I needed, that sick excuse for a human being would be in prison, paying for what he did to Charlie, instead of posing as the big saviour, out to eradicate disease."

"Tell me about this letter," Matthew said.

IT HAD ARRIVED eight months to the day after Charlie's death. She was still living in La Jolla at the time. The envelope had no return address on it, but it had been postmarked from somewhere called "Homewood, IL." Later, Jennifer learned that it was a wealthy suburb of Chicago.

> Dear Mrs. Banks,
>
> I know that I should not be contacting you, but I have been wanting to thank you for so long—without knowing who you even were—that when I came across my father's private files and learned your husband's identity, I simply couldn't help myself.
>
> My father was the recipient of your deceased husband's kidney. The gift that you so generously made—a gift of life to another human being—transformed not only my father's life, but mine and my children's as well. Sadly, Daddy died two months ago. But your husband's kidney gave him six months that we never expected to have. Six months in which we, as a family, were able to heal wounds that had kept us apart for far too long. In the end, Daddy's health problems were just too advanced for him to go on. But I will always treasure those last months with him that your gift made possible.
>
> Money can never take the place of a loved one, but I only hope that the money you were willing to accept to give Daddy another chance helped lessen the burdens you were experiencing. The laws should be changed. Daddy should not have been denied the chance to live simply because he was elderly. But through your generosity and compassion, we had six glorious months together. I pray that the knowledge that your husband's death was not in vain will forever bring you comfort.

I'm sorry that I cannot sign my name, but I'm sure you understand.

God bless you.

Jennifer had read it a dozen times. There was no mistaking what it said. Charlie's kidney had been transplanted into someone else.

When? How? This was crazy. The subject of organ donation had never even been raised, either for Charlie or Stacey. Had it been, Jennifer would have consented, as she knew that would have been both Charlie's and Stacey's desire. It had even occurred to her—too late, after the funerals— that she should have seen to it herself. But she was barely functional in those first days after both deaths, and no one had even brought the subject up. Later, when she finally thought of it, she attributed that to the fact that Chihuilla General was such a small facility they didn't even have donor programs in place.

How then was it possible that Charlie's kidney had gone to this woman's father?

The first call she'd made had been to Dr. Treecedale.

"That's simply not possible," he'd told her. "Even if the potential donor has designated his or her desire to donate on their drivers' license, our policy is that organ donations also require the consent of the next of kin."

Jennifer had lost it then.

"Don't tell me it's not possible," she'd yelled into the phone. "I have a letter saying it happened. Don't you understand?"

"Jennifer, calm down," Treecedale had told her. "I'll look into this, but I'm absolutely certain this is some kind of mix-up. A mistake. I want you to fax me that letter."

She'd faxed it to him. The next day when she'd called, she was informed that Dr. Treecedale was home ill.

"Can I call him at home?"

"No, I'm afraid not. We can't give home phone numbers out."

"Please, can you give him a message? Ask him to call me?" She'd left her number.

When she still had not heard from Treecedale a day later, she'd called directory assistance and asked for his number. It was unlisted.

"But this is an emergency," she'd said.

"I'm sorry. I can't help you," the operator told her.

She'd driven the ninety-five miles to Chihuilla in eighty-two minutes. At the hospital, she was told that Dr. Treecedale was out and not expected to return in the near future.

"How can that be?" Jennifer asked. "I just spoke to him the day before yesterday. He promised he'd call me back."

"Dr. Treecedale is very ill," the nurse had told her. "It was sudden."

"If he's so ill, why isn't he here, in the hospital?"

By now the nurse was growing irritable.

"Where Dr. Treecedale chooses to be treated is none of your or my business."

Chihuilla was a small town. Its welcome sign boasted a population of twelve thousand. Jennifer drove to Bud and Shirley's, where she recognized a waitress she'd come to know during her stay.

"Can you tell me where Dr. Treecedale lives?" she asked.

"The old guy? With the silver hair?"

"Yes, that's him."

The woman called over the counter that separated the dining area from the kitchen.

"Frank, do you know where that nice doctor, you know the older one who comes in after work some nights, lives?"

A faceless voice called back.

"You mean Dr. Treecedale? He lives on Chihuilla Lane. Can't miss it. The big yellow house at the end."

The cook was right. It wasn't hard to find. But when Jennifer pulled in front of it, the house looked deserted. She parked her car, opened the gate to the white picket fence that surrounded the yard, and walked up the sidewalk to the house's porch.

After several minutes of knocking, the front door creaked open. A middle-aged Hispanic woman, wearing an apron, stood before her.

"I'm looking for Dr. Treecedale," Jennifer announced through the screen door.

"Dr. Treecedale is gone. Out of town."

"When will he be back?"

"I don't know. He didn't say."

"Where can I reach him?"

"He doesn't want anyone to bother him," the woman said. Echoing the words of the telephone operator, she then said, "I can't help you," and shut the door in Jennifer's face.

Jennifer drove straight back to the hospital. She walked past the receptionist's desk, as she had for those five days Charlie was there, and got on the elevator. But this time, instead of pressing 3, she pressed the fourth and top floor, where the administrative offices were located.

The secretary to the hospital administrator told Jennifer her boss was out to lunch. It would be a good idea to make an appointment if Jennifer wished to see him.

"I'll just wait," Jennifer had responded.

The waiting room was small, just four chairs and two side tables filled with medical journals and newsletters. Jennifer found herself studying everything from the back of the receptionist's head to the photos and newspaper articles that were framed and hanging on the wall.

One such article was yellowed with age. In it, half a dozen men and women stood behind a ribbon, which one of the men was poised to cut. The caption read:

> Hospital administrator Erland Baldwin and some of his staff
> look on as California State Representative Joseph Engles cuts
> the ribbon that officially opens Chihuilla General Hospital.

It was dated June, 1977. Jennifer recognized Engles. He was now a Senator and one of the most powerful legislators in the country.

Minutes later, when another face from the photo walked through the door, she knew it was Erland Baldwin.

"Mr. Baldwin?" Jennifer said, standing.

Baldwin looked to the receptionist, who was clearly flustered that this visitor had gotten to her boss before she did.

"I'm Jennifer Banks. I drove up from San Diego to talk to you."

Baldwin looked momentarily stunned.

"Well . . . I'm afraid I have an awfully busy afternoon planned. Perhaps you can come back tomorrow. Janice," he said, turning to his secretary, "could you help Miss Banks?"

Having dismissed Jennifer, he continued across the reception area, and was just reaching for the knob of the door marked HOSPITAL ADMINISTRATOR when Jennifer managed to stop him in his tracks.

"It's *Mrs.* And if I come back tomorrow, it will be with the police."

Baldwin froze, then slowly turned, his face now host to a gracious smile.

"Please, come into my office."

While the rest of the hospital appeared to have been untouched since the ribbon-cutting photo on the wall, it was obvious Erland Baldwin's office had recently been remodeled. New carpet, freshly painted walls, higher-quality furniture, and all new windows, which looked out on the sparse desert landscape east of Chihuilla.

"Now, what can I do for you?" Baldwin said to Jennifer once they were seated.

"Explain this," she said, sliding the letter across his desk.

Baldwin extracted it from the envelope and opened it. His face displayed no reaction at all as he read.

"I'm afraid you've been the victim of a prank of some type. A very sick, cruel prank, but a prank nonetheless."

That thought, that someone out there was sick enough to do something like that, had never even occurred to Jennifer.

"You're saying my husband's kidney wasn't removed?"

"Of course not. Your husband died during emergency surgery. Neither of his kidneys were removed."

"How do you know? Have you done an investigation?"

Baldwin's face contorted into a condescending smirk.

"An investigation? I spoke with Dr. Fielding, who, of course, dismissed this entire matter as ridiculous."

"So you knew about the letter?"

"Dr. Treecedale mentioned it to me. Yes."

"Where is he? Where is Dr. Treecedale."

"Dr. Treecedale wasn't feeling well. He's been pushing himself too hard for years now. He's finally taking a much-deserved break. Even if I knew where he is, I would not give you that information."

"I want to see my husband's records."

"Mrs. Banks. I understand the effect receiving this," he gestured with the unfolded letter, "could have on you. But you have to try to hold on to your senses. How could your husband's kidney be removed without your consent? It's Chihuilla General's policy to get the next of kin's consent, even in situations where the deceased clearly indicated his or her desire to donate."

"If it's this hospital's policy to approach next of kin about organ donation, why wasn't I approached? After all, numerous tests had already shown both kidneys to be in good condition."

"I don't know," Baldwin said, his voice rising. "It must have been an oversight. Maybe the nurse on duty didn't think about it. Dr. Fielding isn't a regular here. They were performing emergency surgery when your husband died. Maybe in all the commotion, it simply never occurred to anyone that your husband's kidneys could be used for transplant."

"No. That's not the explanation, and you know it. The reason they didn't ask for my approval to take my husband's kidney after he died was because by that time, *they'd already taken it.*"

"Mrs. Banks, I would suggest you consult a lawyer before you start making such statements. We take our reputation here at Chihuilla General very seriously. It is, I can assure you, unblemished."

"I *am* a lawyer. That's why I know you have to give me Charlie's records. I'm not leaving today without them."

"This is ridiculous. Your husband was a patient here—how long ago? A year?"

"Eight months."

"Records are archived after a patient is discharged. It could take hours to locate your husband's."

"I'll wait."

The first floor of the hospital had a large waiting area. Baldwin had instructed her to wait there, telling her someone from records would be in contact with her.

An hour passed.

Jennifer got up and wandered down a hallway she'd seen numerous hospital employees enter and leave while she'd been sitting there. The first door she came to was the Employee Lounge. Several doors down, a placard read "Records Department." She pushed the door, which was already slightly ajar, open. Inside, a lone desk was unoccupied. A small fan on one of its corners rotated slowly back and forth, raising havoc with papers on its surface, all of which were weighted down with odds and ends—a pen, a coffee cup, and, for the biggest stack, a half-eaten Snickers bar.

There was a door at the back of the room. It was open, but the room or hallway to which it led appeared unlighted.

"Hello?" Jennifer called.

There was no answer.

Other than the chair behind the desk, there was nowhere for Jennifer to sit. She stood there for several minutes, waiting for someone to return, then she crossed to the other open door and again called out.

"Hello?"

A short, unlit hallway led to another room to which the door was half open. Jennifer padded quietly down the hall and peered into the room at its end. It was musty and lit by several lightbulbs hanging from the ceiling and two long, skinny horizontal windows positioned in the narrow space between the ceiling and top of six-feet-high built-in cabinets—housing what appeared to be row upon row of filing drawers—that lined every wall. Jennifer entered the room and did a slow 360-degree turn, taking in the sight.

She glanced back toward the room she'd just left, then reached to open the nearest drawer. Dozens of files were jammed into it, each labeled with a name and year.

She reached for one.

"Rodriguez, 1978."

Nineteen seventy-eight. Baldwin had made it sound as though files from eight months ago were difficult to access. He'd told her it would take hours to find Charlie's and urged her to go home, where he would send the files to her, even, if she insisted, via overnight carrier.

She replaced the file, shut the drawer, and walked to the start of the filing cabinets.

The "A"s took up all of two rows. There was a step stool in front of the third row. Straining to read the label on the top drawer, Jennifer stepped on to the stool.

Babcock–Beam.

She pulled the drawer open and began searching.

She found a *Bank* and pulled the file. It was from 1989. Andrea Bank. She replaced it. The very next file was Banner. No Banks.

She went through the entire drawer again.

Charlie's file was not there.

Maybe, she thought then, the records clerk had removed it and was, at this very moment, looking for Jennifer in the lobby. Maybe they'd crossed paths. Or maybe Jennifer had been waiting in the wrong place.

Jennifer climbed down. She hurried to the waiting area, keeping an eye out for someone who would be carrying a thick manila file, like those she'd just seen.

She got on the elevator and went to the fifth floor, but the door to the administrative offices was closed and locked. She glanced at her watch: 4:15. Pretty early to close down for the day.

Back down on the first floor, she returned to the records department. It was still unoccupied. Jennifer stepped inside. Maybe the file was on the desk. She went around its other side and examined the documents held down by the assortment of paperweights.

Most were internal memos.

The top document on the stack held in place by the Snickers bar was a billing record for a recent patient. Likewise, the pages beneath it all appeared to be billings.

Suddenly, a yellow Post-it note next to the telephone caught Jennifer's eye.

S. Fielding. 432-5522.

Jennifer was reaching for it when a voice behind her caused her to jump.

"Can I help you?"

She swirled and came face-to-face with a woman who had to have come from the room of filing cabinets. She did not appear happy to have found Jennifer at her desk.

As casually as possible, Jennifer slipped the hand holding the Post-it note into the pocket of her blue jeans.

"I'm Jennifer Banks," she said. "Mr. Baldwin told me you'd get me my husband's hospital records. I've been waiting almost two hours now."

"I'm afraid your husband's records are part of the group that we recently moved off premises. Our capacity here is limited. A couple times of year we purge our files and send the old ones to a storage facility. I've called the storage company and requested that they pull your husband's files and return them to us, but I haven't heard back from them yet."

Jennifer's temptation to call the woman on her lie was overpowering. But that would require admitting she'd been snooping through the hospital's files.

"When will you have them?"

"As soon as the storage company gets them to me."

"I'll give you twenty-four hours," Jennifer said. "If I don't have those files by tomorrow afternoon, I'll go straight to the attorney general."

"Do what you have to do," the woman answered indifferently.

"DID THEY GET THEM to you the next day?" Matthew asked, completely engrossed in Jennifer's story.

"Yes. A courier hand delivered them."

"And?"

"And there was nothing to indicate Charlie's kidney had been removed."

"But you're still convinced it was."

"I think the reason Charlie's file wasn't there, in the records department, was that they'd sent it to Sherwood Fielding to make sure there was nothing in it that would cause suspicion. The records clerk was gone when I first went there. The stool—there's no way she could have pulled that file without it; it was in the top drawer and those cabinets are a good six feet tall—was right there, right in front of the drawer where his file should have been. Sherwood Fielding's phone number was sitting on her desk. I think after I left his office, Baldwin called down to her and told her to get that file out of there and get it to Fielding."

"It's plausible."

"It's more than plausible. And there was one thing in the records that convinced me they killed Charlie for his kidneys. Remember I told you that the night Charlie died, the nurse came in to give him a shot—of antibiotics, or so she said? Well, there was no note of it in the records. None whatsoever. There was page after page listing all the medications he'd received, but nothing on that shot. I'm convinced that shot had something to do with what they did to Charlie that night. That it proves they planned to take his kidneys, and that the story about him bleeding internally was just a cover-up."

"Anti-coagulants."

"What?"

"It was probably an anti-coagulant. They didn't want his blood to clot."

An expression Matthew took for shock froze Jennifer's features. Seeing it, he instantly regretted being so blunt.

But his interpretation of Jennifer's reaction was way off.

"You believe me?" Jennifer said softly.

Matthew leveled his gaze at her.

"I believe, from what you've told me, that it's entirely possible. Organ selling is big business these days. The Chinese military's been doing it for years. Executing prisoners and selling their organs to wealthy foreigners—usually Americans—too low on the recipient list to have any priority in the national distribution system.

"And I don't buy that the letter was a prank. Plus people like Dr. Treecedale don't just disappear without a reason. Did you ever confront Fielding? Or make good on your threats to go to the AG?"

"Yes, on both counts. I called the number I got off the desk. I'd expected it to be a hospital or clinic or something, but it had to be his home because the first half dozen times I called I got Fielding's recorded message. Then, finally, he answered. I lost it then. When I realized I was talking to the man who'd killed Charlie, I became hysterical. Called him a murderer. Told him I'd get him, if it took my every waking moment for the rest of my life, I'd get him."

"I imagine he was pleased to hear that."

"He told me he'd sue me if I ever repeated my allegations to anyone else. And then he hung up on me. He disappeared then. I went to Palm Springs, spent a week trying to find him. He'd simply vanished. No trace of him. The next thing I knew of him was almost a year later, when I read about his starting a company in Seattle. BioGentech."

"So that's why you changed your name back to Rockhill."

"Yes."

"And the Attorney General?"

"Never actually made it to the Attorney General. Just an assistant.

She made a copy of the letter, said they'd look into it. A week later I got a letter saying they were sorry that I'd been the victim of such a sick hoax, but they had found no evidence to substantiate my allegations about Sherwood Fielding."

"The last thing the California AG wants to do is ruffle the feathers of a powerful entity like the medical community. That's not to say that if you had hard evidence, he wouldn't pursue it. But with a letter as your only corroboration, it's the easiest, and smartest, response."

"You *do* believe me."

"My instincts are that you're on to something. But we need to know more. It's certainly not enough." He hesitated, then continued, "There is a way to settle this. But I'm not sure it's something you'd consider."

"What?"

"Exhuming the body. Then you'll have your answer, once and for all."

Jennifer laughed.

"I had him cremated. Both Charlie and Stacey." The laughter quickly disappeared from her lips. It had never reached her eyes. "Stacey was so disfigured by the accident—I had to identify her for the coroner—that it just seemed the only thing to do. And then, of course, when Charlie died, I wanted them to be together."

So much for that suggestion.

"After tonight, we know that Fielding's not your everyday, above-board scientist," Matthew said, thinking aloud. He was quiet for a while, then went on, "Sometimes these guys follow a pattern."

"You mean, there could be a connection between what happened to Charlie and what we saw tonight?"

"When a respected professional gets down and dirty, he has to be careful about who he shows his true colors, who he dirties his hands with. In this instance, I'd say that's where the connection might be. The creeps behind the scenes. I can't see there being a direct connection—not if what I think is going on here is, indeed, what's happening."

"What do you think is going on?"

"The rumors I was sent to Seattle to investigate were that BioGentech was doing cloning experiments. Highly advanced experiments. Now I know why they're so secretive," he said, shaking his head in disbelief, as he thought back to what he'd seen earlier that evening, "if the rumors were right—that the work being done is in the cloning arena—then it must be baboons they're attempting to clone. If that's true and they're successful, this would be huge. Much bigger than Dolly or the cloned cows. No one has ever been successful in cloning a primate from an adult cell. No one. But that also pretty much eliminates the possibility that there's a direct connection between Fielding being involved in selling organs on the black market and what he's doing here."

"You're wrong," Jennifer said quietly, almost to herself.

"What do you mean?"

"They're not cloning baboons," she answered.

"They're cloning humans."

FIFTEEN

MATTHEW STOOD STARING at Jennifer. One moment she impressed him with her presence of mind and strength, the next she had him wondering just how stable she really was.

"I saw them. In a barrel," she said.

"The one whose lid was on the floor?"

She nodded.

"I opened it. I opened it, then it splashed on me. And then . . . then . . ." she closed her eyes.

"What?" Matthew asked. "Jennifer, what did you see?"

She opened her eyes and looked directly into his. "Babies. Two tiny babies, floating at the top."

Matthew had stepped forward. His face was just inches from hers now.

"You're sure?" he said. "How can you be sure they weren't baboons? After all, they're remarkably like humans."

"These weren't baboons," Jennifer answered. "Their skin was darkened, almost black, and they were tiny, no bigger than my fist, but that's what they were. There's no way they were baboons."

Matthew studied her. His cynicism about mankind and the atrocities of which it was capable was well earned, perhaps because it was founded upon firsthand knowledge. Still the horrors implicit in Jennifer's statement exceeded anything he'd seen. Anything he'd ever expected to see.

"You have no doubt about that? That they were human fetuses, not baboons?" he asked again.

She shook her head.

"None."

With Jennifer standing against the wall, Matthew, his face drawn into a scowl, began to pace, back and forth, in the small bathroom.

"It just doesn't make sense," he said. "Unless . . ." he stopped. His back was to Jennifer.

"What?" Jennifer asked.

"How much do you know about Dolly?" he asked her.

"You mean the sheep?"

He nodded.

"Just that it was the first time a mammal had been cloned," she answered. "And that she was cloned from an adult cell."

"That's right," Matthew said. "But Dolly didn't just happen on the first try. It took 277 tries, to be exact. And twenty-nine different adult females served as surrogates by having the embryos implanted. You can imagine how many aborted, deformed fetuses they produced along the way, before they ended up with Dolly. Dozens, maybe even a hundred."

"That's what I saw!" Jennifer broke in. "Aborted fetuses. But where are the surrogates?"

Matthew stared at her.

"I think we saw them."

"What?"

"We saw them tonight."

Jennifer's hands flew up to her mouth in horror. "The apes!" she cried.

"Baboons. The closest thing possible to human surrogates. They knew they couldn't find human surrogates to work through this thing—hell, they'd need dozens of them—so they turned to the next best thing. Primates."

"Is that even possible?"

"Before tonight, my answer would have been 'not yet.' They've been coming closer, but most of the transgenic work has been done with pigs. They don't use primates because they're so like us that ethicists consider it immoral to attempt cross-species transplants between humans and apes." A sardonic smile crossed Matthew's lips. "Of course, our Dr. Fielding doesn't seem to get hung up on ethical issues, does he?"

Jennifer fell back against the open door. Matthew reached for her, but she pushed his arm away and abruptly exited the bathroom. He followed her to the kitchen, where she walked mechanically to the stove and grabbed hold of a tea kettle from which a pathetically wispy column of steam rose. Then, as if it were an afternoon tea party, she took two cups and saucers from the cupboard, spoons from the drawer, and honey from the refrigerator—all of which she placed precisely on the table. Without asking Matthew whether he wanted any, she placed a tea bag in each cup and finally, before sitting down, poured steaming water into each cup. The kettle ran dry before she'd finished filling her own.

They sat in silence. Finally Jennifer lifted her eyes to his and spoke. "We have to stop him."

Eureka. It was "we" now.

"We need more information. We need proof. The protocol."

"You mean *you* need the protocol. That's what you're being paid to get, isn't it?"

"Yes," he said. "And if we're right about Fielding, that he's gone from selling organs to human cloning, it will also come in handy when we turn him in to the authorities."

Jennifer fell silent again as she took this into consideration.

Suddenly, watching her play with her tea bag, Matthew was helpless to stop the wave of pity that washed over him. The poor woman had already been through hell, losing both her daughter and husband, and then living with the belief that Sherwood Fielding had stolen her husband's kidney—probably causing his death. While her theory on Fielding was out there, and supported by little more than a letter and an omission in the hospital records, Matthew's instincts were that Jennifer was on to something. But regardless of whether it had actually happened, it was clear that she was convinced of her story's authenticity. Whether Fielding took her husband's kidney or not, she'd lived with the reality that he did for three years. And now she was dealing with another reality—the knowledge that, quite likely, her attempt to bring Fielding to justice had put her own life in danger.

Impulsively, he broke the silence, "You can still get out."

Jennifer looked at him.

"I have nowhere to go," she said.

"I can send you somewhere safe, where they'd never find you."

"Don't you need me? To get the protocol?"

"Yes. I do need you. There's no doubt that my chances of succeeding are better with your help. But I have to make this clear. If you stay you'll be in danger."

"I'm not leaving." Jennifer said matter-of-factly. "I'm going to get that son of a bitch. So, we need the protocol. How do we get it?"

CHAPTER

SIXTEEN

SHERWOOD FIELDING ALMOST NEVER broke a sweat. Even at the club—he could spend half an hour on the treadmill or stairclimber without misplacing a single hair or soiling one of his freshly laundered t-shirts. But the prospect of making this phone call had him wiping his brow and loosening his tie. This was as close as Sherwood Fielding got to losing control, and for the people who worked for him, it was especially unpleasant and unnerving.

It had been a phone call from Preston that had started it off first thing that morning.

Ken, the night guard, had left an urgent message for him in the middle of the night. Just after arriving at work this morning and listening to it, Sherwood tracked Ken down at home and immediately laid into him.

"Why the hell wasn't I called at home?" he wanted to know. "You mean to tell me someone broke in there last night and I don't learn about it until the morning?"

"Well," Ken stammered, "nothing was stolen. I caught up with the guy right away. If it *was* a guy. But it must have been."

"What the hell do you mean by that?"

"It's just that when I first noticed somethin' on the monitor from the lab, it looked kinda' like a woman. I only saw the person from behind for just a second, but I just coulda' swore it was a woman wearing a hat. But then I gotta glimpse of him through the door to the lab—he barricaded it—and saw that it was definitely a man."

"Did you apprehend him?"

"No. He escaped through the skylight. But at least I run him off before he could do anything. I called Ernie in right away and me and him went through the lab and offices. There's nuthin' missing. So I didn't think I should wake you up in the middle of the night."

"You didn't call the police, did you?"

"No, sir. Me and Ernie know better than to call the cops."

"You and Ernie are both ineffectual, fucking morons," Fielding said before hanging up the phone.

Who could the intruder have been? A person the guard took one moment to be a woman, the other a man.

Suddenly, Sherwood Fielding bolted forward. Of course! Who else? Patricia Lukins. She'd been there yesterday, when that fucking courier mentioned the lab in Preston. She'd asked him about it, but had obviously not swallowed the BioSystems ruse he'd given her. No, instead the fucking lesbian had to see for herself. It was just like her.

After a long while spent mulling over the situation—during which he snapped so viciously at Georgie for interrupting him with documents that needed his signature that she was reduced to tears—Sherwood Fielding reached for the phone.

"We need to talk," he said when a voice came on the line. "Things are heating up around here. We may need to move the schedule up. How quickly can you prepare to take delivery?"

When the voice on the other end offered resistance, Sherwood became visibly agitated.

"There are no problems with the experiment. That is coming along fantastically well. All I'm saying is that we may have to make the transfer prior to the actual birth. Of course, in that event our scientist, Dr. Chandra, would accompany the surrogate and stay through delivery of the baby. This would in no way jeopardize or compromise the results. In fact, if you think about it, this provides you with an incredible opportunity. You'd have the benefit, firsthand, of Dr. Chandra's expertise." Sherwood could tell by the thoughtful silence that met his words that this approach had made an impression. "Just think how your scientists could learn from having the opportunity to work side by side with the man who developed the technology you're buying."

Sherwood grew silent as he listened to the voice on the other end.

"Of course, we will also deliver the donor. We agreed on that from the start. How else could you verify the authenticity of the newborn child? That will not be a problem. But we must have your assurances that the donor never resurfaces here. It goes without saying that such an occurrence could become very problematic for me." He thought briefly of Angelique, of the future they'd planned. "I want her out of here, for good."

The conversation was finally going more like Sherwood had hoped.

After receiving assurance on this point, he broached the subject that had been foremost on his mind from the start of the conversation. Money.

"Of course, we'll expect partial payment at the time of delivery," he said. "My suggestion would be to split the payment fifty-fifty. That would mean forty million upon transfer of the surrogate and forty upon birth and subsequent confirmation of authenticity of the clone."

Now a heated discussion ensued. The deal had been eighty million dollars for delivery of the clone and the corresponding technology. None of this—installments, early delivery of a pregnant surrogate who might still abort and fail to produce a viable clone—was part of the deal and Sherwood knew it. But he also knew who he was dealing with. A man who knew no limits in his quest for power and immortality, be they financial or moral. A man who desperately wanted this technology and who, Sherwood was confident, was willing to take a gamble if the odds of acquiring it were even remotely in his favor. Banking on this, Sherwood Fielding would not back down.

"Listen, do you realize how much money I've already sunk into this project? You should count yourself lucky that I didn't demand upfront funding," he said. "The way things are going, I've no doubt I can find another buyer. On these same terms. The choice is yours. Are you in, or do I go underground with this?"

This tactic worked. Having agreed on the new financial arrangements, the two men discussed possible scenarios for the transfer of the surrogate, Dr. Chandra, and the donor. Then, promising to be in contact again soon, Sherwood Fielding hung up the phone and finally allowed himself to sink back in his chair.

Brilliant. He was fucking brilliant. He'd just maneuvered himself from a position in which he'd stood to either win big or lose big—and the odds of doing either were, as he saw it, about even—to one in which he simply could not lose. Under this new scenario, he'd either end up with forty million bucks, or eighty. Either way, he'd be guaranteed enough money for BioGentech to survive at least another two years, which gave him plenty of time to get their anti-cancer therapy to market. A therapy that would ensure him fame and respect, as well as lifetime wealth.

It was just like him to turn a negative—last night's intrusion—into a positive. Now all he needed to do was deal with Patricia Lukins and convince Ram Chandra that a little time in the tropics would be good for him.

DEEP IN THE SOUTH Pacific, equidistant between the cluster of islands that comprise Melanesia and those of Polynesia, lies one of the smallest independent nations of the world. Niupalu consists of four islands, volcanic in origin. Unlike its neighboring islands—the Solomon Islands to the west and Cook Islands to the east—Niupalu had long been considered so hostile and of so little value, economically speaking, that at no time had any of its neighbors or the Western powers that in the eighteen-hundreds colonized the rest of the region displayed any real interest in it. The inaccessibility of its high cliff coasts caused early explorers to pass it by, and when the other islands were being colonized by France, Great Britain, and the United States, Niupalu, with its small native population, went virtually unacknowledged and ignored.

The closest Niupalu ever came to change came in the early 1960s. When the rest of the South Pacific islands began the process of achieving independence from colonization, there was brief talk of Niupalu being incorporated into the government of the Solomon Islands. The fiercely independent natives of Niupalu, led by their newly instated ruler, Tupeni Sanday, met visiting Solomon officials with guns, spears, and piers set aflame to prevent their visitors from docking. They managed to be quite effective in cutting short any such plans.

And so the little nation and its people—distanced from the rest of the world not only by its jagged coasts but also by many miles of rough seas—had always pretty much lived in isolation.

The plain truth was that no one much cared about Niupalu or its inhabitants. In a time when all the islands around it were coming to grips with Western civilization, Niupalu remained peculiarly immune to such changes. The economy had always consisted almost exclusively of subsistence agriculture and fishing. For centuries, life had remained simple.

Tupeni Sanday was the nineteenth king in a line of Niupaluan nobility who, legend has it, originally descended from a Polynesian god of the sea. Because the population of the islands was small, never exceeding its current number of approximately eight thousand, and the islands were so removed from the rest of the world, the kingdomship had rarely been challenged. Also the fact that the long line of rulers had been successful in keeping out outsiders, particularly missionaries—who had succeeded in undermining the authority of nobility on other islands, most notably Tonga, Niupalu's neighbor to the west—had helped maintain the status quo. The commoners never knew enough to question the practice of forced labor for the nobility. Likewise, it simply did not occur to them to question the fact that the majority of land was owned by the king and his family. The nobility of Niupalu had always been smart enough to make certain of two things: that the people remained cut off from the advancements of civilization around them and that, while they could never accumulate land or wealth, the commoners were provided for. With recent developments, that strategy had become especially important.

It had long been believed that the mineral resources of the Pacific islands were limited and that any deposits to be found were only on the larger islands. In the 1980s major gold deposits were discovered on Papua New Guinea and Fiji. Upon receiving this news, Sanday—who a decade earlier had begun a closely monitored program of sending protégés, hand-picked as much for their loyalties as for their abilities, off island, primarily to the United States and England, to be educated and to become his links to the Western world—dispatched one of his nephews to the U.S. for training as a geologist in order that upon his return he could conduct a thorough search of the Niupaluan Islands.

And not surprisingly, when the nephew returned and did, indeed, locate a rich vein of gold, it was royal land upon which it was found.

Tupeni Sanday kept the discovery very hushed. While his and his family's standard of living skyrocketed with the find, life for the rest of the islanders remained basically the same, and they paid little note to the excavation that took place in the mountains of their ruler's private lands. As long as their idyllic world—and idyllic it was, the kind of life for which Fletcher Christian and his fellow mutineers abandoned ship—remained unchanged, there was no reason to challenge the existing system.

From the start, Tupeni Sanday had kept his distance from the people, living behind walls, venturing out only for festivals and religious holidays. This long-held practice enabled him to keep his newfound wealth hidden, in large part, from his people. He simply continued a monarchy of ruling remotely, but with general benevolence.

But Sanday was not, by nature, a benevolent man. Any benevolence with his people stemmed entirely from self-interest. Keep them happy, he knew, and there was little reason for change. However, as Sanday's knowledge of the Western world—aided by what he learned from his returning protégés—and wealth grew, his ego and quest for power expanded exponentially. After he established a market for his gold, which was predicated upon secrecy regarding its origin, the money began pouring in, far faster than Sanday could spend it. With the sale of the first shipment, he purchased a helicopter and quickly dispatched one of his men to Germany for flight training.

The villagers, who had seen planes from a distance, particularly during World War II—when the Japanese invaded the Solomon Islands and United States forces were based on the island of Aitutaki in the Southern Cooks—marveled at the helicopter, but other than their curiosity at its comings and goings, paid it little attention. Sanday had begun offering a public feast each Sunday and in general, life on Niupalu was better than ever.

As a result of his reclusiveness, coupled with his paradoxical desire to know what was going on in the world around him, Tupeni Sanday developed a voracious appetite for periodicals. He became particularly interested in the subject of science. He devoured the science articles in *Time* and *Newsweek* magazines, and, with the aid of one Harvard med school–educated nephew, spent hours digesting the contents of various science journals.

But it had been one article in particular that engaged his interest. It was a *Time* magazine story about the cloning of a sheep by Scottish scientists. He'd read it twice before calling his nephew Tumari to his side.

"This article says that if they can clone sheep and cows, they can clone a human," he stated.

"I beg to differ, Uncle," the nephew responded. "It says human cloning is a theoretical possibility in light of this new development; that, in theory, the technology used to clone the other mammals could be applied to the cloning of humans."

"Find it," Sanday ordered.

"Find what?"

"The technology to clone a human. If it doesn't already exist, then we'll pay someone to create it."

The nephew mounted strenuous objections. It was impossible, in many countries illegal, he argued. What useful purpose would it serve?

But Tupeni was unrelenting.

For Tupeni Sanday, approaching his midsixties, had long been concerned about something. None of his heirs, none of the seventeen sons he'd sired, nor the dozens of nephews that surrounded him daily, had it in them. The ability to rule his country as had Tupeni, to ensure the survival of the monarchy, which, Tupeni knew, was dependent upon maintaining Niupalu's status quo—a daunting challenge in a world where no other nation had been able to resist the changes inevitable once Western civilization was allowed to get a foothold. His sons and nephews were loyal subjects and filled much-needed roles within the monarchy, but capable of accomplishing what Tupeni had? Never. How many times had he looked at one of his sons, admired his handsome features, or another's skills as a fighter or hunter, or yet another's mind, but always come to the same conclusion—that they are not, never will be, Tupeni's equal? There was only one Tupeni Sanday, he'd concluded, and therefore, when Tupeni Sanday died, so, inevitably, would his kingdom.

And then, like a thunderbolt from one of the gods, the answer to this dilemma had been delivered to him. It came in the form of a magazine article. He'd known its significance the instant he'd laid eyes on it.

He would utilize this new technology to produce a clone of himself, and in his remaining years, embue his clone with all the wisdom he'd acquired over forty years of rule. He, Tupeni Sanday, would live on, allowing his people and generations that followed to enjoy the benefits of his leadership long after the aged Tupeni was gone. His memory, his legacy, could live on indefinitely.

Of course, the path he'd set upon was not without obstacles. Eighty million dollars was a lot of money to part with. After much consideration and discussion with his nephew the doctor, they had actually chosen the course that cost more and took longer. The first proposal given him by the American doctor had been to clone Tupeni himself. But Tupeni didn't like the idea of being a guinea pig. What if the experiments went wrong? What if they created a being genetically identical to Tupeni but with some gross deformity or defect? It was too hideous a possibility to even contemplate. No, they'd finally decided, the better part of valor would be to fund the doctor's experiments using another adult donor. If that proved successful, then and only then would Tupeni allow his own cells to be duplicated. Then the solution to all his problems would finally be within his grasp.

In his own lifetime, he'd managed to preserve a timeless world, a paradise, for the people of Niupalu. Soon, according to the American doctor, he would have the means to do so indefinitely.

And at the same time, he would be leaving a living, breathing monument to the great leader he had been.

AT WORK THE NEXT DAY, Jennifer adopted an air of business-as-usual, but she kept her eyes and ears open, watching for signs that her involvement in the break-in at Preston might have been discovered. Last night, before he left her apartment, she and Matthew had discussed the wisdom of her returning to BioGentech. The guard, they'd reasoned, had never seen her. If he had, he would have pursued Jennifer, and not Matthew. Still, Jennifer was looking over her shoulder all day and the one cup of coffee she'd had on her way to work was not enough to explain the jittery state of her nerves.

She'd called Patricia Lukins twice already during the morning to suggest that they meet on the balcony, but Patricia hadn't answered either time and she did not want to leave a voice mail. As Jennifer walked to the library, she was in the process of thinking about how to contact Patricia when she saw the notice. It was taped at eye level to the wall between the elevators. In bold print, it announced:

Presentation
"The Bystander Effect"
Drs. A. Mannington and P. Lukins
Wednesday 1 p.m. in the auditorium
(all employees encouraged to attend)

Jennifer looked at the agreement she held in her hand, which she'd just received that morning from one of the scientists. He'd already signed it and was about to return it when, as an afterthought, he realized he should have run it by Jennifer first. The antibody production and immunological services it provided for were to begin the following Monday. If there were a problem with the agreement, she would have to address it immediately. However, after reading the first page detailing the polyclonal antibody production work that the BioGentech scientist wanted to hire out—a page in which she was introduced to terms such as *hybridoma cell line development, ascites fluid production, polyclonal antisera,* and numerous other penta- and septasyllabic words she couldn't even begin to pronounce, much less understand—she'd grabbed the agreement and headed for the library, where she planned to work through it with the help of a medical dictionary and research journals.

She looked at her watch: 12:55. Then she read the notice again.

Patricia's lecture. Or the agreement. Which would it be?

It seemed ludicrous to worry about work right now, not after last night. The agreement could wait.

She headed down to the auditorium on the fifth floor.

The auditorium only seated eighty, but as with everything else at BioGentech, it was state-of-the-art all the way. A sunken podium, backed by a movie-theatre-sized screen, faced rows of comfortably padded chairs, all of which had drop-down desktops attached to the right arm.

By the time Jennifer arrived, the room was full. Prominently seated in the front row were half a dozen unfamiliar faces whom Sherwood Fielding was in the process of introducing. Visiting execs from Roslyn and Roslyn. On the stage, facing the audience, were three chairs. In one was seated Patricia Lukins. The other was occupied by Angelique Mannington. The other must have belonged to Sherwood Fielding, whose final introduction had just elicited a round of applause for the visiting dignitaries.

When Jennifer caught Patricia's eye, she gave her a thumbs-up. Patricia nodded in response.

Dave Maynard, who was seated in the middle of one of the last rows, noticed Jennifer looking for a seat. He stood and signaled for her to join him. The seat next to his was one of the last still available.

"Thanks," Jennifer whispered as she squeezed by Dave, then settled in.

Sherwood Fielding had already begun his introduction to the lecture.

"It's an amazing world we live in," he started. "Ten years ago, who would have guessed that gene therapy would show such promise as a weapon against cancer? When the ability to engineer genes first came on the scene, the interest in it was focused exclusively on curing genetic diseases. Today, we know that engineered cells are effectively treating cancers that used to be untreatable. Last year, of the one hundred four experiments approved by the National Institutes of Health Recombinant DNA Advisory Committee, sixty of them were human gene therapies aimed directly at tumors. Only twenty-nine were aimed at the inherited diseases. Cancer, we are finding, is a logical and promising target for applications of gene therapy."

As he spoke, Sherwood Fielding was working the room with his eyes, putting on a show for their guests. Guests with deep pockets. The lecture was probably planned more for the purpose of impressing R&R than sharing Patricia's findings with other BioGentech scientists. If it weren't for Patricia Lukins, Jennifer would be tempted to sneak out at the first opportunity. But as the scientist sat on the stage, waiting to be introduced, Jennifer could almost see Patricia's excitement at the opportunity to present her work. It annoyed Jennifer to see Angelique Mannington alongside Patricia. If she were in Patricia's shoes, she would not have as benevolent an attitude about Angelique's being up there, sharing in the recognition of this important work.

"Now," said Sherwood Fielding, "here at BioGentech, we have the distinct privilege of sponsoring research in a cutting-edge area of gene therapy aimed at the treatment of cancer. And here to explain what is now commonly known as the 'bystander effect' is one of the talented researchers heading that project for us. Ladies and gentlemen, it is my honor to introduce to you," he said, turning now in the direction of the two scientists seated behind him, "Dr. Angelique Mannington."

So shocked was she at these words that Jennifer's breath escaped in an audible huff of disbelief and indignation, turning several heads. Patricia Lukins, seated on the stage, looked equally stunned.

Angelique Mannington strode to the podium.

"Thank you, Dr. Fielding," she said.

"Molecular surgery is the newest weapon in the battle against cancer. We are finding that it can prolong, even save, lives." She paused. "It was

Dr. Culver's brilliant work several years ago that first brought to light the bystander effect. He came up with the idea of a 'suicide gene' that makes tumor cells vulnerable to a killer drug. Dr. Culver injected a gene from the herpes simplex virus into hard-to-reach brain tumor cells and then dosed them with ganciclovir. And it worked. Amazingly well. But what really surprised and delighted Dr. Culver and other research scientists was the fact that, along with the cells that incorporated the HS-tk gene, all of which were tumor cells, many other malignant cells, which did not carry the herpes virus, were also eradicated by the ganciclovir. For some reason, their mere physical proximity to the cells that had taken up the virus caused them to be wiped out as well. Thus, the name, the 'bystander effect.' "

Jennifer had not taken her eyes off Patricia Lukins, who sat stone still, expressionless, her hands clasping notes on her lap. She had worn a pantsuit today. Navy gabardine jacket and pants, with a white silk blouse. And blue, two-inch pumps. That fact, that Patricia had dressed up for the occasion, added to the poignancy of the moment. With every passing second and each of Angelique Mannington's well-chosen words, Jennifer felt her anger rising to a new level.

"What causes this effect?" Angelique Mannington continued. "Several theories have been proposed. One involves intercellular communication. Another possibility is that destruction of the circulatory system within the tumor, caused by the ganciclovir, starves to death those tumor cells that do survive the drug. We have been examining both theories and believe we are on the right track. I think you'll find my presentation of our findings quite interesting. After the presentation, Dr. Lukins would be happy to answer the questions that I'm sure you'll have. Now, if someone will please dim the lights," she looked to a man standing at the back of the room, "I'll begin with the slides."

The lights went out, and as Angelique fumbled to find the switch to operate the projector, a dark shadow crossed behind her at the podium. When the side door opened, Jennifer could see Patricia Lukins framed in the light from the hallway. The scientist was leaving the auditorium.

Jennifer jumped up and began excusing herself as she squeezed her way back to the aisle. By this time, in preparation to take notes, several of the scientists had raised the desktops attached to the arm of their chair and she had to wait as one after another, with obvious displeasure at the inconvenience, lowered the desktop for her to pass.

By the time Jennifer reached the hallway, Patricia had disappeared.

Suddenly it came to Jennifer—where to find her friend. She hurried to Patricia's secret balcony. But when she opened the door off the storage room, it slammed into something. Tom, the maintenance man, was seated on the balcony's cement floor eating his lunch.

"I'm really sorry," Jennifer said hurriedly. "I'm looking for Dr. Lukins."

"Haven't seen her," Tom said through a mouthful of sandwich as he rubbed the leg where the door had connected.

Jennifer turned and headed for the seventh floor. Once inside her office, she tried calling Patricia again. This time she left a message.

"Patricia, it's me, Jennifer. We need to talk."

"CHANDRA HERE," THE VOICE emitting from the transmitter announced.

Matthew reached for the volume knob and turned it up. He'd heard the scientist moving about in his office for a while now—the shuffling of paper, opening and closing of drawers and cabinets, the moan of his lab stool—but this was the first vocal transmission he'd picked up since he'd set up his listening post at just past eight that morning. His car was parked a quarter of a mile away from the secret facility, on one of the narrow dirt roads that turned off the gravel one on which the building and grounds were located. He'd driven up and down several almost undetectable off-shoots until he found what he was looking for—a location higher in elevation than the lab itself and one to which the path from the lab was relatively unobstructed by buildings or hills. This spot fit the bill. With the flip of a switch, he was able to hear everything going on inside the office in which he'd planted the transmitters the night before.

Chandra had just answered the ringing phone.

"It's me," Matthew heard the caller say. "I heard about what happened last night. What's your take on it?"

"I've been waiting for your call," the first voice, already identified as belonging to Chandra, responded. "Well, according to the guard, there was just one person involved. He didn't get anything. I've gone through everything—all my files, specimens. As far as I can tell, there's nothing missing. The most disturbing thing, however, is that the lid to the preservative solution had been removed. He may have seen the contents."

"Which were?"

"Which were two aborted fetuses."

"*You've got to be kidding.*"

"No," said Chandra. "Unfortunately, I'm not. As I informed you in the report I couriered to you yesterday, both Tea and Pamela aborted earlier this week. That, of course, did not come as a surprise. But I hadn't disposed of the fetuses yet because I was planning to do autopsies today."

So the caller was none other than Sherwood Fielding. The report must have been the package the courier had delivered the day before, the one that sent Jennifer to Preston in search of the secret lab.

"What about the other one?" Fielding asked. Matthew could sense the urgency in this inquiry. "What condition is she in?"

"Ursula or Angel?"

"Which one's carrying the adult cells? That's the only one I'm interested in now."

"Angel? She's doing very well. I'm confident she'll carry to term. Or at least baboon term. Plus, if we're lucky, with the newest techniques for delaying the onset of labor, another month. That should practically guarantee survival."

There was a pause in the conversation, then Fielding voiced another question.

"How would travel affect her," he said, "affect Angel? And the fetus? Is she up to it?"

"Travel?" Chandra parrotted, his voice suddenly rising an octave. "What kind of travel?"

"By sea."

"Now? But I thought . . ."

"Yes, now. Just answer my question."

"Well, travel can be stressful. But Angel's in excellent condition, and the pregnancy is far enough along now that, with reasonable precautions, travel shouldn't jeopardize it. But see here," Chandra said firmly, "I'm not about to part with Angel now. I intend to see this through to its completion."

"Oh, you'll see it through all right. Right to the end. You'll be going with."

"You don't mean to Niupalu!"

"That's exactly what I mean."

"Are you out of your mind? I'm not going to that barbarian island. And neither is Angel. That's never been part of the deal. The deal was we deliver the clone and the technology."

"That was before last night. We have to get Angel out of there. The sooner, the better. You can see her through the rest of her pregnancy in a tropical paradise. Doesn't sound that bad to me."

"Last night?" Chandra responded. "What happened last night doesn't warrant such insanity. Who's to say our visitor last night wasn't one of those animal rights activists? After all, nothing was taken."

"Our visitor was no animal rights activist. Our visitor was one of your colleagues. Patricia Lukins."

Chandra cursed in Hindi, then switched back to English. "This can't be. The guard said it was a man. He pursued him."

"He pursued someone who *looked* like a man. Sounds a lot like Lukins to me."

"But how would she have found out about this place?"

"She overheard the courier yesterday. I was in a meeting with her when he delivered your report. Ironically, it was a meeting about her blood samples. She's cutting us off."

Chandra fell silent.

"If it was Dr. Lukins and she saw the aborted fetuses, she's probably already deduced what we're up to," he finally said, then he paused. "Still, I have my doubts. I'm going to talk to the guard again and see just how good a look he got at the intruder."

"Well, regardless of what he says, our plans have changed. Angel is going to Niupalu."

"Increasing security makes more sense than this plan of yours. It's crazy."

"Let me just explain a few things to you . . ."

Matthew listened as Sherwood Fielding told Chandra about the new payment arrangement. Then Fielding appealed to the scientist's ego, telling him how enthused Tupeni Sanday was at the opportunity to have his scientists observe the work of such a genius.

"Don't you see?" he said. "We're guaranteed a minimum of forty million this way—when, under our old arrangement if Angel failed to deliver a live clone, we'd get nothing. Nothing. And I've made a decision. Since it entails this added burden on you, it's only fair to increase your compensation. Instead of receiving two million for your part, I'll pay you five. Two and a half when we make the transfer, the other two and a half when I receive final payment."

Chandra remained silent.

"Angel is going," Fielding said flatly. "Whether you choose to accompany her or not."

Matthew, who'd earlier flipped another switch to record the conversation, sensed that this last statement was Fielding's trump card.

"No!" the scientist said. "No one but me lays a hand on Angel." He was quiet for several seconds. "All right," he finally conceded. "If there's no other way, I'll do it. But when?"

"When is yet to be determined. My guess is any time after two weeks from now. They'll need at least that much time to get a steamer prepared and up here. And you'll need that much time to assemble equipment and supplies."

"I thought that delivery of the donor was part of the deal."

"It is," Fielding responded impatiently. "Don't worry about that. And

Sanday has also given me his word that once she gets to Niupalu, she'll never leave. I'll take care of her. You just take care of the baboon. Listen, I've already told Jim Wilkes to get over there. Until we make the transfer, there will be increased security. But you keep your eyes open, too. Let Jim know if you notice anything the least bit out of the ordinary."

"This is outrageous," Chandra said before hanging up. "Simply outrageous."

Matthew could hardly believe what he'd heard. So they were selling the clone and the technology to Tupeni Sanday, the Niupaluan ruler. He had already been in power almost two decades when Matthew left the CIA. During that time the agency had attempted to keep an eye on him, compiling a dossier on his mediocre human rights records, but the details had always been very sketchy. High tech was of little assistance in penetrating the island, and its natives virtually never left—eliminating the possibility of acquiring information from defectors. The agency had long ago concluded that the little kingdom posed little threat to anyone other than its inhabitants, and even that was hardly worth bothering with. But there was a periodic review of the situation and Matthew could remember, just before leaving the service, there being some concern that Niupalu might be impacted after gold was discovered in neighboring islands. Obviously the ruler had acquired sudden, immense wealth—eighty million dollars for the purchase of Chandra's cloning technology indicated as much. Matthew wondered just how current the agency's file on Tupeni Sanday was.

He spent the better part of the day at his post, monitoring transmissions from Dr. Chandra's office, but the only other one of significance was a conversation between Dr. Chandra and Jim Wilkes, the security person Fielding had promised to send to Preston.

"Hope you like dogs," Wilkes had said to Chandra.

"Dogs?"

"Yep. We're having two Dobermans delivered this afternoon. These are trained guard dogs," Wilkes continued. "You'll have to have a short session with their handler when he arrives. These animals can be dangerous if you're not educated as to their training."

"I don't want them anywhere near the vivarium," Chandra responded testily. "Primates and dogs are natural enemies. We must be certain they're kept out of the baboons' sight. We can't allow anything to upset Angel, particularly now."

Matthew knew the scientist was thinking of his conversation earlier that morning with Fielding. It wouldn't do to have Angel abort now.

"That shouldn't be a problem," the other voice answered.

•   •   •

MAYBE IT WAS his imagination, but when Jennifer's car pulled up beside his, Matthew could have sworn she looked relieved to see him. Neither spoke as he followed her to the front door.

Stepping inside her apartment, she turned to face him.

"Why am I not surprised to see you here?"

"Like a bad penny, huh?"

"Kind of."

They went to the kitchen, where she offered him a soda.

"Any beer?" he asked.

"No beer."

He took the soda.

Matthew could feel her eyes on him as he sloshed it down.

"What?" he said. "Am I drooling or something? You're staring."

"I'm just trying to figure you out."

"Good luck," he said. "Actually, I'm not that complicated."

"Did you sleep with Georgie Hill?"

"Yes."

"Just to get information from her?"

"Yes."

Jennifer fell silent.

This was not the start he'd hoped to get off to.

"I went back to Preston today," he said, changing the subject. "Yesterday I planted a couple bugs in the office next to the lab with the baboons. Overheard some pretty interesting stuff."

He was baiting her. He could see Jennifer struggling with her mixed feelings about him. A part of her, he knew, found him and what he did repugnant, but another side recognized what he might be able to do for her. In light of her zeal for her mission to avenge her husband's death, he was banking on the latter side winning out.

It did.

"*Tell me,*" Jennifer said.

Matthew told Jennifer what he'd overheard earlier that day out at Preston. The only thing he refrained from telling her was the part about Sherwood Fielding suspecting Patricia Lukins to be the intruder. Matthew had been quite pleased to hear that Fielding was focusing his suspicions on someone other than Jennifer. It just gave them that much more breathing room. But he knew Jennifer would feel compelled to do something about it if she knew.

"You mean he's selling it?" she asked. "He's selling the clone?"

"Yes. But even more important is the fact that he's selling the technology. To Tupeni Sanday, the ruler of a small South Pacific island called Niupalu."

"I've never even heard of it. Or him."

"That's not surprising. Little is really known about Sanday. He's somehow managed to preserve the isolation that his islands and their inhabitants have known for centuries. That takes some doing in this day and age."

"Then how do *you* know so much about him?"

"I used to be in the CIA," he said.

Jennifer's expression, a half smirk of undisguised disgust, actually caused him a flicker of anguish.

"What's wrong? Government doesn't pay enough for skills like yours? Business better in the private sector?"

"Don't go there," he told her, suddenly angry.

He rose from the table, and reached for the car keys he'd placed on it.

"Please," Jennifer said, "don't leave."

Matthew froze and directed piercing eyes at her.

"How does it feel to have cornered the market on morality?"

Jennifer blushed.

"I'm sorry. It's just that I've never met someone like you. Someone who . . ."

"Say it. Someone who makes a living doing all the things good girls like you were taught never to do."

"Yes. But . . ."

"But you need me now. Don't you? So now it's okay."

He lowered himself back into his chair, bringing the two of them eye-to-eye.

"Let's get something straight. You don't have to respect me. You certainly don't have to like me. But if you think I'm going to subject myself to your scorn every time I see you, you're wrong. Don't think you know what I'm about, because you don't. And if you have any interest in working together, you'll keep your condescending attitude to yourself."

"I'll say it again. I'm sorry. And yes, I do need you. I need you to help me get that bastard for what he did to Charlie."

Matthew stared at the keys in his hand as he fingered them, thinking. Then, decisively, he plopped them down on the table and pushed back in his chair.

"Now," he said, "where were we?"

He could swear he heard a sigh of relief from across the table.

"Tupeni Sanday," Jennifer replied.

"That's right. Fielding has arranged a rendezvous at sea with him, where he'll transfer not only the baboon, Angel, but the donor as well, to Tupeni."

"The donor? Who is it?"

"*That* we don't know," Matthew answered, though from Fielding's comment about Patricia Lukins' refusal to give more blood, he thought he knew the answer. "At least, not yet. But if Fielding has his way, who-ever it is should be packing for a long trip. Fielding made it clear that the donor won't be resurfacing in this country."

"Do you suppose the donor has agreed to go along with Fielding's insane plan?" Jennifer asked.

"Hardly. It seemed pretty clear from the conversation that the donor doesn't even know he or she has been cloned. They'd hardly agree to be sold to Tupeni Sanday."

"So Fielding is planning to kidnap the donor?"

"Yes."

"We have to warn whoever it is," Jennifer said after a long silence. "The donor. We have to go to the police."

"No. We can't go to the police. We still don't have proof," Matthew said, "not one thing they would take seriously."

He did not disclose the fact that he'd actually taped Sherwood Field-ing's conversation that morning with Chandra. A conversation that surely would have prompted an investigation were he to proffer the tape to the authorities—which, of course, he could not do because at that point, the point at which they went to the authorities, Matthew knew that he would be cut out of the loop. He would no longer stand to obtain the information WTI was paying him to obtain.

And he also knew one more thing. That if the police were brought into this now, they would bungle this thing. There was no way they were prepared to handle it. No, this was way beyond them. Even the CIA—the best and brightest—had been known to blunder something this big. Matthew knew that, only too well.

"First we have to find out who the donor is," Matthew said. "We have to get the files on Angel. But I have to get back in that lab to learn more."

"I had an idea today," Jennifer said. "It might work to get you into Preston. But first, I want some assurances."

"About?"

"If I help you, what are you going to do to help me?"

"It goes without saying that if we're right about what Fielding's up to now and can prove it, he'll be put out of commission for a long time. More like forever."

"That's not enough. He has to pay for what he did to Charlie."

Matthew didn't usually make promises.

"I'll not only help you, I'll give you my word. If Sherwood Fielding did what you think he did," he said to Jennifer, "I'll make sure he pays. In fact, it will be my pleasure."

JENNIFER WAS UNABLE to sleep, despite the fact that she'd had less than two hours the night before.

Sherwood Fielding was not only cloning a human being, but was selling the technology to some little-known ruler—whose purpose for obtaining it she could only guess.

Of course, Matthew probably had some ideas about that, but, not surprisingly, he hadn't shared them with her.

Matthew. Spy for a British pharmaceutical company. Former CIA agent. And the first person who seemed to believe her about Charlie.

To say Matthew was turning out to be more complicated than she'd expected was a bit of an understatement, wasn't it? What made a man like that tick? And why was she willing to trust him with the only thing that mattered to her anymore—avenging Charlie's death?

But there was more than one man's death at stake now. If Matthew's assessment was correct, some other poor soul was in grave danger. Soon to be kidnapped, and sent off to a South Pacific island with a demented ruler who would do who-knows-what with him or her. Jennifer squeezed her eyes closed, in a vain attempt to keep out the images that these thoughts gave rise to.

Images of Angel.

Something about Angel had caught Jennifer's eye when she'd broken into the Preston lab. Despite the crazy circumstances, she'd found herself pausing at the ape's door, drawn to her. She could still see the expressive brown eyes, imploring Jennifer somehow. She still remembered the feeling that prompted her promise to the furry creature. *"I'll be back for you."*

And plans were now being made to transfer Angel, to sell the form growing within her. Along with the donor.

It was then that the words came back to her.

"Sherwood's always saying he wishes he could clone me."

SEVENTEEN

MOST MORNINGS DIMITRIUS, a Seattle Pacific University intern who ran the mail room, delivered the mail. But since Jennifer's office was on the seventh floor and therefore one of the last stops on his route, sometimes—if she were in a hurry to get it—she dropped by the mail room first thing to pick it up herself. Which is why she knew it was likely she'd find the small, cluttered room empty, like now.

A large, wheeled pushcart that would be used later that morning for deliveries sat in the middle of the room. Inside its green canvas dump bin was an assortment of mail—large manila mailers, letters, an occasional small box. Larger boxes, many of which contained bold warnings regarding their contents and were destined for the labs, were stacked on the worktable.

Jennifer eyed the ten or twelve boxes, looking for a good candidate. Then she stuck her head out the door to make sure the hallway was empty and snatched one marked CAUTION: BIOLOGICAL MATERIALS in bold red letters. She slid it carefully into a brown paper bag—one of the new kind, with handles, that all the grocery stores now offered—which she'd brought with her that morning from home.

Hurriedly, she exited and, carrying the bag by the handles, headed for the stairwell. Just before she reached it, she noticed Dimitrius approaching from the other direction.

"Morning, Ms. Rockhill," he called as Jennifer struggled to push open the door into the stairwell, which seemed to be stuck. She looked down at the bag. The prominent red warning, also posted on the box's top, stared back at her. "You need help with that?"

Just before Dimitrius caught up with her, the door gave way. Jennifer flashed him a big smile.

"No, but thanks."

"You bet," he said. "Do some shopping on your way to work?"

"Yes, I did. Just some snacks to keep in my office. I can never find anything I like in those vending machines."

"Tell me about it," he said good-naturedly as he continued past her to the mail room. "Now I'll know where to go when I get the munchies."

"Anytime." Jennifer forced a laugh as the heavy door closed behind her.

Back in her office, she made room for the box in one of her file drawers, lowered it inside, and locked the drawer. Tonight she would tell Matthew that she was ready to set their plan in motion. If all went as planned, tomorrow would be the big day.

She tried to immerse herself in the stack of files that had become a permanent fixture on her desk, but when she found herself reading the same paragraph over and over with absolutely no comprehension, she reached for the phone and dialed Patricia Lukins' extension. She was worried about Patricia. Two days earlier, the last time they'd talked, Patricia had set last night as the night they would go to Preston to try to find the lab the courier had mentioned. She hadn't returned Jennifer's call from yesterday, which meant Jennifer hadn't even had a chance to tell her about her own visit to Preston. Maybe Patricia was just so upset about Sherwood Fielding and Angelique Mannington upstaging her yesterday that she'd forgotten their plans. But it was hard to imagine Patricia Lukins forgetting something like that.

As had been true for two days now, Patricia did not answer.

"Hey there," Jennifer told her voice mail. "I was wondering whether you had time for a quick break. Call me. Okay?"

But she did not hear back from Patricia.

Lunch could not come fast enough. She hadn't planned to leave the building, but the urge to get away had her out of there at twelve sharp. Since she wasn't hungry, she decided to take a drive around the lake. Anything to get her mind off what was happening. She pulled out of BioGentech's offices and headed north on Eastlake. At the second light, the car behind her blasted its horn. She looked up at the signal, expecting to see that it had turned green. But it was still red. Irritated, she looked in her rearview mirror to see what kind of maniac would be honking at her when she didn't even have the light.

It was Patricia Lukins.

Jennifer rolled down her window.

"Pull into that Seven-Eleven," the scientist yelled, pointing ahead.

When the light turned green, Jennifer did as instructed. Patricia, driving a weathered Jeep, pulled up beside her and got out of the car. Instead of coming around to Jennifer's window, she reached immediately for the handle on the passenger side of Jennifer's Volvo. Jennifer unlocked it and Patricia climbed inside.

"What's going on?" Jennifer asked. Patricia looked wild-eyed and disheveled.

"Drive," Patricia said.

Jennifer pulled back on to Eastlake and negotiated her way through the lunch hour traffic, sneaking an occasional glance at Patricia, who was clearly agitated.

"Are you going to tell me what's going on?"

Patricia clenched her hands into tight fists.

"That fucking bastard," she said. "I want to kill him."

They'd crossed the Ballard bridge. Jennifer turned into a residential area and pulled the car over onto the side of the road.

"Listen," she said, reaching for Patricia's arm. "You have to calm down. Then tell me. Tell me *who* did *what*."

Patricia, fists still clenched and resting on each thigh, stared straight ahead.

"You're right," she said. "I have to get a grip. But I tell you, I've never been so angry in my entire life."

"Tell me."

The scientist shifted her back against the car door to face Jennifer.

"It's David."

So much had happened to preoccupy her in the past forty-eight hours that it took a moment for Jennifer to register who David was. Patricia's brother.

"He's been kicked out of the trial," Patricia continued. "*He* did it, he's responsible."

"Who?"

"Fielding. The study director visited David in the hospital this morning. Poor kid, he's been sick as a dog from the treatments, hasn't been able to leave the hospital, so I've been spending the last couple nights with him. Anyway, the director comes in and tells us that he'd just become aware of the fact that I've been working on the bystander effect studies. There's a rule that prohibits relatives of researchers from participating in related clinical trials. It's a conflict-of-interest type thing. He kicked David out of the trial."

"But why did they let him in then in the first place?"

"He lied on the forms. I told him to. Our last names aren't the same.

We had different fathers. When I found out about the clinical trials at UW, I made him apply. I knew he had no chance of getting in if he told the truth."

Jennifer fell back against her door.

"But how did they find out now? I mean, he's been in the trial a while, hasn't he?"

"Four months," Patricia answered. "I'll tell you how they found out. Sherwood Fielding. He told them."

"But why?"

"To get back at me. We had this big blowout after the lecture. He called me in to his office and told me how my walking out during the lecture and leaving Angelique to answer questions—which, of course, she didn't have a clue how to answer—had embarrassed both the company and Angelique. Told me I would be the one responsible if R&R decided not to go forward with the joint venture."

"What did you say?"

Patricia dropped her face into her hands.

"I lost it. I was still so pissed off. I told him to go fuck himself." She looked up at Jennifer then. In her eyes, Jennifer saw absolute, unconditional misery. "And I came this close," the scientist held up a hand with her thumb and forefinger separated by the thinnest margin of air, "to accusing him of killing your husband. But I didn't."

"Thank God."

"*I* did this to David. If I'd just kept my mouth shut, this wouldn't have happened."

"Stop that," Jennifer said. "Don't you do that to yourself. How could you possibly have known this would happen? Anyone in your shoes would have done the same thing after what happened at that lecture."

"But it didn't even matter, not really," Patricia moaned. "I don't give a damn who gets credit for this work. The only reason any of it even mattered to me was David. And others like him. Who cares if Angelique Mannington horns in on it? I've always thought I was superior to the rest of them. That it wasn't about ego for me. But then look how I reacted."

Jennifer placed a hand on top of Patricia's and squeezed.

"You're only human," she said. She was silent for a moment. "I don't see how in good conscience they can do this. I don't mean Sherwood Fielding. I mean the UW. David's been responding so well to the treatment, hasn't he?"

Patricia nodded.

"There's been a seventy-five percent reduction in tumor mass."

"Then how can they do this? I can see if they have rules in the first place not letting him participate, but after he's taken the treatments and responded like this?"

"I pleaded with the study director, told him it was all my fault. But I have to say, I really can't blame him. He felt horrible about it, but he said his hands were tied. The rules suck, but rules are rules just the same and as he pointed out, the consequences, if they knowingly disregarded them, could even affect their federal funding. Other patients could lose the chance that this study stands to give them. I can't let that happen. David wouldn't allow that."

"Did he say it was Fielding who told him?"

"He didn't have to. You and I both know that's what happened. Firing me wasn't enough for Fielding. He wanted one more way to get even."

"*Fielding fired you?*"

Patricia laughed, a bitter, caustic laugh.

"Didn't you know?"

"No. I had no idea. I'd just left you a message this morning. I got your voice mail. No one told me you were fired."

"That's their MO," Patricia said. "They'll wait a while, then make some kind of announcement that I'm *no longer with BioGentech.*" She drew quotation marks in the air. "Actually, Angelique came in during my meeting with Fielding and tried to stop him from firing me. I don't know whether she had a sudden fit of conscience or whether she knew she still needed me to complete the bystander effect studies, but either way, she did stand up for me. Told Fielding he was making a mistake. But you don't tell Sherwood Fielding to go fuck himself without paying for it. I tried to call you this morning, from the hospital, but apparently they've told Zelma not to let my calls through. I'd been waiting outside, hoping you'd leave for lunch, for over an hour."

"I am so incredibly sorry," Jennifer said. "I wish there were something I could do to help."

She could feel Patricia's eyes on her.

"*There is.*"

Jennifer straightened in her seat.

"What? What can I do?"

"They've locked me out of my lab. It's imperative that I get in there. Or . . . that someone gets in there for me."

"I don't understand."

Patricia shifted forward, narrowing the distance between them, her eyes leveled on Jennifer.

"I have to get that cell line. The HS-tk line."

"Do you mean the genetically engineered mouse cells?" Jennifer asked. "The ones that contain the herpes virus?"

"Exactly."

"But why?"

"Because it's David's only hope now. I can duplicate the clinical trial. If I get my hands on the cell line."

"You mean . . . ?"

"Yes. I mean I can give David the injections myself. I'd rather a neurologist administered them. But I am, after all, a trained surgeon. I can get my hands on all the equipment I need, even the ganciclovir. And I have a friend who will open her clinic to me, assist me, at night. I have everything—everything but the cell line containing the virus. And it's right there, in the lab. If I'd only thought to take it with me yesterday when Fielding fired me. But I didn't. It didn't become important until today, when David was kicked out of the study. But there's no way they'll let me near the cell lines now. I made it as far as the lab entry today and when I tried to get through the monitor, the guard showed up and escorted me out of the building. That's when I started waiting outside for you."

"I'll do what I can," Jennifer said.

"Thank you. I don't mean to put pressure on you, but you're our only hope. And I want you to know, I'll do anything I can to help you. Starting with going out to Preston tonight."

"There's no need for that."

"I don't understand."

"I've already been out there. I saw it, Patricia. There *is* a secret lab out there. And if what we think is going on there is actually what's happening . . ."

"Wait a minute," Patricia interrupted. "Who's we?"

Starting with their encounter at Larry's, Jennifer told Patricia about Matthew Pace.

"You mean he's some kind of spy? For hire?"

"Exactly."

"And you took him with you to Preston the other night?"

"No. I had no idea he was following me. But now, I have to say, I'm glad he was. This is too big for me. Too big for the two of us, you and me, to handle alone."

"What's too big? What did you see out there?"

Jennifer described the lab. Its unmarked site, deep in the woods. Then she described what she saw inside. The baboons. And then the human fetuses.

"Holy shit! Are you absolutely certain? That they were human, not primate?"

"Absolutely," Jennifer answered.

"The son of a bitch is cloning humans! Especially if it's Ram Chandra running that lab. He was always obsessed with the idea. He told me once that if anybody could do it, he could."

"That's Matthew's theory, too."

Patricia grew silent, but Jennifer could see the fury churning in her veins.

"I'll get that bastard," the scientist said. "If it's the last thing I ever do."

Now there were two of them who felt it.

"You have to take me there. We have to get proof."

"Matthew and I have a plan. If it works, we'll have the proof we need. Just sit tight for another day or two. Take care of your brother."

Before Jennifer dropped Patricia Lukins back off at the 7-Eleven, the scientist grabbed a gas receipt that was sitting on the Volvo's console. She pulled a pen out from her shirt pocket, and scrawled a number on the paper.

"Here," she said, pushing it into Jennifer's hand. "If you can't reach me at home, try this. It's the number of my friend. The one who's willing to help me with David. She used to be my significant other. She loves David almost as much as I do. And she's a damn good doctor."

MATTHEW SHOWED UP that evening again, as he had the past two nights. He never called first, never gave any warning, just showed up at her door as if it had been prearranged.

"Are we set to go tomorrow?" he asked.

"Yes. I took a box of lab materials from the mail room today. I've got it locked in my desk."

"No sign of anything unusual there today?"

Jennifer snorted a short, sarcastic laugh.

"At BioGentech? Only another firing. This time it was my friend— my *only* friend."

Matthew leaned across the kitchen table and glared at her.

"What do you mean she was fired?"

"Take it easy. It has nothing to do with us. Absolutely nothing to do with what we found out at Preston."

She proceeded to tell Matthew about Patricia Lukins.

"And she wants you to help her? To get the cell line so she can treat her brother herself?"

"Yes."

"Well, you can't do it."

"What do you mean I can't do it?" Jennifer snapped at him. "Her brother's life is at stake."

Matthew reached across the table and grabbed her forearm so roughly it hurt. Jennifer tried to pull away, but his grasp only tightened. His strength, and the look on his face, frightened her.

"Listen to me, Jennifer," he said. "Your friend's brother isn't the only one whose life is in danger here. Do you hear me? This isn't some fucking game you've wandered into. You can't afford to be playing Superwoman. So get any thoughts of breaking into a lab out of your mind, right now. Do you hear?"

It was something in his eyes, something she hadn't seen there before, that told her.

"You know something, don't you? What? What is it?"

Matthew relaxed his grasp.

"Yes. I did some digging today. I told you I'd help you find out what happened to your husband, didn't I?"

"What did you find?"

"Not a whole hell of a lot. But enough to know that you could be right. Hell, you probably are. And, if you are, it's bigger than what happened to you."

Jennifer found herself struggling to catch her breath.

"Tell me," she practically whispered. "Please, tell me what you know."

"Two months ago a wealthy land developer from Idaho died of AIDS. Turns out he'd contracted it from a kidney transplant he received four years ago, about nine months before your husband's death, at the Alpha Dialysis Center, a respected Southern California dialysis and transplantation center."

"I can't believe I never read anything about it. This kind of thing would be huge in the media."

"It never made the news. The moment the recipient got sick and learned he'd contracted AIDS, he knew it had to have been from the transplant. He went after the Alpha Center. But there was a problem. You see, he bought the transplant—he wasn't sick enough to be on the priority list, so he paid for what he needed. A kidney. Only what the poor fucker really bought was a death sentence. Still, he'd broken the law by buying a human organ, and he didn't want to spend whatever time he had left in a courtroom or jail, so he never went to the police or the media. The Alpha Center settled with him and managed to keep the whole thing quiet."

"So how did you find out about it?"

"After he died, his wife went nuts. Called the papers. The CIA got involved then."

"What happened?"

"The Alpha Center had no record of the transplant. Denied any involvement. They invited the reporter she'd talked to to come in and go through all their records. He couldn't find anything to substantiate the wife's accusations. Without any corroboration, the story just died. The paper knew that if they printed it, they'd be hit with a huge libel suit and with what they had, it wasn't worth risking."

"But you just said her husband did have the transplant at the Alpha Center."

"I believe he did."

"Why wouldn't they have record of it then?"

"Records are easy enough to destroy. Or, as in your husband's case, alter. Or, in certain cases—and I suspect this was the way the Alpha Center operated—easy to dispense with keeping altogether."

"You make it sound like it happened routinely."

"That I don't know. All I know right now is that the CIA has heard of two other instances in which it was alleged a kidney was purchased for transplant and that each alleged transplant took place at the San Diego Center. Because of the Chinese military scandal, they've been called in to investigate, to make sure there isn't some connection."

Jennifer felt her chest tightening with rage.

"You mean the CIA knows about this, but they haven't done anything?"

"According to my contact there, they haven't come up with anything substantive yet. But there's another factor, one that my contact doesn't even want to discuss."

"What's that?"

"I did some research on the Alpha Center. Turns out the majority owner is the family of Senator Joseph Engles."

Jennifer gasped.

"I saw his picture! On the wall of the administrator's office at Chihuilla General. He was cutting the ribbon at the hospital's opening ceremonies." She shrunk back then as another thought came to her. "And I think I saw it on Sherwood Fielding's office wall. Only I couldn't get close enough to be sure."

Matthew, surprised, let out a low whistle.

"Engles is a big-time CIA supporter. In today's climate, where everyone's calling for funding cuts, the agency needs people like him. When I found out that Engles owned the Alpha Center I called my contact back to confront him with it. His take was that if there were anything to the allegations—and he specifically denied the CIA's knowledge of the existence of any hard evidence—the agency was confident that Engles had no personal involvement. Engles has assured them he'd look into it and be relentless in determining whether there's any truth to the allegations. In a situation like that, the agency might just choose to look the other way, let Engles handle it internally, rather than embarrass—maybe even bankrupt—a big supporter by going in there heavy handed. But now we find out that Engles had a direct tie both to Chihuilla General and Sherwood Fielding. Makes his claim that he had no personal involvement a little harder to buy, doesn't it?"

Jennifer had read about people who died, then came back to life, and how during those first seconds after death, they frequently reported a sense of being outside their body, watching as frantic resuscitation efforts took place. It was like that now. She was there in body, listening to Matthew, but her spirit was hovering overhead somewhere, observing, as she learned that her suspicions about what happened to Charlie were true.

"Who knows how many times it might have happened? After all, the only cases the CIA's heard about are the ones where something went wrong. Where someone died. Kidney transplants are pretty successful these days, especially with the anti-rejection drugs they've developed. They're so effective anymore that the screening to find matches can be a lot looser. So for every case that's been reported, most likely there've been dozens of successful transplants. It's the perfect setup. Someone with money gets turned down for a kidney. Desperate, they start looking for other options. Engles hears about it through the Alpha Center. A legitimate, well-known transplantation center. He recruits Sherwood Fielding to find the kidneys. Sends him out to little hospitals like Chihuilla General, where Engles already has connections. No records are kept, to protect the Alpha Center and the recipient, both of whom have broken the law. The perfect setup," he repeated.

"Until something goes wrong," Jennifer injects. "Like the letter I got."

"Exactly. Then, people like Dr. Treecedale, who from all I could find has a perfectly clean, even distinguished, record, begin disappearing. Engles starts calling in his cards. Uses his clout to keep the agency off his back."

"Would the CIA actually turn its head like that?"

Matthew was slow to respond.

"I'm not the right person to ask what the CIA is capable of."

MATTHEW CHECKED HIS WATCH. Just past noon. Jennifer should be placing the call any time now. For the sixth time in less than an hour, he extracted the cell phone from his shirt pocket and looked for the blinking power squares to be certain it was on.

After she did it—after she determined that Sherwood Fielding and Georgie had both left for lunch and she placed the call to Double S Courier Services—Jennifer was to call him on the cell phone. Sherwood always left for lunch at twelve sharp, she'd told him. And Georgie usually just a few minutes later.

Matthew was experiencing something so foreign to him that he had trouble pinpointing it. Anxiety? Should he have allowed Jennifer to return to work? Was she taking too great a risk in helping him? After today, he would insist that she leave town. He could send her to his house in Phoenix, where she would be safe. Of course, it was highly unlikely she'd go along with that. The first chance she got, she'd probably put as much distance between the two of them as possible.

These thoughts were interrupted by the phone.

"Yes?"

"He's on his way" was all she said. In an early morning call to her apartment he'd instructed her to keep her communication brief—last night on his way home from Jennifer's he'd felt certain he was being followed again. Undoubtedly the same person who had tailed him the night he'd broken into BioGentech. CIA? The route he'd taken to Preston this morning was so convoluted he was confident he'd have lost anyone tailing him, but there was no sense taking chances by divulging information over the airwaves.

"Everything go as planned?" he asked.

"Yes."

He pressed the red "end" button and replaced the phone in his shirt pocket.

Now he would wait for the cream-colored van that carried the package Jennifer had arranged for the courier to deliver to the Preston facility.

When it came into sight only forty minutes later, rounding the bend at a pace that sent gravel flying in every direction, Matthew was ready. He dropped to the ground and quickly centered the approaching vehicle in the eyepiece of the rifle he'd earlier set up on a tripod. Zeroing in on the van's front right tire, when it was twenty yards from him he squeezed the trigger.

He didn't wait to watch what happened next. As he jumped up and ran toward his car, which he'd left hidden several hundred yards down the road, in the woods beyond the curve the van had just come around, he could hear the decisive "pop" of the tire's rubber being followed closely by the screeching of brakes and the sound of the vehicle skidding on gravel as it spun sideways.

Less than five minutes later, he pulled up alongside the van in his rental car. Its young driver, clearly the same one Jennifer had described to him the night before—the one she'd spoken to just days earlier when he was delivering a parcel to Sherwood Fielding—was down on his knees examining the pancaked tire.

"Need some help?" Matthew asked, approaching.

The kid looked up.

"Scared the holy hell out of me," he said. "A blowout. Came out of nowhere."

Matthew bent next to him and pretended to study the tire. As he knew would be the case, it was so flattened that the three-millimeter puncture left by the bullet would be nearly indistinguishable.

"Must have hit one hell of a pothole," he said. "Need any help changing it?"

The kid looked at his watch. Time was money for couriers and Matthew knew it.

"I own a garage," Matthew continued. "Change at least a dozen of these babies a week. I can get you back on the road in five minutes."

"You really don't mind?" the kid asked, more than a little tempted by this generous offer.

"Not at all. I'm in no big hurry. You just point me in the direction of the jack and spare."

When the pock-faced kid turned and walked toward the back of the van, Matthew drew his Glock and with one quick, precise movement, struck the back of his skull with its handle. This was in direct violation of his promise to Jennifer that he would not hurt the boy, that he would instead, at gunpoint, bind his hands and legs. But he'd known Jennifer would never go along with the plan if he hadn't agreed to handle things her way.

And he also knew how to administer a blow without causing serious injury.

The lanky body crumpled to the gravel. Matthew grabbed the van's keys from its ignition, opened the back door, then hoisted the boy's form over his shoulder and heaved him into the body of the van. Then he went to his car, removed duct tape from his trunk. Leaving the car's trunk open, he climbed back into the van and pulled the door shut. Minutes later he emerged wearing the boy's uniform and hat. He carried the boy, now dressed only in boxer shorts, his legs and arms bound with silver tape, to the car, which he'd parked on the side of the road, and placed him in the trunk. Then he slammed it shut.

Next he set about changing the tire on the van.

The entire process took less than ten minutes.

At exactly 12:52, Matthew pulled the van up to the front gate of the Preston lab.

A voice from the intercom on the security post called out.

"Identify yourself."

"Double S Courier Services," Matthew said. "I have a package from BioGentech for Dr. Chandra."

There was a pause during which Matthew knew he was being observed via the camera mounted on the gate. He was banking on a different guard, the day guard, from the one who'd caught a brief glimpse of him in the lab Tuesday night, though with the uniform and hat pulled down over his eyes, chances were he wouldn't be recognized anyway.

"Pull around back," the voice finally said.

The gate silently swung open and Matthew eased the van onto the premises. He pulled around to the back door, the one he and Jennifer had used to gain entry the night before last, then reached for the box labeled CAUTION: BIOLOGICAL MATERIALS, which the courier had already placed on the passenger seat. On the box was a new mailing label, placed there that morning by Jennifer, indicating the sender to be Sherwood Fielding. It was addressed to Ram Chandra.

With the package and shipping labels in hand, Matthew approached the door.

It opened before he could reach for its handle.

"Where's the regular guy?" a short, plump, and hardly threatening man in uniform said. Matthew was relieved to see it wasn't the same guard from the other night.

"He had a little accident," Matthew replied. "Nothing serious."

The guard reached for the clipboard Matthew had placed on top of the package. "I'll sign for it," he said.

"Sorry," Matthew said. "Dr. Chandra has to sign." He made a face that indicated his distaste for such foolish formalities, then nodded toward the box. "I guess this is one of those high-risk shipments. Probably some deadly virus or something," he joked. "You're probably better off not being in the loop."

The guard looked at him skeptically.

"I've always been able to sign before," he said.

Matthew raised his shoulders in a "beats me" kind of gesture but still, he stood his ground. In the moment that they were standing there waiting for the guard to decide whether to accommodate Matthew's request, a burst of deep, fierce barking suddenly signaled the approach of two enormous Doberman pinschers, who were racing in the direction of the men, having just emerged from the woods surrounding the building.

The guard raised a whistle that hung from a cord around his neck and blew, emitting a shrill, high-pitched blast. "Halt," he called loudly. The dogs froze, not more than ten feet from where the two men stood.

"Don't mind them," the guard said to Matthew with exaggerated nonchalance. Having established his control over the menacing dogs, he suddenly became more benevolent and cooperative. "Okay. Wait here. I'll get Chandra's signature."

"Wait a minute," Matthew said as the guard pulled the door shut. "You're not leaving me out here with *them*."

The guard turned and snickered. Matthew could see the man—who probably had a Napoleonic complex about his height—was pleased that Matthew, who towered over him, was afraid of the dogs.

"Okay," he said, pushing the door back open.

Once inside, Matthew followed behind the guard just long enough to make a quick assessment. No one, it appeared, was around. Before they'd reached the first turn, he pulled out the Glock.

This time its victim let out a loud groan before folding to the tiled floor. And this time it took far greater effort on Matthew's part to lift his victim off the ground.

Matthew had drawn a mental layout of the building that, pieced together with his earlier foray there, had caused him to conclude the security station was most likely straight ahead—near the front entrance and past the turnoff to the lab. With the portly guard slung over his shoulder, he picked the box back up and made his way in that direction, pausing first to listen before crossing the turnoff to the lab.

He found the door, marked "Security," wide open. Inside, on the desk, sat a steaming cup of coffee and a *Playboy* magazine opened to the

"Forum" section. Above were the three television monitors, showing the front gate, the hallway he'd just come down, and the lab. The third monitor, of the lab, was the only one showing any activity. Matthew watched as a tall, skinny, dark-skinned man, no doubt Dr. Chandra, took the blood pressure of a baboon who lay on the exam table—the table Matthew had used to blockade the door—while the animal played with something that looked like a child's toy.

He reached up and turned the volume knob clockwise.

"That's my girl," he could hear Chandra say to the ape as he was deflating the rubber cuff around her arm. Finished with this test, he placed the cuff on the tray next to the table, then, using one hand to tickle her, he used the other to make an entry in a file that lay open on the table. He closed the file, then proceeded to carry Angel to her cage and place her inside.

Before closing the cage door, he reached inside one last time to pat her on the head.

"I'll see you after lunch," he promised.

Chandra then took the file from the exam table, placed it in the top drawer of a three-drawer cabinet that backed to the wall, and left the room.

Faced with the possibility that the scientist would soon be walking by the security room on his way to his car—which was undoubtedly one of the two vehicles Matthew had observed in the small lot in front of the building—Matthew hurriedly dragged the guard's limp form behind the door, all the while keeping an eye on the monitors. Chandra came into view almost immediately on the second monitor, the one showing the main hallway. Having no time to hide elsewhere, Matthew ducked behind the door with the unconscious guard. He could not see the monitor without poking his head out, but he could hear the approach of the scientist's footsteps. He drew his gun and waited behind the door.

"Out for lunch," a thickly accented voice called into the room as it passed, but the footsteps did not slow.

"Right," Matthew grunted back.

He heard the front door to the building open, then click closed. He stepped out from behind the door and fixed his eyes to the first monitor. Once Chandra's BMW passed through the security gate, Matthew rummaged through the guard's desk for something to use to bind the man's hands and legs. He found two twelve-inch bungee cords, which if stretched to their limits, would have to do the job. The guard had begun to moan again, so after tying the bungee cords around his ankles and wrists, Matthew gave him another good blow on the head. Then he removed the large ring of keys from the guard's belt and headed to the lab.

Everything looked much as it had two nights earlier, except that the skylight was boarded over, and in the corner, near a long, horizontal freezer, a stack of small, empty boxes lent the only touch of chaos to the otherwise sterile lab. Matthew moved quickly, walking directly to the filing cabinet. It was arranged alphabetically and under the heading "Angel" he located two thick files. He removed both, then headed to the building's back exit, where his van was parked. But halfway down the last length of corridor he stopped and turned heel. He retraced his steps to the security room, bent down over the unconscious form of the guard, and removed the whistle from around his neck. Then, once again, he headed for the van.

As he opened the door at the back of the building, the sharp brown muzzle of one of the dogs immediately tried to push through. Matthew opened just wide enough to stick his face out and give a short blast on the whistle.

Both dogs froze.

He slid outside, never taking his eyes off either dog and slowly, surely walked between them.

"Stay," he ordered, establishing eye contact with the larger and more dominant of the two. They obeyed at first, but when he turned to open the door of the van, the larger one sprang at him and before he could climb inside, it had him by the ankle. His hands were full with the files, which he did not dare allow to fall to the ground, but as he raised himself onto the seat, Matthew kicked at the snapping dogs—the other had by now joined its leader—with his one free foot. When he landed a good shot on the big dog's head, it let loose its grip on his right ankle, which enabled him to pull his foot in and slam the door.

"Motherfuckers," he murmured. His pants were torn, blood beginning to soak through the fabric.

He'd planned on using the guard's keys to unlock the gate at the front entrance, but the dutiful dogs had chased the van, managing to keep up with it the entire length of the long drive, so instead of risking another encounter with them, as he drew near the gate, he pushed his aching foot to the metal and braced himself for the impact.

The gate did not budge.

He backed the van up again then put the pedal all the way to the floorboard.

This time the gate jolted loose from its hinges. Matthew backed just one more time and on this, his third try, finally sailed through.

On his way down the hill, he passed the car with the delivery boy still trapped in the trunk.

Gonna be hot in there, he thought to himself as he flew by. He reached for the cell phone and dialed Jennifer's number at BioGentech.

"Damn," he cursed when he got her voice mail on the first ring.

"Get out, *now*," he said curtly to the recorder.

JENNIFER HAD FOLLOWED their plan to the letter. Up to a certain point. After she'd called for the delivery and given the box to the courier, she'd placed the call to Matthew. She was supposed to return to her own office and wait for Matthew's call. Once he'd informed her that he'd completed his mission, she was to leave the building immediately and head directly to his apartment.

When she returned to her office, she'd only used the phone once, to try to reach Patricia Lukins. Jennifer knew that once she left the office today, she would never return to the BioGentech building again. If she were to help Patricia, it had to be now. Matthew had given her firm instructions not to delay her departure. The last words he'd said to her again this morning when he'd called had been, "Forget about your friend for now. We can't help her. Do you understand?"

Jennifer could not forget about Patricia, nor her brother, David. But when Jennifer dialed the number of Patricia's apartment, the telephone rang over a dozen times without an answer. Immediately after hanging up, Jennifer noticed that her message light was blinking. Matthew had called while she was trying to reach Patricia.

She dialed her access code and heard his terse "*Get out now.*"

Jennifer had a decision to make.

She grabbed her briefcase, which she'd already filled with several files she thought might be valuable in making a case against Fielding, and headed down to the third floor. Angelique Mannington would most likely still be out of the office, on one of her long lunches with Fielding.

As she approached the security door to the labs, Jennifer saw the young scientist who had not allowed her access two days earlier emerge. She stopped in the hallway and began rummaging through her briefcase, keeping her head down, until he'd passed. Shortly after he'd disappeared around the corner, the door opened again.

"Hold that," she called to the young woman exiting.

"Uh . . ." the girl stammered. "We're not supposed to let anyone in. You need to get cleared by the monitor first."

Jennifer stepped forward and grabbed the open door.

"I don't have time for that," she said authoritatively. "Don't you know who I am?"

The girl shook her head sheepishly.

"No, I'm new here."

"Well, I suggest you learn who the key players around here are. I'm the company attorney."

Without another word, Jennifer walked through the door, past the girl—who stood for a moment looking confused, then finally continued on down the hall.

Inside, the hallway was empty.

The cell line, Jennifer knew, would be frozen. She'd been in and out of the labs a dozen times and had never seen a freezer. There were closed doors on either side of the hallway. She began opening doors as she walked toward the large central lab, which was located at the end of the hall.

The first two doors she opened revealed well-lit rooms with hooded worktables that provided ventilation for scientists working with noxious or toxic materials. The next door was marked "Caution: Radioactive materials." Jennifer opened it to a room that looked much like the first two. There was only one more door along the hallway. Inside, Jennifer found a room-sized linen closet. Rows of white lab coats hung from hangers. Boxes of gloves were stacked neatly on shelves.

When she reached the lab, she was pleased to see that only a few scientists were working over the lunch hour. It was generally a busy area, with people constantly coming and going—which probably explained why no one seemed to pay any attention to her. And, after all, Jennifer had been a frequent visitor in the months she worked there. As she swept her eyes across the room, looking for signs of a freezer, she tried to look purposeful. She remembered seeing multi-volumed research journals on a shelf in the corner where Patricia Lukins had worked. Heading there, she withdrew one of the heavy books from the shelf, placed it on the counter, and opened it. Pretending to read—even scribbling an occasional note on a legal pad—she dropped her head, but every few seconds she glanced up, trying to figure out where the freezers might be located.

At the far end of the next row of counters, the ring of a phone broke through the drone created by the assortment of high-tech laboratory machinery and the dozen or more computers scattered about. Jennifer saw a young Asian woman dressed in a lab coat rise from her stool and walk to a door along the far wall.

"Phone's for you," she heard the woman say after she'd opened the door.

Jennifer, still hunched over the book, dropped lower. The woman, standing in the doorway, had her arm braced against the door, holding it open. Through the window created by her arm, the door, and, on the other side, the door's frame, if she stooped low enough, Jennifer could see a man wearing some odd kind of headgear and long, bright blue gloves. He was standing at a large steel container. Its lid was open. Clouds of what looked like steam billowed out, in a scene reminiscent of Halloween.

Liquid nitrogen.

Jennifer did not hear the man's response, but she watched as the woman retreated and picked up the phone she'd left lying on the counter.

"Can he call you right back?" she said. "He's retrieving vials right now."

In a couple minutes, the door opened again and the man she'd seen emerged with two vials in his hand. He stopped to pick up his message, then exited the lab.

There were now only two other scientists, the woman who'd answered the phone and an older, ponytailed man at the far end. Without looking in either of their directions, Jennifer strode to the door from which the man had just emerged with the vials and, without looking back, entered the room.

Inside, she paused behind the closed door, her heart beating wildly as she waited to see if anyone would appear and challenge her authority to be there.

There were six large appliances in the room, all apparently freezers. Three were upright and looked identical to the one she and Charlie had had in their garage, except that on the front door, a sign declaring "Minus 20" had been taped. Two were long, horizontal models labeled "Minus 70." The sixth, from which she'd seen the man withdrawing samples, looked like something straight out of *2001: A Space Odyssey*—a huge, sleek stainless steel cannister that came up to Jennifer's waist. Its lid was ringed with a blue rubber seal. In the corner, feeding the freezer via a thick black hose, was a tank labeled CAUTION: NITROGEN. The headgear—a plastic shield that looked like something a welder might wear—and padded gloves the scientist had been wearing when Jennifer saw him were now hanging from hooks above the appliance.

Jennifer had no idea where to start. She knew that cell lines would be kept frozen, but she hadn't anticipated this—having to choose between three methods. Minus 20 degrees, minus 70, and liquid nitrogen.

She opened a door to one of the uprights. Inside were four shelves, all the space on which was filled with short, square cardboard boxes, stacked as many as four or five high. She pulled a box off the top of one stack and removed its lid. Inside, a grid held thirty-six small vials. She began withdrawing vials. Each was labeled with notations that made absolutely no sense to Jennifer.

*B*16, *RXP/rj/5/22*

*L*7, *micro/ss/6/3*

One after another, she withdrew the vials and scanned the labels. The situation quickly began to look hopeless. It would take her hours to go through the entire inventory in all six freezers and even if she had the time, the labeling was such that Jennifer feared she would not even recognize Patricia's cell line if she saw it. If only she'd been able to reach Patricia on the phone.

When she heard the door open behind her, Jennifer caught her breath and turned. It was the man who had just left minutes earlier.

He studied her for a moment, as if trying to place her. Jennifer could not be sure if she'd ever seen him.

"Can I help you?" he said. His voice was friendly, but there was a note of suspicion there, too.

Jennifer grimaced.

"I told Dr. Mannington I'd pick up a vial for her while I was down this way and I don't have a clue where to find it." She smiled at him, then, trying to look as relaxed and confident as possible. "I'm the company attorney, Jennifer Rockhill. Have we met?"

The man continued to stare.

"Seems kind of odd for her to ask you to do that," he said.

"Oh, she didn't ask. I volunteered. I was coming down here anyway, to pick up some things of Patricia Lukins," Jennifer used a conspiratorial tone that, were he aware of Patricia's firing, would indicate her proximity to the situation. "But I didn't think to ask her which freezer to look in."

"What study is it?"

"Something to do with a herpes virus. I think she said it was work Dr. Lukins was doing."

"Oh, you mean the HS-tk cell line. You're in the wrong freezer." She seemed to have allayed his suspicions. "That's in what we call the 'deep freeze.' I was just going back in there myself."

With Jennifer standing by watching, he grabbed the gloves, slipped the headgear on, and opened the top to the mammoth silver freezer. Clouds of liquid nitrogen instantly spilled out, causing Jennifer to fall back.

The man's head disappeared momentarily into the mist, then reappeared. He'd hooked his finger around a metal ring and as he lifted his hand, from out of the cloud appeared a rectangular "box." It housed two dozen tiny drawers, labeled "A" through "X." They were secured by a long metal rod that ran the length of the box. He balanced it on the edge of the freezer and removed the rod. Then, he pulled out the drawer labeled "H." Like the boxes Jennifer had opened from the refrigerator, it held a grid filled with vials. He lifted one after another, then let out a "Voila!"

In his hand was a vial marked *HS-tk/pl/6/4*.

"Thank you so much," Jennifer said, reaching to take it from him.

"No problem," he said, sliding the rod back in place and lowering the box back inside the freezer. "You know, you might want to put a lab coat on if you ever volunteer to come in here again. That suit of yours could get stained."

"Thanks for the advice," Jennifer said, smiling again. "And thanks so much for the help."

Wasting no time, she hurriedly exited the room with the vial and crossed the open lab. As she was passing, the phone rang again.

"He's in the freezers," the same scientist who answered before reported, her voice holding a note of exasperation. "I'll have him call you back."

Jennifer was almost to the corridor, when she heard the woman's next words.

"Oh, sorry, Dr. Mannington. I didn't recognize your voice. I'll get him for you right now."

MATTHEW HAD TORN a sleeve off the courier's shirt and wrapped it around his ankle, but by the time he got off the bus at the bottom of Queen Anne Hill, blood had soaked through the makeshift bandage and mottled the leg of his tan slacks. As he stepped down to the curb, pain shot up his calf. Still he jogged up the hill, stolen files in hand, toward his apartment.

Foremost on his mind was whether he would find Jennifer there.

Last night he'd given her a key to his apartment—an act that, in his entire lifetime, was unprecedented, but seemed to have made scant impression on her—and as he rode the elevator up to the penthouse he hoped to find her already ensconced safely behind his locked door.

But the apartment was empty. He went right to the phone and dialed Jennifer's number at work. After four rings, he listened to her recording, which instructed the caller to press the star key for "immediate assistance." He punched the star impatiently.

"BioGentech," a live female voice announced. "How may I help you?"

"I'm trying to reach Jennifer Rockhill."

"Jennifer has left for the day."

Matthew looked at his watch. Two-forty-five. He'd left his message telling her to get out of the office at around twenty past one. Plenty of time for her to make it over to his apartment. Where had she gone?

He reached for the files. He would keep busy reading while he waited for her.

THE FIRST FILE CONTAINED a mixture of photocopies and lined yellow pages filled with Ram Chandra's loose, flowing script. The pages that had been copied, thought Matthew as he skimmed through, probably represented studies or portions of the process that had been used repeatedly, perhaps with all the surrogates he'd seen in Preston; while the handwritten entries would be unique to Angel's file.

Matthew was already familiar with much of the scientific procedure in the documents, having read everything published on the PPL experiments that culminated in the birth of Dolly, as well as the subsequent cloning research conducted at the University of Hawaii—however, Dr. Chandra had had to make adjustments to accommodate the subject of this experiment. Human beings.

While udder cells had been used for Dolly, Chandra had chosen cervical cells. *Cervical cells previously extracted from Donor B and frozen were placed in Solution E* read one handwritten entry. According to the file, there had been several different formulas ("A" through "E") used for the culture without success, until a formula denoted by Chandra as "Formula F"—most likely that devised by and stolen from Gregory Gallagher—finally proved successful. It achieved that delicate balance that deprived the cells of nutrients needed for the cell division process but provided adequate nutrition to keep them alive and healthy. As Dolly's creators had discovered, this quiescent phase effectively switched off all active genes in the adult DNA, in effect resetting the DNA—turning back its clock—and allowing it to be born all over again.

Next Chandra removed the nucleus of an unfertilized egg cell, this one from Donor A, and placed the empty egg cell—which still had intact all the cellular mechanisms for producing an embryo—next to the nucleus of the cell from Donor B. A gentle electric pulse applied to the culture solution caused the egg to accept the Donor B nucleus, with all its DNA, and at the same time triggered the cell division process.

A week later, the process called for the growing embryos to be implanted in the uterus of a baboon.

Behind the first set of pages describing the cloning process in general, which were neatly stapled together and attached to the left side of the file by a two-pronged clip, Matthew found a set of photocopies.

This second set focused on xenotransplantation; the transplantation of an organ—or, in this case, an embryo—of one species into another. Less familiar with this subject, Matthew settled back to read closely the dozen or so pages.

They consisted of medical journal articles reporting the results of recent studies—information, Matthew would soon see, that Chandra had used to create his own cutting-edge technology.

The first article described a first-of-its-kind experiment—the transplant of a baboon's bone marrow to a patient dying of AIDS. In theory, the transplant would provide the patient with a facsimile of a baboon's immune system, which had proven to be particularly resistant to HIV and which would mature into HIV-battling cells within the recipient's own immune system. Earlier transplants of baboon tissue to AIDS patients had failed when the foreign tissue was rejected by the recipients, but it was hoped that the recent discovery of what had been labeled "facilitator cells" would increase the odds of this transplant's success. A special filtering process that allowed scientists to separate mature baboon bone marrow cells from younger cells was believed to reduce the chance of rejection because the younger cells, being less highly developed, would be less likely to provoke an immune reaction. Chandra had highlighted this last sentence, about the lessened chance of rejection, in yellow and above the words "younger cells," which he'd drawn lines through, he had written "embryo?"—an indication he suspected that, as with the younger, less-differentiated cells in the study, the recipient's immune system would be less likely to attack undifferentiated embryonic cells.

A topic of grave concern to the scientific community followed: the potential of such transplants to spread baboon diseases to humans. The danger of cross-species viral transmission occurring was not to be taken lightly, not when both Ebola and HIV were believed to have originated via cross-species transmission: HIV when an African villager ate a monkey carrying it; and Ebola from people eating infected chimpanzees.

Because of the fear of cross-species viral transmission, scientists had focused on pigs for xenotransplantation. The relationship between baboons and humans was just too close for comfort—the similarity in biological characteristics between the two species greatly increasing the chance of a virus crossing over. With pigs, dissimilarities worked against viral transmission. Pig-to-human transplants would soon be commonplace.

Splashes of yellow highlighter and margins crowded with comments indicated the last two articles had sparked a fire in the scientist. An English biotech firm had genetically manipulated pigs to incorporate material "friendly" to humans, creating "transgenic" animals that tricked the immune system of the human recipient into accepting the transplanted tissue. *Angel!* Chandra had scrawled at one point in the margin. The article stressed the importance of screening donor pigs for infectious organisms. Handwritten notes alongside this paragraph appeared to have been whited out.

The last article talked about a study in which patients weaned themselves off anti-rejection drugs, which have a high degree of toxicity and present dangers of their own, when grafted organs contained bone marrow stem cells. As the stem cells mature inside the recipient's circulatory system, they teach the body to tolerate the transplant. At the bottom of the second page, Chandra had theorized: *injection of human stem cells into host system: same effect?*

A later notation declared: *Additional samples may be necessary, P. L. P. L.*

It took Matthew a moment to understand the significance.

Patricia Lukins. They were using blood samples from Patricia Lukins to build tolerance to human tissue in the baboons!

Finally, the journal articles ended and the subsequent pages, labeled **THE PROTOCOL**, reverted to the practiced script of Dr. Chandra.

> Current study incorporates three leading-edge technologies: the use of animals genetically engineered to incorporate human immune system characteristics into their DNA, lessening the chance of rejection of human fetuses; treatment with powerful anti-rejection drugs; and the study director's own program of tolerance-building injections.

The study director was Chandra. Continually referring to himself in the third person—"the study director"—he went on to describe his innovative program.

Four weeks prior to implantation of the embryo in Angel, Chandra began a series of injections that cleverly combined two of the studies Matthew had just read about in the journal articles. Based on the work done with facilitator cells, Chandra had separated mature human plasma cells from undeveloped, less-"offensive" cells. Then, utilizing the research that showed the host's immune system can be trained to tolerate a transplant when it receives small amounts of the donor's immature bone marrow stem cells, he injected steadily increasing amounts of separated, immature human plasma into the baboon.

Angel's immune system, it seemed, was part baboon, part human.

If successful, the process should enable Chandra's baboons to acclimate to the foreign cells gradually and avoid the dramatic hyperacute rejection—a process in which the blood flow is shut off to the donor organ, causing it to blacken and die—that had plagued research of this nature in the past.

So that's why Jennifer described the human fetuses she'd seen the other night as being almost black in color, thought Matthew. Apparently Angel was the first of the primates with whom Chandra had tested his new program.

Interestingly, Chandra's own notes *(baboons are the preferred surrogates because they are less susceptible to hyperacute rejection)* made no mention whatsoever of the dangers laid out in the journal articles. Nowhere was there any reference to any efforts on his or anyone else's part to screen the animals for infectious disease. Matthew was sure that the danger had never, and would never, be communicated to Tupeni Sanday; nor, despite the scientist's obvious awareness of it, been given more than fleeting consideration. No, from what Matthew was reading, it appeared that rejection of the implanted embryo was the only real concern for Chandra. Unless . . . Matthew lifted the file to get a closer look.

Yes, there it was. At the top of the file, wedged between two pages. A slender remnant of paper, indicating a page had been torn from this section. Why had it been removed? Did the fact that his actions could unleash another AIDS- or Ebola-like plague on the population of Niupalu, and conceivably even the world at large, fail to register with Chandra? Or, more likely—in light of the inclusion in the file of articles on the subject—had it failed to matter?

The files contained everything that Matthew had been hired to obtain. As he continued leafing through them, running his eyes down entries on charts, daily data recordings, in-depth protocols for every procedure utilized by Chandra both in earlier trials leading up to the work with Angel and with Angel herself, Matthew Pace realized that his job was done.

EIGHTEEN

AS SHE ENTERED the stairwell, Jennifer took another look in her briefcase to be certain the vial containing the cell line was upright—once outside the lab, she'd hurriedly slid it into an empty leather ring designed to function as a penholder—then she began descending, as quickly as her high heels allowed, to the basement parking garage. As she stepped out into it, she wished she'd parked closer; but newer employees were assigned spaces at the far end, near the ramp that led to the street.

The parking garage had always given her the creeps. It was cavernous and cold, running the entire length of the building, and gave one the feeling of being completely shut off from the outside world. Lighting was fluorescent and, in most areas, poor. The entire garage seemed to vibrate from the near deafening thrum of the massive HVAC unit located directly overhead. Even on dry days, water dripped from pipes running the length of the ceiling.

Most employees either stayed at BioGentech for lunch or walked to one of several restaurants and delis nearby, so Jennifer was not surprised to find herself alone amongst the cars—a concentration of Jaguars, Mercedes, and high-end sports utility vehicles nearest the elevator and stairwell, giving way to the Fords and Hondas driven by lab workers and support staff. Still, it was possible she'd come across someone, so focusing on the far end where she had parked, she fought back her instinct to run.

The instinct grew especially acute when she thought she heard something behind her. Footsteps?

She turned, but saw no one. She must just be jumpy, that's all. Still, it occurred to her that the cement beams designed to support the building were big enough for a person to hide behind.

When her car finally came into sight, she couldn't help herself. She began to run.

Immediately, unmistakably now, she heard another set of footsteps fall in behind her. Terrified, this time she did not turn to look. Instead, she clutched the briefcase to her chest and sprinted toward the Volvo.

In the next instant, her pursuer's footsteps were drowned out by a new sound—that of a car's tires screeching as, rounding a distant corner, they attempted to gain purchase on the cement floor. With both pursuers narrowing the distance between them, she realized that she would never have time to unlock her car and get inside. Her best bet would be to race toward the garage door, which, miraculously, at the top of the ramp, she could see to be open. If she could make it to the street, she might be safe.

It was just twenty yards ahead. Then fifteen. She might just make it.

And then yet another sound sent shivers of terror down Jennifer's spine. A mechanical sound this time, louder and more metallic than that of the air-conditioning system.

The garage door was lowering, trapping her inside.

MATTHEW CLOSED THE first file, stood, and tossed it down on to the wet bar. He walked over to the sliding door that led to the balcony and looked down. He was hoping to see Jennifer pulling up in her car. But the green Volvo was nowhere in sight. Where the hell had she gone? He glanced at the clock on the VCR. Almost four o'clock.

He dialed her apartment again but this time did not leave a message. Grabbing both files, he hurriedly scribbled two words on a sheet of paper and placed it in the middle of the dining room table, where, amidst the stark order of the apartment, it stood to draw Jennifer's attention immediately.

Stay here, it said, both words underlined for emphasis.

Then, heaving a sigh both of frustration and disbelief—for never before in his history would he, at a time like this, when success was all but guaranteed, have so risked jeopardizing it—he headed out in search of Jennifer.

Her car was missing from its customary spot under the long carport; her apartment appeared empty, which he quickly confirmed by his easy entry via the flimsy lock on her sliding patio door. An assortment of personal items, which he recognized from the night he'd rummaged through her briefcase, lay scattered on the kitchen table. Her bed was still unmade from that morning. It was obvious she had not returned home after leaving BioGentech.

He headed back into Seattle and cruised slowly by BioGentech, turned around at a parking lot half a block away, then drove by again. A security guard stood smoking a cigarette at the open garage door that led to the underground employee lot, putting to rest Matthew's impulse to look for Jennifer's car there.

Reasoning that it was still too early to jump to the conclusion something had happened to her, he decided that he had two choices.

He could either head straight to Interstate 5 and Sea-Tac Airport, knowing that he'd completed his mission and that, if he felt compelled to do so, he could continue to try to reach Jennifer by phone from London—and that each moment he delayed doing so put him and this assignment's success in unnecessary jeopardy.

Or he could return to his apartment and hope to hear from her soon.

He drove to his apartment.

Back in his penthouse floor unit, with his anxiety and adrenaline building to an almost intolerable level, he felt like punching the wall. Instead, he dropped to the floor and began pumping out push-ups. But the pressure this position placed on his ankle forced him to quit and turn his attention to his wound. He stripped off his pants, then went in to the bathroom, where he cleaned and wrapped the wound inflicted by the Doberman's teeth with fresh gauze.

As he finished taping the gauze in place, it suddenly occurred to him. The donor. Nothing he'd read in the file identified the donor. Not that it would matter to WTI. The protocol and all the research going into it were laid out with great detail and clarity. His employer would not care who the donor had been.

But he knew Jennifer would not rest—that he would have no chance whatsoever of persuading her to leave Seattle—before she'd warned the donor of Fielding's plan. And so, after dressing his ankle and slipping on a pair of Levis and army-issue boots, Matthew returned to the living room and the files he'd stolen from the Preston lab.

He dropped into the black-leather chair that had come with the furnished apartment. As he leafed through both files, he glanced occasionally to the street below, looking for Jennifer to make her arrival.

The first file repeatedly referenced a Donor A, from whom the oocyte had been extracted, and a Donor B, the person whose cells had been cloned. But it contained no information that might identify Donor B. In his preliminary review of the material he'd stolen from the lab, Matthew had quickly perused the second file and come away with the belief it contained nothing more than several dozen pages of data entered, apparently on a daily basis, by Dr. Chandra—data that the scientists at WTI would undoubtedly scrutinize closely in their analysis of the cloning technique, but which, in its raw form, held little meaning to Matthew.

But this time, he carefully turned each page of the laboriously organized file.

Tell me, how did you sickos go about getting a donor?

Page after page contained columns of readings. Charts and graphs, row after row of recorded vital signs. Detailed analyses of Angel's blood, which was being closely monitored to allow quick recognition of and reaction to any signs of rejection, and also to detect any problems with toxicity that could result from the administration of the heavy-duty anti-rejection drugs being utilized by Chandra. But nothing that would disclose the identity of the donor.

He was almost to the back of the inch-thick file, and had come to the exasperating conclusion that the donor information must be included in another file—one he must have overlooked in his hurry to get out of the lab—when he flipped over a page that looked much like all those before it and immediately, his eyes fell to the bold print at the top of the subsequent sheet of paper.

Donor B Data
Subject: female, 43 years, 5' 7", 135 lbs.

The hairs on the back of Matthew's neck had begun to bristle, stand on edge.

Characteristics: Brown hair, blue eyes
IQ: unknown (above average)

As he read the next entry, sick dread filled every pore, every fiber of Matthew's being; but it was all taking place on some safe, subconscious plane. Until he read the next line, he'd managed to avoid giving form to the hideous cloud that had taken hold of his mind in the last thirty seconds.

Family: none (husband deceased);
                 no children, no siblings or
                 parents

"No!" he called out loud.
"*No!*"
The donor was *Jennifer Rockhill.*

CHAPTER

NINETEEN

SEVEN, AND STILL no word from Jennifer. Waiting had grown intolerable. Matthew grabbed the files and slid each into a gallon-sized zipper-locking freezer bag. Then he went out onto the balcony, carefully lifted one of two large wooden planters positioned at each end of the balcony by its rim, and slid the files into the planter's false bottom. He'd chosen this apartment because the building sat at the apex of Queen Anne Hill. The fact that there were no other high-rises facing his building, combined with the dramatic drop in elevation just below, gave him total privacy and eliminated having to worry about being seen. He'd also chosen the building for its enhanced security, but that didn't guarantee that whoever was following him couldn't get inside and ransack his apartment in search of the protocol. Still, he felt confident he hadn't been followed home yet—undoubtedly due to the fact that each time he returned there he first drove a circuitous route designed to shake anyone tailing him—and believed it safer to hide the files in the planter he'd painstakingly built just the week before than to carry them around.

The files safely tucked away, he headed out to find Jennifer. He drove directly to BioGentech and parked his car along the curb. In the past, he'd taken every precaution to avoid being seen anywhere near the BioGentech building. But his desperation to find Jennifer and the knowledge that one way or another he was out of there soon, out of Seattle, gave him a new freedom. He walked boldly around the side of the building to the garage door, which was down, and began pounding on it, the metal amplifying the sound of his fists hitting its surface.

In less than a minute the smaller door opened and a uniformed guard appeared.

"What the hell do you think you're doing?"

"Looking for my old lady," Matthew answered. "She never made it home from work. I can't find her anywhere. I want to see if her car's still here."

The guard studied him.

"I was a real jerk last night," Matthew explained, donning a sheepish expression. "Don't blame her if she just took off. But now I'm worrying myself crazy about her. You know how it is? I just want to know if she's okay. Can you do it? Just let me take a look to see if her car's here?"

The guard's expression mellowed just a bit, perhaps in understanding, as if he, too, knew a little about mistreating a woman.

"Describe the car," he said.

"Green Volvo, 1994 or 5. Wagon. California plates."

"Wait here."

Minutes later the guard was back.

"Still here," he said. "Where does she work?"

"BioGentech," Matthew answered.

"She's not up there, I can tell ya. I already did my rounds up there. Place is empty. She musta gone home with someone," the guard suggested. "Or maybe she walked, or took a cab somewhere. Just how big a jerk you been?"

Matthew ignored that.

"You sure no one's up there?"

"Dead sure."

Nodding a thanks, Matthew returned to his pickup.

So Jennifer hadn't left BioGentech in her car. Had she done something along the lines of the guard's suggestion, taken a cab somewhere to disappear for a while? It was possible, but unlikely. She was too determined to blow the whistle on Fielding and she couldn't do that without Matthew and the information he'd set out today to obtain. Besides, as she'd told him, she really had nowhere to go, no one to turn to.

This very fact had actually been acknowledged in the file. No family, no children, no parents or siblings. Perhaps it helped explain Jennifer's selection as the donor.

The other rationale for her selection had also been set forth in Chandra's file:

> All previous cloning attempts have utilized embryonic cells, with results ranging from immediate failure to early onset rejection by the surrogate. It is unknown whether these failures stem from the process itself or from deficiencies within the

donor cells. The choice of a mature donor, in this case a female
43 y.o.a., is of interest due to the theory that use of a mature
donor assures the study director that he is working with a
proven entity, one whose viability and desirability have already
been established.

Matthew had read this paragraph over half a dozen times, amazed
each time at the tone of utter detachment from the reality that the subject
of this intellectual assessment was a human being. Let alone Jennifer.

If Jennifer had not taken flight on her own, that left one possibility.
Something had happened to her. Something no doubt involving Sherwood
Fielding.

There was only one redeeming consideration if that were true: Fielding would not harm her. Not before he'd delivered her, along with Angel
and Ram Chandra, to Tupeni Sanday.

But where could he have taken her?

When Matthew had first arrived in Seattle, before staging his meeting
with Jennifer, he'd thoroughly checked Fielding out. It was routine procedure. He'd followed Fielding home from work, learned he lived in a
brick three-story mini-mansion in Magnolia. Three days of staking out the
house had given him plenty of information on the personal life of Bio-
Gentech's founder and CEO. For one thing, he had a wife whom Matthew
would not have wished on his worst enemy, the kind of woman who had
long ago set Matthew on a course of lifelong bachelorhood. This one, with
her expensive cars and clothing, her gardeners and maid service, had few
redeeming qualities that Matthew could see, and she had one hell of a
vicious tongue. He'd witnessed the verbal lashing she'd given a Hispanic
gardener one day. The front of the house was lined with neatly sculpted
bushes and the worker had apparently trimmed one down further than
suited Fielding's wife's whims. Matthew, who'd taken to jogging through
the neighborhood—a tactic that worked well in this city of hiply fit yup-
pies—could hear her berating the worker from half a block away. The
little ice queen had a mouth on her, and obvious contempt for anyone of
the gardener's status. But on the two occasions he'd observed her with
Fielding, she'd been the picture-perfect doctor's wife—attractive, well
dressed, reserved, but still, openly adoring and proud of her accomplished
husband. And in addition to the wife, Fielding had a young boy. Blonde,
cherubic. Always dressed like a fucking ad from a Nordstrom catalogue.

As Matthew contemplated the possible scenarios surrounding Jennifer's disappearance, it was easy to conclude that there was no way Fielding

would be holding her hostage at his house. No way Fielding would introduce his other life—the baseness of it—into this perfect little Stepford-world existence.

Where then? The answer came to him with such clarity that he cursed himself for not having thought of it sooner.

Preston.

JENNIFER CAME TO in a state of drug-induced confusion aggravated considerably by her circumstances. Her head ached. The tissues of her throat and nose burned. She opened her eyes to such total blackness that she actually tried to reach up and touch their lids to see if, indeed, they had opened, or if perhaps they were covered with a blindfold. But her hands were bound behind her. After a while, her pupils adjusted and she could see enough to know she was imprisoned in what she first took to be a box of some sort. It took her foggy mind a few more seconds to realize she was in the trunk of a car—a small car. She was lying on her right side. Her knees were pressed into her chest and when she tried to extend her legs, there was nowhere for them to go. Rolling over was also impossible, so tight was the space.

Someone had bound her mouth with a cloth and wide tape. She attempted to scream through it and then, with her knees, started pounding awkwardly against the roof of her prison, but when she stopped, she was greeted by nothing but silence. Feeling her anxiety building, fearing she would have a heart attack if she did nothing to stem it, she called upon the breathing techniques she'd learned sixteen years earlier during the Lamaze classes she and Charlie had taken in preparation for Stacey's birth. Of course, the short "hee-hee-hee" exhalations were impossible through her taped mouth, but she improvised and soon the increased oxygen, as well as the distraction offered by the process itself, had calmed her somewhat.

Then, suddenly, she heard the hum of a motor, which she recognized to be a garage door opener, and the metallic clanking of the door itself as it lifted, followed by footsteps on cement and the sound of two doors opening—one on each side of the car—then closing.

As the car backed out of the garage, Jennifer could hear no conversation taking place inside. She, too, remained silent.

The car made several turns, then picked up speed, indicating to Jennifer that it had accessed a highway. Still no sound from the driver or passenger, though a radio had been turned on. KJR. Something called "Sportsradio." The announcers were complaining about an ump's call that had cost the Mariners the game against the Anaheim Angels the night before.

"These assholes don't know what the fuck they're talkin' about," a gruff voice—presumably, from the direction in which it came, that of the driver—finally said. "I saw that play. Vaughn was safe by a mile."

His passenger did not respond.

The voice struck a chord in Jennifer's memory, but she could not place it. Of one thing she was certain. It was not Sherwood Fielding. Perhaps Fielding was the passenger.

The silence of the car's occupants was enough to make her crazy. But finally, an hour or more into the trip, a second voice sounded. This one she recognized.

It was Angelique Mannington.

"This is ridiculous. We should've just taken the ferry over."

"Too risky," the driver responded. "If she'd raised a fuss while we were waiting in line, or at the pay booth, we could've had real trouble." He paused. "She's awfully quiet back there. 'Spose she's okay?"

Angelique's laughter sent chills down Jennifer's spine. She had heard hints of it before, but nothing that compared to the sound now coming to her from the front seat.

"Got the hots for her, do you?"

"No, darlin'," he answered. "Only for you."

"Fat chance of anything coming of that."

They fell into silence again.

A short while later, the car crossed what seemed to be a long bridge. Another half hour and it turned, slowed, and then stopped several times in succession.

Traffic lights, thought Jennifer. She now tried to tune out the radio and pick up any sounds coming from outside. When the time was right, she would try to get someone's attention; but she knew she would be allowed no more than one opportunity to do so and she did not want to waste it by choosing the wrong moment.

The car turned, and Jennifer slid forward, her face smashing against the trunk's front wall, as it eased down a hill. Then there was the crunch of gravel under tires.

"There. The one at the end," Jennifer heard Angelique say. "Therapy."

What could she be talking about? Were they at some medical buildings?

This could be the moment she was waiting for.

"Got the keys?" the driver asked.

"Yes. Here they are. I'll meet you at the beach a quarter of a mile past the lighthouse in half an hour. Look for my headlights—if the coast is clear, they'll be on. If not, cruise on by and come back half an hour later. I'll use the same signal each time. And keep your cell phone on. Sherwood wants us to be within reach at all times."

"Got it."

Both car doors opened simultaneously. Jennifer waited and listened. Were they leaving her there, in a parking lot, while they both went somewhere? She could only hope so.

But then she heard the two exchange a few more words outside, which she could not make out, and someone get back in the car, on the driver's side.

She couldn't stand it any longer. This might be her last chance. When the car started to back up, Jennifer began screaming again—a scream in large part absorbed by the gag—hoping to attract the attention of a passerby. At the same time, she repeatedly butted both the top of her head and her knees against the top of the closed trunk, producing a series of thuds that did not do justice to the pain she was inflicting upon herself.

At this, the car jerked violently into reverse and rocketed backward. Then, turning, it shot forward with equal force, throwing Jennifer first in one direction, then the other, like a limp ragdoll.

"*Shut the fuck up!*" an outraged voice screamed.

It belonged to Angelique Mannington.

Jennifer kept up the commotion a bit longer, but when the car gained more speed, she knew they'd entered another highway. Her chance had passed.

Angelique's laughter from the front of the car made Jennifer wish with all her might that her hands were free to press them to her ears and block out the sound.

"Have a nice nap?" the scientist asked. "Ready for your big adventure?"

Jennifer began her breathing exercises again. Slow, deep inhales; long, measured exhales.

This time it didn't help.

The realization that Angelique was part of the repulsive scheme—part of Fielding's plan to sell a cloned human being—had a devastating effect on Jennifer. She'd actually been concerned about the scientist's safety, planning to warn her.

As if she could read Jennifer's mind, Angelique again began her taunts.

"So tell me, who is it? Who's in this with you? Someone you're fucking? That's it, isn't it?"

So, they didn't know about Matthew yet.

"It has to be. Cause I know you. All those barriers you put up, but once you let them down, I bet the sky's the limit."

Soon, the car turned off the highway and traveled only a short distance—no more than a mile—before coming to a stop. Jennifer heard Angelique get out of the car and walk around back.

"I'll be back in a minute," she told Jennifer through the trunk. "Go ahead and scream your heart out. No one's around to hear."

Her sheer pleasure in the situation, which was audible in her voice, terrified Jennifer. Right now Jennifer knew two things with a certainty: that her captor was not only totally void of conscience, but also brilliant. A frightening combination.

Soon the other voice, that of the male driver, could be heard approaching along with Angelique, and in just seconds the trunk was opened, blinding Jennifer momentarily with brilliant daylight. Rough hands reached for her and as she blinked in the late afternoon sun, she was finally able to match the male's voice with an all-too-familiar face. Jim Wilkes, head of security at BioGentech.

"Come on, out of there," Wilkes ordered. Bound as she was, Jennifer was in no position to either help or hinder the process of removing her from the trunk. Wilkes grabbed her under the armpits while Angelique Mannington took her ankles, raking Jennifer's spine against the edge of the trunk as they lowered her awkwardly to the ground. She lay there, utterly defenseless and still feeling the effects of the chloroform they'd used to knock her out in the BioGentech garage.

"We'd better untie her," Wilkes said. "I'm not about to try to carry her all the way to the dock. Besides, someone might come along and see her like this."

He bent and brought himself face-to-face with her.

"Don't try anything funny. Understand?"

Jennifer nodded, her eyes wide with terror.

Now Angelique stepped around, coming into Jennifer's line of vision for the first time.

"Hey there, girlfriend," she said. "You better listen to Jim here. He has some very imaginative ways to force cooperation. And I'm sure he'd just love to try them out on you. Wouldn't you, Jimbo?"

As he stepped over Jennifer's form, Wilkes responded with a lascivious laugh. Soon she could feel him sawing with a pocketknife at the tape that bound her ankles. Her wrists were next, and finally, the gag came off. Jennifer rolled to her knees, then stood, stumbling at first from the numbness that had crept into her legs and feet—which, having lost her shoes somewhere along the way, were bare, except for her hose.

Wilkes gave her a shove and she followed as Angelique led the way down a short grassy embankment to a long dock, at the end of which was tethered a large white yacht.

Therapy.

They were within a couple yards of the vessel when, from the two-lane road behind, Jennifer heard the approach of a vehicle.

Darting under the arm of Wilkes, who was following closely behind her, Jennifer sprinted back down the length of the dock. The vehicle, a beat-up pickup truck, was fast approaching a point where it would be dead even with the dock, but the public landing's parking lot would still separate them by more than fifty feet, and much of the dock was hidden by the embankment. Jennifer knew the odds of being seen from the road were slim. If she had any hope of being rescued, she had to get up the short hill before the pickup disappeared around the curve.

Her action had taken both Wilkes and Angelique Mannington by surprise, but before she could top the grassy knoll, Wilkes tackled her, throwing her to the ground face first with enough force to render her momentarily unconscious. She came to with Wilkes still beside her on the ground and Angelique Mannington straddling her, her face wild with rage.

"You bitch!" Angelique screamed, bending to slap Jennifer across the face.

"Not here," Wilkes ordered, rising and swiping at the dirt on his pants. "Let's get her onboard. Then you can slap her around all you want."

Each grabbing an arm, Wilkes and Angelique clamped Jennifer in a viselike grip and dragged her as she struggled against them—hoping to slow the process enough for another car to pass by—the entire length of the dock.

Both her captors seemed rattled by Jennifer's lack of cooperation.

Jennifer put up as much a fight as she could, but in the end, no more cars came along.

They wrestled her on board. Then, as Jennifer stood at the door to the aft cabin, Angelique pushed her down the four stairs, sending her sprawling on the carpeted floor. The scientist immediately descended upon her, kicking at her as she lay curled in the fetal position, her hands covering her face.

"You screw this up for us and you're dead. *Dead*," she screamed. "Do you hear?"

Wilkes stood at the top of the stairs, watching in amusement, as Jennifer, who had now had enough, began to fight back. Fueled by her anger and also convinced that she had little to lose, Jennifer lunged for Angelique, pulling her down by a handful of hair. Both women were still dressed in the skirts they'd worn to the office and what Jim Wilkes witnessed, no doubt with considerable appreciation, was an entanglement of long legs, arms, and lots of hair—Angelique's blond mane starting out on top, but soon replaced by the auburn locks of Jennifer. Despite the ordeal she'd been through, Jennifer was actually gaining the advantage when Wilkes stepped in.

"Party's over," he said, waving a gun over the two women and prying them apart with one foot. "We've got to get this baby out to sea before someone comes along."

THE SUN WAS JUST dropping into the jagged peaks of the Olympics as Matthew sped south down Interstate 5 toward the I-90 floating bridge that would take him east, over Lake Washington and into the foothills of the Cascades. Long stretches of shadow darkened the roadway once he exited 90 at Preston. As he raced up the gravel road toward the renegade lab, Matthew passed the car in which he'd left the courier earlier that day.

As he'd expected, the gate he'd battered with the courier van was once again closed, though he detected a slight lopsidedness to it. There were no other telltale signs of his escape that afternoon. Matthew fully expected the place to be on high alert, especially if Jennifer were being held hostage there. But as he drove by, something told him things were not as he'd expected.

He was ill prepared to make entry onto the property again, but he had his gun and this time he would silence the fucking dogs for good. That, at least, would enable him to get within close proximity of the building, where he could then reassess things. For once, he was not worried about his suspected CIA tail. A backup, even one he usually considered his antagonist, might just come in handy.

He had one objective and one objective only. To find and recover Jennifer. Why he was taking this risk, he did not know. It wasn't part of the job description.

He parked his car on the cutaway that Jennifer had used the night she came to Preston, then went to the trunk and removed the silver case containing the listening equipment. Back in the car, he flipped the monitor on and adjusted the volume. Telltale static indicated the voice transmitter was still functioning, but the only sounds being transmitted were a few short, mournful wails, undoubtedly the baboons, coming from the lab next to Chandra's office. It did not seem Chandra, or anyone else, was in the office. Impatient, Matthew climbed out of his car and hoisted himself over the chain-link fence. Then he gave it a good rattle and stood, his Glock drawn, ready for the dogs.

But they did not come.

The grounds were large, but regardless, dogs like that would detect his presence almost immediately. Were they inside now, perhaps guarding Jennifer?

Matthew weaved his way through the darkening woods that encircled the warehouse-like facility. Still no sign of the dogs. He would have preferred to confront them away from the building itself, where he could more easily dispose of them without drawing attention to himself.

His approach brought him in line with the back of the building. He cut south, toward its front, in order to survey the situation, see how many cars were out front.

Oddly, there were only two: the beat-up Toyota that had been there earlier that day, which he assumed to be the guard's, and the BMW he'd seen Chandra leave in at lunch. It was parked at an angle, and the driver's door appeared to be open, though from where he was viewing it he couldn't be certain. In light of the silence in Chandra's office, it struck Matthew as odd that Chandra's car was even there.

Matthew was turning toward the back of the building when a glimmer from the paved driveway that led to the front gate caught his eye. He squinted to get a better look. Barely distinguishable in the twilight was a dark form that blended in with the blacktop, and would not have caught his attention were it not for the reflection of the building's floodlight in a pool of liquid in which the form was lying. Matthew crept forward and within a dozen steps, realized that he was looking at one of the Doberman pinschers. It lay still, in a pool of blood. Someone had beaten him to it.

From there he could see that Chandra's car door on the driver side was, indeed, open, indicating the scientist had either been in an awfully big hurry when he returned to work or . . . had he been accosted before he had the chance to get out of the car?

Remaining behind the veil of trees, Matthew quickly retraced his steps. He still had the keys he'd taken earlier from the guard. Emboldened by a sudden sense of urgency, he crossed the clearing to the back door, then one by one, tried each key, but even though one fit, the door's knob would not turn without a passkey.

He walked to one of the dumpsters, and began pushing it, wheeling it over the rough, dry ground cover to finally shove it up against the windowless west wall of the building. Before climbing on to it, he strode back to the clearing's perimeter, where he stooped and picked up a softball-sized rock. He placed it on top of the dumpster, hoisted himself up on top of the the big green container's lid, then tossed the rock on to the building's roof. It landed with a thud. He did not wait for a response from inside, but instead, standing on his toes on the dumpster, stretched his hands upwards, toward the roof's edge, which was still at least a foot and a half out of reach. He sprang, but failed to get a grip. The second time he managed to grasp the strip of metal securing the roof's tar-papered surface and, putting his daily push-up regimen to good use, Matthew pulled himself slowly up. Once his chin rested on the roof's surface, it took just one more surge to swing his legs over the roof's edge.

Now he waited. Had the building's air conditioning obscured his noisy ascent? Or had he announced his arrival, in which case, someone would soon materialize to investigate?

There were two skylights on the roof. One, still boarded up from the night he'd used it to escape, he knew to be the lab. After two or three minutes of complete silence and seeming inactivity in and around the building, he picked up the rock and headed toward the second skylight. He peered over its edge into darkness below. A line of light along the floor indicated a doorway to the lighted corridor. The room appeared small. Perhaps a storage room of some sort. Raising the hand that cradled the rock, Matthew brought it smashing down. It shattered, sprinkling the floor below in a harmonic chorus of glass hitting tile.

He dropped into the room, glass crunching under his weight, pressed his ear to the door, then opened it just enough to see down the length of the hallway, toward the front entrance and the guard's office. Nothing. No sound. No sign of activity, nor of the other Doberman.

He stepped out into the corridor. The guard would either be sitting at his desk or patrolling the building. Better, Matthew decided, to take him by surprise than risk the guard coming upon him as he prowled the building in search of Jennifer. He headed stealthily toward the security office.

The door stood wide open, giving him a view of the desk—which looked exactly as he'd seen it earlier in the day—as he approached. The guard, Matthew concluded, had to be on patrol. But then a narrow red streak—no wider than that left by a magic marker—drew his eyes downward, to the floor. A trickle of blood, dried now, originated somewhere on the other side of the door and dead-ended in a bell-shaped pool at the seam between the office's linoleum and the corridor's surface. Matthew stepped inside the office and pulled the door toward him. Behind it, in the very position in which he'd left him earlier, lay the guard, still bound. But now, like the Doberman outside, he lay in a pool of blood. He'd been shot in the temple, at close range.

Matthew's eyes shot up to the monitors above the desk. All, including the lab monitor, were eerily devoid of activity. Matthew reached into the guard's shirt and yanked on a silver chain around the dead man's neck. A passkey, like Jennifer's, soon appeared. Matthew ripped it off its chain and headed down the corridor toward the lab. The door to Chandra's office was open, but there was no sign of the scientist.

At the lab door, Matthew used the passkey. Stepping inside with his gun drawn, the first thing he saw, protruding from behind the exam table in the middle of the room, were two tan suede Hushpuppies. Their positioning suggested they weren't attached to the same body.

By now, Matthew knew what to expect. He stepped around the table.

Ram Chandra lay on his back, his long, skinny body grossly twisted, his expression contorted in either horror or pain, or, quite likely, both. One arm lay behind his neck, forcing his chin forward onto his chest, but Matthew knew from the amount of blood, and the trail it had left, that the scientist's throat had been slit. He had bled to death.

The same mournful sound he'd heard minutes earlier over the transmitter drew his eyes from the gruesome scene on the floor to the wall of cages. He didn't know why he hadn't noticed it in the TV monitor, but now, the open door and empty cage at the end of the row were almost blinding in their significance.

Angel was gone.

The low moan sounded again. It came from one of the other baboons, all of whom were strangely still and watchful.

Whoever had killed Chandra and the guard had already fled, with Angel. Had they also taken Jennifer? Perhaps she was still in the building. Matthew hurriedly searched the rest of the large warehouse-like facility, but nowhere was there a sign of Jennifer. Chandra's murder had vaporized his belief that Jennifer was, for the time being, safe—for Chandra had been as integral a part of the deal promised to Tupeni Sanday as had Jennifer. Did the scientist have a change of heart that prompted Sherwood Fielding to have him killed? If so, what would happen if Jennifer, too, put up resistance?

He was just heading back toward the guard's office from the rear of the building when, ahead, the front door opened. Darting down the hall-way to the lab, Matthew ducked into Chandra's office and, having no other options, climbed under his desk and pulled a wheeled stool in behind him for cover. Footsteps, running, followed just seconds behind him. They passed the open door to Chandra's office and went directly to the lab. As soon as the door to the lab squeaked open, Matthew heard an anguished, "My God."

He recognized the voice, but could not immediately place it.

The footsteps soon signaled the newcomer's entry into the office in which Matthew was hidden and then Matthew, still crouched beneath the desk, found himself staring at linen trousers and Gucci loafers. Sherwood Fielding! He was using the phone on the desk above him.

"Give me Wilkes," Sherwood's voice, out of control, shouted into the phone.

After a short pause, it continued.

"Chandra and the fucking guard are dead. *Dead*," he shouted. "And the baboon is gone."

From under the desk, Matthew could detect the frantic tone of the voice on the other end but could not make out its words.

"No. I've been trying to reach someone out here on the phone for the past couple hours. Georgie called me at the start of my dinner—tonight was my big dinner with the team from R&R—to ask whether I'd called the courier service today. She said they called her just before she went home and said their van had never made it back from a delivery they were supposedly making out here from our offices. Georgie told them we hadn't even called for them, but then she started thinking something might be up, so she called me at the restaurant. I kept trying to get ahold of someone out here to make sure everything was alright, but couldn't get an answer. I finally made up an excuse about my kid being sick so I could drive out and see what the hell was going on." His fingers drummed frantically on the desktop overhead. "It's a fucking bloodbath out here. Who could have done this? I thought once you took care of that meddling bitch things would settle down out here."

Fielding listened to Wilkes' response, presumably speculation about the murderer. The only two words Matthew picked up caused his heart to lurch. *Jennifer Rockhill.*

"They were obviously in this together," Fielding responded. "Why else would she have had those cell lines in her purse when you caught her? But there has to be someone else involved, too. This looks like it happened in the last few hours, after you called to tell me you'd kidnapped her. And a frozen corpse sure as hell can't have done it. Pick me up at Pier 73 at ten o'clock. She knows who did this, and where Angel is. We'll get it out of her."

"The fucking dogs are dead, too," Sherwood screamed wildly into the receiver. "What the fuck kind of guard dogs did you get us?"

He slammed down the phone.

Matthew watched as the linen pants turned and exited the room at a run. Then he backed out from under the desk.

All he could hear once Fielding had departed was "*once you took care of that meddling bitch*" and "*frozen corpse.*"

Those words ringing over and over in his ears, with robotic preciseness he stood and walked toward the door to the lab. Hadn't he seen a freezer in there on his last visit?

He opened the door.

Yes, there it was. In the far corner. Long, longer than an ordinary freezer. And capable, he knew, of freezing its contents in a fraction of the time ordinary freezers took to do the job. The boxes that had been strewn on the floor next to it earlier were now nowhere to be seen.

Matthew crossed the room, then, bracing himself for what he would find, he reached for the stainless steel handle. He hesitated just a moment before lifting up on it, and closed his eyes.

Slowly, he opened them.

If it weren't for the crust of white crystals lining her nostrils and at the corners of her lips, she would have appeared to be sleeping. Patricia Lukins lay, face up, hands crossed peacefully across her oxford shirt. The freezer was long enough for her to have been stretched out full length, but apparently, because this was the lab's only freezer, her knees had been bent and pressed up against her folded arms to make room for a dozen or so boxes—all of which were jammed to overflowing with test tubes and plastic zipper-locking bags occupying the rest of the freezer.

Matthew, of course, had never seen the BioGentech scientist before, so he could only guess that he was looking at Dr. Lukins. He was fascinated by her clothing and shoes—wing tips, which appeared to be almost identical to a pair he himself frequently wore. A hurried examination revealed only a lump on the back of her head. Nothing that would kill her. More likely she'd been knocked unconscious and put there to freeze to death. The crystals indicated she'd still been breathing when put in the freezer. Perhaps, Matthew thought, Fielding planned to use her corpse. Could frozen organs be thawed and transplanted?

Lowering the freezer door again, Matthew returned to Chandra's office. He hadn't realized his hands were shaking until he reached for the mouse on Chandra's computer and actually had difficulty moving the cursor to click open the file menu.

They hadn't killed Jennifer.

The more the realization hit him, the more violently his hand began to shake. He paused to take a deep breath.

Of course, he realized, any sense of relief was premature. If Patricia Lukins was dead, then Jennifer must be the one being held somewhere by the person Fielding just talked to. With Chandra dead and Angel gone, Fielding was obviously a desperate man. If he didn't find Angel soon, he would have no choice but to get rid of Jennifer.

Matthew had to find her.

But before leaving Preston, he had one more job to do.

He reached into his pocket and extracted a computer disk. Jiggling the mouse caused the screen saver—a view of Seattle's skyline, with a bolt of lightning cutting the sky behind the Space Needle—to disappear and allowed Matthew to see the file labeled "future patent application" that Chandra had been working on. He scrolled up and saw that the file related to the scientist's work with Angel. The man must have been delusional—he was actually planning for the day that he would patent this process for cloning human beings.

Matthew inserted his floppy disk and downloaded it.

CHAPTER

TWENTY

AT JUST BEFORE 10:00 P.M., a twenty-meter Baglietto pulled quietly in to the waters just off Piers 72 and 73. Pier 73 was home to several tugboat services and on this night its entire four-hundred-meter length was occupied by the small squat vessels, which were called upon to man-uever immense oceangoing freighters into the Port of Seattle's crowded docks.

Three hundred twenty-four meters of the next pier, Pier 72—for all practical purposes its entire length—were taken up by a Russian super-tanker that would be leaving in the morning with its cargo of sixty thou-sand tons of wheat. Aside from a watchman on the bridge, the huge vessel was quiet this night, its crew out on the town before embarking on the grueling voyage back home.

A shadowlike form moved silently through the waters beneath the watchman, barely visible against the vessel's vast hull. Only a small patch of forehead between the mask and diving hood worn by Matthew Pace distinguished him from the black lower half of the tanker.

Matthew had mistakenly headed to the downtown piers, which were located behind Park Place Market, immediately after leaving Preston. It turned out to be a stroke of luck. At the last pier, when Matthew enquired as to the whereabouts of Pier 73, a sidewalk musician had pointed north, toward Myrtle Edwards Park. He'd headed down the park trail at a full run and had actually passed the little shack bearing a sign "Scuba Equip-ment Rentals." Several yards later, as the significance of the shop sunk in, he'd turned and headed back. It had already been closed for hours, but the park was empty so he didn't have to worry about anyone seeing him. Getting inside took next to no effort. Finding the equipment he would need for a free-dive was easy—snorkel, wet suit, mask, and fins.

Matthew could see the distant lights of the approaching Baglietto as he stripped off his clothes on the beach 120 yards from the Piers prominently labeled 72 and 73. Donning the equipment and leaving behind his Glock, which was too large to tuck inside the wet suit and could well prove useless when wet, he slipped into the water and remained near the surface, hidden by darkness, for the first 100 yards.

The Baglietto anchored offshore, unable to pull up to the dock to pick up its passenger, Sherwood Fielding, whom Matthew, from his position in the water alongside the Russian tanker, could see pacing between tugs. Two figures lowered the yacht's dinghy into the water. The plan, it seemed, was to taxi in and pick up Fielding.

As soon as Matthew saw one of the figures climb into the dinghy and heard the fifteen-horsepower motor engage, he submerged once more and headed out toward the yacht, using the snorkel for a short distance, then dropping to a depth of twenty feet before the dinghy passed, directly overhead.

He surfaced on the far side of the yacht—a luxurious sleek Italian model—and surveyed the situation from several yards out. The night was still. A half moon, sliding in and out of clouds, provided ample light to read the boat's name. *Therapy*. Matthew would have laughed had the situation been less dire. A single figure on the aft deck watched the dinghy progress toward shore. Matthew approached from the port side. A small ledge on the yacht extended around both sides from the back swim step, tapering out after eighteen feet. Matthew could see rows of waves—created by the wake of the Seattle-to-Bainbridge Island ferry, which had passed minutes earlier—approaching. He waited for them to set the *Therapy* rocking gently, then, using the ledge, he raised himself out of the water. Bracing against the ledge, he pushed himself silently up and grabbed hold of the port rail with the other hand. His finned foot took purchase on the ledge, which was no wider than a matchbook. He inched forward, toward the boat's stern. When the ledge tapered off, he raised himself and, for the first time, peered over the side. He was opposite the main cabin now, but through its windows, he could see the figure he'd observed earlier, still on the rear deck looking out over the water, toward shore. For the first time, he saw that it was a woman. Her hair was piled on top of her head, but long blond locks had fallen to her shoulders. He hoisted himself up, over the railing, and onto the walkway alongside the cabin. Flattened against the deck, he crept forward. Soon he could hear the approach once again of the dinghy, and then, across the night's water, voices.

Matthew raised himself and peered back. There were two figures now in the small vessel, outlined against the piers lit behind them. He looked to the flybridge and debated briefly about hiding there. He'd watched the dinghy being lowered from that level, which meant that upon their return, Fielding and his chauffeur might reposition it there, but as he assessed the situation, he realized he had few other options. With the woman at the back of the boat, eliminating the possibility of taking cover inside in one of the cabins, it was either the flybridge or the wide-open front deck. Slipping the fins off, he continued forward, passing another cabin, whose window shades were drawn. Once at the front of the boat, out of sight of the woman, he began to climb.

On the flybridge, he found that in addition to the wooden dinghy, *Therapy* was equipped with a Zodiak, a motorized rubber raft that was secured to the top deck by several ropes and covered with a canvas tarpaulin. As he heard the taxi pull up to the yacht, Matthew hurriedly loosened the ropes anchoring the tarp and rolled into the Zodiak.

Fielding seemed to disappear into the cockpit immediately upon boarding. Matthew listened as the other two hoisted the dinghy onto the back deck, where they decided to leave it for the time being, and pulled up anchor. Then footsteps sounded on the stairs leading to the flybridge. He watched as sneaker-clad feet passed him for the skipper's chair. Moments later the grating "Grrrrkkk" of *Therapy*'s bow-thruster filled the night's silence as the captain engaged its help in manuevering the vessel through Elliott Bay's night traffic.

Matthew pulled tight once more on the ropes anchoring his hiding place, then waited to see what came next.

IN *THERAPY'S* FORWARD CABIN, which Jim Wilkes had led her to at gunpoint, Jennifer lapsed in and out of a mental state that was as much a loss of consciousness as it was a drug-induced sleep. Before leaving her, Wilkes had once again bound and gagged her. The boat had cruised in what seemed to Jennifer—in her more lucid moments—to be a helter-skelter, zigzagging course.

Then, sometime after dark, the yacht suddenly changed course. And an hour later, when Jennifer heard the familiar mournful wail of first, one passing ferry, then, minutes later, another, she was certain they'd re-entered Elliott Bay. Alert now, she waited to see what happened next.

Soon *Therapy* stopped, still offshore, and the motor went silent. She listened and soon heard the hum of a smaller motor—a dinghy?—as it started up, then receded into the distance. Someone had apparently left the yacht. But outside her window just minutes later, the sound of light footsteps indicated she was still being watched closely.

In less than five minutes the dinghy returned and she heard a new voice—this one unmistakably that of Sherwood Fielding—onboard *Therapy*. She could hear Fielding's feet on the metal stairs as he descended to the main cabin, then his rapid approach to the stateroom in which she lay.

The door burst open.

"Where is she?" he demanded. The room was dark. He stood in the doorway, framed against the lighted cabin behind him.

Jennifer, still gagged, was unable to answer. In two giant strides Fielding crossed the room and began pulling at the duct tape that was wrapped over her mouth and around the back of her head.

He jerked the last section of tape off her face, taking a clump of hair with it and leaving a swath of red, raw skin.

"Where is she?" he repeated.

Jennifer lay on her side, looking up at him.

"Who?" she asked. "I don't know who you're talking about."

Jennifer had no idea who the "she" was Fielding referred to. Patricia Lukins?

Fielding grabbed her by the shoulders and shoved her up against the cabin's wall, into a sitting position. Then he backhanded her across the face.

With this blow Jennifer knew that what she'd experienced with Angelique and Wilkes was child's play compared to what this man was capable of.

"Don't give me that," Fielding said. "Where's the baboon? Where's Angel?"

FROM HIS POSITION in the rubber raft, Matthew had a window about two inches high from which to determine the course being taken by the *Therapy*. They first headed north in Puget Sound, then veered west, in the direction of the Strait of Juan de Fuca. They were about a mile and a half offshore. Across the water, he could make out the lights of a small town, most likely Port Townsend. The yacht's speed had dropped from eighteen knots to no more than half that speed and the same sneaker-clad feet passed by once again, then descended from the flybridge, the skipper having apparently decided to join the boat's other occupants inside, where calm waters would permit navigation from the cockpit.

As far as Matthew could tell, other than himself, the boat had only three occupants—the woman, the skipper, and Fielding. He could hear voices, raised, as if in argument, coming from below. He climbed out of the rubber dinghy and crept forward on his stomach, to the edge of the flybridge. Seeing the aft deck empty, he stood and slowly walked the perimeter of the upper level, his eyes searching the decks beneath him. Retracing the route he'd used to ascend to the upper level, he slid on his rear end by the cockpit and down the glass of the forward cabin, onto the deck. The voices originated there, inside the first cabin.

He crouched outside its curtained window, and immediately recognized Fielding's voice.

"Where is she?" he was shouting. "Where is Angel?"

At first there was no answer, only a sound that Matthew interpreted as a hand striking flesh.

The next voice brought a visceral reaction from Matthew.

"Why would I tell you?"

It was Jennifer.

"Why would I tell you *anything?*" she repeated.

Her voice sounded strong and angry. And terrified.

Matthew had to fight his instinct to rush the room. Decades of experience in situations like this—albeit situations in which he'd had little-to-no emotional involvement—had taught him the value of patience. Fielding might hurt Jennifer a little, but he needed her. He was obviously convinced she knew where Angel was and wouldn't risk serious injury to her until he got the information he needed to salvage his deal with Tupeni Sanday. Which gave Matthew time to assess the situation and come up with a plan.

"Because if you don't, you'll die," Fielding said calmly in response.

"Like my husband died? Will you take my kidneys, too, you bastard?" he heard her rail. "Sell them to your powerful friend?"

Even from his position outside, Matthew could feel the weight of the silence that ensued on the other side of the window's glass.

When he next spoke, Fielding's voice had climbed an octave.

"*Who are you?*"

"Does the name Banks mean anything to you?" Jennifer answered. "Charlie Banks was my husband. Or don't you remember? Have you murdered so many times that you can't even keep track of your victims?"

"*You're* the one who called me," Fielding shouted in response. "You're the reason I had to leave Palm Springs. You and that fucking Treecedale."

When Fielding struck again it was with such force that Jennifer's head flew back, hitting the glass—just inches from Matthew's face—and cracking the thermal pane.

Matthew jumped up, seized with fury.

Outside the aft cabin, he noticed a plastic toolbox, velcroed to the inside starboard railing. He opened it and withdrew a wrench, then stole silently down the cabin stairs. At the bottom, he could see through to the saloon and cockpit, where Jim Wilkes steered the boat, which had now entered the Strait of Juan de Fuca.

Just before Matthew got to him, Wilkes caught Matthew's reflection in the window and swung around to face him.

Switching the wrench from right hand to left, Matthew delivered a right cross that caught Wilkes in the Adam's apple and sunk the skipper immediately to his knees, his hands clawing frantically at his neck, as if attempting to clear a passageway for oxygen. Then Matthew raised his left hand and brought the wrench to bear on Wilkes' skull. Wilkes slumped over and lay motionless, blood spurting from the head wound.

Dropping the wrench, Matthew patted Wilkes down, looking for a gun, but found none. A scream—Jennifer's—from the forward cabin sent him running down the hallway unarmed.

Fielding held a knife to Jennifer's neck as Angelique Mannington restrained her from behind. Jennifer had closed her eyes and ceased struggling.

For a moment, Matthew held back in the shadows. Fielding's knife was just inches from Jennifer's throat, while Matthew had an entire room to cross before he could get his hands on the bastard.

But when Fielding said, "Still not willing to cooperate? Well, then, let's see just what it takes to make you talk," Matthew dove into the room.

Angelique Mannington saw him first and let out a scream. The knife fell from Fielding's hands as Matthew wrestled him to the ground and began to unleash his fury on him. Blow after blow, Matthew pummeled Fielding's face and skull with his fist.

"Matthew, the knife!" Jennifer yelled from behind him. "She has the knife!"

Angelique Mannington had spotted the knife and picked it up. She lunged for Matthew, but thanks to Jennifer's warning, he managed to grab Angelique's wrist before she met her mark. With his free hand, he punched the scientist squarely in the face, smashing her nose and sending her flying back, on to the cabin's other bed.

He crossed the room to Jennifer.

"Are you alright?"

She nodded, keeping an eye on Fielding, who was still stirring on the ground.

He used the knife to cut the binding from Jennifer's wrists and ankles.

Jennifer climbed off the bed, stumbling a bit from having been bound so long.

"I need you to find something to tie them up with," Matthew ordered. "Rope, wire, cable. Anything. I'll keep an eye on them while you do."

She nodded, then disappeared down the corridor.

Only moments later Matthew felt the boat pitch, then heard a loud thud. Leaving both Fielding and Mannington semiconscious, he raced down the corridor. In the cockpit, Jennifer and Jim Wilkes struggled against the yacht's wheel. The boat had turned sharply starboard and dead ahead, through the window beyond, Matthew could see they'd entered the path of a supertanker bound for the Sound.

MATTHEW GRABBED WILKES from behind to disengage him from Jennifer, but Wilkes would not release his hold on her and together, the three of them tumbled backward. Wilkes had apparently decided that Jennifer was his best defense, for he clamped onto her, molding himself to her body in order to make it difficult for Matthew to throw a punch without risking hitting Jennifer. The supertanker had by now detected their presence and let out several loud warning blasts.

When Jennifer kneed Wilkes in the groin, he released his hold on her. She slithered out from under him and left the two men rolling around the cabin floor as she bolted for the yacht's helm. Alerted to the impending danger by the tanker's blasts, she began turning *Therapy* hard to port. With the larger vessel in *Therapy*'s lee and only fifty meters separating them, *Therapy* cleared the supertanker's path.

Matthew soon rendered Wilkes unconscious—if not dead. Leaving him on the cabin's floor, Matthew grabbed a coil of one-half-inch line stowed behind the steps and headed back to Fielding and Angelique Mannington.

The door to the cabin was now closed, with something propped up against it from the inside. On his second try, he succeeded in kicking it open, just in time to see Angelique Mannington disappearing through the cabin's window. He grabbed hold of a slender ankle, yanking her back inside.

"Let go of me, you bastard," Angelique screamed, flailing at him.

Matthew used the rope to hurriedly bind her to the bed, then he climbed through the window, which she and Fielding had apparently shattered with a chair that now lay on top of the bed. He could see the lights of the tanker receding into the night as it continued toward the Sound.

Where was Sherwood Fielding?

He circled the lower deck, pausing to look in the cabin window to be certain Fielding hadn't reentered the cabin. Jennifer stood where he'd left her, at the helm. He climbed to the flybridge. No sign of Fielding anywhere.

On his way back down to the aft deck, it occurred to him. The dinghy. He'd seen it earlier on the deck, just above the swim step. He returned there now and confirmed his suspicions. It was gone.

They were still almost a mile from shore. He scanned the water, but clouds now blotted out the moon, lowering visibility. He circled the deck again, this time at a run, his eyes still trained on the strait's black expanse. Running back down the steps and into the cabin, he began opening cabinets, looking for binoculars.

"What is it?" Jennifer asked when she saw him.

"Fielding. He's gone."

"Oh God. The dinghy?"

"Yeah."

On the flybridge, Matthew used the binoculars he'd found in a cabinet to scan the horizon, 360 degrees. Nothing. No dinghy in sight. Could Fielding have been sucked under the supertanker? He would not have had a chance if he'd put the dinghy in too close to a moving vessel that size.

Or had Fielding managed to escape? Was he out there somewhere, drifting seaward in the blackness of the night? Or headed toward shore?

Matthew instructed Jennifer to turn *Therapy* toward shore. As they cruised at just five knots, both he and Jennifer studied the water's surface. When they were within fifty yards of land, they doubled back and again, coasted, searching for Fielding and the dinghy.

Nothing. No sign of him anywhere. And no sign of debris from a collision with the supertanker.

Jennifer zigzagged away from shore, then back, two more times. Finally, they headed back toward Seattle. Before entering Elliott Bay, Matthew nodded at Wilkes on the floor.

"Guess I better take care of him."

Jennifer's eyes locked with his.

"Let me."

Matthew took over the wheel and watched as she wrapped Wilkes' wrists, then ankles, and pulled the rope binding them together as tight as her strength, fueled by fury, allowed. Matthew couldn't help but think that the woman he watched, her usually lovely face crusted with blood, bore little resemblance to the woman he'd stood next to in Larry's lunch line.

Matthew steered them toward Pier 77. Just as Wilkes and Angelique Mannington had done earlier, he dropped anchor offshore. Then, with Jennifer's help, he lowered the rubber Zodiak from the flybridge into the water and climbed into it. Jennifer followed.

They motored over to the pier lined with tugs. Matthew tied the Zodiak to the first tug and helped Jennifer climb onto and cross it to reach the pier. Once on shore, they headed toward the beach where he'd left his clothes.

As he dressed, Jennifer dipped her hand into the water and washed the blood from her face and neck.

Then, looking like they'd just come from a playful tryst on the beach, they stepped out on to Elliott Avenue and hailed a passing cab.

TWENTY-ONE

BACK AT HIS APARTMENT, the first thing Matthew did was open a bottle of Wild Turkey. Then, he led Jennifer to the dining room table and placed a shot glass in front of her.

"Sit."

She lowered herself into the chair, but Matthew remained standing, pacing first one way, then the other across the table from where she sat. He stopped, turned, and, placing his hands on the table's edge, leaned toward her.

"I have news that will shock you."

Jennifer, whose eyes had not left Matthew since he took her into the dining room, let out a short, sarcastic laugh.

"Nothing can shock me anymore."

"Don't be so sure."

He walked around the table then, and pulled out the chair nearest hers. Seating himself, he turned to her and leveled his gaze at hers.

"Your friend, Patricia Lukins. Describe her to me."

"Short brown hair, five-six, a little on the stocky side."

"Dress like a man?"

"How did you know?"

"Because I found her tonight. When you didn't show up, I went out to Preston to look for you. Chandra and the guard were dead, their throats slit. And Angel was gone."

Jennifer had pressed a hand to her chest.

"Patricia?" she said, her voice high and squeaky.

"She's dead."

"No. No . . ." Jennifer's eyes were wide with horror as she backed into her chair. "She can't be. I told her not to go there, to wait. I told her we had a plan."

Tears rolled down her face, pooling briefly along her jaw before dropping to her blouse.

"Why couldn't she have waited?" she cried. "Why?"

"I don't know," Matthew answered.

How could he tell her the rest?

"Wait a minute," Jennifer said suddenly, struggling for answers, "it must have been *Patricia*. That they cloned. She was so upset when I told her what we'd seen out there, when she realized what they were doing. Maybe that's because she knew they'd used her cells; that she was the . . ."

"Patricia isn't the donor," Matthew said somberly, cutting her off.

"You're wrong," Jennifer said. "It all makes sense now. Don't you see? She told me they were taking her blood, that she'd refused to give them any more. She must have gone out there to stop them."

Matthew reached across the table and grabbed her wrist.

"I got the files today," he said. "I've read them, everything in them. They contain everything—the protocol, research leading up to it, all the data on Angel . . ."

"And the donor?"

Matthew's eyes shifted away, momentarily.

"Yes. They identify the donor."

He brought them back to her face.

"And it's not Patricia?" her voice rose in disbelief.

Her eyes searched his with such complete and shocking innocence, such genuine grief and anger for her friend, that his next words came near to choking him.

"It's you. *You* are the donor."

Jennifer's gasp was unlike any other sound he had ever heard—raw in its emotion, the sheer repulsion and horror of it.

"No," she said, standing, then backing away from him, as if he were somehow responsible. "No."

He stood, but she held out her hand to stop him.

"No. Leave me alone. Just leave me alone."

She turned and fled. He heard the bathroom door close and lock. He went and stood outside. Inside, he could hear her retching. Matthew lowered himself to the hallway floor, waiting.

Eventually, the entire apartment grew silent, then finally, the door opened.

"Give me a gun," she said.

•   •   •

MATTHEW HAD ACCOMPANIED HER, and though she'd feigned indifference about it, secretly Jennifer felt relieved to have him along. But with or without him, nothing would have stopped her now.

"You're out of your mind," he'd said when she told him her plan.

"No. I'm the one person in this whole perverted mess, maybe the only one, who's perfectly sane. Now, give me a gun."

"You're not going anywhere without me."

"Suit yourself."

After failing in his attempt to talk her out of it, he'd handed over one of his lightest revolvers and followed her outside.

"Planning to walk?"

Her car, after all, was still parked in the BioGentech garage. Without responding, she'd opened the passenger door to his Taurus and climbed inside.

Matthew parked across the street and watched, hidden by darkness, as Jennifer, hand in pocket, strode to the front door of the BioGentech building and pressed the buzzer. The same guard Matthew had spoken to earlier that evening appeared.

He yelled at Jennifer through the door.

"What do you want?"

"I left my car here, in the parking garage," she said. "My name's Jennifer Rockhill. I'm the company attorney. My garage door opener is in the glove box. Can you let me in to get my car?"

Jennifer knew she looked like hell from her ordeal on Sherwood Fielding's yacht. Matthew had also told her about his exchange with the guard earlier. She could use her appearance to her advantage.

"Please," she said through the glass. "My boyfriend beat me up. I have to have my car to get out of town. *Please.*"

The guard shook his head in disgust as he made the connection between her and his earlier visitor. She could see him muttering angrily under his breath as he pulled on the giant key ring, which was attached to his belt by a retractable wire, to raise the key and open the door for her.

"So you're the one," he said. "That son of a bitch came here earlier, looking for you."

He held the door open for her.

"Come on in," he said kindly. Then, after she'd passed inside, he turned his back to her to relock the door.

Jennifer had just the briefest pang of remorse before pulling the gun out of the pocket of her blazer.

"*Don't move.*"

The guard swiveled.

"What the hell . . . ?"

Matthew appeared instantly on the other side of the door. Holding the gun on the guard, Jennifer nodded in Matthew's direction.

"Unlock it."

Now the guard turned back toward the door.

"I'll be damned," he said upon seeing Matthew. He looked back to Jennifer. "You don't want to do this. It's him, isn't it? He's making you."

"Open the door," she said, lifting the revolver level with his forehead.

"Take it easy. Take it easy. Okay, I'll open it."

His fingers, trembling visibly, failed him as he tried to insert the key back into the hole. By now, on the other side of the door, Matthew had also drawn his gun, which he held close to his body to avoid being seen by passersby. It was almost dawn, though, and the streets were empty.

The guard finally succeeded in opening the door.

Once they were all inside and out of sight of the street, Jennifer said, "Fourth floor."

Leading, with the guard behind her and Matthew, his gun in the guard's back, bringing up the rear, Jennifer steered the trio onto the elevator.

At the entry to the fourth floor lab, she turned to their captive.

"Get us in."

Offering no resistance, the guard stepped in front of the security monitor and stared into the camera, enabling it to register his identity.

The small black screen mounted above the door handle flashed ENTRY APPROVED.

Once inside, Jennifer again led the way, turning on lights as they entered the lab. She crossed immediately to the room where the freezers were located. Matthew stood outside with the guard as she disappeared inside.

She donned the gloves and eye shield and opened the liquid nitrogen freezer. The thought had occurred to her that the vial she'd already stolen for Patricia could be the sole vial of the genetically engineered mouse cells. But common sense, and the sheer volume of vials in sight, told her that probably wasn't the case.

A strange sense of calm had descended upon her. Her focus on the task at hand was the only way to block out the hideous news Matthew had just delivered. It was difficult to see through the gaseous cloud enveloping her. She plunged into it, reaching down and waving at it to clear a glimpse inside, where she saw more than a dozen of the long boxes with rings attached to their tops. She methodically lifted one after another from the freezer, then walked over and placed it on a counter, where she pulled out the drawer labeled "H" and examined vial after vial, looking for the one that represented Patricia's brother's only chance of survival.

Three boxes and nearly a hundred vials later, she found it.

"HS-tk/pl/6/4."

She kept on and ended up with five vials marked with the HS label. She slid the drawer all the way out of the box and then, one by one, removed all the other vials, placing them gently but hurriedly on top of the boxes still in the freezer. One rolled off. Jennifer could hear it break as it hit the metal bottom of the tank. Had she just been exposed to some deadly virus? She dropped the gloves and headgear to the floor and exited the room, drawer in hand.

Outside, in the lab, she saw that Matthew had bound and gagged the guard. The telephone had also been ripped from its mounting on the wall and lay in the middle of the floor between two rows of laboratory counters.

"Let's get out of here," Matthew told her.

"Not yet," Jennifer replied.

On the elevator, she punched six. Gun drawn again, she led the way to the lunchroom. There she opened the refrigerator. Several Tupperware containers held partially consumed lunches. She dumped the contents of the largest one on the floor, then opened the freezer and filled the container half full with ice. She eased the tiny drawer containing the vials down into it and sealed the lid, then, reverting to her days as a wife and mother, raised a corner to release its air.

They made it back to the street without incident. In the car, as Matthew headed south on Eastlake, Jennifer balanced the box containing the vials on her lap.

"What do you expect to do with those now?" Matthew asked.

"Stop at that pay phone."

She got out and dialed the number given her by Patricia Lukins two days earlier.

A woman's voice, groggy with interrupted sleep, answered after just two rings.

"You don't know me," Jennifer said after introducing herself. "But I'm a friend of Patricia Lukins. We work together." She could not bring herself to use the past tense. "I have terrible news."

The line grew silent, weighted down by dread on both ends.

"Patricia is dead."

The other woman let out an anguished moan.

"How?"

"I don't know," Jennifer said. "But two days ago, Patricia gave me your telephone number. I think she had a premonition. She had asked me to help her get the cell lines for her brother. I have them, right now. But I need to get them to you immediately. I'm in danger myself. Can you meet me in the parking lot at Husky Stadium?"

"Of course. I'd do anything to help David. Patricia knew that."

"You might want to pick up some dry ice along the way."

TWENTY-TWO

IF FIELDING DOESN'T have her, who does?"

After they'd returned from their rendezvous with Patricia Lukins' friend, Matthew had retrieved the untouched Wild Turkey from the dining room and now, sitting in the living room, on either end of the couch, they both held full shot glasses.

Matthew threw back his before answering.

"There are a couple possibilities that I can see," he said. "Maybe Tupeni Sanday decided eighty million was a little on the high side. Just the other day Fielding told him things were going well, that he was ready to deliver the surrogate. Why pay if he doesn't have to? Maybe Tupeni sent his boys up here to get Angel, and the protocol, which, of course, they couldn't find cause we beat them to it."

Jennifer considered this possibility, which seemed to make some kind of sense—at least in the frame of reference of this new world she'd now entered.

"You said you had a couple different ideas."

"I do," he answered, then paused. "But the other one doesn't really add up." Again he grew silent, working through the situation in his mind. "Someone—someone good, a professional—has been following me for weeks now. I've assumed it's CIA. That, just as WTI did, they got wind of something happening at BioGentech and that they also learned I was in town."

"Why would the CIA be involved?"

"That's what they do now. Economic espionage is one of their primary focuses these days. They know what I do and have been trying to catch me at it for years now."

"You're sure of that?"

"Oh yes, I'm sure. This isn't the first time I've had them on my ass. I know when they're out there. And I still have a contact within the agency who has warned me in the past when they were getting a little too close for comfort."

"But your contact didn't warn you this time?"

Matthew shook his head.

"Not this time."

They both grew silent. Jennifer sipped sparingly at her whiskey. She needed to keep a clear head.

"But why would they take Angel?" she said. "If it's you they're after, why wouldn't they just wait and get you?"

"That's a good point, and it's one of the reasons this scenario—the CIA taking Angel—doesn't add up."

"One of the reasons?"

"The other is the way they did it. Killing both the guard and Chandra. That doesn't carry the print of the CIA. Not unless they put some rogue agent on this. But even then, what I saw out at Preston was pretty extreme." He paused. "Unless . . ."

"Unless what?"

"Unless they're planning to frame me for the murders. I could see that happening. There are a couple old-timers there who would do just about anything to get me."

She studied him.

"Why?"

"That's a long story" was all Matthew said.

"A long story?" Jennifer parroted, feeling, quite suddenly, the onset of a loss of composure. "Another long story? How many long stories do you have? Is that all this is about? You and your fucked-up life?"

Matthew was quick to level his steely gaze at her.

"I had nothing to do with Fielding choosing you as the donor. You understand that, don't you? Yes, I came along, and my presence here might have complicated things for you, but with or without me, that ape would still be carrying your clone."

He was right. Fielding certainly hadn't chosen her because of her relationship with Matthew. In fact, her physical exam, the pap smear and blood samples taken by Dr. Cannon—while slumped on the floor in Matthew's bathroom she'd realized that had to be how they got hold of her cells—had taken place before she'd even met Matthew. Actually, the very day. If Fielding had known anything about Matthew, he wouldn't have touched Jennifer with a ten-foot pole.

She could blame Matthew for many things, but not for that. Not for the one fact whose existence she truly could not bear to acknowledge. That somewhere a female baboon—Angel, she even knew her name, knew exactly what she looked like—was out there, in hostile hands, carrying Jennifer's identical twin.

"You're right. But without you, maybe I would never have found out," she said.

"That's what you wish? That you knew nothing about Angel? That you could just live in blissful ignorance of the fact that she's out there somewhere, carrying your genetic duplicate?"

"I don't know what I wish," she answered. "Besides, what's the point? That's not how it is. How it is is I *do* know. And now she's gone, and we have to figure out what to do about it."

"What do you *want* to do about it? If we're able to find Angel, what then? Have you thought about that?"

Jennifer dropped her face into her hands. "I can't stand to. I can't stand the thought, that that baboon is carrying my, my . . ."

"Clone."

"Yes, my clone. *Me.* She's, in effect, carrying me. You might as well say it. It's so hideous, so nightmarish. The very thought of it being born, of living the rest of my life knowing that somewhere out there, a child will be growing up who looks identical to me, who . . ."

Matthew's eyes bore down upon her.

"Are you saying you want to destroy it? Destroy Angel and the fetus?"

Jennifer did not avoid his eyes when she answered.

"Wouldn't you?" Her gaze was dulled with shock, and pain. "Maybe it's best like this. Not knowing. Maybe she won't make it. Maybe they've already killed Angel and this whole nightmare is already over. Maybe you should just take what you have—it's all they wanted you to get, isn't it, the protocol, the files?—and go home. Go to WTI. You'll be a hero."

"I could do that," Matthew answered. "But just how will you feel a year from now. Two years from now. Ten? Do you honestly think you can ignore the possibility that she's out there somewhere? Do you honestly think you'll not care—not even worry for her—just a bit? Wonder whether or not she's well cared for, safe? Healthy? Is that what you really want?"

There was a long, drawn out silence between them.

"No." Jennifer's voice was weak.

Matthew would not let up. "And what about what brought you here in the first place? Are you willing to walk away from that?"

She might have some ambivalence about Angel, but not about this subject. Nothing would stop her from bringing Fielding to justice for what he had done to Charlie. And now Patricia. If her determination was passionate before, now it was obsessive. Fielding's organ-selling operation was just the tip of the iceberg. They had enough evidence about the cloning to bring him down, but she still had nothing to prove her theory about Charlie.

"Of course not." Matthew was right, she had to pull herself together. "So what do we do?"

"We find her," Matthew answered. "Before Fielding gets his hands on her again and either delivers her to Niupalu or destroys her."

"How do we go about doing that, finding her?"

Matthew was silent for a moment, then he answered.

"It may not be as hard as you think."

THE PLANE WAS SCHEDULED to depart at 12:15. It was a non-stop flight, to Phoenix. They'd registered in their true names, using Matthew's American Express card to pay for their tickets. Over Matthew's protests, Jennifer had insisted on going to her apartment that morning. She knew it was unlikely she would ever return to Seattle and she was not about to leave pictures of Stacey and Charlie, as well as other keepsakes of them, behind. Jennifer could sense Matthew's impatience as he watched her race through the apartment, throwing things into a duffle bag.

"Pack light," he'd said. "You won't need much in the way of clothes."

That was an understatement. They were headed to the desert in the middle of the summer. At the airport Matthew bought a *Seattle Times* that listed Phoenix's temperature the day before at 120 degrees.

When Matthew was using the rest room, Jennifer had picked up the *Times* and scanned its front page. A single column was headlined "Local Company Searches for Missing Employee." The article detailed the mysterious disappearance of the Double S Courier Service employee.

The moment he emerged, Jennifer had lashed out at him.

"You promised he wouldn't get hurt," she'd fumed, thrusting the newspaper in his face.

Matthew had taken it and calmly read the article.

"They've probably found him by now," he said when he was through.

"*Found* him? You mean his body?"

"No, not his body. *Him.* I had to lock him in the trunk of a rental car. By now, someone's found him. Aside from being a little stiff, he'll be fine. Maybe even something of a hero."

She'd decided to let it be. But when she excused herself to use the rest room before boarding, she went instead to a pay phone and placed a call to Double S.

"The missing courier is in the trunk of a rental car," she said hurriedly. "Near the BioGentech lab in Preston."

She hung up and returned to Matthew just as they were beginning to board.

Despite the resistance she'd put up, she was actually relieved to be leaving Seattle. Maybe some distance would make it all seem less real.

Going to Phoenix had been Matthew's idea. During their discussion about how to find Angel, he had proposed it.

"The only way we'll find Angel is by first finding her abductor," Matthew had said. "But I have a feeling that won't be too hard. In fact, the more I think about it, the more certain I am. All we have to do is be patient."

"Patient?" Jennifer had asked.

"Yes. Angel has no value to anyone without the protocol. And without you. She's just a pregnant ape. Even if she delivers a healthy human baby, there's no way anyone can duplicate that without the protocol. And without you, there's no way to prove the baby is even a clone."

Every time they discussed this subject, Jennifer felt sickened.

"There's no need for us to go looking for Angel's abductors," he'd continued. "They'll find *us*. We'll go to Phoenix, wait for them to follow."

"But we can't leave Seattle," she'd argued. "We have to get Sherwood Fielding first. You promised. We can't let him get away with what he did to Charlie."

"Jennifer, Sherwood Fielding is long gone by now. Believe me. Once he realized who you were, once he escaped from his yacht, do you think he'd actually stick around for you to bring the authorities down on him again?"

"You promised," she'd found herself sobbing suddenly. "You said you'd help me get him."

Once the floodgates had opened, she was helpless to stop.

Afterward, she couldn't remember at what point Matthew had reached for her, but she knew that she sat there in his arms, weeping unconsolably, for a long while.

"We'll get Sherwood Fielding," Matthew promised. "But we can do it from Phoenix. In fact, we're closer to all of it there. Listen to me, once we get there, we'll find Dr. Treecedale."

Jennifer had drawn away from him to get a good look at him.

"Fielding mentioned Treecedale," she said. "On the boat. He blamed him for what happened."

"I heard. We'll find him. Find Treecedale. Maybe he can help us piece this together. Or maybe Fielding won't be willing to give up his deal with Tupeni Sanday and he'll come after us. But either way, staying in Seattle does us no good. In Phoenix I have the advantage. They won't be able to take me by surprise. Not there. Here, everyone's a stranger to me. There, I can pick out a strange face."

"But what if they don't follow? What if they can't find us?"

"Oh, they'll find us. Don't worry about that."

A BLAST OF COOL air met them when they stepped into the house. Nan had been looking after it in his absence and she always had the tendency to overdo things, including, it appeared, air-conditioning. Of course, the midafternoon heat was so brutal that the muggy taxi they'd stepped in to at the airport had even seemed invigorating.

He led Jennifer directly upstairs, where he opened double french doors to the master bedroom.

"You'll stay here."

"But isn't this your room?" she asked, looking around at the spacious room, with its adjoining bath and jacuzzi.

"No," he said. She probably thought he was angling to sleep with her. "I sleep in the next room. I like the view better."

She seemed to accept his answer, and after he placed her bags on the bed, she began unpacking. As she lifted a stack of clothing from her suitcase, Matthew caught the glint of a gun barrel peeking out from under a sweatshirt. On the way to the airport in Seattle, he'd asked her about the gun he'd given her to break into the BioGentech lab.

"I think I should keep it," she'd said.

He'd decided she was right.

He left her there, closing the doors behind him, as he took off to prowl first the house, which seemed in order, then, stepping outside into blazing heat, the grounds.

Furnace-like waves of air radiating off the cement patio assaulted him as he stepped out the back door. Every other house in the desert had foliage placed strategically in front of windows and patios to help block out the white-hot rays of the desert midday. But not Matthew's. Trees and shrubs provided not only shade, but, more importantly, cover. He did not want one thing, living or otherwise, to obstruct his view from the house to Lookout Mountain and the strip of desert flanking it. Nor to provide concealment for uninvited visitors.

He looked up at the mountain. It had always amazed him how small and totally void of even a hint of color it could appear at times, like now; while at others (this evening was sure to be one) it would loom, brilliant as an artist's acid-induced trip on canvas, deep clay orange, and massive—a formidable armed sentry standing guard over what was once a wasteland, but had now become a haven for the moneyed, and almost moneyed.

In his quest for privacy, Matthew did not even have his swimming pool maintained by a pool company. He'd just dipped his hand into its waters, which were almost two feet low—finding it tepid, and the quality more than a little suspect—when he heard a car pull up out front. The slow flop, flop of thong-type sandals turned his attention to the gate at the side of the house. A scarfed head soon appeared. He recognized it to be Nan.

Busy fumbling with the lock, she had not even looked up.

He approached the gate from the other side, silent, then said quietly, so as not to startle her, "Hello there."

Nan's head jerked up. She looked little more than a skeleton—her nose and cheekbones considerably more prominent than the last time he'd seen her—and the sight of her, her floral scarf hiding her bare head, pierced him.

"Matthew!" she squealed, her efforts to unlock the gate growing frantic in her desire to get to him.

Matthew pushed down on the latch, opening the gate from the inside. She rushed through and they embraced. She felt noticeably smaller, more frail than he remembered, and he held her tight for as long as he could to prevent her seeing the shock on his face.

"When did you get home?" she finally asked, pulling back.

"Just a little while ago," he said. He saw then that Nan's eyes had been drawn to something behind him.

He turned. There stood Jennifer.

"I'm sorry," Jennifer said, turning to go. "I didn't realize you had company."

"No," Matthew said. "Stay. Please. This is my sister, Nan."

Jennifer approached hesitantly, extending her hand.

"Nice to meet you," she said. "I'm Jennifer."

Nan looked from Jennifer to Matthew and back, and broke into a smile.

"Hi, Jennifer. Nice to meet *you*."

No one said anything for an awkward moment.

"I was just coming over to check on the pool," Nan explained.

Matthew looked at her disapprovingly.

"I told you I didn't want you bothering with the pool," he chided. "I just asked you to look in from time to time. Make sure the place hadn't burned down. I didn't want you out here in the sun."

They'd begun walking toward the backyard now.

"Obviously, I haven't done much with it," Nan laughed, nodding at its murky water. "But I knew it needed a good cleaning and some chemicals. And since you're so stubborn about hiring someone to get it done," she looked at Jennifer and added the aside, "As if he couldn't afford it," then back to Matthew, "I thought I'd better come take a look. And you know, for some reason, I half suspected you'd be showing up one of these days."

Despite her obviously worsened health, Nan seemed inordinately happy to see her brother.

"But since you're home now, I'll run along and leave the work to you. I have groceries to pick up on my way home."

"No way," he said, grabbing her elbow. "You'll stay and have a drink with us."

Nan looked to Jennifer.

"Yes," Jennifer said, smiling. "Please. Stay."

They started out inside, sitting on stools at the kitchen counter, sipping margaritas. Jennifer and Nan seemed to hit it off immediately, taking the pressure off Matthew, who had no patience for the small talk such a situation called for, but who very much wanted his sister to stick around. Around six o'clock, he left the two women alone together while he went to pick up a pizza and some groceries.

He returned and at sunset, they moved out on to the patio. This was Matthew's favorite time of day.

"Listen you two," he said, "would you mind if I got a little run in?"

"Go ahead," both women urged.

Matthew went to his bedroom and changed into running gear. Then he took off.

His outing had dual purposes. He was sprung tight and needed the release that exercise always provided. But in light of the new situation, he also wanted to reassess the house's security and he was grateful for Nan's presence so that he would not have to leave Jennifer alone. He started down the street, then soon cut between two of his neighbors' matching pink stucco homes, on an easement that was routinely used to access the mountain trails.

Already feeling the relief of the approaching desert night, as he started up Look Out Mountain's rock-strewn trails Matthew broke into a slow jog and realized that, at that moment at least, he was pleased to be home.

Seattle was okay, especially in the summer, but he'd never seen sunsets to rival these. This one looked especially promising—the mountains to the north black now against a sky the color of smoldering embers, while the peaks most distant and to the west, a light charcoal against butter yellow. In between, the sprawl that had become Phoenix, its few sky-scrapers catching, then throwing back the last rays of the sinking sun.

A kestrel flew low overhead, landing a short distance away at its nest in an arm of one of many saguaro cactuses populating the mountain's slopes. Matthew had seen everything from rattlesnakes to quail to mule deer along this trail. Every night from his bed he could hear the coyotes' plaintive cries. Anyone who thought the desert barren of life was out of touch with reality. Nine months of the year, Matthew almost envied the wild creatures their existence. These three, he did not. But despite the unbearable days, the evenings were almost routinely pleasurable—the air, especially in contrast to that of Seattle, having a smoothness to it that was almost palpable.

He turned around about three fourths of the way up. He wanted it to be dark by the time he got back down but did not want to stay on the mountain so long that he risked twisting his already injured ankle or stray-ing off-trail into a jump-happy choya in the dark. When he reached the bottom, he cut away from the well-worn path, heading directly west along the swath of desert along which backed his and his neighbors' homes. When he found himself opposite the back of his house, he stopped. He could hear the scurrying of some small creature, most likely a jackrabbit made nervous by his presence. Coyotes had begun to call to one another in short, staccato yips.

The only barrier between his house and where he now stood was a black wrought-iron fence, which by tomorrow would be equipped with a surface stress sensor. As a backup, he would also bury an area intrusion detector that would provide warning if someone came within fifteen feet of the fence. That, he thought as he stood watching Jennifer and Nan—who had moved back inside and now sat in plain view in the living room—was really about the best that he could do.

As he stood observing, thinking, he decided that he would not even bother putting up curtains to hide the fact of his and Jennifer's presence. After all, they were here to set a trap.

And Jennifer was the bait.

TWENTY-THREE

S HERWOOD FIELDING WAITED for the sun to break through the morning mist each day before taking his coffee out to the veranda. The afternoon would bring eighty-degree weather and warm, penetrating rays to deepen his already near-perfect tan. But mornings could be downright chilly.

He had to admit. His self-imposed exile hadn't been entirely unpleasant. Thank God he'd had the presence of mind to withdraw a large sum of cash from the bank—an account his wife knew nothing of—before leaving Seattle. But his stay at La Brescia had been costly. By the time he figured room service in, the ocean-side European-style hostel located in Del Mar, playground of the very rich, cost him upward of seven hundred dollars a day. But he had no regrets as he sat watching the Pacific hurl its powerful waves against the rocky shoreline below.

In fact, the time he'd spent there had served him well. It had allowed him to think about his situation. A situation that at first seemed hopeless, but now, now he had an idea. A brilliant idea.

It was time to go home.

As the last of the coastal haze gave way to another idyllic morning, he carried the telephone outside with him and placed it on the wrought-iron table next to his favorite chaise lounge.

He worried briefly that he wouldn't get an answer, but Jim Wilkes picked up on the first ring.

"Hello?" His voice held a note of disbelief. No one but Fielding had this number.

"It's me."

"Where the fuck are you? We thought you'd drowned."

Fielding chuckled.

"Hardly. Decided I'd better get out of town for a while. What's happening there?"

"What's happening is we've been trying to keep the company from crashing down around us at the same time I've been trying to keep the authorities off my back."

"What do they know? The authorities?"

"Not much. After they found me and Angelique tied up on *Therapy*, they spent two days combing the waters for you. Called the Coast Guard in. Then a couple kids finally found the dinghy, upside down, ten miles outside Port Townsend. They've decided you drowned."

"What about Preston? What do they know about that?"

"Only that someone killed Chandra and the guard. They don't know why. I cleaned up any sign of what we were doing out there before I called them to report the murders. If you were alive, why the hell have you waited so long to call? I could've used some help these past few days. At least some advice about how to handle things."

"What about Patricia Lukins?" Fielding said, ignoring his question.

"So far she's just been reported missing. They think her disappearance might be connected to the murders, but until they find her—which is not gonna' happen—they won't know."

"Tell me what you told them about Preston. How did you explain it?"

"Just that it's a vivarium to house the baboons we use in research. That we've kept its location secret to avoid animal-rights nuts finding it. The police's latest theory is that someone knew BioGentech had a facility like this, but not where. They followed the courier to Preston, then, for whatever reason, killed Chandra and the guard. The courier gave them a description of the guy who stole the van. Fits Jennifer Rockhill's friend. The police think whoever killed Chandra also kidnapped us while we were boating. That's where their theories end."

"Any publicity?"

"Some. A double murder doesn't go unreported. But the papers are as clueless about a motive as the police."

"That's perfect."

"What do you mean it's perfect?"

Wilkes sounded as though he thought Fielding had lost his mind.

Fielding took a slow sip of the vanilla latte he'd ordered with his breakfast, then continued.

"I want you to call that reporter from the *Seattle Times*. The one who did that article a couple years ago when we were getting started. Give him this number." Fielding recited the number of his pager. "Swear him to absolute secrecy until he's talked to me."

"Would you care to explain?"

"Of course. What's been our biggest problem at BioGentech?"

"I'd say three bodies ranks right up there."

"No. I mean before. Before all this happened. What's been the thing that's held us back the most?"

"Money."

"Exactly. Money. If we had enough money, our problems would all be solved. None of this would ever have happened. And how do you go about getting that. Money?"

"What is this? A fucking quiz show?"

"Just answer me," Fielding said. He was enjoying himself. "How do you raise money for a company like BioGentech?"

Wilkes let out a weary sigh.

"Investors. Joint ventures." He paused, apparently giving the question some thought. "Public offerings."

"*Exactly.*"

"You're out of your mind. A stock offering? Now?"

"That's right. I've had a lot of time to think. And one thing I've realized is that I'm not ready to give up. I worked hard to build something there in Seattle, at BioGentech. I'm not going to let that bitch take it from me. She ran me out of Palm Springs. It's not going to happen again. So once I came to that conclusion it meant I had to solve a couple problems.

"The first is money. Now that the deal with Tupeni Sanday's been lost, I had to come up with something else. I spent days thinking, plotting how I could find another buyer for Chandra's technology. But that wouldn't be easy, especially without the protocol. Then it came to me. I had to go back to the basics. A stock offering."

"Who's going to buy stock in a company whose CEO has disappeared and whose employees keep turning up murdered?"

"That's the beauty of it all. I'm coming back. To Seattle. We're going to use the media. Turn what's happened into a cash cow."

Fielding glanced to either side. Only four suites at La Brescia faced the ocean. The verandas on either side of him were empty. At the last suite, a lissome blonde had just walked outside in a thong bikini. She waved at him, as she had each day. He nodded in her direction, and, lowering his voice, continued.

"I'll talk to the press. Tell them I've been in hiding because I believe my life is in danger. Blame it all on economic espionage. I'll let it be known that we've been working on some very promising therapies, so promising that we believe our competitors may have sent spies to Seattle to uncover our secrets. They'll draw the conclusions. That the secrets are so valuable people are willing to kill for them. Just a hint of that in the papers and by the time we make the offering, BioGentech stock will have been driven through the roof."

Wilkes paused.

"You know. You might having something."

"Of course I do."

"What technology will you tell reporters our competitors are after?"

"We won't have to disclose that, make it public. After all, that's proprietary. We'll just keep feeding them tidbits about how promising our results have been. So promising that the heavy hitters—especially foreign pharmaceutical giants—are feeling very threatened by it. At most, we'll have to share our technology with the authorities. Needless to say, if any evidence of Chandra's work still exists, I want you to destroy it.

"The truth is, we do have some extremely promising therapies in the works. With the money we'll make in a stock offering, we'll be able to finance the clinical trials and the development we need to get them to market. It will work. I'm convinced of it. If we're smart about it, we can solve all our problems at once. Get the authorities off our backs by giving them a focus for their investigation—which, of course, will lead nowhere. And fund BioGentech indefinitely. As far as I can see, there are only two problems. And I'm counting on you to take care of them."

"What's that?"

"I can't let my past catch up with me. Once I return and play this thing up for the press, we can't risk any complications, any bad publicity before the offering." Fielding's eyes strayed to the woman on the other veranda. She'd rolled onto her stomach, revealing a nicely rounded rear end. "There are only two people who stand to make trouble for me. Treecedale and Jennifer Rockhill. I want you to find them and get rid of them. Once and for all."

He wondered whether the sunbather was watching him watch her. She faced his direction, but dark glasses hid her eyes.

"Treecedale's easy," Wilkes said. "We've known where he is for a long time. But Jennifer Rockhill, that's another story. That may take some time."

"I don't *have* time," Fielding said, his fine mood souring at Wilkes' resistance. "I want to come home. I want my life back. *Find them.*"

"You're really something, you know that? Calling all the shots. What am I? A fucking hitman? You think I get off on killing people?"

Sherwood Fielding turned away from the woman and sunk deeper into the chaise lounge, bringing the phone's mouthpiece in contact with his lips.

"I think," he said, exaggerating every word, "that you're in this so deep that you know there's no way out. I think you want to salvage things as much as I do. Because you know you'll be compensated nicely if we do. And the alternative—if we don't shut Rockhill up—could be time in prison."

Wilkes did not respond right away. Fielding let his words hang there.

"I'll get right on it," Wilkes finally mumbled.

"Good. Give that reporter my pager number. I'm laying low until you call me back to tell me you've done your job."

He was about to hang up when something occurred to him.

"By the way, you haven't told me what you did with Patricia Lukins. I assume you got rid of the body."

"Actually, I thought you might want me to keep it. I moved it somewhere safe. It's still frozen."

Fielding couldn't help but chuckle. He had to give Wilkes credit. He really was good at what he did.

TWENTY-FOUR

ASIDE FROM THE HEAT, she was holding up well. Despite Matthew's seeming indifference to his own home, Jennifer found it lovely. She had never spent time in Phoenix before, but she'd always loved the desert. And though their outings now were pretty much limited to trips to the grocery stores, from what she had seen so far she'd concluded it would be a nice place to live were it not for the fact that merely stepping out of the car and walking the ten or twenty yards to the store's entrance was like stepping into an oven.

Her relationship with Matthew had settled into a comfortable routine. Though she had yet to let on as much to him, slowly, she was beginning to accept his past, the way he earned his living. Maybe it was the fact that they were faced with atrocities of such incomprehensible magnitude that his sins had, in her eyes, shrunk by comparison. Or maybe it was the fact that he'd saved her life and seemed now, for some reason, willing to risk his own in order to see this through with her.

Or maybe it was how he was with Nan.

Nan was, without question, the highlight of the week Jennifer had spent in the desert. Jennifer had known the young woman was dying the moment she laid eyes on her. Even if she had not, Matthew's expressions, which Jennifer caught time and again when the three of them were together, would have told her as much. And perhaps because of that tragedy, perhaps because both women either had or were about to deal with that most painful of life's twists—death's separation of mother from child—they'd developed an immediate kinship, a bond that was one of the closest Jennifer had ever experienced. Nan had become a daily visitor, leaving always before dinner to be with her sons when they arrived home from summer school and work.

After she'd left that afternoon, Matthew had turned to Jennifer and asked: "Is it my imagination, or does she seem to have put on a little weight since we got here?"

The hope that she saw in his eyes had touched Jennifer. She suddenly found herself fighting back unexpected tears.

"She does seem to have better color, doesn't she?"

They were planning to go to Palm Springs the next morning. Jennifer had not badgered him about it. She had come to trust that Matthew was a man of his word and that, when he felt the time right, he would carry through with his promise to find Dr. Treecedale. Maybe he sensed she needed the reprieve that the past few days had given her. Away from Seattle, from the grisly events of the past weeks, Jennifer almost felt human again. In fact, the company of both Nan and Matthew—though the actual conversation that went on between Matthew and her in one day could be condensed into the duration of a seventh-inning stretch of one of the many ballgames she'd been subjected to since coming to Phoenix—had given her more normalcy than she'd experienced in years, ever since Charlie and Stacey's deaths.

Perhaps Matthew knew that she needed this time to recuperate, to regain her spiritual and physical strength, before she reentered the world of Sherwood Fielding.

MATTHEW WAS ALWAYS UP before her. This morning she awoke to her alarm, which she'd set the night before for five-thirty. In the kitchen, she found him already drinking his coffee and reading the sports page.

"We need to be on the road in fifteen minutes" was his only greeting.

"No problem."

The drive to Palm Springs took less than three hours. At any other time, the sunrise they experienced would have enchanted Jennifer, but today there was a rock sitting dead center in her gut and she did not even notice the soft pastels the rising sun had painted across the barren landscape and cloudless sky.

All she knew about their trip this day was that Matthew had located Dr. Treecedale. He didn't say how, though she suspected it was through a friend of his at the CIA. That—his past with the CIA—she now knew to be a sore point with Matthew, one she avoided questioning him about. The old Jennifer would have wanted answers to everything, would have pressed for reassurance that their actions were reasonable and justified. But she was no longer that person. This Jennifer knew things were not cast in black or white, that right and wrong were now relative, and that success—and ultimately survival—dictated a new, looser set of rules.

A set of rules, she realized—and the irony of this was not lost on her—more in line with those by which Matthew lived and worked.

"Where are we going?"

It was the first time either of them had broken the silence since they'd stopped for Jennifer to use a rest room at a gas station in Blythe, but Matthew had just surprised her by breezing past all of the freeway exits marked "Palm Springs."

"Just a little further," he'd answered. A short while later, he took the Highway 62 exit, and headed north. In twenty minutes, just past Yucca Valley, Matthew turned off again. The road was a dusty, narrow two-laner now. The first intersection they came to was preceded by a weathered sign saying "Viejo." Matthew slowed, then turned west, following the sign's arrow.

Viejo. Old. The town they soon came upon had been aptly named. It was little more than half a dozen cinder-block buildings—a bar, general store, gas station, a post office—stuck in the middle of some of the bleakest landscape Jennifer had ever seen.

Matthew pulled in to the gas station and, with the sun now beating relentlessly overhead, left his Jeep running with the air conditioner on while he went inside. Jennifer could see him talking to a man just inside the door, who never bothered getting up from where he was seated. It was amazing, she thought, that they actually had a gas station in a place like this. She found herself wondering how often he had customers, whether he just sat there like that all day. She watched as the man gestured, pointing up the road.

"What was that all about?" she asked when Matthew returned.

"Directions" was all Matthew answered.

"I thought you already knew where Dr. Treecedale lived."

"They don't exactly have addresses out here. All I know is that he lives outside the town of Viejo."

Great. Jennifer had been confident that when Matthew said he'd found Dr. Treecedale, he'd actually found Dr. Treecedale. This sounded like a wild-goose chase.

"Did he know? Does he even know who Dr. Treecedale is?"

"He said a gringo drives by here once in a while, in a big expensive car, but he never stops in town. He thinks he lives up ahead, in those hills." Matthew pointed north and west.

"That's it?" Jennifer could hear her voice rising. She told herself to stay calm, if for no other reason than to avoid antagonizing Matthew.

Matthew glanced sideways at her.

"No, that's not it. He told me to try turning at the big saguaro."

"You've got to be kidding."

The giant cactuses dotted the landscape every direction she looked.

Jennifer could feel her spirits take a nosedive. They continued down a road that, were another car to come in the other direction, would now force one of them off to the side, passing several offshoots along their way.

"*There*," Jennifer said, "that road has a saguaro right next to it."

"It's no bigger than the rest," Matthew answered, passing the turnoff.

They'd gone several miles, climbing steadily, when they crested a hill and both spontaneously said, *"There it is."*

It was a huge, magnificent specimen, over a century old, sporting at least a dozen L-shaped arms, most of which had in turn produced a new generation of offshoots.

Immediately past the giant cactus, there was a gravel road, at the mouth of which they saw an unmarked mailbox. Matthew stopped and opened it, but found only a candy wrapper inside.

Two-tenths of a mile down the new road, the Jeep crested another hill and they were met by another startling sight. The blanched, colorless midday desert all around suddenly gave way to lush greenery—grass, flowers, palm trees. An oasis. A small oasis—no bigger, thought Jennifer, than her own yard in La Jolla—but in this context, the power of the display, after their having just driven through mile after mile of seeming nothingness, was considerable.

In the middle of the oasis sat an adobe structure, a house. The door to an attached garage stood wide open. Inside they could see a white Cadillac Seville.

At the house's front door, Matthew pressed the doorbell. Despite the absolute quiet that is characteristic of the midday desert, they did not hear the bell sound inside. When no one responded, Matthew tried to open the wrought-iron security door that barricaded them from the innermost, oak door, but its knob would not turn. He reached through its bars and rapped decisively on the wood. Again, there was no answer.

"Stay here," Matthew told Jennifer. Stepping off the front step, he crossed the grass to the garage.

Jennifer followed close behind.

Matthew shook his head, chagrined, when he looked back and saw her enter the garage right behind him, but he did not bother to object. He crossed the cement floor to the door leading to the house and tested the knob. It turned. Opening the door slowly, silently, they stepped into a laundry room. Inside, a TV blared from somewhere toward the back of the house.

"Shouldn't we call out to him?" Jennifer whispered.

"No," Matthew mouthed.

The flooring in the laundry room and hall consisted of oversized taupe-colored ceramic tiles that looked like they hadn't been swept in weeks. As they crept toward the sound, Jennifer could feel and hear the blood pulsing through her temples. Her feet felt heavy and slow, like when she wore ankle weights to work out. They passed a living room and dining room, both of which were empty. Ahead, beyond Matthew, who had pulled his gun from its shoulder belt and who periodically reached back to be certain she stayed within the zone of protection offered by his body, Jennifer saw that the hallway opened to a kitchen. Even before they reached it, she could see dirty dishes and pans stacked haphazardly on its counter.

A melodramatic soap opera theme song blasted from the TV on the counter. Dr. Treecedale sat at the far end of the kitchen table, facing the television. His head had fallen forward, so that his chin rested on his chest. His eyes were closed. It looked as though he'd been frozen in that position for some time.

"Dr. Treecedale!" Jennifer called out, rushing to him.

He lifted his head slowly. Recognition came instantly.

"Jennifer," he said, a weak smile cracking his leathery face.

Jennifer was shocked by the change in his appearance. It had been three years since she'd last seen him, but he had aged a dozen. She was surprised to see him unshaven. His hair—brown, streaked with gray when she last saw him, but now a shocking white—appeared not to have been combed in days. His clothes, however, as had always been true those five days back in Chihuilla, were spotless and still fit as though custom-made.

"I wondered if I'd ever see you again," he said softly. Then he turned his eyes questioningly to Matthew.

"Is anyone else here?" Matthew asked.

"No. I'm all alone now," Treecedale answered.

"I KNEW SOMEONE WOULD eventually find me. I just wasn't sure who it would be." Dr. Treecedale smiled again at Jennifer. "You, my dear, are a far nicer surprise than what I'd been expecting."

At Treecedale's insistence, they'd moved into the living room, which, though dusty, was a vast improvement over the cluttered kitchen. The three of them now sat around a coffee table.

"How did you know that?" Matthew asked. "That you'd have company?"

"Because of Helen's obituary."

"Helen?" Jennifer asked.

"My wife. She died three weeks ago. She passed away here, at home. I don't know how the paper learned about it. I had her cremated at a little funeral parlor in Yucca Valley. No service, no announcement. Still, her death somehow made its way into the *San Diego Star* obituaries. I saw it myself. Last Sunday's edition. I have the Sunday paper mailed here. So I knew it was just a matter of time before they started looking for me."

"They?"

"Fielding or Engles. Or Baldwin."

"Have you been hiding from them all this time?" Jennifer asked. "Ever since you left Chihuilla, after Charlie's death?"

"No. Not really. I didn't have reason to hide, not until Helen died. They knew they were safe until then. That I wouldn't turn on them while Helen was still alive, when she still needed me. They had that all figured out. I think they knew it from the start, from the very day I arrived at Chihuilla General. That Helen was my Achilles heel. The key to my cooperation."

Jennifer leaned forward, reaching across the table to touch the old man's bony knee.

"Tell us, Dr. Treecedale. Tell us what you mean."

Treecedale's eyebrows shot up, as though he were confused. For a moment, Jennifer wondered whether all his mental capabilities were still intact. Would he be able to help them? The way the house looked and his own appearance were so at odds with the Dr. Treecedale she'd come to know years ago. But once he began speaking, it became apparent she had nothing to worry about.

"It was when we were still living in San Diego that Helen was first diagnosed. Alzheimer's. There had just been a few signs back then, nothing too alarming. She'd always been a little on the forgetful side, so at first I didn't really think anything of it. But then one day she left to meet friends for lunch. That night she never returned home. The next day, twenty-four hours later, the police found her wandering around Del Mar. She couldn't tell them who she was. I'd of course called the police and within an hour, they'd matched Helen with the description I'd given them. A day or two later she was back to her old self, but I insisted on a battery of tests.

"When we learned the diagnosis, we decided to move away, somewhere quiet, where I could slow down some and spend more time with her. I accepted the job at Chihuilla General and hired a nurse to take care of Helen when I was gone. It was right about then, when I hired the nurse, that I made a promise to her. That I would never, ever put her in a home. I promised her that I would take care of her for the rest of her life.

"When I made that promise, I had no idea how costly it would end up becoming. Shortly after we moved to Chihuilla I discovered that Helen, who had always handled the family finances—quite competently, I might add—had made a number of bad financial decisions in the year before she was diagnosed. The stock we had, at one time worth almost two million dollars, had become virtually worthless. We were forced to live off my salary, which at a small-town hospital like Chihuilla General was not enough to cover the medical costs Helen was mounting.

"I've given this a lot of thought over the past couple years, and I've decided that that was when I made my biggest mistake. The turning point. When I went to Erland Baldwin and told him about my situation. He told me he'd try to think of a way to help. And then, about a month later, it happened for the first time."

"*What* happened?" It was Matthew speaking now.

"A patient of mine had just died from head injuries. They asked me to discuss organ donation with his family, which I did. The family was happy to give its consent. They signed all the necessary forms, agreed to the secrecy provisions that are part of any organ donation. Baldwin brought in a Palm Springs doctor, Sherwood Fielding, to remove the kidneys. The kidneys were both in great condition. It's one of those situations where, as a doctor, you have such mixed feelings. Some doctors grow accustomed to losing patients, but I never could. But the knowledge that two more lives are being saved does a lot to offset those other feelings. I get a lot of satisfaction from that, and I wanted to follow through. Find out a little bit about who received the organs, what the treating physicians thought their chances were."

"And?"

"And I was told by Baldwin to butt out. Still, it didn't register with me. Not until it happened again. And again, I was cut out of the loop the moment I'd gotten the signatures on the consent form."

"The organs weren't going into the national donor network," Matthew said. "They were selling them."

"Exactly. But by the time I figured that out, I'd already become an accomplice—an unwitting accomplice, but they were able to convince me that I'd have a hard time proving that. And they also managed to mount a pretty effective argument for what they were doing, though later I realized it was all hogwash. I've never approved of the regional system for organ distribution that went into effect a few years back. Used to be the sickest patients got the organs. As far as I'm concerned, that's how it should be. And the ironic thing is, now there's talk of returning to that system. But back in the early 1990s, they established regional organizations, more than sixty of them, that decided who within their area would get organs. It became a political thing. Hospitals make big money off transplants. They have no trouble manipulating some of the criteria for determining who should get an organ—they put patients in the hospital before they really need to be hospitalized, things like that. A hospital in Newark can transplant all the livers it gets, into its own patients, even with a much sicker patient waiting just across the Hudson River, in New York. People who could live years before becoming seriously ill receive new livers that should go to patients about to die. Fielding told me it was those patients—the sickest patients, the ones who just happened to live in the wrong place—they were trying to help.

"I never knew—never wanted to know—the details of the transactions. But I knew it was illegal, and I should have done something to stop them. But that's where Helen came in. They knew my financial situation. They offered me money, enough to cover the nursing care that Helen needed, to simply turn my head. And between my determination to keep Helen out of an institution and my being able to rationalize that this scheme of theirs was actually helping people who'd become victims of the system, I decided to go along with them."

Jennifer could hardly believe what she was hearing.

"You mean you let them take organs from patients before they died? You didn't do anything to stop them?"

"No!" Dr. Treecedale strained forward, adamant about his response.

"I would never have allowed that. Never. As far as I knew, organs were only taken after a patient died a natural death, and with the consent of the family. I believed that the only deviation from what takes place every day at every major hospital across this nation was in what happened next. Instead of going through the national donor network, Engles had everything arranged for the transplant to take place at the Alpha Center in San Diego." He reached across the table for Jennifer, but she had drawn back, away from him. "Jennifer, I give you my word. I am guilty of a terrible transgression, a crime, but it wasn't until Charlie died that I ever had reason to think they'd actually caused a patient's death. One of my own patients." He shook his head in dismay and grief. "Your husband."

Jennifer did not trust herself to speak, so powerful was the turmoil she felt at hearing Dr. Treecedale confirm the suspicions that had driven her for the past three years. So angry was she to know that he could have stopped it before her Charlie became a victim.

"Go on," Matthew ordered.

"When I left for Santa Barbara that day, for my granddaughter's graduation, I was optimistic about Charlie's chances, far more optimistic than I let on to you," he nodded Jennifer's way. "I really felt that he was going to make it, even thought that by the time I returned he might have come out of his coma. I didn't share that with you, because I didn't want you to get your hopes up. But I remember how good I felt that day on my drive north. Charlie was a special patient to me. Of course, I never got a chance to know him. But I was so impressed with you, Jennifer. So moved by the sight of you at his bedside. So heartsick about your loss of your daughter. I would have done anything to save him. For you."

The old man began to shake then, a barely perceptible tremor at first, but as he continued telling his story, continued confessing his guilt, it grew more noticeable.

"I was in denial. When I came back and heard he'd died, I was stunned, but I tried to push any thoughts that their version of what had happened—that Charlie had started hemorrhaging and they'd operated to save him—was anything but the truth out of mind. And then you called, many months later, and accused us of taking his kidney. And I knew, right that instant, what had happened. What they'd done."

"For God's sake, why didn't you do something?" Jennifer's own body trembled now.

"I went to them. Demanded answers. They denied it, of course. I told them that I didn't believe them, that this time they'd gone too far. I was going to the authorities."

Seeing her tears, Treecedale reached into his pocket and withdrew a white handkerchief, which he placed on the table in front of Jennifer.

"They laughed at me. They told me they'd bring me down with them. That no one would believe I hadn't been part of it. After all, I very conveniently left Sherwood Fielding in charge of Charlie, and they could show I'd been taking money from them. They said Helen would spend the rest of her life in some overcrowded state institution while I spent the rest of mine in prison. Then they gave me a choice. They offered me money to leave Chihuilla. Enough to find a comfortable home for Helen. Enough to live on.

"Nothing I could do would bring your husband back. And I was convinced that Helen would not survive in an institution—any institution, but certainly not a state facility. So I took their money. Since I was no longer working, I was able to take care of Helen myself. The last couple years, it's been just the two of us, here, where no one bothered us. She passed away in her sleep, peacefully. That's all I'd ever wanted. For her not to suffer."

"And you got your wish," Jennifer responded emphatically, bitterly. "Didn't you? So now it's time for you to help me get mine. You have to help me get Fielding and Engles. They *have* to be punished for what they did to Charlie."

Dr. Treecedale shrunk back in his chair, looking even older than he had just minutes earlier when they walked in on him sleeping.

"You're right, of course," he said quietly. "What can I do?"

"There must be some kind of evidence. Something we can take to the authorities."

"Oh, no. They were very clever about that. No paperwork. Not a thing to trace what happened. Even with this Stowe fellow, they were very . . ."

"What do you mean?" Jennifer said, practically jumping out of her seat as she cut him off midsentence. "Who is this Stowe person?"

"*Was,*" Treecedale said. "Was. I believe he was the man who received your husband's kidney. But I have no proof. That's all I have. A last name. It might not even be the right one. I should never have mentioned it. Really, I'd consider it almost worthless."

"How did you get it?" Matthew asked, his own posture falling just short of Jennifer's as he leaned across the table toward Treecedale.

"After I'd confronted Fielding, when he denied taking Charlie's kidney, I went down to San Diego. To the Alpha Center. You see, that day I left for Santa Barbara, the day Charlie died, I drew blood samples from him and sent them to the lab for routine tests. When I returned and learned that Charlie had died, I retrieved some of that blood. I wasn't even sure why I was doing it, because as I said, I didn't want to even consider the possibility that Charlie's death was related in any way to the earlier incidents. But for some reason, I had it frozen. Stored it at a lab. And then when you called, I knew why my instincts had told me to keep the blood. I went down to the Alpha Center.

"I knew a clerk there, a woman whom I'd heard Fielding talk to on the phone a couple of times. I'd had dealings with her before, when I'd referred patients of my own there, and we'd always gotten along well. I knew the illegal transplants were arranged through the center and that someone there had to be involved in the administrative end of things. You know, organizing things. Passing messages. Ordering the necessary supplies and scheduling procedures. It was just a guess, but I figured it might be her. I went to her, pretended I was in on it, and told her I needed the files on the kidney transplant Fielding had done around the time of Charlie's death. She said something like 'You mean the Stowe transplant?' Then suddenly, she clammed up, realized she'd probably made this colossal blunder. She told me she didn't have any idea what I was talking about. I couldn't get anything out of her after that. In fact, before I'd walked out of her office, she'd already picked up the phone. There's no doubt in my mind whom she was calling. Engles. Or Fielding."

"What were you planning to do with it, if you found it? With the file?" Jennifer asked.

"I hadn't decided that yet. Maybe nothing. Or maybe preserve it to turn over to the authorities once Helen died. It was one of those things where I was just following my instincts. I hadn't thought it through. I just had to know what really happened."

"What about Charlie's blood? Why did you have it frozen?"

"I guess on a subconscious level I thought it might be useful some-day."

"A DNA analysis?"

"Yes. A comparison of Charlie's DNA to the DNA of the kidney in the man who supposedly received the transplant," Treecedale answered. "You see, my dear, I may have gone along with Fielding and Engles, but there was always a part of me that planned to get them someday for what they did. But, unfortunately, the blood's useless without tissue to compare it to. In fact, I recently received a bill from the lab. For its storage. I've been paying it on a yearly basis. This time I didn't bother."

"What was the clerk's name?" Matthew asked then. "At the Alpha Center. Do you remember it?"

"Cathy something. I long ago stopped trying to remember last names of nurses and clerks."

"But the name she used to refer to the transplant? That was Stowe?"

"Yes. I'm fairly certain that it was. But if you think they have record of it down there, you're wrong. Especially after my visit. You can be sure they destroyed anything even remotely capable of connecting them to Jennifer's husband's kidney. These are clever people you're dealing with. Far too clever to leave a paper trail."

"Then it will be up to you to convince the authorities." It was Jennifer speaking again. "To tell them everything you know. We'll take you back with us."

"Now?" Treecedale, wide-eyed, asked.

"Yes," Matthew said. "Now."

"I can help you pack a few things," Jennifer said, standing.

"But if I let you take me to the authorities, they might arrest *me*."

Jennifer's eyes did not evade his. Nor did they display any trace of sympathy. Understanding, perhaps. Sympathy, no.

"That's right. Will you come with us?"

Treecedale's gaze held hers a long while. Jennifer sensed him searching for a sign that he could trust her.

"Yes," he finally answered. "I'll come with you. But give me a little while. Alone, please. An hour, no more. Let me pack a few things and arrange for Helen's garden to be watered. She dearly loved her garden. Let me say good-bye to this place. It wasn't exactly what she and I had planned for our last years together, but in a way, it was very special to both of us."

"We'll wait right here," Matthew said.

"No," Jennifer pronounced. "Let's give him his privacy. We'll come back for you, Dr. Treecedale. In one hour."

"WHY DON'T YOU start the car and get the air going?" Matthew said to Jennifer, handing her the keys, as they walked away from the house. For once, Jennifer didn't question him.

He could hear the Jeep's engine turn over as he lifted the hood of the white Cadillac. Reaching under it, he sliced a wire and the radiator hose with the pocketknife he'd opened. Then he joined Jennifer in the car.

"Are you out of your mind?" he turned to ask her.

"For agreeing to leave him alone? No, I think he wants to do the right thing. Besides, we can't *force* him to talk to the authorities. If he's right, that there's no evidence anywhere of Fielding and Engles' kidney-selling operation, then we'll need his cooperation. Treating him like a human being is a good place to start. Besides, where can he run?"

Not far without a car, thought Matthew. He backed the Jeep out of the driveway and headed back down the dusty access road. He turned on to the road leading to Viejo, then pulled over, and repositioned his rear-view mirror to allow him a view of the big saguaro.

"What are you doing?" Jennifer asked.

"Just playing it safe."

They sat there, silent, for about half an hour. Then Jennifer told Matthew she needed to go to the bathroom.

"Again?"

"Yes, again. It's been hours."

Matthew nodded toward the window.

"Go behind those rocks over there. I won't look."

"And get bitten by a rattlesnake or tarantula? No thank you. Take me to town, to that little gas station where we stopped before."

Matthew looked in the rearview mirror. He'd seen to it that Treecedale wasn't going anywhere. And Jennifer was probably right. Either the old man was willing to help or not. They could forcibly turn him in, but without his cooperation, the authorities would release him faster than spit dried in the merciless desert sun beating overhead.

Matthew parked in the shade of the gas station and, after Jennifer disappeared into the women's room, decided he needed to relieve himself, too. Two minutes later they were both back in the car and headed back out to Treecedale's.

The silence that met them when they stepped inside the laundry room was the first sign that something was wrong.

"Wait here," Matthew told Jennifer.

The fact that she obeyed told him that she felt it, too.

MATTHEW RETURNED IN just minutes.

"Let's go," he said, grabbing her by the arm.

"What happened?" Jennifer said, resisting. "Where's Dr. Treecedale?"

It was one of those questions you really didn't want answered.

"Dead. Shot himself."

Jennifer jerked away from Matthew and headed in the direction from which he'd just come. He grabbed her again.

"Don't go in there. It's too late. He's gone."

She turned to Matthew, tears streaming down her cheeks.

"That son of a bitch. That son of a bitch."

"Let's get out of here."

"Shouldn't we call the police? We can't just leave him here."

"Do you know what will happen if we do? If you get dragged into this now, this kidney-selling thing, you'll have them crawling all over both of us. And do you know what that would mean? Do you? That Angel's captors won't come anywhere near us. That we might as well kiss goodbye any chance we have of finding Angel."

Jennifer, wiping her tears with the back of her clenched fists, took one last look in the direction of Dr. Treecedale's bedroom.

"Okay. Let's go," she said.

•   •   •

ON THE WAY back to Phoenix, Jennifer sat, stone still, eyes fixed forward, consumed with anger and grief.

"He was our only chance," she said despondently.

Matthew's response was a long time in coming.

"Maybe not."

"What do you mean?"

"Didn't you tell me the envelope for the letter you received came from a suburb of Chicago?"

"Yes. Homewood."

"Well, there can't be that many Stowes in Homewood, Illinois."

Matthew was right. Treecedale may have taken the cowardly way out, but before doing so, he'd given them a piece of information that could turn out to be very valuable. The name Stowe. Before, all Jennifer had was a postmark without a name. A postmark coupled with a name presented entirely different possibilities. Of course, what were the odds of the daughter of the kidney recipient having the same name as her father? Or even that she'd stayed in Homewood? It had, after all, been over two years since she'd written the letter to Jennifer.

They were back in Phoenix by early evening. Nan had left a note on the counter, but Jennifer was glad to have missed her. She had one thing, and one thing only, on her mind.

With Matthew seated next to her at the kitchen counter, Jennifer picked up the phone and dialed directory assistance.

"Have a first name?" the operator asked curtly when Jennifer gave her the name.

"No. Just tell me, are there *any* Stowes in Homewood?"

"Three of them. Mark, Elijah, and an S. Stowe. Have a street address?"

"No."

"Want to try one of these?"

"Can you give me all three?"

"Nope. Only one. Take your choice."

"Okay. S. Stowe."

"Hold for that number," the operator responded in a mechanical voice.

Without hanging up, Jennifer dialed.

An elderly man answered.

"You don't know me," Jennifer said. "But I'm looking for someone named Stowe who wrote me a letter two years ago. You don't by any chance have a relative who received a kidney transplant?"

"You mean Elijah? He received a kidney. But he died anyway. A couple years ago."

Jennifer felt her breath leave her.

"Does Elijah have a daughter?"

"That would be Kate."

"And where might I find her?"

"She's living in Elijah's place now. Who is this?"

"I need to talk to her. Can you give me her phone number?"

"I don't know if I should do that. What do you want with her?"

Jennifer hung up without responding and dialed directory assistance for the number of Elijah Stowe.

After three rings, a woman answered. She sounded about Jennifer's age, maybe a little younger.

"Is this Elijah Stowe's daughter?" Jennifer asked.

"Yes. Who's calling?"

"This is Jennifer Banks. Do you remember me? You wrote me a letter two years ago."

The line was silent so long that Jennifer wondered if they'd been disconnected.

"Hello?" she said.

"Yes," the voice said softly. "Yes, of course, I remember you. How did you get my number?"

"That's quite a story . . ." Jennifer began.

She told Elijah Stowe's daughter everything that had happened. About the fact that Charlie's kidneys had been taken without her knowledge or consent. About Dr. Treecedale and Jennifer's belief that Charlie had been killed for the kidney that Elijah Stowe received. Throughout Jennifer's discourse, the other woman remained silent.

"What do you want from me?" she finally said, when Jennifer had finished.

"In your letter you said you found my husband's name in a file. They actually gave him that information? He knew what they were doing?"

"My father believed your husband had already died when they took the kidney. The possibility that he was still alive had never entered his mind, believe me. He was a good man, good-hearted. Many times he said how badly he felt for you, and how he hoped the money he paid for the kidney helped you out. They told him you were destitute."

"How much did he pay? Do you know?"

"Over $150,000. But money wasn't a big issue for him. He was a very wealthy man. And very used to getting his way. He told me they refused to give him the information about the donor at first, but he persuaded them. That means he probably paid them for it. Daddy was always very thorough. He had everything they told him checked out, made sure your husband and Daddy really were good matches. It was all in the file."

"Do you have that file? The one with my husband's name?"

"No. I destroyed it. I knew that what Daddy did was illegal and I certainly had no use for it. But when I was going through his things and came upon the file, when I saw for the first time that the donor was an actual person—that he had a name, a wife—I just felt this rush of gratitude and emotion. That's when I wrote you. But it's gone now. So you see, I can't help you. I'm sorry."

"Yes, you can," Jennifer said.

"How?"

"By telling the authorities what you just told me."

"But that doctor—Treecedale, was that his name?—he can tell them."

"Dr. Treecedale is dead. He killed himself. Right after giving me your father's name."

Jennifer's entire being felt numb, suspended in time, as she waited for the woman's response.

"Please," she begged. "Please help. I've lived with this for three years now. The only way I'll ever be able to put it behind me is by bringing the people responsible to justice."

The voice, when it spoke again, was barely more than a whisper.

"I can't do that," it said. "I can't do that to my children. I've just been through a divorce. It's been hard on them. I don't want them dragged through some tawdry scandal now, over something their grandfather chose to do. I'm sorry. I really am. But I have to think of my children."

Jennifer was certain that the other woman would hang up on her, cut off her only hope of proving what Fielding had done. But for some reason she did not. Jennifer could still hear her rapid, shallow breaths.

"Please," Jennifer said. "Please give it more thought. Let me give you a number where you can reach me." She read her Matthew's phone number, then paused before continuing. "But I want you to know something. If you can't do it, I'll understand. I had a child, too. And I would have done anything to protect her."

"Had?"

"Yes. She died in the same accident that put my husband in a coma."

Jennifer heard an anguished, stifled sob, then the line went dead.

Jennifer replaced the phone carefully in its handset, then, utterly defeated, lowered her head into her hands. She would not cry. She was tired of crying. Tired of feeling.

Yet, the next moment, when Matthew placed his arm around her shoulder, when he comforted her, she did feel something.

"I'm sorry," he said. "We'll figure something out."

His voice was sincere. And kind. She raised her head to look at him and then, without a word, without forethought, she kissed him. It was a simple, spontaneous reaction. She wanted to thank him, to show him her appreciation. But the moment she touched her lips to his, the moment she came close enough to inhale the salty scent of the day they'd just spent in the desert on his skin, it became something else entirely. *Jennifer* became someone else entirely—someone who, if only for the moment, had shed her pain, and who had a desperate need to prolong that state.

Her actions must have shocked Matthew as much as they did her, because at first he seemed not to comprehend what was happening. But it didn't take long for him to catch on, and when he did, it immediately became clear that he would be more than willing to oblige Jennifer in her quest.

She was not even aware of, did not even hear, her own low moan as she parted her lips to make way for his probing tongue. And as he pulled her to him, as he lifted her onto his lap, where she could feel his hardness, the strength of his desire for her, the only conscious thought she had was that she could not allow this to end.

"You make me crazy," he murmured into her hair. "Fucking crazy."

His hands groped for her, reaching in and under her shirt, pulling at it as his lips explored her neck and shoulders. His breathing seemed easily as ragged as hers, and when she had helped him unbutton her blouse and she reached behind to unfasten her bra, freeing her breasts, she heard the moan. This time it was his.

He carried her down the short hallway to a bedroom.

He settled on the edge of the bed and, positioning her before him, between his muscled legs, he pushed the shirt off her shoulders, then followed with the bra. He took her hands and placed them on his shoulders, and with the palm of each hand, he reached out and lightly brushed her nipples, teasing them with rhythmical circular motion, making them achy and hard.

She watched him, fascinated and wildly excited, as he removed her shorts and panties and explored, with eyes and hands, her body. She was already wet when he probed between her thighs and finally, his fingers penetrating her, his eyes came up and met hers.

"You're ready for me, aren't you?"

He slid his jeans off and pulled her to where he sat on the bed. She straddled him, opening herself fully to him and then, his hands guiding her hips, he lowered her onto him. She gasped as he filled her, reaching deep inside her, deeper than anyone had ever been, causing her pain and anguish, and making her want more. Much more.

They made love for hours. Perhaps Matthew sensed her need to make it last. Or perhaps he always had that kind of stamina. It didn't matter. All that mattered was that *she felt*. Pain, pleasure, longing.

For a short while, she was alive again.

THE PHONE WOKE them at six-forty-five the next morning. At some point in the night, they'd moved to Matthew's bedroom and, until interrupted by the sharp ring, had slept curled together, Jennifer's back to Matthew's front.

Matthew answered, then immediately handed it to her.

"Mrs. Banks?"

Jennifer recognized the voice from last night.

"Yes?"

"I've been thinking about what you asked me. I couldn't sleep all night." The words came in a rush. "You've been through so much already, and whether you agreed to it or not, your husband's kidney changed my life. Reunited me and my children with my father and gave us time together before he died. It's because of that time we spent together that I'm able to get by now. Daddy left us his house, and the money that enabled me to finally walk away from a husband I should have left years ago, but was too penniless and scared to. It wouldn't have happened without your husband dying."

Jennifer was afraid to speak. Afraid to interrupt her caller, for fear of changing the course of what might be happening.

"I was being selfish last night," the voice continued. "I didn't want to go through any more pain. But then I thought of what *you'd* been through, especially when I heard about you losing your daughter, and I realized that I couldn't live with myself if I didn't help you."

Matthew had moved away from her, but Jennifer could still feel his presence, somehow knew that he was watching her.

"You mean you'll do it? You'll tell the authorities what you know?"

"Yes," Elijah Stowe's daughter said. "You can count on me. I'll help you in any way I can."

When Jennifer hung up the phone and told Matthew the news, his reaction disappointed her.

"What is it?" she asked. "Why do you look like that?"

"Because without evidence, I don't trust the authorities to take any of it seriously."

"But we don't *have* evidence. Everywhere we look, we find it's already been destroyed."

"Maybe. But maybe not. What about your husband's blood?"

Jennifer bolted upright in bed.

"Oh my God," she cried. "You're right. Now that we've located Elijah Stowe, a DNA analysis could prove that he got Charlie's kidney!"

She was out of bed and dressing as she gabbled excitedly.

"The lab bill. Remember what Dr. Treecedale said? He hadn't paid it yet. Maybe it's still there, at his house. Did you see what a mess it was? It didn't look like he'd taken the trash out in weeks. Maybe it's still there."

Naked, Matthew walked across the room to his closet and reached blindly inside for a shirt.

"We'll know soon enough," he said.

THE CAR SAT out front in plain sight.

"Maybe it's the police," Jennifer said. "Maybe someone found his body."

"That's not the police."

They had just crested the final hill leading to Treecedale's house. Easing the car into reverse, Matthew backed slowly, quietly out of sight.

He opened his glove compartment and withdrew a gun. A snub nose. Quickly he loaded it and turned to Jennifer.

"You know you should wait for me here."

"And you know that I won't."

He pushed the gun into her hand.

"That's what I thought you'd say. Here, use this if you have to. And stay behind me."

Returning on foot to the crest, Matthew dropped to the sand and surveyed the house and grounds. There was no sign of activity.

The desert offered little in the way of a hiding place. Knowing the house as he now did, he decided the best strategy was to approach it straight on. And quickly.

Jennifer kept up with him in a sprint to the garage. The door to the laundry room was ajar. They crept down the same hallway they'd used the day before, but this time Matthew stopped before the doorway to the study where he'd found Treecedale's body less than twenty-four hours earlier.

As they stood there, Matthew could hear someone rummaging about inside. He pushed Jennifer flat against the wall, then before she could get in his way, pivoted, gun at chest level and aimed straight ahead, into the open doorway.

"*Don't move,*" he ordered.

The man standing at an opened wall safe, his back to them, froze. Papers were strewn everywhere across the floor. Tossed haphazardly from open desk drawers during the intruder's search, some had even landed on Treecedale, who was in the same position in which Matthew last saw him—sitting at his desk, his head thrown backward so forcefully by the bullet he'd put through his mouth that the only portion of his head that could be seen from this view was the bottom of his chin. All color had by now drained from his face and hands, and the splatters of blood on the wall, desk, and floor had dried.

Matthew did not recognize the intruder until he ordered him to put his hands up and turn slowly.

By now, Jennifer had come to Matthew's side.

"Jim Wilkes!"

Wilkes betrayed no emotion, not even surprise, upon seeing them.

Matthew approached him and removed Wilkes' pistol from its shoulder holster. As he patted him down, out of the corner of his eye, Matthew could see Jennifer still in the doorway, holding the snub nose on Wilkes. He started at Wilkes' waist and worked down to his shoes.

When he'd finished, in one continuous, swift motion, Matthew stood and swung his right fist squarely into the underside of Wilkes' jaw.

The sound of breaking bone was unmistakable.

Wilkes fell back against the wall, cowering as he held his jaw.

"*Talk,*" Matthew ordered.

When Wilkes did not, he went at him again. Jennifer had by now entered the room. Matthew heard her gasp at the sight of Treecedale, but she immediately turned her attention back to Wilkes, never dropping the revolver from its position, trained on Wilkes.

It only took one more assault for Wilkes to crumble.

"Okay," he sputtered through bloodied lips. "I'll talk."

Matthew backed away.

"What are you doing here?"

"Fielding sent me."

"Why?"

"To kill Treecedale." His eyes strayed to the corpse. "But you beat me to it."

"We didn't kill him," Jennifer said, her voice rising with indignation. "We're not murderers. That's *your* domain. Yours and Fielding's."

Wilkes ignored her, his eyes trained only on Matthew.

"Why did he want Treecedale killed?"

"To shut him up."

"About the kidney-selling operation?"

"Yes."

"What else?"

"What do you mean what else?"

"Tell us what else you know."

"Nothing. There's nothing else."

"Where's Fielding?"

When there was no answer, Matthew raised his Glock—just slightly, just high enough to take aim at the toes of Wilkes' right foot—and pulled the trigger. Wilkes crumpled to the ground, screaming and grasping his foot in agony.

"Where's Fielding?" Matthew demanded.

"I don't know where he is," Wilkes wailed. "I only have a pager number for him."

"What's he up to? Why did he suddenly decide to have Treecedale killed?"

It was apparent that Wilkes was about to pass out. Blood was seeping from his leather shoe onto the floor.

"It wasn't just Treecedale he told me to kill," Wilkes groaned. "It was her, too." He nodded Jennifer's way. "He wants to go back to Seattle. Take BioGentech public, have a stock offering. He wants to go back home. And he thinks the two of them are all that stand in his way."

At first Matthew thought he was mistaken. That it couldn't be laughter he heard from Jennifer. But when he turned to her, he saw a big grin on her face. She looked half deranged, standing there, still holding the gun on Wilkes.

"A stock offering?" she snorted. "A stock offering." The smile evaporated from her face then, leaving no lingering trace. "You tell that son of a bitch that he'll never be able to return to Seattle. You tell him that we have proof now, proof of what he did to Charlie. Dr. Treecedale gave it to us, before he killed himself. Names, dates, witnesses. *Everything.* You tell him that he's going to have to spend the rest of his life running from us and from the authorities. And that we'll find him. And when we do, he'll pay for what he did to my husband. He'll rot—either in jail or in Hell. You tell him *that*."

"He won't be able to tell Fielding *anything* when I'm done with him," Matthew said, approaching Wilkes again.

"*No*," Jennifer shouted. "No. Let him go. I want him to go back to Fielding and give him my message." She lowered her gun and turned away. "This one's not even worth worrying about. He's pathetic."

Matthew caught her eye then, as she was turning.

"Are you sure?"

"Yes, I'm sure."

He reached down to the ground and grabbed Wilkes by his collar. Limp, almost lifeless, Wilkes offered no resistance as Matthew dragged him down the tiled hallway and thrust him out into the garage, where he dropped in a heap on the cement floor.

When Matthew returned to the study, Jennifer was on her hands and knees, searching frantically through the papers strewn everywhere. Just as he stooped to join her, she let out a shout.

"Here it is! The bill from the lab. For a year's storage." She continued reading from her position on her knees. "It says it will destroy the sample if he doesn't pay within fourteen days."

"What's the date on it?"

Jennifer scanned the document.

"The eighth," she said. "Today's the twenty-first!"

Matthew glanced at his watch as he reached for her arm to help her up.

"If we hurry, we might be able to make San Diego before they close."

CHAPTER

TWENTY-FIVE

YOU LOOK BEAUTIFUL," Sherwood Fielding said.

Angelique Mannington gazed at him from across the table at the diner to which he'd taken her directly from LAX. Her flight from Seattle had arrived half an hour earlier.

She'd been so relieved to hear he was alive. After she and Jim Wilkes had been discovered onboard *Therapy* and the search for Sherwood had turned up only the overturned dinghy. She, too, believed he had drowned. After all, if he were alive, surely he would have contacted her.

His call to her apartment last night had left her with mixed emotions. She felt angry and hurt. He'd deserted her that night on the yacht, then not called to let her know he was alive and well. But still, her predominant emotion, at first, had been relief.

"I can't explain over the phone," he'd told her from a pay phone. "I need you to get down here right away. On the first available flight. And don't let on that you've heard from me."

"That's good," he'd said when Angelique told him the authorities still believed him dead. "That's very good."

Now they sat face-to-face again and he had begun telling her about his plan, about her role in it, and the future it would ensure for the two of them.

Angelique watched him carefully, trying to pinpoint what—besides this cheesy diner, a place so tacky she couldn't believe Sherwood had chosen it—was wrong with this picture.

When he lifted his hand and pushed back a lock of errant hair—also a first—she realized the answer. A ring of perspiration darkened the underarm of Sherwood's raw silk shirt. And Angelique realized in that instant what had struck her as being so incredibly out of whack from the moment she stepped into his arms at the airport.

Sherwood Fielding was frightened. Scared shitless.

"I've been thinking," Fielding was saying. "Yes, without Angel, we lose any hope of getting the eighty million we'd agreed to." Fielding's eyes brightened as his grasp on her hand tightened across the tabletop. "But there's no reason we can't still get the first installment. The forty million."

"Are you crazy? I thought the deal was that he pays you the forty million when you deliver Angel, the protocol, and the donor."

"That's almost right," Sherwood answered. "In truth, all Tupeni really wanted to begin with was proof that the clone was genuine, that the donor and clone match up. It was my idea that he actually take possession of the donor. It killed two birds with one stone—provided him with the means to prove the authenticity of the clone and also got Jennifer Rockhill out of our hair. But what if I got him to agree to our merely providing *cells* from the donor—cells that he would keep to match up against the clone when it's born?"

"You're not making sense. The clone will never *be* born if we don't deliver Angel."

"But he won't know that. At least not when we make delivery."

"Delivery of *what?*"

"Delivery of a pregnant baboon whom we claim to be carrying a clone. Just think about it. Ursula is still pregnant. She's on her way here right now. I'm having her shipped to me. She's fine. Healthy. Pregnant. What has Tupeni agreed to? He's agreed to pay us the first half upon our delivering a pregnant baboon and the protocol."

"And the donor."

"Yes, and the donor. But I'm confident I can convince him to accept verification that comes in a different form."

"You still have some of Jennifer's cells?" Angelique asked. "From her pap smear?"

"Yes. But we can do better than that. We'll surely have to. We can allow them to actually examine the donor, to take their own cell samples, which they'll store for comparison with the clone, after it's born. If I can give them that, I'm certain I can get him to go along with my new plan."

"We don't even know where Jennifer is. What makes you think you'll find her, and if you do, that you'll be able to get her away from G. I. Joe?"

Fielding smiled, but it wasn't the same cocky smile Angelique had seen countless times before. This smile left her feeling unsettled, even a bit creeped out.

"We don't even *need* Jennifer," he said. "Don't you see? Since there's no clone, what difference does it make who we identify as the donor?"

"I guess you're right." He had a good point. She had to admit it was a clever idea. "But who? Who will we say is the donor?"

Fielding gave her hand an affectionate squeeze.

"*You*. We'll say it's you." When she jerked away from him, he reached back across the table to her. "Why not? In a sense it's true, after all, isn't it? If Chandra had succeeded in cloning the cells *you* donated, it would be you they wanted. Of course, I would never have agreed to that. All I would ever have agreed to, if your cells—instead of Jennifer's—had been the ones to survive nuclear transfer, would have been a sampling, for verification purposes. And that's all they'll get now. That's all you'll have to do. Allow them to take a cell sample back to Niupalu with them. Forty million dollars, Angelique. Forty million. Think of it. Isn't it worth it? They're expecting a woman. I've already told them that much. All you have to do is put up with a physical exam. I'll be right there, making sure there's no funny business." He paused, letting his words settle in. "Just think what we can do with that much money. What a difference it would make. For us. You and me. Please. Say you'll think about it."

"But what about the protocol? They infected Chandra's computer with a virus and stole the files. The protocol is gone. We don't have it, in any form. They won't pay us without the protocol."

"We make one up. We have time. I brought everything we need, files from old projects, the ones Gallagher had worked on. We know the basics of this stuff, both of us do. We can come up with something that will pass their preliminary scrutiny. We'll write it at sea."

"*At sea?*"

"Yes. I've chartered a boat for us. We leave tomorrow. I've thought all of this through. It's perfect. You can also fill in for Chandra. We'll tell them he fell ill, but that you've been working with him all along and that you're as familiar with the protocol as Chandra. See the beauty of it? You're not only the donor, but one of the scientists as well. Hell, it's pretty damn close to the truth. They'll think it was a brilliant touch using someone like you—beautiful, intelligent—as the donor. What?" he said suddenly. "What are you smiling about?"

"You're really something, you know that?" Angelique said, her voice rising enough to draw the attention of a couple at the next booth. "You actually think I'd fall for this? That I'm so fucking blinded by love for you that I couldn't see through it? Do you actually think I'd trust you, that I believe you'd so much as bat an eye before leaving me with them so they could wait for the baby to be born to prove I was the donor? You're fucking out of your mind."

Fielding groped frantically for her hand, which swatted him away like some disgusting insect.

"Angelique, darling. Don't do this. Don't you see? We can be together. I'd never betray you."

Angelique had grabbed her purse from the seat beside her and started to rise, but then she thought twice about it. Dropping back into the seat, she leaned forward and glared at Fielding.

"You are scum," she said. "Pure scum."

"Angelique," Fielding, desperate, pleaded. "Please, you have to help me. I can't go back to Seattle. I've lost everything. My company. My family. Even Wilkes has abandoned me. All because of that bitch. All because of Jennifer Rockhill. Please, you're my last hope. I need you to make this plan work. I've already told Sanday you'll be coming."

She had always hoped that she would one day have the ability to move Sherwood Fielding to tears. *This*, of course, wasn't exactly what she had in mind, but the tears of desperation spilling over from his sleep-deprived eyes as he sat across the formica tabletop from her would just have to do.

"I hope you drown at sea" was all she said before she left him there.

TUPENI SANDAY DREW on his cigar as he sat waiting for his nephew, Tamasese. He'd sent his servant to rouse the young man from bed after receiving a call from the United States.

Of all Tupeni's sons and nephews, Tamasese, a stout, solid man in his midtwenties, was the first to whom the king turned when faced with a difficult decision. He knew Tamasese to be not only exceptionally bright and well educated—he had two degrees from UCLA, an MBA, and a bachelor's in world affairs—but also possessed of an uncanny sixth sense about people and situations. It was this, this extrasensory faculty, that Tupeni wished to call upon now.

"Sit. Take coffee with me," Tupeni ordered his nephew when he arrived at Tupeni's bedside.

Once the servant had filled Tamasese's cup, Tupeni dismissed her.

"I have received a call from the American doctor," Tupeni began. "He wants to make the exchange immediately, as soon as we can get our ship to the designated pickup."

"I thought that's what you had already agreed," Tamasese said. "To move the transfer up."

"It is. But now he informs me that Dr. Chandra is deathly ill, so he's sending another scientist, one who worked side by side with Chandra. And listen to this, this new scientist—a woman—is also the donor."

"This woman, the donor, the American doctor says we can keep her? Take her back to Niupalu?"

"Yes. He says she will return with us, so that we can do tests after the birth. After that, she is mine, to do with as I please."

Tamasese sipped at his hot coffee.

"Let me ask you something, esteemed Uncle. What would prevent him from delivering a fake donor? After all, we will not be able to confirm the clone's authenticity until after the ape delivers. By then you will already have parted with a great deal of money."

"That is what is troubling me."

The two sat in silence.

"You can back out now," Tamasese suggested.

"No," Tupeni was adamant. "This is too important. If I have to risk losing the forty million dollars, it's worth it to me. I must have this technology. But, of course, I do not like risks."

Tamasese fell deep into thought for a while.

"What about this: you hold both the Americans, Sherwood Fielding and the scientist he says is the donor, bring them back here, until the clone is born and we confirm its authenticity."

Tupeni Sanday's wide smile exposed a row of perfect front teeth, all of which were capped in gold.

"Now that is a very good idea." His laughter came from deep in his belly. "Then when the clone is authenticated, Fielding gets full payment. Eighty million dollars, for I am a man of my word."

"And if he double-crosses you? If the clone turns out to be other than what they say it is?"

"He has not done his homework if he thinks that he can trick Tupeni Sanday. That would make him a very stupid man. Wouldn't it?"

His nephew nodded in agreement.

"Anyone who tricks Tupeni Sanday would have to pay the price. Anyone who tricks Tupeni Sanday," he said, misstating, as he often did, a typically American adage, "would not live, I think, to regret it."

TWENTY-SIX

THE WEATHER WAS unusually cool for early July in Phoenix, and Jennifer had taken advantage of that fact by taking her morning coffee outside, to drink by the side of Matthew's pool.

The same mockingbird that had warbled a multitude of songs to her yesterday morning was back again today, perched on top of the cement fence that separated Matthew and his neighbor. Jennifer was happy for the diversion, anything that would take her mind off her situation. She felt as though she were living in some kind of twilight zone, a state of constant limbo. Waiting. For the results of the DNA analysis. For Angel's captors to show up.

She'd slept with Matthew again the night before. They had not made love. After a late dinner, they'd each gone to their separate bedrooms, but once there, Jennifer had been unable to sleep. She found herself thinking about Matthew, thinking about the charming man who first appeared in Seattle, then soon transformed into the menacing, frightening figure who'd confronted her that day on the running path. Both those men were long gone now. What she saw in their place was a quiet, rather strange man, uncomfortable not only with her, but with his sister—and himself— as well. It was hard to tell what went on inside that head of his. Why he had stayed with her. Why he hadn't taken the easy way out.

Maybe the whys didn't matter anymore. She felt too old, way too disillusioned, to believe in fairy tales and princes anymore. Maybe someone solid and resilient was enough.

When she'd turned to the bedside table and saw that she had been lying there, trying to fall asleep, for more than two hours, Jennifer's analytical mind finally clicked off and without more deliberation, she'd thrown back the covers, risen, and padded barefoot down the short hall-way separating the room in which she slept from Matthew's.

His door was closed but not locked. She'd opened it and stood for a moment, framed by the light from the hallway. Matthew was lying on his back, his arms crossed over his chest, his eyes open. His head turned her way.

She'd walked slowly toward him. He lifted up the covers for her and she climbed under, as if she had done the same thing many times before.

"Not a good idea to walk around barefoot. Scorpions" was all he said.

She'd nodded, then kissed him at the base of his neck. And then they'd both fallen asleep. And awakened, less than an hour ago, with his arm draped over her midsection and her foot tucked behind her, between his ankles.

At the sound of the patio door opening, she turned. Matthew emerged from the house. Shirtless, wearing only gym shorts, he was a magnificent sight, but the look on his face cut short Jennifer's admiration.

He grabbed a chair from the patio table and pulled it up beside Jennifer's. Despite the degree of intimacy they'd recently achieved, she'd noticed he still chose to sit beside her instead of facing her.

"Cogswell just phoned," he said. Cogswell was a forensic pathologist that Matthew had called to exhume Elijah Stowe's body, someone he'd worked with before, while he was with the CIA. Matthew had felt confident Cogswell would be willing to help them, and that, if asked, he would also do so in secrecy. "He told me that yesterday he faxed the DNA analysis of Elijah Stowe's kidney to the lab in San Diego, the one doing the analysis on your husband's blood. He just got a call from them, from the lab."

Jennifer knew that this was it. The moment she had been working toward for two years. With the exception of the effect it was having on her heart, it seemed oddly lacking in drama.

She placed her hand on Matthew's forearm, forcing him to meet her eyes while he delivered the news.

"It's a match," he told her. "A perfect match. The kidney they took from Elijah Stowe's exhumed body was your husband's."

"That son of a bitch" was all she said.

"You have a decision to make." Matthew had turned back away from her now. She watched him in profile as he spoke. "We can turn this in now. Take it to the CIA. It's proof positive, they'll jump right on it. Engles' position and power would mean nothing in light of this. He and Baldwin will be arrested right away, and Fielding, if they can find him."

"Or?"

"Or we can wait. Until we find Angel. And her kidnapper."

"You still believe that if we go to the authorities now, we'll never find her? That it will scare off Angel's captors?"

"It's a possibility."

"I need time to think about this."

"Take all the time you need."

HE HAD NOT told her. That if she chose to go to the authorities now, he would have to leave. He'd thought long and hard about this. Without any evidence to the contrary, the moment the CIA became aware of Ram Chandra and the guard's death, Matthew would be their number-one suspect. They knew who he worked for, what he did now, and for years had been trying to put him out of business. His enemies at the agency would jump for joy at this development. Even his comrades would be hard-pressed to support him when sound thinking dictated the logic of his being a suspect.

If Jennifer went to the authorities, brought them into her life, their life, now, he would have to disappear. The only way he could wriggle out of this one and manage to stay in the States was if he could produce the killer.

Maybe, he'd considered, it was time to go. He could return to WTI, buy a place in London. What was stopping him?

Jennifer had apparently begun to figure it out, too, for when she entered the living room later that day and asked him to mute the sound on the Diamondback game, she said, "When the CIA finds out about Ram Chandra and the guard being killed, they'll try to pin it on you. Won't they?"

"Most likely."

"You'd leave before you let that happen, wouldn't you? Go to London."

"I don't see what other choice I'd have."

"So we have to find Angel's kidnapper, the murderer, don't we?"

Matthew hit the remote's "off" button.

"No. We don't have to. All you have to do is answer this question. Do you *want* to find Angel? Or are you ready for this to end? You have what you started out for, the proof you were seeking about what happened to your husband. You can turn it in and walk away. Let the authorities handle it from here."

"But then I'd never know about Angel."

"That's right. You'd never know what happened to her, or to the baby. Could you live with that?"

"I don't think so. As disturbing as I find the whole thing, I can't turn my back on her now. Not when she's carrying a fetus that originated from me, from my own body. It would be like turning my back on my own child. And if we don't find her, Fielding might. I can't let him get away with what he had planned. I won't allow another of his horrific schemes to succeed."

"Then I think you have your answer."

Jennifer sat quietly, studying him.

"You've thought about this, haven't you? About leaving, especially if I decided to go to the authorities now."

"Yes. And if you'd chosen to go that route, I probably would have. But that's not what I want."

"What *do* you want?"

"I want to find Angel. I think you need that. I don't think you'll ever have peace of mind until we do. I want to nail Fielding, to destroy him."

"It would be so much easier for you if you just left. Why are you willing to do this, to stay here with me, when you've already got what WTI is paying you to get?"

"I've never looked for easy ways out. I'm not about to start now. Plus the only way to clear my name is to find who killed Chandra, and stole Angel."

He could have given her another answer, but he didn't. He could have said that he did not want to leave her. That it was worth taking risks just to be with her.

But before he could say these things to Jennifer, he would first have to admit them to himself.

TWENTY-SEVEN

AFTER HIS MORNING WORKOUT, Matthew's routine was to open his laptop on the dining room table and log on to the Internet, where he caught up on the news, followed his favorite baseball teams, and, in an effort to keep abreast of the latest developments in his field, often spent hours reading scientific articles.

He was in the middle of just such an article, entitled *Neural Growth Factors: Do They Protect against Parkinson's?*, when his eye was drawn to the lower-right-hand corner of the screen. A flashing white envelope signaled that he'd just received an e-mail.

Curious—despite the fact that he had an e-mail address through his Internet server, the only e-mailing Matthew ever did was via another secured network designed and accessible only by employees of WTI— Matthew exited the biotech article and slid the mouse over to the envelope. He clicked it open.

Skimming over the mumbo jumbo describing the path the message had taken at the top of the screen, Matthew's eyes came to rest on the lines directly above the message itself:

Date: 25 Jul; 08:27:20
To: mpace@aol.com
From: sunshnbkr@halcyon.com
Subject:

Who was "sunshnbkr"? The subject box had been left blank. The message itself followed:

Who but a Frenchman would kill for a fungus? Beware: he has the
black truffle and has now come for the recipe.
Relax not, die not.

Matthew stared at the screen. It was a warning of some sort. But from
who? And why?

He read it again.

Relax not, die not. It was a phrase familiar enough to him—as it was
one he himself had coined, and used often, during his agency days when
he was conducting counterintelligence training at the Farm.

The CIA. Could the warning have been sent from someone in the
agency—the same agency that he feared, if given the chance, would
charge him with the deaths of Ram Chandra and the Preston guard? The
use of the saying itself, plus the reference to the black French truffle,
indicated the sender was familiar with Matthew's background—knew
he'd spent enough time in France to understand the reference to the
knobby fungus that was so prized by French gourmet chefs it actually
triggered the infamous "Truffles War." Its reference, obviously an analogy
of sorts, indicated the sender had to be familiar with the prized fungus as
well; perhaps because he or she, too, had at one time been assigned
French duty.

But why would anyone within the CIA issue him a warning? In the
past, on two separate occasions, Jack Eberhardt had warned him when his
name had come up as a target of agency interest, but Matthew was convinced Jack had no knowledge of his current activities. They'd long ago
established a rule: that when Jack provided Matthew with assistance, it
was without questions. The less Jack knew of Matthew's activities, the
less risk he was exposed to from helping Matthew. Matthew had decided
that the fact that Jack was out of the loop on what was happening at
BioGentech could be attributed to one of two things. As a matter of prac-
ticality, not every agent was privy to all agency activities, and it could be
a natural result of that fact. Or it could be that the agency was finally wise
to the fact that Jack and Matthew's friendship had survived Matthew's
tumultuous departure from the agency and they had therefore deliberately
kept Eberhardt in the dark. At any rate, if the warning had come from
within the agency, it wasn't from Jack.

Who then? And what exactly did it mean?

Now Matthew turned his attention to what at first had seemed gib-
berish to him—the technical language describing the course the message
had traveled to reach him.

At the very top of the screen were the words:

Received: from iceland.it.earthlink.halcyon.net (iceland-c.it.eartlink.
halcyon.net [204.119.177.23]

The next four lines were different variations of the above, with
long series of unintelligible numbers interspersed, including one
(<*103020900b0d863a79b04@[602.63.32.61]*>) labeled "Message Id" that
meant absolutely nothing to Matthew.

He rose and went into the kitchen, where Jennifer was making coffee.

"How about going for a ride?" he said to her.

"A ride?"

"I'll explain in the car."

He drove west four blocks, stopped briefly at the end of a dead-end
street that ran the length of a city park, then pulled his Jeep up over the
curb, on to the sidewalk and crossed over to the parking lot, which was
not otherwise accessible from the direction he'd come. From the parking
lot he had access to Tatum, a major thoroughfare that could take him east,
toward Scottsdale. Without his little shortcut, he would have to have
driven more than a mile, a mile in which he could easily have been followed, to access Tatum from his house.

He chose the noisiest and busiest intersection along Tatum—the
noise would mask his conversation in the event someone were trying to
pick it up via an acoustic transducer—then pulled into a 7-Eleven. He
got out of the Jeep, walked to a row of pay phones flanking the store's
exterior, and dialed a number written on a piece of paper he withdrew
from his pocket.

"Pace here," he said when a familiar voice answered. "I need help.
I want to trace an e-mail transmission. The message I.D. number is . . ."
Slowly he read the thirty-one-digit number from the same piece of paper.
"I need to know who sent it, and from where. Can you do that for me?"

"You bet," Billy Key answered.

Matthew had known Billy when he served in the Air Force as an
information specialist. He'd now gone into business for himself.

"That's what you pay me for. But I need more information. Do you
have a printout of the message in front of you?"

"Yes."

"Okay, read me everything. I need as much information as you can
give me, so I can hack backwards to figure out who sent it."

Matthew remembered Billy telling him about the time he and a team
of officers had used the "hacking backwards" method to catch a British

teen who'd broken into the military's computer system. It had taken them two solid weeks, during which they'd slept under their desks.

He read Billy the pathway printed at the top of the page.

"That should do it," Billy said when he'd finished. "Still have the same pager number?"

"Yes."

"Okey, dokey. I'll page you when I've got it."

THEY HAD JUST FINISHED a late lunch when Matthew's phone rang. Jennifer knew by looking at Matthew's expression that the call was about Nan.

"She's in the hospital," Matthew said when he'd hung up. "That was Luke. They rushed her there by ambulance."

"Let's go," Jennifer said, reaching for her purse on the counter.

At the hospital, they were directed to the third floor, where, in the waiting room, two boys sat side by side, heads down.

The older of the two—a tall, nice-looking kid with the closely cropped hair of an athlete—glanced up upon hearing Matthew and Jennifer's approaching footsteps.

"Uncle Matt," he said, standing. Apparently not knowing what to do with them, he placed his hands awkwardly on his hips.

Matthew reached for him and briefly pulled him close.

"Hi Luke," he said. Then he turned to the younger boy—a freckled redhead with bloodshot eyes.

He placed a hand on the boy's shoulder.

"How are you, Tommy?"

The boy's eyes misted over.

"Okay," he said, looking back down into his lap.

Matthew introduced both boys to Jennifer, then, unable to find words of comfort, disappeared in search of Nan's doctor.

Jennifer felt such grief at the mere sight of the two boys that she wondered if she had it in her to sit there with them.

"Have you had anything to eat all day?" she asked.

Tommy shook his head no.

"Not really very hungry," Luke answered.

"I tell you what," she said. "I'll find the cafeteria and bring you something. How does that sound?"

They both nodded.

She found the cafeteria in the basement and was pleased to see a wide assortment of choices. She selected several sandwiches—a turkey, a roast beef, and a sub—as well as juice, two apples, and two chocolate brownies.

Despite the indifference they'd shown, the boys seemed pleased to see her return. She pulled a veneer-topped coffee table over to where they sat together on the couch and spread her purchases before them, then, silently, they ate it all.

"I can run down and get some more," she offered.

"Nah, that was enough," Luke said.

She had never, in her entire life, had such a need to hold anyone as much as she did those boys at that very moment. She could see their fear and devastation, and it occurred to her that of the three of the children— these two boys and her daughter—maybe Stacey was the luckiest. For Jennifer had come to believe that dying could not possibly be as painful as being the one left behind.

And so she rose from the chair in which she sat and eased herself in between the two of them on the couch. She placed one hand on Luke's knee, which he did not resist, and the other around Tommy's shoulder. She did not say a word, for she knew all too well there was nothing she could say to make them feel better. But neither boy stirred, neither tried to slide out from under her touch, and she took that to mean they were comforted by it. And so they sat like that for a long while, until Matthew reappeared.

"She wants to see you now," Matthew said to the boys.

He took them down the hall to Nan's room, then returned to Jennifer.

"How is she?" Jennifer asked.

He shook his head.

"Not good. But she's being strong. We had a long talk about the boys, what she wants for them."

Jennifer felt the lump in her throat that always preceded tears.

"She told me how happy she is that I came back. And how much she likes you." He turned away for a moment, then said, "I think our being here made a difference."

"How much time . . ." Jennifer started, but she could not say it.

"The doctor said it could be any time now. Or she could hang in there for a day or two. But soon."

They sat another hour in near silence, Matthew flipping through an old issue of *Time*, but appearing not to actually read it. And then Jennifer heard an insect-like buzz from Matthew's waist.

He reached back and removed his pager from his belt, read the number of his caller, and stood.

"Listen, I have to go make a call. I'll be right back."

"Is it that important? That you have to return it now?" Jennifer asked, then immediately regretted it. She did not need to make him feel guilty, on top of everything else.

"Yes. It is."

"Then go ahead. I'll stay here, in case the boys need anything. I'll do what I can to help them."

HE CALLED BILLY back from a phone in the lobby.

"What did you come up with?" he asked.

"Plenty," Billy Key reported. "Your message hopped around plenty, but it initiated through a server in the New Mexico area. It's a small network, so it wasn't that hard to hack back to the sender, but this guy or gal is security conscious. They even used their on-line name, Sunshine-baker, to register for the service."

"I didn't think the providers allowed that."

"They don't. Not unless the customer has some governmentally authorized security status."

"CIA?"

"Could be. But it didn't go through an agency network. If the sender is CIA, they deliberately chose to go outside to send this to you."

"A precaution."

"I'd have to say yes. You know how it is. If you wanna send something private, better not do it from work, especially if you work for Uncle Sam."

"So we don't really know much."

"Au contraire. I got an address, but as it turns out, this transmission didn't originate at the sender's registered home or business number. That was the tricky part, tracking down its origin. Took some doing on my part, cashing in on a couple of IOUs, but I was finally able to trace the transmission to your neck of the woods."

"Phoenix?"

"Just down the road a bit, in Carefree."

"You got the phone number?"

"Better than that. I got an address."

Matthew pulled the same piece of paper he'd read to Billy from that morning out of his pocket and held a pen to it, poised to take down the information.

"Two-zero-one-one-one Carefree Highway. From the numbering, sounds like it might have come from a business there, in which case, your e-mail pal is probably already long gone. But maybe if you hustle out to Carefree, you'll have some luck."

"Hey listen, thanks. I owe you. This one's important."

"Glad to help out," Billy said, then paused. "A word of warning."

"What's that?"

"If I can get this information, can trace the origin of e-mails you're receiving, someone else can, too. They'd have to be good. Or they'd have to have damn good contacts, but it could be done."

"Warning duly noted," Matthew said, hanging up the phone.

THE SUN WAS DROPPING quickly in the sky behind him as Matthew headed north to Carefree. The road, Cave Creek Highway, was a narrow two-laner, with lots of sudden dips that, at the speed he was traveling, sent him airborne several times. Saguaro cactus stood out against the dry, sagebrush-filled landscape on either side of the road. A lone horse, skinny, stood nose to the ground, trying to find even a single blade of grass, but apparently—from the sight of its ribs—having had little luck of late.

Carefree, mostly a resort town and home to some of the more wealthy recent immigrants to the area, lay ahead, nestled against the boulder-strewn hillside. As Matthew approached, high in the hills he could pick out the sprawling rooflines of homes of the mega-wealthy. At the junction of Cave Creek and Carefree he turned east and after a mile, began looking for the address.

A lone gas station signaled his entrance into the city limits. Next, a motel. "Shady Rest." He slowed. 20111.

He pulled into the parking lot, which was empty of all but one car. A black sedan that looked like standard agency issue.

It was a seedy place, one that no doubt managed to stay in business solely to serve clientele whose needs were for a room for an hour or two at a time. And this time of the year was not exactly the height of tourist season. Matthew sat, trying to figure out which room his man, or woman, was in—if, indeed, he or she had not already departed. But the car made him think whoever it was remained inside. There was no sign of life in the office.

As daylight quickly waned, Matthew waited for a light to go on and help him narrow the possibilities, but only a single light in the office, as well as a spotlight over the parking lot, had gone on.

Of the twelve rooms he'd counted, only two, one upstairs and one down, had curtains drawn. Knowing the agent mentality would dictate choosing the upstairs room over one on ground level, he finally got out of his car and crossed the lot. He moved along the dark lower level to the stairway, then headed up the cement steps to the second floor. Once there, he moved silently to the room with the closed curtains, putting his ear to its door. He thought he heard something inside but he could not be sure.

He reached for the doorknob and turned, expecting it to be locked, but once he turned it, the door creaked open on its own. He stepped inside, into darkness. A laptop sat open and on, in the middle of a cheap table, its screen providing the only lighting in the room.

Matthew drew his gun.

Then he heard it again—the same sound he'd heard through the door, only then it had been muted. A groan. No, a gurgle. Stealing forward, he passed two double beds, then continued toward the bathroom. The bathroom window, which was wide open, threw soft light across the floor and as soon as he came around the partition separating the sleeping area from the single sink outside the room, he saw it. A body sprawled face-down across the floor—half in the bathroom, half out.

He grabbed it by the shoulder and turned it over and saw the same handiwork he'd seen used on Ram Chandra—a knife wound across the neck, from one ear to the other. But this victim's eyes were open and still showed signs of life. He was a man in his early thirties. He looked vaguely familiar to Matthew, but his grotesque expression made identification difficult.

Matthew reached behind the man's neck to support his head as his lips moved in his struggle to say something. The life was draining from him quickly and Matthew knew instinctively that it was too late to call an ambulance.

"Who did this to you?" he asked.

"Frenchman," the dying man whispered.

"French Intelligence?"

"No." He coughed, spurting blood from the neck wound. "Private. Biotech," he managed to say, his voice not even a whisper. Matthew leaned closer to try to read his lips.

But he'd grown silent. Matthew took his wrist then and searched for a pulse. It was so weak as to be almost impossible to detect.

As he did so, Matthew heard the hiss of another forced breath.

"He has her."

"Has *who?*" Matthew answered.

The man tried to swallow, but could not. He mouthed, "The ape."
Angel.

"Now he wants . . . Jennifer." *So, he knew Jennifer by name.* "He. . . . knows. . . . where you live."

At this mention of Jennifer, Matthew had a momentary start, but then he remembered that Jennifer was safe, at the hospital. He stared at the man for a moment, as his lids closed again on glassy eyes.

So, just as he'd long suspected, he had been followed. But not just by the CIA, he'd been followed, probably all along, by a French biotech spy as well. An obviously ruthless—and highly skilled—spy, whose company had apparently heard the same rumors that had sent WTI to Seattle. Why hadn't he thought of it? He knew the French intelligence service was one of the most aggressive in the world. And that the techniques they utilized were alleged to be reminiscent of the KGB. This American agent lying before him in a pool of blood had undoubtedly been assigned the job of counteracting both Matthew's and the Frenchman's activity.

But why then had he sent Matthew a warning?

Matthew went to the bed and yanked the cover off. He laid it over the agent, whose body was cooling as it drained of blood. As he did so, the eyes flickered open again—one last time—and Matthew drew his face within inches of the other's.

"Why?" he asked. "Why did you warn me?"

The man tried to speak but could not. His lips moved in silence and Matthew could have sworn that the words they formed were: "three," then "sixteen."

Suddenly Matthew recognized him. He couldn't remember his name, but something about his expression—the eagerness to be heard, understood—triggered the memory of a young recruit sitting at a desk, raising his hand in response to a question asked by Matthew.

"You were in my training group, weren't you?" Matthew said. "At the Farm."

Momentarily energized by Matthew's recognition, the corners of the young man's mouth actually lifted in a half smile before he uttered the last words that would ever part his lips.

"You were my hero," he said softly before dying.

BATALLION 316. THREE SIXTEEN.

In looking back on the CIA's history and performance, Retired Adm. Stansfield Turner, former CIA director from 1977–1981, stated:

> In the first 29 years, under the intensity of the Cold War, we
> didn't bother to check on the CIA an awful lot and, even if we

had, we would have condoned most of the things it did, maybe
all, because we were willing to sacrifice our ethical and moral
standards in order to win.

Matthew had laughed when he recently read that quote in a newspaper article about today's CIA.

"You sorry bastard," he'd said aloud to no one in particular. But Jennifer had heard him and asked what he meant. He'd, however, pretended
not to hear Jennifer.

It was perhaps during the 1980s that the greatest sacrifices, in terms
of the ethical and moral standards referenced by Admiral Turner, were
made by the CIA. For it was during the early 1980s that the agency
collaborated with a secret Honduran military unit known as Battalion 316.

The number of Honduran citizens thought to have been kidnapped,
tortured, and even executed at the hands of this unit counted in the
thousands. All of this was common knowledge within the CIA, yet it
continued to develop, train, and equip the counterinsurgents and lend
strong support to the chief of the Honduran army, who was also the director of Battalion 316. Back in those days, agency training manuals, designed for training security forces allied with the United States'
anti-communist crusade in Central America, taught torture techniques.

For a short while, Matthew Pace conducted surveillance courses con-
sisting of three weeks of classroom instruction, followed by two weeks of
practical exercises, for Batallion 316 members brought to the states for
training. However, early on Matthew registered his opposition to the
CIA's involvement and as a result, he was relieved of training duties and
returned to the field. His ascent within the agency's ranks came to a halt;
still, his effectiveness in intelligence gathering and a penchant for putting
his own life in danger to carry out a mission earned him widespread, but
widely unexpressed, admiration. In 1988 Matthew was called upon, along
with the deputy director for operations, to provide secret testimony con-
firming the CIA's involvement with Batallion 316 before the Senate Select
Committee on Intelligence. His testimony was honest and accurate. And
apparently anything but secret. Immediately thereafter the full wrath of
the agency, for what it perceived as insubordination and betrayal, was
dealt. Matthew was assigned to a desk job.

He resigned the next day, officially an embarrassment, but for many
who shared Matthew's repugnance for this ugly period in the agency's
history but had never dared speak out—including Jack Eberhardt and,
apparently, the dead man he'd left behind at the Shady Rest—he'd become something of a hero. Someone that other agents felt indebted to for

the role he played in changing the course of the agency, getting it back on track.

The hero thing bothered Matthew. For, if the truth be known, if he had it to do over again, Matthew wasn't so sure he'd take his stand. As far as he was concerned, it had accomplished nothing but his ouster from a life that he loved.

And now a man had lost his life because of it.

Poor sucker, thought Matthew as his Jeep literally flew over a section of highway on his return to Phoenix.

He'd stopped at a gas station at the intersection of Cave Creek and Carefree Highways and called 9-1-1 with instructions to check out room 11 at the Shady Rest. Then he'd climbed into his Jeep and was now headed back to the hospital.

He was terribly worried about Nan and saddened by the death he'd just been witness to, especially in light of his own role in the turn of events that led up to it.

But he had, at least, one consolation: his plan to draw Angel's kidnappers to them had apparently worked.

TWENTY-EIGHT

JENNIFER SAT ALONE in the otherwise empty waiting room. The boys had not yet returned from seeing Nan, and Matthew's phone call had taken him off somewhere. He had been gone well over an hour now.

This sitting, waiting, was driving her mad. Just stepping inside the hospital had stirred such awful memories for her. She'd been keeping her eyes fixed on the hallway for sight of Matthew.

But it was Luke who appeared first.

"Where's Uncle Matt?"

"He had an errand to run. I'm sure he'll be back soon. How's your mother?"

Luke smiled, but it could not be mistaken for anything other than a boy's attempt to hide what he was really feeling.

"She says she's hungry. She couldn't eat that hospital crap. Sorry 'bout my language but you should have seen what they brought her for dinner. But she hasn't really eaten anything much in days anyway. I think she just wants to be sure Tommy and I have something. Anyway, I'm going to Taco Louie's and wondered if you'd like something, too."

"That actually sounds pretty good," Jennifer said, wishing he'd invite her to go with so that she wouldn't have to sit there alone. She simply had to get out of there, get some fresh air. Without thinking it through, she blurted out, "Hey, I have an idea. Why don't you stay here and let me get it?"

The moment the words left her mouth, she realized they were a mistake.

"Really?" Luke said. "That'd be great. The truth is, I don't really want to leave Mom now. You sure you wouldn't mind? You can use my car. Can you drive a stick?"

Luke's response made it difficult to take back her poorly thought out offer.

"You bet," she said.

As he handed her his keys, he recited their order. "Two chicken burrito meals and a soft beef taco. And two super-size Cokes."

"Got it."

"My car's a dark blue Toyota. I parked on the first floor, right side. You can't miss it. The plates say 'Hoopstr,' " he said proudly, spelling it out for her. "You sure you know your way around?"

"Yes," Jennifer said. "I remember seeing Taco Louie's. It's on the way to your uncle's place, isn't it?"

"That's it," Luke answered.

Her misgivings soon gave way to a tremendous sense of relief as Jennifer walked out of the hospital. Night had fallen and she should have felt some apprehension at walking through a deserted parking garage, but the truth was, she did not. She had been living like a prisoner since they'd come to Phoenix and she'd about had it. She was beginning to think Matthew was wrong about Angel's captors following them to Phoenix. Besides, there was just so much a person could stand and today's turn of events—with Nan falling so ill, and hours spent waiting in a hospital, just as she'd waited three years earlier for word of Charlie—had pushed her perilously close to her limit.

Luke was right, the personalized plates made it easy to find the blue Toyota. And as she climbed behind the wheel and pulled on to the highway, the simple act of being out by herself, driving, felt like being set free from a ball and chain. Matthew would be furious if he found out, but she wouldn't worry about that now.

She had no trouble finding Taco Louie's. In a concession to Matthew's concern, she decided to use the drive-thru window. She placed the order given her by Luke and added two burritos for when Matthew returned. When she finished, the voice on the intercom said, "That'll be fourteen fifty-four. Please pull up to the first window."

She pulled the Toyota up to the window, where a teenage girl wearing a headset was taking the next car's order. Jennifer reached in her purse, which sat on the passenger seat, for her wallet, but she could not feel it anywhere in the open-topped bag. She pulled the purse on to her lap and, while the girl waited with hand extended for payment, began frantically rummaging through it, but the wallet was not there. Had someone stolen it? Then it occurred to her. The day before Matthew had received a Sundance catalogue in the mail. Jennifer fell in love with a silver keepsake—a Guardian Angel that reminded her of Stacey—and had decided to order it over the phone. She'd removed the wallet last night when she needed a credit card to place the order.

Embarrassed, she looked to the girl.

"You won't believe this," she said. "I've left my wallet at home."

The girl just stared at her as if she'd heard this one many times before, and offered no suggestion.

"Can you hold it?" Jennifer asked. "Hold the order? The house is just five minutes from here. I'll be right back to pay for it."

"Sure," the girl finally said. "What's the name?"

"Rockhill."

"It'll be waiting behind the counter. But you'll have to come inside to pick it up."

How accommodating, thought Jennifer. Still, she thanked her, then headed toward Matthew's.

She was glad that just the other day, she'd insisted on being given a key. Matthew had resisted.

"Why would you need one?" he asked. "If you think you're going out alone, you better think again."

Just the words to trigger a fight. Now it had become a matter of principle. She wanted a key.

An entire day of avoiding him—other than during Nan's visit, which had been shorter that day than usual—and Matthew had finally handed one over. She reached for her purse again to be sure she had it with her.

Phew, she thought with relief when her hand closed round it. She would have hated to return to the hospital empty-handed.

She punched in the four-digit code that opened the gate to Mountain Estates and eased the car down the street and into Matthew's driveway. The light outside the garage was on, as was the front-door light, both of which were on automatic timers, but inside, the house was dark. She inserted the key and, stepping into the two-story-high entryway, flipped the light switch. She started for the kitchen, then remembered that when she'd placed the order last night she hadn't wanted Matthew to know what she was doing—if he knew he'd probably give her a lecture about why she couldn't have anything delivered to the house—so she'd placed the call from the bedroom. She must have left her wallet there, on the bedside table.

It was just before she reached the top stair that Jennifer was seized with a sense that something was wrong. She stopped on the stairway and listened. She thought about turning and getting out, but she could see the bedroom, where her wallet lay, a mere ten steps away. She thought then of Nan and the boys, waiting for her to return with their meals.

She took the last step. Nothing. *See. There was nothing to be afraid of.* She was letting Matthew's mentality get to her. They had not seen one sign that they'd been followed, and surely Matthew would know, surely he'd have some warning if, indeed, Angel's kidnappers had found them.

She stood outside the bedroom and reached inside for the light switch. When she flipped it, light flooded the room and she stood, examining it, for a long moment before entering. The bedside table was in the far corner. She saw her wallet lying open, as she'd left it the night before, and she began to cross the room.

She was almost to the table when the door slammed shut behind her. She whirled, and there stood a man, medium in build, dressed in denim shirt, sleeves rolled up, and khakis, as if he were on his way to the local bar to meet friends for drinks.

But across his front, both his shirt and pants, was a spray the color of rust, which Jennifer knew immediately to be blood.

"Where's Matthew?" she demanded.

He smiled, and approached her slowly.

"Mr. Pace?" he responded, continuing to narrow the distance between him. His accent, French, was subtle. "I'm afraid he's indisposed at the moment."

"You killed him," she gasped, staring at his blood-stained clothing. "You bastard. You fucking bastard."

She went after him, kicked and pummeled him with her fists, hysterical now. She wanted to kill him. Never before had she felt such fury. He'd grabbed her by the hair, but that didn't stop her, she brought her knee up, hoping to connect with his groin, but he stood, holding her away from him with one hand like some oversized fish he'd just caught, then, with the other, he landed a right hook squarely on her jaw.

She went immediately slack. He let go of her hair and she slumped to the ground.

"Nicely done," he said. "You're quite the little tiger, aren't you? That's good. But there's no one to save you now. Your boyfriend is dead. Slit his throat." He gestured toward his clothes, as if he were modeling them for her. "Messy way to die, don't you think?"

Matthew was dead.

With that confirmation of her worst fears, the last ounce of resistance, the last ounce of anything resembling spirit, simply drained from Jennifer. She would not look at him.

"What do you want?" she asked.

"The protocol, of course," the Frenchman answered. "But first, I'd like to get to know you better."

• • •

WHEN HE FOUND the third floor waiting room empty, Matthew took off down the hall for Nan's room.

Inside, Luke sat on one side of Nan's bed, Tommy on the other. Jennifer was nowhere to be seen. Nan appeared to be resting comfortably. Her eyes were closed, but her left hand held Tommy's.

From out in the hallway, Matthew signaled for Luke to join him.

"Where's Jennifer?" he asked softly.

"She went to pick up some dinner for us. I let her use my car," Luke said, then added, "It's taking her a lot longer than I thought it would."

"Where?" Matthew said. "Where did she go for dinner?"

"Taco Louie's. You know, down by your house."

"You're sure?"

"Yes."

"How long ago?"

Luke, thinking, turned his face toward the ceiling.

"I dunno," he said. "Maybe half an hour. Maybe even forty-five minutes."

Shit. Matthew wanted to slam his fist into a wall. But instead he placed a hand on his nephew's shoulder.

"How is she?" he asked, nodding toward the room.

" 'Bout the same," Luke answered. "They gave her a shot that kind of knocked her out."

"If she wakes while I'm gone, tell her both Jennifer and I will be back soon. Okay?"

"With the food?"

"Yes," Matthew answered. "With the food."

He turned and walked stiffly past the elevator, to the stairwell. He looked back. Luke was still standing in the hall, watching him. Matthew raised his hand in a relaxed wave, then opened the door and stepped inside.

Once out of Luke's sight, he bounded down the stairs, four and five at a time. In his entire career, never had he felt such agitation. He was furious with Jennifer for having left the hospital alone. He had just one consolation right now, and that was his belief that at this very moment, the French agent was most likely at his house, waiting for them to return, and not out stalking Jennifer.

His logic was based on the conclusion he'd come to while driving back to Phoenix: that the Frenchman had been inside the motel room when he'd first arrived at the Shady Rest. Two things pointed toward this.

First, the CIA agent's condition. The neck wound was such that the agent could not have survived more than a few minutes after its infliction. The second was the open window, which had undoubtedly been the Frenchman's escape route.

As Matthew saw it, the Frenchman had been inside when he first pulled up. Seeing Matthew's arrival, the foreign agent had disposed of his American adversary posthaste, perhaps in revenge for the agent's having sent Matthew the e-mail warning just that morning, and had then been forced to flee through the window, unintentionally leaving the agent still alive—which was contrary to the standards of someone like this, but with Matthew literally at the door, a necessity. Once he'd made his getaway, Matthew further reasoned, the Frenchman—knowing he'd left Matthew behind at the Shady Rest—would head directly to Matthew's house, where he hoped to find the two things he'd come to Phoenix seeking. The protocol. And Jennifer.

But he would be disappointed, for Matthew had not left Jennifer at the house. She was at the hospital.

Or at least that's where she was supposed to be. Wouldn't you know she'd choose this moment to pull a stunt like this.

Matthew pulled into the parking lot at Taco Louie's. When he did not see Luke's blue Toyota, he parked and ran inside.

"I'm looking for a woman," he said to a teenaged boy working the counter. "Brown hair, five foot seven. Pretty. She would just have been here, in the last half hour. This is important."

The boy looked at him, his face expressionless.

"Haven't seen anyone like that," he said.

"You the only one working the counter for the past hour or so?"

"Yep," the kid answered. "Maybe she used drive thru." He nodded toward a girl standing at a window at the back of the kitchen area.

"Get her," Matthew said.

The kid looked at him for a moment, obviously trying to decide whether he had to take orders from a customer.

Matthew reached across the counter and grabbed him by the collar. "*Now.*"

"Okay, dude," the kid said. "Chill. I'll get her. Hey Cindy, come here."

Cindy raised a finger, telling him to wait while she listened to an incoming order.

"Now!" the kid said, keeping a nervous eye on Matthew.

Cindy removed the headset and ambled over.

"Did a fortyish brunette come through the drive-in?" Matthew asked. "She would have been in a blue Toyota. Maybe half an hour ago."

"Yeh. She was here," Cindy answered. "Her order's still waiting."

She pointed to a bag that Matthew hadn't noticed sitting on the counter. Scrawled across it was the word *Rockhill.*

"*Why?* Why's her order still here?"

"'Cause she didn't have money with her," Cindy answered. "She asked me to hold it while she went to get some."

"Went to the bank?" Matthew asked hopefully.

"Nah. She was gonna go home and get some. She said she only lived five minutes from here."

Before she'd finished her last sentence, Matthew had already disappeared out the door.

TWENTY-NINE

HE WAS TOYING with her. In the past ten minutes, the "I'd like to get to know you better," which had succeeded in sending ripples of terror throughout Jennifer's entire being, had been followed by several other such statements—all designed to make her believe he intended to sexually assault her.

And if Matthew were dead, why not? No one but Matthew knew she was there. No one would come to her rescue. He had all the time in the world for his sick little game.

But his actions belied his words. Either he had no sexual interest in females—even in the form of sexual violence—or he was in too big a hurry to make good on his threats. Jennifer was beginning to suspect the latter was true and that the threats were being used solely to frighten her into cooperating as quickly as possible.

"I told you," she said, "I don't even know where it is."

She had repeated this denial time and again as he waved his gun at her, telling her she had no choice but to turn over the protocol.

"If I leave here without it, I'll be leaving behind your corpse," he'd said. "Your *defiled* corpse." He laughed then. "Do you know what necrophilia is?"

His accent would have lent him an air of dignity had it not been for the things that came out of his mouth, the product, clearly, of a dangerously sick mind.

Jennifer shuddered, fighting the urge to be ill. Maybe that was more his style, for she had begun to feel confident he would not carry out his threats of forcing himself upon her—at least not now. Maybe after he'd killed her. For if he were to be believed, death would surely come if she failed to produce the protocol.

She was seated on the end of the bed. She kept her eyes downcast, was now only aware of his movement—pacing back and forth as he played his game, the cat stalking its defenseless prey—through her peripheral vision.

"Look at me," he commanded.

She brought her eyes up.

He stood before her. He took the gun he'd been waving at her and reached behind him, placing it on the table next to the TV. Then both hands went to his belt buckle, began unfastening it.

Maybe I was wrong, she thought.

His next words confirmed it.

"Strip."

Had she been standing, her legs would have given out. As it was, her entire body began to tremble. She felt she was losing control of all voluntary muscles, and when he screamed it again—"*Strip!*"—her fingers would not work right as they struggled with the row of buttons down her sleeveless blouse.

His belt in hand, he stepped forward and with a single forceful swipe, ripped open the rest of the buttons.

"Take it off," he commanded.

She would not look at him. She slid her blouse off her shoulders, then, when he reached for her bra strap, she slapped at his hand—which caused him to laugh—and removed her undergarment herself.

"You're a pretty thing," he commented, standing there, watching her. He had not removed anything other than his belt.

"All of it."

She had to stand to remove her shorts and panties, and after she'd stood, when she was bent over, awkwardly sliding her shorts down her legs while trying to cover her chest as best she could, his belt ripped into her flesh.

Searing pain shot across her back and shoulders, and she fell back on to the bed.

She rolled into a ball on her side and, using her hands and arms to cover as much of her exposed flesh as possible, lay there, silent, as he brandished his leather belt on her again. She prayed for unconsciousness, but it did not come, and after two more lashes, he stopped and grabbed her by the shoulder, forcing her to look at him again.

"I can do this all night," he hissed at her. "Do you hear? All night long. The choice is yours. Are you going to help me, or do I keep at it?"

She could hardly bear to look at him. She closed her eyes, then at his squeeze of her shoulders—his demand for an answer—opened them again. It was then that she saw movement behind him. Outside, on the balcony.

"Tell me what it is you want," she said, trying to keep him focused on her. *Had she imagined that just now?* "Describe it. Maybe if I knew what it looked like, I could help."

He released her and stood back, studying her.

"Don't play fucking games with me," he said, uncertain as to whether she'd actually had a change of heart and was now willing to cooperate, or whether this was a ploy on her part.

"I'm not," Jennifer said, covering her face with her hands, as if cowering, in fear of his striking her again. Now, through the space between her fingers, she could clearly see outside to the balcony.

On which stood Matthew, holding his Glock in one hand and the index finger of the other hand to his lips to caution Jennifer against alerting her captor to his presence.

He was alive! Unable to help herself, Jennifer let out a sob of relief.

This seemed to infuriate the Frenchman and he flipped the belt back behind him again, in preparation to strike once more. Jennifer cringed, ready for its razor sharp sting.

Just as it landed on the top of her thigh, the entire room exploded.

Glass—from the sliding door to the balcony, which Matthew had crashed through head first—flew everywhere as Matthew lunged in fury at Jennifer's tormentor. Matthew's gun, ensnared by the cord for the levelor blinds when he charged through the window, dangled inches above the floor.

Jennifer rolled off the bed, on to the floor. She lay for a moment, stunned. As Matthew and the Frenchman boxed and grappled and rolled over the shattered segments of glass, she grabbed for her blouse. Slipping it on, she eyed Matthew's gun hopelessly. She would have to make it past the two men to get her hands on it.

The Frenchman had landed a bone-shattering blow to Matthew's jaw, stunning him momentarily into inaction.

"Matthew, the gun!" Jennifer yelled as the Frenchman turned toward the table where he'd earlier placed his own gun.

Matthew rallied from the floor and dove at the other man's knees, bringing him down; but in his fall, Matthew's amazingly resilient opponent had reached for the table and grabbed hold of its edge. It teetered, and the gun slid down its surface, toward both men. With the speed and reflexes of a bird of prey, the Frenchman's hand shot up to catch it by the barrel. In one continuous motion, he turned and brought its butt down on Matthew's skull.

Matthew fell still.

Jennifer had started toward the dangling Glock but drew up when she saw the Frenchman's gun now turned on her.

"You said you killed him," she spat at him, unable to contain her scorn. When she believed that—that Matthew was dead—she'd lost all will to put up a fight. But it was a different story now.

The Frenchman continued to hold the gun on her as, with one foot, he rolled Matthew over, on to his back.

"You're better off without him, believe me," he said, reaching for the Glock, then tossing it out into the night. "Actually, as it turns out, this is much better anyway. This way you'll get to watch him die."

Jennifer stared at him defiantly.

"You'll have to kill me first."

He smiled.

"No, I'm afraid not. You see, I need you."

"But you said . . . you told me you were going to kill me if I didn't tell you where the protocol is."

"Yes, I did say that. Didn't I? At the time, it seemed like the best means of persuading you to cooperate. But now I have something better. Now I have him."

Matthew had begun to regain consciousness. His groan earned him a kick in the stomach.

"Yes, that's it. Wake up," the Frenchman said. "Your girlfriend and I were just getting to know each other when you interrupted us so rudely. Now you'll have the privilege of watching."

He redirected the gun toward Matthew on the floor and pulled Jennifer to him.

"You'll cooperate," he whispered in her ear, "or he dies."

He pulled Jennifer's back up against him, then began running his free hand under the shirt she'd just put back on, but had not yet had a chance to button.

Jennifer did not move as his hand roamed up her stomach and over her breasts. She pressed her eyes shut. When she opened them, she saw Matthew, still on the floor, watching. His expression was that of a wild animal.

"*Stop.*" Matthew had risen to his knees. "I'll get it for you. But if your hand moves so much as one more inch, not only will you never see that protocol, I swear I'll rip your fucking arm out of its socket."

The Frenchman cocked his head and grinned.

"Big talk for a man with a gun pointed at his head."

"You're not going to use that thing. Not until you get your hands on the protocol."

"You're right, of course," the Frenchman said. He pushed Jennifer away, toward Matthew, who, by now, was standing.

It was then, when she went to join Matthew, that it occurred to her. *There was a gun under her mattress.*

Her first night in Phoenix she'd loaded it and placed it between the mattress and box springs. Yet, incredibly—in the chaos of the past hour—she'd forgotten all about it until that very moment.

"Let's go," the Frenchman said, waving them out of the room with his gun.

Matthew started forward, but Jennifer, behind him, stood her ground.

"Not until I get dressed," she said. She still had only her blouse and panties on. Her bra lay in the middle of the bed, her shorts on the floor.

"No way," the Frenchman sneered.

Matthew turned toward Jennifer and said, "Go ahead. Get dressed."

The Frenchman neither said nor did anything further to stop her.

Jennifer grabbed the shorts off the floor, then pretending to be too modest to dress in the open, took them around the side of the bed. She sat down on the bed and bent forward, stepping into the shorts, but at the same time, running her hand along the bottom of the mattress. Where was the gun? The thought that she might have hidden it on the other side of the bed suddenly hit her. Her mind began spinning dizzily in panic as she tried to remember where she'd placed it . . . and then, suddenly, the tip of one finger hit something hard and cold.

"Let's go," the Frenchman said again impatiently.

"I'm almost ready," Jennifer said.

Matthew, who had been watching her closely, suddenly swung back around toward the Frenchman, distracting him from Jennifer and even managing to knock him off balance by stumbling into him.

The Frenchman recovered quickly and leveled the gun between Matthew's eyes.

"That was not smart," he said. "Now, now that I know the protocol is here, somewhere in the house, you will die."

The sound of the trigger being cocked seemed to reverberate throughout the room.

"Not if I shoot first."

It was Jennifer's voice.

As the Frenchman stood with a gun to Matthew's head, she, in turn, had a pistol pointed at his.

"Well, well," the Frenchman said. "Mother Theresa she isn't."

"Lower your gun," Jennifer ordered.

The Frenchman snickered.

"Lower it, or I'll use this."

"Don't do it, Jennifer." It was Matthew speaking now. "He's not going to kill me before he has the protocol."

"But once you hand it over, he will. He'll kill both of us."

"Actually, no." It was the Frenchman speaking now. "That's not quite correct. I have no intention of killing you," he said to Jennifer. "You see, I've made arrangements to step in for your employer, Sherwood Fielding. By the way, did you know that he had a terrible accident at sea? Such a pity. A real blow to mankind. I wasn't able to cut quite the deal the former Dr. Fielding made with Tupeni Sanday, but, of course, that's because I won't be able to deliver Dr. Chandra. Shot myself in the foot with that one, didn't I? I'll only be delivering the protocol. And you. And, of course, Angel."

Jennifer startled at these last words.

"*Angel!*"

Matthew's eyes locked with hers. "He has her. He has Angel. That's why you can't kill him. Don't you see? If you do, we'll never find her. Don't do it, Jennifer."

Matthew might be right. But of one thing, Jennifer was convinced. The Frenchman would kill Matthew. Before the Frenchman left the house that night, taking Jennifer along with him, Matthew would be dead.

Her finger tightened on the trigger.

"*Don't do it. Jennifer. Don't shoot.*"

She saw it then. It was just the slightest of movements, just the tiniest lift of his arm, the slightest increase in tension in the Frenchman's grip on the gun, but instinctively she knew—he was about to pull the trigger.

She beat him to it.

EPILOGUE

THE NEWSPAPER ARTICLE was an obscure one, hidden back, many pages distant from the big news stories of that day. It was already ten days old, but that was always true of the time it took for the printed media to reach Niupalu. Tupeni Sanday had already read it, but as he awaited his nephew's return, he could not help but read it carefully, with intense focus on every word, once more:

Cloning Takes New Turn
by Rick Weiss
The Washington Post

It sounds like a recipe for a witch's brew: Scientists in Wisconsin have mixed ear of pig and egg of cow—also ear of rat and egg of cow and a variety of other cross species combinations—to clone living embryos of rats, pigs, sheep, and monkeys. The series of experiments represents a new and surprising twist on the cloning techniques that led to the birth of Dolly the sheep.

The article went on to describe scientists' discovery that natural chemicals in the cow egg were able to activate the foreign species' genes, producing an embryo that—after being allowed to grow in a laboratory dish—was ready for transfer to a surrogate mother animal.

Tupeni had just finished reading the article for a second time when his nephew, Tumari, the medical doctor, returned to the royal study. A short while earlier an emergency appendectomy had interrupted their weekly meeting and sent Tumari scurrying to the hospital.

"Have you read this yet?" Tupeni quizzed him. "They've now used an egg from a cow to create a clone of a monkey. Did you know that?"

"No, Uncle," Tumari said. "I did not."

Tumari picked up the article and read. The entire time, his uncle studied his face, watching for his reaction.

"It's much like what the American doctor was doing," Tupeni pressed. "Isn't it? Using two species to produce a clone. His technique looked like it would have worked. Doesn't it?"

It was clear this was a topic that caused Tumari some distress—but equally clear was his uncle's enthusiasm for what he'd just read. In his response, Tumari chose his words carefully.

"There are some significant differences between this method and what we knew about Dr. Fielding's techniques, but, yes, it would indicate he was on the right track."

This answer pleased Tupeni. He hadn't given up on his plan, despite the double blows it had recently been dealt.

First, the deal with Sherwood Fielding had fallen through when Fielding was supposedly killed in an explosion at sea, presumably on his way to meet Sanday. It puzzled him that he had read nothing of it in the papers; however, he believed it to be true as the Frenchman who delivered this news seemed to know everything about Tupeni's deal with Fielding. He also had startling information—that Fielding was planning to double-cross Tupeni Sanday by delivering the wrong ape. The Frenchman, as it turned out, claimed to have the right ape—the one carrying the clone. He also had the protocol, and the real donor, and he had cut Tupeni a much better deal than Fielding anyway. But as fortune would have it, the Frenchman had also disappeared. Simply failed to show up at the appointed time and place.

That deal, Tupeni had finally concluded, must have lacked the favor of the gods.

But he would not be deterred. And with every passing week, just as the *Washington Post* article proved, more developments in the field of cloning were being reported. All of which served to confirm his belief that if he could just remain patient his plan was sure to one day succeed.

He was, after all, only sixty-four years old. The way he saw it, he had at least two more decades of good health. Two decades in which to raise and nurture his heir, confer upon him the hard-earned wisdom of Tupeni Sanday. And ensure the success of Tupeni's quest for the only thing that this life had previously threatened to deny him.

Immortality.

•   •   •

ANOTHER NEWSPAPER ARTICLE sat on the front seat of Matthew's Jeep. This one was front page material. It had, in fact, made headlines around the world. Jennifer had read it to Matthew on their way to pick up the boys.

Senator Engles Indicted in Kidney-Selling Scheme
by Heidi Emily
USA TIMES

Prominent Republican lawmaker, Senator Joseph Engles from California, whose family owns a majority interest in a San Diego transplant facility, has been indicted for illegal selling and transplanting of kidneys. Also indicted were Erland Baldwin, Administrator of Chihuilla General Hospital, and Dr. Sherwood Fielding, CEO and founder of BioGentech, a Seattle-based biotech company. The twelve-count indictment alleges that the three worked together to fraudulently obtain consent from the family of deceased patients, then sold the organs to wealthy recipients not sick enough to have high priority within the national organ distribution system. Donor family members were unaware that the organs were sold and that the three men profited—as much as $150,000 per organ—from the donated kidneys. Engles and Baldwin have been arraigned. Both have posted bond. Fielding's whereabouts are unknown.

There are unconfirmed reports that murder charges may also be brought against the three men reportedly arising from a case recently brought to the attention of authorities in which a comatose patient's kidneys were removed, allegedly causing his death.

In a related development, Fielding is reportedly also wanted for questioning regarding a scheme involving human cloning experiments. A source close to the investigation has confirmed that authorities have acquired credible evidence that seems to indicate that Fielding's efforts to produce a first-ever human clone may have succeeded. Information regarding the status or whereabouts of the clone is unavailable.

Jennifer had been quick to lay the newspaper down on the seat when they stopped to pick up Luke and Tommy.

At the graveyard, Jennifer was the last to climb into the Jeep. She'd lingered at Nan's burial site, in order to give Matthew a chance to talk to the boys alone. She knew he was feeling the need to establish some relationship with Luke and Tommy independent of the one he and Jennifer had forged in the past week. Frequently during the past few days, she could feel him watching her, observing how well the boys responded to her efforts to comfort them, almost as though he were studying the process, in the hope that he might learn it himself.

The sympathy she felt for Matthew was keen.

He, too, was suffering over Nan's death and needed the comfort of their shared grief, yet it had been Jennifer to whom the boys had turned. Of course, Jennifer understood that. They'd just lost their mother and right now, Jennifer was the closest thing to Nan. But she couldn't help but think Matthew felt especially alone at this moment. And since Nan's death, Jennifer's concern for Luke and Tommy had taken precedence over any attempts to console Matthew.

As she settled into the front seat of the car and buckled into her seat belt, she looked over at him. It was amazing how her perception of him— and her feelings—had changed over the span of their relationship. A mere four months. But time would never be an appropriate measure of what they had been through together. Four months in which she'd gone from suspicion, even hatred, of a man who stopped at nothing to achieve his coldly calculated objectives, to *this*—compassion, and affection for a man she was just beginning to know.

Matthew turned her way then, and caught her studying him.

"You okay?" he asked.

"Yes."

The Jeep pulled on to the highway, heading south, back toward Phoenix. At Nan's request, she'd been buried in a small desert graveyard that sat on a hilltop overlooking the entire valley. Now they were headed back to her house, where Matthew had moved some of his things. He would be living with the boys, at least temporarily. The three of them had asked Jennifer to move in also, but she had declined. She felt Matthew needed time with his nephews alone.

And the truth was she needed time alone, too. Being with Tommy and Luke, sensing they needed her, had changed her. Given back her sense of purpose. It would be easy to fall into a familial relationship with all of them. But Jennifer knew that what lay ahead of her—the issue of Angel still weighing heavily on her heart and mind—was a burden she could not place on those two boys.

And there was something else. She couldn't afford to let her affection for the boys dictate the direction of her relationship with Matthew. She had to take it easy where he was concerned. Take her time.

When they pulled in to Nan's driveway, Matthew turned to her.

"Will you stay for dinner?"

The plans had been for her to drop them off, then borrow Matthew's car to begin her search for an apartment.

She looked at him a while before answering. She always enjoyed looking at him.

"Why don't you?" Luke said from the backseat.

"Please," Tommy chimed in.

Matthew reached across the space between them for Jennifer's hand. She gave it to him and he squeezed it, long and hard.

"I'd like that," she finally said.